WESTERN

Rugged men looking for love...

A Maverick For Her Mum
Stella Bagwell

Her Hometown Cowboy
LeAnne Bristow

MILLS & BOON

Stella Bagwell is acknowledged as the author of this work
A MAVERICK FOR HER MOM
© 2023 by Harlequin Enterprises ULC
Philippine Copyright 2023
Australian Copyright 2023
New Zealand Copyright 2023

First Published 2023
First Australian Paperback Edition 2023
ISBN 978 1 867 28919 7

HER HOMETOWN COWBOY
© 2023 by LeAnne Bristow
Philippine Copyright 2023
Australian Copyright 2023
New Zealand Copyright 2023

First Published 2023
First Australian Paperback Edition 2023
ISBN 978 1 867 28919 7

MIX
Paper | Supporting
responsible forestry
FSC® C001695
FSC
www.fsc.org

Published by
Harlequin Mills & Boon
An imprint of Harlequin Enterprises (Australia) Pty Limited
(ABN 47 001 180 918), a subsidiary of HarperCollins
Publishers Australia Pty Limited
(ABN 36 009 913 517)
Level 19, 201 Elizabeth Street
SYDNEY NSW 2000 AUSTRALIA

Cover art used by arrangement with Harlequin Books S.A.. All rights reserved.

Printed and bound in Australia by McPherson's Printing Group

A Maverick For Her Mum
Stella Bagwell

MILLS & BOON

After writing more than one hundred books for Harlequin, **Stella Bagwell** still finds writing about two people discovering everlasting love very rewarding. She loves all things Western and has been married to her own real cowboy for fifty-one years. Living on the south Texas coast, she also enjoys being outdoors and helping her husband care for the animals on the small ranch they call home. The couple has one son, who teaches high school mathematics and coaches football and powerlifting.

Dear Reader,

When rancher Dale Dalton walks into Kendra's Cupcakes, he isn't looking for love. Especially not with a divorced mother of a seven-year-old daughter. But one look at the pretty baker has him deciding one or two dates with her couldn't possibly put his bachelorhood in jeopardy.

After a short failed marriage, Kendra has moved to Bronco, Montana, for a fresh start in life. Presently, she has no wish to jump into another relationship. Her life is consumed with raising her young daughter, Mila, and running her bakery. She doesn't have time, or courage, to search for love. But when Dale walks in to collect an order of cupcakes, she takes one look at the sexy cowboy and begins to dream about having a big, loving family.

Meanwhile, Mila wants a father and the child is interviewing any and every bachelor who crosses her path for the job. Trouble is, the girl thinks cute cowboy Dale is all wrong for her mother. Can he prove to Kendra and Mila he's the right man for the role of father and husband? He believes so—until Kendra's ex-husband shows up in Bronco and puts the meanings of love and family to the test.

I hope you enjoy visiting Bronco and dropping into Kendra's Cupcakes for a tasty treat while you read Dale and Kendra's love story.

Best wishes,

Stella Bagwell

DEDICATION

To the big sky country of Montana and the
rugged cowboys who work the open range.

CHAPTER ONE

DALE DALTON WAS a cowboy. He wasn't the kind of guy who walked into a bakery and asked for cupcakes. If he wanted dessert, he'd eat whatever his mom served at home on the ranch, or order pie at one of his favorite restaurants.

But Dale wasn't making this stop at Kendra's Cupcakes to satisfy his own personal sweet tooth. He was doing it as a favor to his brother Morgan and sister-in-law, Erica. Otherwise, he'd hardly be wasting his time driving the streets, searching the upscale business district of Bronco Heights for a fancy bakery-café.

He located the shop in a narrow building jammed between an antique store and a beauty salon. The front was constructed mostly of plate glass framed with red brick. The words *Kendra's Cupcakes* were painted in red cursive lettering across the wide window, while a second sign with the same name hung beneath a small red-and-white-striped awning that shaded the entrance.

Inside the bakery, Dale took his place behind a line of customers and glanced curiously around the spacious room filled with the mouthwatering smells of baked goods and deep-fried pastries. The floor was a checkerboard of red and white tiles, while on the left side of the room, several wooden tables and chairs were grouped in front of the plate glass window that overlooked the sidewalk. Presently, all the tables were occupied, and that surprised him. He didn't have any idea cupcake shops were such social spots. Did they serve beer in this joint?

He was studying a large menu displayed on the wall, when the person ahead of him moved forward to give Dale a direct view of a long, glass display case. But it wasn't the sweet treats inside that caught his immediate attention. It was the blond woman working behind the counter that had him staring and wondering.

Who was *she*? And why hadn't he seen her around Bronco before now? Because she was married? He didn't want to consider that possibility.

Standing in line normally irritated the heck out of Dale, but this evening he was more than happy to endure the wait. It gave him more time to watch the woman as she sacked up treats and dealt with the cash register.

Even though he was several feet away and peering around the heads of the customers in front of him, he could see she was darned attractive. The top of her head would probably reach the middle of his chest and her slender curves would fit right into his hands. Wavy blond hair was pinned atop her head in a messy bun, but he could easily imagine pulling the pins and coaxing the silky strands to fall upon her shoulders. A red-and-white-striped apron covered most of her blouse and jeans, yet as far as Dale was concerned, the casual clothing only made her sexier.

As customers collected their orders and departed the sweet shop, Dale mentally went over every line he'd ever handed a woman, but once his turn came to step up to the counter, all he could do was stare at her sky-blue eyes and the smile tilting the corners of her plush pink lips.

"Hello," she greeted. "May I help you?"

He cleared his throat, but the reflexive action didn't seem to help loosen his partially paralyzed tongue. "Uh— yeah. I'm here to pick up an order."

"Name?" she asked.

"Oh. Yes. My sister-in-law—she called in the order."

The pretty blonde continued to smile at him and Dale could see a bit of humor had crept into her expression. Did she think he was funny-looking or something?

"And your sister-in-law's name?" she prompted.

Dale felt hot color creeping up his neck. "Uh—sorry. Erica. Erica Dalton."

Nodding, she said, "Oh sure. I have her order ready."

She turned away from the counter and walked over to a long table situated against the wall behind her. Dale used the moment to slide his gaze over her pert little bottom and shapely legs inside the skinny jeans.

That part of her looked more than fine, he thought. But he still hadn't had a chance to get a full view of her left hand. If he spotted a wedding ring, then all his admiring and ogling would be for naught.

She returned and placed a large paper bag with the name *Kendra's Cupcakes* stamped on the side onto the check-out counter. "Two dozen cupcakes of mixed flavors," she stated, then asked, "Is there anything else you'd like?"

Dale could think of plenty of things he'd like from her, none of which he could say out loud. The decadent thoughts were going through his head as her left hand finally came into view. Ridiculous relief poured through him as he saw there was no ring or even a pale circle of where one used to be.

Without bothering to consider what he was actually doing, he gestured to the glass display case situated on the right side of the checkout counter. "You know, I'm feeling mighty hungry this evening. You might box me up a dozen of those cupcakes with the swirly stuff on top."

She stepped over to the case and slid open a door at the back. "The chocolate or vanilla?" she asked.

"Uh, which one tastes the best?" He realized there were customers behind him and he was taking up her time, but he had to grab the chance to talk with her. Even if the conversation was only about cupcakes.

She let out a soft chuckle and the sound floated over him like a warm, dreamy cloud. What in heck was wrong with him, anyway? He'd been around plenty of attractive women. So why was this one making him feel like an addled fool?

"Depends on a person's taste," she told him. "Frankly, I like the vanilla, but I'm a plain Jane."

Her comment very nearly made him laugh, but he stifled the reaction. There was nothing plain about this lady. "Okay, I'll try the vanilla."

She quickly placed the cupcakes in a special holder, then carefully eased the whole thing in a sack that matched the one with Erica's order.

When she stepped over to the cash register and began to punch the keys, she said, "So you're Erica's brother-in-law?"

Could she possibly be the teeniest bit interested in him? He could only hope. "Yes. I'm Dale Dalton."

"Nice to meet you. I'm Kendra Humphrey."

She totaled up the amount due for his order and he handed her enough bills to cover the cost.

"Kendra," he repeated thoughtfully, then his gaze fell to the name on the sacks and the connection clicked. "You own this bakery?"

"I do." Her smile was edged with pride as she counted his change. "I hope you enjoy your cupcakes. Thank you for coming in."

Dale was all set to continue their conversation, but she was already moving over to where the next customer was eyeing rows of apple fritters.

Realizing the short moments he'd had with her were over, Dale turned away from the counter feeling oddly bereft. He'd exchanged a handful of words with a woman he'd never met in his life, yet he felt like he'd just said goodbye to one of his arms or legs.

Damn! He must be losing it, he thought. Love at first sight didn't happen in real life. Especially not to Dale Dalton. He was too happy playing the field. Still, a date or two with the pretty baker would be mighty nice.

As Dale skirted around the line of waiting customers and made his way to the front, he was so preoccupied with the notion of asking Kendra Humphrey for a date that he very nearly collided with a little girl who'd pirouetted directly into his path.

Somehow he managed to do a quick sidestep to avoid the crash, while the child, seemingly unaffected by the near miss, stopped and stared curiously up at him. Dale's first instinct was to hurry on past her and out the door. He wasn't good with kids. Except for the limited time he spent with his nieces and nephews, he wasn't around children very often. But something about this girl's sweet little face made him pause.

"Hello," she said brightly. "What's your name?"

Somewhat nonplussed by her bold approach, he answered, "Dale Dalton. And let me guess. Your name is Princess."

Her little nose wrinkled with disapproval. "My name isn't Princess. Why would you think that?"

A fluffy pink skirt partially covered the top portion of a pair of black jeans, while a purple T-shirt with a cartoon dinosaur in bright lime green completed her colorful wardrobe. A small rhinestone tiara adorned the top of her blond hair.

He gestured to the head decoration. "You're wearing a crown. Princesses wear those things, don't they?"

Her expression said she'd already summed him up as being a silly man and as Dale noted her wavy blond hair and blue eyes, he was knocked a bit off-kilter. This girl clearly resembled the owner of the bakery.

Quick to correct him, she said, "This is not a crown. It's my tiara. My name is Mila Humphrey and I'm seven. Do you live around here?"

"I live on a ranch. Dalton's Grange. It's a few miles out of town," he answered, while the child's last name spun through his head.

Dale glanced over his shoulder to where Kendra continued to take orders from the waiting customers, then back to the charming child standing in front of him.

Mila didn't give him a chance to question the connection—she lifted her chin to a proud angle and stated, "That's my mommy and this is her bakery. She makes money selling good things to eat."

So Kendra had a daughter. Did that mean she was married? In spite of her not wearing a wedding ring? He could ask the girl an offhand question about her father, but that would make Dale a creepy jerk. Besides, there were plenty of reasons Kendra might not be sporting a ring. She might be allergic to precious metals. Or maybe she didn't want to get her diamonds all gooey when she mixed pastry dough. And no doubt her wedding ring would be full of diamonds, he thought. A man lucky enough to have her for a wife would give her nothing less.

Realizing his mind was on a runaway fantasy, he gave himself a mental shake and smiled at the child. "I'm sure everything your mommy bakes is delicious."

The girl regarded him skeptically. "Are you married?"

A bit taken aback, he said, "No. Are you?"

"I'm too young," she explained. "And I don't have a boyfriend yet."

"I'm sure you'll have one soon enough," he told her.

She tilted her little blond head to one side as she continued to regard him with big blue eyes. And even though Dale was telling himself he needed to be headed home to the ranch, there was something about Mila that made it impossible for him to walk away.

"I'll bet you have lots of girlfriends," she said suddenly. "Cute cowboys usually do."

Was that how this rosy-cheeked cherub saw him? He was thinking she might be smarter than he first imagined when she promptly added, "My mommy goes on dates—sometimes. But I don't think you should bother asking her to go on one."

Dale was thrilled to hear Kendra Humphrey was single and dated occasionally. But he wasn't at all sure he liked having a seven-year-old read his mind. And where did she come off giving him romantic advice?

"Why not? I'm a nice guy."

She shrugged. "You're just not her type. She likes men who wear glasses and read books."

The nerdy type? Kendra hardly looked like a woman who'd want to spend an evening discussing literature with a man, Dale thought. It was difficult for him to imagine those luscious pink lips talking instead of kissing.

He said, "Uh, don't you think you should let your mommy decide whether she likes cowboys?"

She shrugged both shoulders, then reached up and carefully adjusted the rhinestone tiara on her head. "Well, she might like cowboys. But only the kind who want to settle down and have kids. And you're not that kind. I can tell."

Dale had to admit there was nothing bratty or purposely impolite about Kendra Humphrey's daughter. But just the same, her comments were pushing his buttons. How did this child know he was the free-roaming type? Did he have it written across his forehead? And even if he did, could a seven-year-old read?

He was wondering how he could respond to the girl, or if he should even try, when a soft, female voice sounded behind him.

"Mila! Are you harassing Mr. Dalton?"

Dale glanced over his shoulder to see Kendra, looking somewhat exasperated, hurrying toward them. At the same time, he noticed the customers had cleared away from the display counters and now the only patrons left inside the bakery were the ones seated at the tables.

"No problem." Dale flashed Kendra his most charming grin. "Your daughter and I were just having a— Well, an enlightening discussion about cowboys."

Groaning with embarrassment, she leveled a stern look at her daughter, then turned an apologetic smile on Dale. "I'm so sorry, Mr. Dalton—"

"Oh, no one calls me Mr. Dalton. I'm Dale to everybody."

Smiling, she took a step closer and rested a hand on her daughter's shoulder, and as Dale took in the image of the two of them together it was hard for him to imagine why there wasn't a man in the family. What kind of fool would give up these two? Or perhaps he'd not given them up. Maybe the man had died an untimely death.

"Okay, Dale. And I apologize for Mila. She can be, uh, very pushy sometimes and unfortunately she says exactly what's on her mind."

Which appeared to be screening men for her mother's potential boyfriends. Judging by the way Mila was carefully taking in everything he and Kendra said to each other, she probably held these question-and-answer sessions with suitable male customers on a daily basis.

"Don't give it a second thought. I welcome a girl's dating advice no matter what their age," he joked.

Kendra let out another embarrassed groan. "I'm sorry about this, Dale. Please let me give you some extra cupcakes to make up for my daughter's behavior."

"That's thoughtful of you, Ms. Humphrey. But it's not necessary," he told her.

The smile she flashed him said she was grateful he wasn't taking Mila's chatter to heart. It also told Dale he couldn't possibly rest until he saw this woman again. Especially without a seven-year-old chaperone.

"Call me Kendra. And it's necessary to me," she said. "I'll be right back."

While Kendra went to fetch the cupcakes, Mila used the time to practice her pirouettes, only she wasn't balanced on the toes of ballet flats, she was wearing a pair of sparkly pink cowgirl boots. Dale couldn't imagine how it would be to parent such a precocious child. His brother Morgan did a great job dealing with his little daughter, JoJo. But Dale had never imagined himself as a daddy.

"I've been taking dance lessons," she told Dale. "Someday I might dance on a stage. Mommy says anybody can do what they really want if they try hard."

"Your mommy is right."

She stopped her whirling and leveled a curious look at him. "Are you trying to do something?"

The simply spoken question caught Dale off guard. What was he trying to do in the greater scheme of things? Sure, he was helping to keep the family ranch, Dalton's Grange, intact and profitable. He was doing his part to make sure his mother remained healthy and happy. But in regard to his own life, he couldn't think of one single thing he was trying to do, except enjoy himself.

"Well, I guess I try to do lots of things," he told her. "When I'm at work on the ranch."

She didn't appear to be all that impressed with his answer, but she remained silent. Probably because her mother had just walked up to join them.

"Here's the extra cupcakes, Dale." She handed the sack to him and he could tell by the weight that she'd been very generous. "I hope my pestering daughter won't keep you from visiting the bakery again."

He could tell her that a herd of wild horses couldn't keep him away, but he kept the thought to himself. He didn't want to give Mila reason to shoot him a look of disapproval, or give Kendra the impression he was overeager.

"Like I said, she hasn't been a bother. You'll be seeing me again. And thanks for the extra cupcakes."

"You're welcome," she told him, then purposely wrapped a hand around Mila's shoulder. "Come on, sweetie. I have a job for you back in the kitchen."

Mother and daughter walked away and Dale forced himself to leave the bakery, but as he made the long drive to Dalton's Grange, he continued to think about Kendra and little Mila. A fact that surprised him. He'd never thought of himself as a family man, yet something about Kendra and her daughter had him wondering how it might feel to be a husband and father.

THE KITCHEN AREA at the back of Kendra's Cupcakes wasn't large, but the space was efficiently equipped with everything Kendra and her helpers needed to get the daily baking done. At this time of the evening, the ovens and deep fryers were shut down and Jackie, a twenty-five-year-old woman with vivid red hair, cut in a pixie style, was busy mopping the floor.

She looked up as Kendra marched Mila over to the end of a work counter and lifted her onto the top seat of a step chair.

"Uh-oh. Looks like someone is in trouble," she said slyly. "Who did she ambush this time? A married minister?"

"I only wish it had been," Kendra told her assistant. "This time Mila had to pick on one of the Dalton brothers. An unmarried one."

Shaking her head, Jackie leaned on the mop handle. "You made a big mistake, Kendra, when you allowed Mila to go with you to Audrey Hawkins and Jack Burris's wedding. Now the child has weddings on the brain."

Unfortunately, Jackie was right. Ever since they'd attended Audrey Hawkins and Jack Burris's beautiful wedding, Mila talked incessantly about brides and grooms, flower girls and ring bearers. Each time an opportunity presented itself, she announced to their friends, and even strangers, that her mommy was going to get married—soon! It was beginning to be a very frustrating problem for Kendra. Especially when she had no plans to even look for a boyfriend, much less get married.

"Well, that can't be all bad," Jackie said. "The way I remember, there's not one ugly Dalton in the bunch."

Kendra helplessly rolled her eyes. "Jackie, you're no help at all!"

With a mischievous chuckle, Jackie continued with her mopping, while Kendra turned an admonishing look on her daughter.

Mila carefully smoothed her pink tulle skirt before she leveled an innocent smile at her mother. "What do you want me to do sitting here, Mommy?"

"I want you to explain what you were doing with Mr. Dalton. I know you haven't forgotten what I told you about talking to the male customers—about asking them personal and embarrassing questions. I've told you it's rude and not to be doing it. So what do you have to say for yourself?"

Seemingly unfazed by her mother's interrogation, Mila said, "I wasn't being rude. Dale liked talking to me. I could tell."

The moment Kendra had spotted the Dalton brother sauntering into the bakery, she had to admit, she'd taken a second and third peek at the tall, good-looking cowboy. Dark hair, blue eyes and a killer smile. He'd had that look of a charming rascal. Exactly the sort of guy she didn't need in her life. But that hadn't stopped Kendra from snatching a few more glances at the man while she'd tended to the other customers.

While she'd dealt with Dale's order, he'd been polite and friendly. He hadn't ogled her as if he wished she was a part of the dessert menu and Kendra had appreciated his gentlemanly attitude. So when she'd looked up a few moments later to see her daughter had waylaid the sexy cowboy a few feet from the door, she'd been totally mortified.

Turning her focus back to Mila, she asked, "Really? How did you decide that Dale liked talking to you?"

Mila's lips pursed together before she finally spoke. "Well, he was smiling and he wasn't saying anything mean. And he wasn't rolling his eyes or looking bored."

Kendra let out a long sigh. She didn't know where her daughter had gotten the ability to size up people, but usually Mila was spot-on in her assessments. And to be fair, Dale hadn't appeared to be all that irritated with Mila's foolishness.

"And I suppose you asked him if he was married or had a girlfriend."

Mila nodded. "Why not? He's cute. We needed to know if he had a wife. And he doesn't. But don't worry, Mommy. I already told him that he wasn't your type."

Oh Lord, this was worse than Kendra had first thought. "Mila, you didn't!"

Seeing the anger on her mother's face, Mila held her palms up in a defensive gesture. "Well, I had to set him straight. Because I could see he wasn't the kind of guy who'd want to get married and have kids."

There was no point in asking her daughter how she'd reached such a conclusion about Dale Dalton. Frankly, Kendra had concluded the same thing, but that hardly meant it was right or proper for her daughter to be discussing such issues with a strange man.

"Mila, I realize you'd like to have a daddy and that you want brothers and sisters. But you need to understand how things like this work. You can't just go around picking out a man to be your mommy's husband. It doesn't work that way. A man and woman need lots of time to discover if they're compatible and if there's chemistry between them before they can, um, get together."

A puzzled frown wrinkled Mila's forehead. "Does that mean you need to find out whether you like each other?"

"Well, that's a simple way of putting it, but yes. And finding out whether you'd like someone for a lifetime doesn't happen overnight."

With an exaggerated sigh, Mila folded her arms across the dinosaur on her chest. "Well, it won't happen with you at all, Mommy, 'cause you're too busy. That's why you need me to help you find a boyfriend. One that'll want to be my daddy."

There was no way Kendra could stay angry with her

daughter. Hearing Mila's wish for a father always tore at her heart. It also left her feeling like a failure.

Damn Bryce! She'd given her ex every opportunity to be a part of Mila's life. She'd tried her hardest to make him see how much his daughter needed her father. But he'd always been too self-absorbed to ever acknowledge Mila, much less give her attention and support.

Sighing, Kendra reached out and patted Mila's cheek. "I know you mean well, sweetie. But you need to let me choose my own boyfriend. Okay?"

Mila frowned. "Okay. But I don't think you'll really start looking for one."

Her daughter knew her well. Kendra had little interest in finding a boyfriend. Her marriage to Bryce had been humiliating and heartbreaking. He'd broken every promise he'd ever made to her and squashed every dream she'd ever had for a family. She didn't need a man waltzing into her life and messing it all up for a second time.

Hearing the jingle of the outer door of the bakery, Kendra quickly lifted Mila off the seat and set her back on the floor. "Come on. We have customers waiting."

Three hours later, Smitty, the young man who worked as the bakery-café's barista, along with Andrea, a part-time college student who worked as a server and all-around helper, had already left for the night. Kendra was getting ready to close up shop when she spotted a frequent patron attempting to enter the bakery. Because the woman was elderly and walked with the aid of a cane, she oftentimes struggled with the door, so Kendra hurried over to give her a helping hand.

"Let me hold the door for you, Mrs. Garrison. The wind is strong tonight."

"Bless you, Kendra. Are you about to close?"

"Don't worry. You have plenty of time to get whatever you'd like," Kendra told her.

Just as the woman hobbled over the threshold, an orange cat zoomed past her legs and straight into the bakery, causing both women to let out shrieks of surprise.

"Oh my goodness!" Mrs. Garrison cried out.

Kendra stared after the flash of ginger fur racing across the bakery floor.

"It's that darned cat again!" she exclaimed.

Racing after the animal, Mila shouted, "Mommy, it's the orange kitty! He's come back to see us. Can I pick him up?"

"No, Mila!" she called out, but Mila was already chasing the cat around the display cases and through the door of the kitchen.

With the customer safely inside, and the door shut behind her, Kendra said, "Excuse me for a minute, Mrs. Garrison, I'd better see about our unannounced visitor."

Kendra hurried back to the kitchen to find Mila peering beneath a rolling cart that was sandwiched between the refrigerator and a cabinet.

"He's hiding under the bottom shelf, Mommy!"

Jackie, who was standing directly behind Mila, glanced over her shoulder as Kendra approached them. "I don't think the cat is too happy about being in the kitchen," she told her.

Kendra walked cautiously over to the cart and squatted on her heels to get a better look at the cat. At the moment, the animal was peeking timidly out at the unfamiliar surroundings.

"Hello, pretty guy," she gently said to him. "What are you doing? Looking for a meal, or a girlfriend?"

The cat's big green eyes blinked once as he made a

skeptical study of Kendra, but he didn't make a move to crawl from his hiding place to greet her.

"Can I give him some milk, Mommy? It might make him come out and let me pet him."

Kendra had seen the cat at the back of the bakery on different occasions. Probably because Mila had been secretly tossing it food. And once he'd dashed into the bakery's entry, but during those visits, he'd never stuck around long enough for the animal-rescue organization to catch up with him.

"Okay. A small bowl of milk. But don't scare him. Animal rescue needs to collect him."

"I'll pour the milk for Mila to give him," Jackie said. "Go ahead and finish whatever you were doing."

"Thanks, Jackie."

Kendra returned to the front to deal with Mrs. Garrison. The woman's order turned out to be an extra-large one and Kendra carried everything out to the woman's car.

Once she helped the faithful customer to her vehicle, Kendra waved goodbye, then hurried back inside to call animal rescue. When a man answered, she quickly related the situation.

"The cat you're describing sounds exactly like Morris. The feline who went missing in July."

"Morris," Kendra repeated thoughtfully. "Yes, I recall seeing a poster on a missing cat by that name. You think this might be him?"

"Possibly. We've been getting calls of sightings around town, but no one has managed to corner him," the man replied. "He escaped an apartment fire and hasn't been located since."

"Morris or not, this cat is right here in my kitchen," Kendra explained. "It's past closing time, but I'll be glad to stay here until the rescue unit arrives to collect him."

"Thank you, Ms. Humphrey. Someone will be there in just a few minutes."

At some point during the phone call, Mila had appeared at Kendra's side. Now, as Kendra hung up the phone, her daughter tugged on the leg of her jeans and looked up at her with pleading eyes.

"Mommy, why does someone have to get the cat? Why can't we take him home with us? He looks nice. And remember, you said I could get a pet pretty soon."

Kendra wearily pushed at the strands of hair that had tumbled loose from the bun atop her head. She'd been going since four o'clock this morning and the day had been a long one. Now, with a wily cat to deal with, the day was growing even longer.

Suppressing a sigh, she looked down at her daughter's eager face. "I haven't forgotten my promise to get you a kitten or puppy. But this cat belongs to someone else. He's been lost and people are looking for him so they can take him to the home where he belongs."

Mila looked crestfallen. "I guess he does need to be with his family. But he should've walked to his own house instead of coming to the bakery."

"He's probably confused and doesn't know where his house is." Kendra patted her shoulder. "Now I need to finish packing up the leftover pastries. You'd be a big help if you'd go sit by the door and watch for the animal-rescue people."

"Okay, Mommy."

While Mila stood sentinel at the door, Kendra went to work. Each night, on her way home, Jackie dropped off the surplus of baked goods at a local charity house or nursing home. Kendra liked to think the donated food was enjoyed by folks who were especially in need.

As she packed up a cardboard box, Kendra's thoughts

unwittingly drifted to Dale Dalton. Until he'd walked into the bakery, she'd never seen the man before. But that was hardly surprising. She was usually too busy to attend many social events around Bronco and those that she did take in were usually family-type outings. Not the sort of entertainment a good-looking bachelor like him would find interesting.

Before he'd explained to Kendra that he was picking up his sister-in-law's order, she would've never guessed he was a member of the Dalton family. Except for Morgan Dalton, who was married to her friend Erica, she wasn't personally acquainted with the Dalton brothers. She'd often heard Erica talk about living on Dalton's Grange with her husband, however, Kendra had never seen or visited the property located on the outskirts of Bronco. From Erica's comments, Kendra knew the ranch was very large and supported huge herds of livestock.

During Mila's earlier chatter about Dale, Kendra had learned he worked on the ranch. Which meant it was probably safe to assume he lived there too. He'd also told Mila he didn't have a wife, which hardly surprised Kendra. From the looks of him, she figured his romantic involvements were the brief kind without promises or strings.

Kendra, why are you thinking about Dale Dalton? He isn't your kind of man. Besides, you don't want a man in your life, remember?

Pushing back at the annoying voice in her head, she started to carry the box of leftovers back to the kitchen, when Mila sang out.

"Those people are here, Mommy! And they have a little cage with them!"

After placing the box on the counter, Kendra walked to the door to meet a young man and woman, both wearing polo shirts with emblems that read Bronco Animal Rescue.

"Thank you for coming so quickly," Kendra told them. "The cat is in the kitchen—hidden under a table. Follow me and I'll show you."

The group entered the kitchen and Mila immediately pointed to the table where Morris had remained since the rescue service had been called.

"He's under there," Mila told the rescue workers. "We gave him a bowl of milk and he drank all of it. He was hungry."

The man cautiously approached the rolling cart, then kneeled down and looked under the bottom shelf. "I don't see any kind of cat under here."

"What?" Kendra practically shouted the word. "He was there not more than five minutes ago. I saw him. A big orange cat."

Mila raced over to the cart and, lying flat on the floor, peered beneath it. "He's not here, Mommy!"

"Well, he has to be here in the kitchen somewhere," Kendra said. "He couldn't have gotten out."

She'd barely spoken the words, when Jackie entered the back door of the building. The redhead was carrying a large plastic bucket. She glanced nonchalantly at the group.

"Did you get the cat?" she asked.

Kendra walked over to where Jackie was placing the pail in a storage closet. "No. The cat isn't under the cart, where we left him," Kendra told her. "Have you seen him?"

As she waited for Jackie to answer, the rescue pair began to search the small nooks and spaces around the room.

Puzzled, Jackie nodded. "He was here a couple of minutes ago. I saw him before I went out to the dumpster. Maybe—" Her mouth formed a perfect *O*. "Do you think he might have run out the door?"

Kendra passed a weary hand over her forehead. "Did you leave the door open while you went out?"

A look of guilt crossed the redhead's face. "I'm sorry. I wasn't thinking. I mean, we don't normally have a cat in the kitchen."

"We don't normally have *any* animal in the kitchen!" Kendra exclaimed, then, with a rueful shake of her head, she patted Jackie's arm. "Don't feel badly. I imagine the cat will turn up somewhere sooner or later."

Hearing Jackie's admission about the door, the two rescue workers decided to search the back alley, but several minutes later they returned to announce Morris was nowhere to be found.

After the rescue workers departed and Jackie left with the box of pastries to be donated, Kendra began locking the doors for the night.

Mila trailed after her. "Mommy, why did Morris run off? Didn't he like us?"

Pausing, Kendra stroked a hand down the back of Mila's blond hair. "Well, he wasn't with us long enough for him to decide whether he liked us. And I suspect he's just trying to find his way back home."

"Like we found our home here in Bronco?"

Smiling now, Kendra bent down and placed a kiss on her daughter's forehead. "That's right, princess."

Mila giggled. "Dale said my name was Princess. Because I'm wearing my tiara. That's funny."

Kendra slanted her a curious glance. "I thought you decided Dale wouldn't make a good boyfriend for me."

Tilting her head from side to side, she said, "Well, he wouldn't make a good one for you. But he is cute."

Yes, Dale was charming, cute and sexy, Kendra thought. Everything she didn't need in her life.

CHAPTER TWO

BY THE TIME Dale drove home to Dalton's Grange, and then headed to Morgan's house, night had fallen and so had the temperature. Long before he pulled to a stop in front of the rock-and-log structure, he spotted smoke spiraling up from the chimney. Dale hardly considered the weather cool enough this late summer evening for a fire, but the air was a bit chilly, and he figured his brother had built it for Erica. With her being pregnant with their second child and currently on bed rest, Morgan was doing all he could to make his wife comfortable.

Dale walked across the wooden porch and knocked briskly on the door, then, without bothering to wait for an answer, stepped inside.

"Hey, anyone home?" he called out.

From his seat in a large leather recliner, Morgan motioned for Dale to join him. Dale walked over and deposited the large sack of cupcakes on a low, pinewood coffee table, then eased onto the end cushion of a long couch.

"You've surprised me," Morgan said. "I thought you'd stay in town and have a beer or something before you came back to the ranch."

"I wasn't much in the mood to hang around town," Dale told him. "And I didn't want to drag in here with the cupcakes about the time you and Erica were getting ready to go to bed."

Morgan pulled a rueful face. "Erica is already in bed. Remember?"

Dale nodded. "I haven't forgotten. How's she doing?"

"Okay. Just tired of being in bed and staring at the walls. She watches TV, reads, eats and does it all over again."

Dale could see the worried look on his brother's face, and he knew the situation with his wife and unborn baby had to be putting a load of stress on Morgan's shoulders. He was crazy in love with Erica and this second baby she was carrying was the first biological child for him. Not that this child was any more precious to him than little Josie, or JoJo as everyone called her, who'd been born shortly after Morgan and Erica had married.

Dale admired his brother for being such a good, dedicated family man. Dealing with his little daughter seemed to come natural to him. So did his ability to keep a loving smile on Erica's face. But Morgan's success at being a family man didn't necessarily mean Dale was cut out for such a life. No, sir.

Dale replied, "Well, as long as she and the baby are healthy that's all that matters."

"Exactly. Just getting them safely through the next few months means everything." Morgan raked hands through his dirty blond hair, then rested his elbows on his knees and looked at Dale. "Seen Holt or Boone today? I was out most of the day riding fence on the north range. Did Holt go to the horse sale at Kalispell? He was all worked up over that cutting horse he'd found in the consignment catalog."

Dale's chuckle was wry. "He'd need more than that to get worked up. That mare will probably bring six figures. The ranch can't afford her and neither can Holt. But, yeah, I think he went to the sale. I saw Boone earlier this morning. He was headed into town for vet supplies."

Like Morgan, both Holt and Boone were older than

Dale and, like Morgan, were married to women they were gaga about. Boone had married Sofia Sanchez, a fashion stylist for BH Couture, a high-end fashion boutique in Bronco Heights. Holt was married to Amanda Jenkins, who worked in marketing. Together they were raising Holt's ten-year-old son, Robby.

Presently, Dale and Shep, the two youngest sons of Neal and Deborah Dalton, were the only ones who were still single and living at home. And though Dale couldn't speak for Shep, he had no intentions of changing the direction of his life anytime soon. Even though their dear mother would love to see the last of her boys married and raising babies of their own.

In an effort to push that unwanted scenario from his mind, Dale glanced around the room and noticed the TV was on, although the sound was turned down too low to hear. A coloring book and a box of crayons were on the floor in front of the fireplace, but JoJo was nowhere to be seen.

"Where's my little niece?" he asked.

"She took her mommy a plate of cookies for dessert. But you can bet JoJo will do all the eating," he said with a fond smile. "When she finds out you've delivered the cupcakes, she'll be begging for one. By the way, thanks for picking them up for me."

JoJo was starting her first day of nursery school tomorrow and she was supposed to take cupcakes. Since Erica was on bed rest and Morgan couldn't cook a piece of toast without ruining it, they'd called in an order to Kendra's Cupcakes.

"No problem," Dale said. "In fact, the bakery trip turned out to be a pleasure of sort."

"Oh. Let me guess. You bought a half-dozen donuts and ate them on the way home?"

Dale grinned and waggled his eyebrows. "No. But I met the tasty-looking blonde who owns the bakery."

"You're talking about Kendra?" Morgan asked.

Hearing his brother speak the woman's name caused Dale to sit straight up. "Yeah, that's who I mean. You know her?"

"Only slightly. Erica knows her very well. She's been going to the bakery since Kendra first opened it."

Dale felt like groaning out loud. Three long years Dale could have been walking into Kendra's Cupcakes and getting to know her. So much wasted time.

"Do you know anything about her?" Dale asked him.

Morgan shrugged. "Not much. Erica said she's been divorced for a while. And she has a little girl. I saw her once when we ran across them at a burger place in town. Cute kid."

Yes, Mila was a mini-replica of her mother, Dale thought. Which made her very cute. But he considered her far too precocious for a child of her age.

Dale said, "I met Mila this evening when I stopped by the bakery. I've never met such an outspoken kid. She gave me an earful."

Puzzled, Morgan asked, "What was she doing having a conversation with you?"

Dale grimaced. It still got his goat to think how the seven-year-old had ruffled his feathers. He was a grown man, for Pete's sake. A child's opinion should roll right off his back, not stick him like a knife blade.

"Apparently when she grows up she has plans to write an advice column for the lovelorn," Dale answered wryly. "She informed me that I'd be wasting my time to ask her mother for a date. I was cute, but not the sort of guy her mother goes for."

Morgan threw back his head and laughed. "Must be a smart kid."

"Hey, hey, Morgan. This is your brother, Dale, you're talking to. What's wrong with me?"

Morgan shook his head. "Nothing. You're just not Kendra Humphrey's type."

Dale snorted. "Mila implied her mommy wants a husband and babies."

Morgan shot him a droll look. "And what's wrong with the woman wanting those things? You'd rather Kendra be the one-night-stand type?"

"No!" The mere notion of that blond angel flitting from one man to the next made Dale a little sick to his stomach. "Not at all. But what would be wrong with her liking a gentleman cowboy? Enough to go on a date with him?"

"Nothing. If that's all you wanted from her."

Morgan's comment caused Dale to pause and stare at his brother. Did he think sex was all he ever wanted from a woman?

Well, to be fair, you sure aren't looking for love or marriage. What's left? Conversation and hand-holding?

Dale gave himself a mental shake in an effort to rid his head of the annoying voice.

"You make me sound like some sort of playboy," Dale said distastefully. "I'm not that kind of guy."

"I'm glad to hear it. Because I don't think Kendra needs another heartache."

Dale arched his eyebrows at Morgan. "Another heartache? You're implying she's already had one."

Morgan shot him an impatient look. "She's gone through a divorce, Dale. Don't you figure that was a heartache? Or maybe you consider the end of a marriage a laughing matter?"

Shaking his head, Dale said, "Oh, come off it, Morgan.

I mention a woman and you start giving me a moral lecture. What's wrong with you, anyway?"

A resigned grin on his face, Morgan rose to his feet. "Sorry, Dale. I guess I've forgotten how it is for a man to be single and looking. And you're my brother. I don't want to see you get tangled up in a relationship that might hurt you."

"Don't worry about me. I'm not going to get tangled, period."

"Good. So let's go to the kitchen. I'll make coffee and you can have a cup with me before you head home."

Chuckling, Dale rose from the couch. "Wrong, brother. I'll make the coffee. You can't boil water."

A FEW DAYS LATER, on a sunny, but particularly cool day for the first Saturday in September, Kendra parked her white SUV a couple of blocks away from the city park, which was located across the street from the city hall. Bronco's back-to-school picnic was held every year around this time and the event was something that Mila waited eagerly to attend. Her daughter loved being outdoors and especially enjoyed the chance to see all her friends she'd be reuniting with once school opened.

Kendra had to admit there was still enough of a kid in her to enjoy going to the park. And this particular gathering gave her a chance to chat with friends and acquaintances she didn't get to see on a regular basis.

"Maybe you'll run into plenty of cute guys at the park today, Mommy. I'll bet they'll all be looking at you too. 'Cause you're so pretty."

Kendra doubted there would be many single guys present today. Not unless they were widowed or, like her, divorced and a single parent.

She glanced over at Mila, who was happily swinging

her arms to and fro and alternating her forward movement with a skip and a walk.

"I think you're a little biased, sweetie. But thank you for the compliment."

Mila looked at her. "What does *biased* mean? Does that have something to do with chemistry and compat-i— Well, whatever that word was?"

So her daughter had listened to at least part of the lecture she'd given her over this idea she had of finding Kendra a husband. She could only hope that enough of these talks would convince Mila to drop this obsession she had of getting her mother married. "Not exactly. It means you think I'm pretty just because I'm your mommy."

"That's not being bad, Mommy. You are pretty. And you wore your sweater today that I like the best."

Kendra glanced down at the Fair Isle sweater she'd pulled on over a pair of flare-legged jeans. The jewel-necked garment was done in autumn shades of gold and brown that complemented her blond hair. At least, that's what her friends told her. Kendra had donned the sweater mostly so she'd be comfy and warm without having to wear a jacket. She'd certainly not dressed to attract a man's attention.

For some reason she didn't want to analyze, the idea of attracting a man had her thinking of Dale Dalton. Since he'd come into the bakery to pick up Erica's cupcakes, he'd not returned. Not that she'd expected him to show up again. It had been fairly obvious that he wasn't a bakery-café-type guy. Still, she had to confess that a few times this past week, she'd caught herself glancing around and hoping she might see him walk through the door.

"Oh wow! Look at all those people!" Mila exclaimed. "I'll bet lots of my friends are here. Louisa and Violet said they would be here. Do you think we can find them?"

The park consisted of a wide expanse of lawn area surrounded by tall cedars and thick fir trees with a few hardwoods mixed in. Presently, there were crowds of people milling about the lawn and gathered beneath the trees. At one end of the park, portable tables had been erected to hold food and drinks for anyone who wished to partake. From the looks of things, there were plenty of people piling finger food onto paper plates and filling foam cups with soft drinks.

Kendra reached for Mila's hand just to make sure the girl didn't dash into the crowd ahead of her. "We'll work our way around the park," Kendra told her. "I'm sure we'll run into your friends along the way."

More than a half hour passed before the two of them reached the opposite side of the park. By then, Kendra had spoken with several of her daily bakery customers and a neighbor who lived across the courtyard from her in the same apartment complex. Mila had run into Violet, and the two girls had chatted up a storm until Violet's parents had announced they had to leave.

"Gosh, the picnic is just getting started," Mila complained as she watched her friend disappear into the crowd. "I wanted Violet to stay longer."

"I know you did. But Violet's mom and dad had an important appointment they couldn't miss," Kendra explained. "I'm sure you'll find another friend. Are you getting hungry yet? We could walk over to the refreshment tables."

"Okay. But I'm not hungry yet. Do we have to eat right now?"

"No. We can eat later. But most of the picnic crowd is gathered around the tables. Maybe you'll run into Louisa or some of your other friends over there."

They had almost reached the refreshment area when

Mila pulled her mother to a stop and pointed toward an-
other group of people gathered near a stand of tall fir trees.
"Mommy, look at that pretty black-and-white dog. Wow,
I'd really love to have a dog like him."

"He is very pretty." Kendra gave her an indulgent smile.
"What happened to wanting a cat like Morris?"

Her daughter continued to gaze longingly at the energetic dog, which looked to be a border-collie mix. At the
moment, the canine was zooming in happy circles around
a boy, who appeared to be somewhat older than Mila.

Flashing Kendra an impish grin, she said, "Well, a dog
would be good too. But a dog *and* a cat would be the best!"

With a hand on her shoulder, Kendra urged her daughter forward. "That's a pretty tall wish, but we'll see. Come
on. Let's walk on and maybe you can get a closer look at
the dog."

The two of them were maneuvering through the people scattered across the open lawn when Kendra lifted her
gaze to the distance and spotted *him*.

Black cowboy hat, broad shoulders covered with a blue
plaid Western shirt and long legs encased in faded denim,
he stood out from the rest of the crowd.

Dale Dalton.

What was he doing at a picnic for schoolchildren? More
importantly, why was her heart suddenly beating a mile a
minute? Other than his name, she hardly knew the man.

Mila must have spotted him too. She stopped in her
tracks and pointed in Dale's direction.

"Mommy, there's Dale. The cowboy in the bakery."

Kendra was staring directly at him when he suddenly
turned his head and looked straight at them. Did he recognize her and Mila? she wondered. Or had he already
forgotten his visit to the bakery?

She didn't have long to wonder as he suddenly lifted a hand to acknowledge them.

"We don't want to talk to him," Mila said and gestured to a spot at the opposite end of the park, where only a handful of people were milling about. "Let's walk down there and sit on a bench."

Since Mila rarely wanted to sit for any reason, Kendra knew she was purposely trying to avoid Dale. It wasn't unusual for her daughter to develop strong opinions about people, but Kendra found it a bit odd that she viewed Dale as a threat to the wedding plans she'd been making for her mother.

Kendra tried to keep her admonishment gentle. "Walking away from a friend who greets you is rude behavior, Mila. What if you waved at Violet and she took off in the opposite direction?"

"I'd be sad. I'd think she didn't like me," Kendra answered.

Hoping Mila was getting the message, she said, "Okay. We don't want Dale to think we don't like him. So let's go say hello."

Mila hesitated. "Mommy, do you like Dale?"

Even though Kendra was puzzled by her daughter's question, she tried not to show it. "Why, yes, Mila. I do like him. He seems to be a nice guy."

Mila shrugged both shoulders. "I guess he's nice. But he doesn't look anything like my daddy."

Kendra wasn't expecting that sort of thing to come out of her daughter's mouth. Mila hadn't seen her father in a long time. Not since they'd moved to Bronco. Yet, in spite of his neglect, Mila had this fairy-tale image of her father. She often gazed at his photo and talked about how perfect it would be if the three of them were a family again.

The idea sickened Kendra, but she made sure she didn't

criticize Bryce in front of her daughter. Mila needed to learn for herself exactly what sort of man her father really was.

"No. Dale doesn't look like your father. He's not supposed to." She gave Mila's hand a little tug. "Come on. Let's go say hello."

CHAPTER THREE

— ATTENDING THE BACK-TO-SCHOOL picnic at the Bronco town park had never been something on Dale's to-do list. Especially since he had no children of his own. But this year, Holt and Amanda had invited Dale to join them and their ten-year-old son, Robby. And because he hadn't wanted to let down his nephew, Dale had made an effort to make an appearance at the function.

He'd not planned to spend the whole day at the picnic and had been on the verge of telling Holt he was going to head back to the ranch when he'd spotted Kendra and Mila in the distance.

If Dale had been thinking clearly, he would've already guessed that she and her little girl would be at the picnic today. Now, as he watched the two of them turn and walk in his direction, he was so thrilled he wanted to shout with joy.

When they finally reached him, he encompassed them both with a friendly smile. "Hello," he greeted. "I wasn't expecting to see you two here today."

Kendra smiled back at him. "We weren't expecting to see you, either."

➤ From the corner of his eye, Dale could see Mila was sizing him up, as if she wasn't quite sure she was in favor of spending any time in his company. The idea annoyed him. Especially when he'd not done one single thing to make the child dislike him. Other than be a cute cowboy, he thought wryly.

After clearing his throat, he said, "Well, I'm here for my little nephew, Robby. The brown-haired boy with the dog. I imagine by now you've seen the two of them running around here somewhere."

"Actually, we have. Mila was infatuated with the dog."

"That's Bentley. He's quite a character," he said, then asked, "How's the bakery business been going?"

Kendra said, "The bakery has been extremely busy. I think the cooler the weather gets, the more people want to eat sweets and drink coffee."

Dale didn't know what it was about this woman, but the moment he'd first spotted her behind the counter, he'd felt extraordinarily close to her and he was getting that same odd feeling today. It made no sense whatsoever.

"The cupcakes were delicious," he told her. "I shouldn't admit it, but I ate all of them except for the two Mom ate."

Her gentle smile was full of appreciation. "I'm glad to hear it."

Dale leveled a friendly smile on the girl. "Hello, Mila. Are you excited about starting school?"

Mila nodded. "Yes. I get to see my friends and learn all kinds of new things. And I got a bunch of new school clothes to wear."

Dale glanced over at Kendra's amused expression.

"You can't leave fashion out of the equation," Kendra explained.

As Dale's gaze swept over Kendra, he thought how she looked as warm and inviting as a fire on a cold night. He could only imagine how it would feel to cuddle her close and have her soft lips pressed to his.

"Mila would probably enjoy spending time with my

sister-in-law, Sofia. She's a fashion stylist at BH Couture. Ever shop there?"

"Only occasionally. Whenever I need something sort of fancy to wear. Otherwise, I stick to discount stores in Bronco Valley."

He winked at her. "Smart girl. The discount stuff looks just as good to me. But I'm only a cowboy. I don't know a thing about clothing. Except that my mother enjoys filling her closet. And Dad enjoys giving her the money to do it."

She smiled. "Your father must be a thoughtful man."

Thoughtful? Yeah, Dale thought bitterly. Neal was considerate of his wife's feelings now. But it had taken nearly losing her to teach him a hard lesson. After Deborah had learned her husband had cheated on her, she'd suffered a heart attack and Neal had spent the past several years trying to make the mistake up to her.

"He, uh, I guess you could say he's learned how much his wife means to him." He inclined his head toward Holt and Amanda, who were seated several feet off to their left. "My brother and sister-in-law are Robby's parents. I'd like for you to meet them. Or maybe you already know Holt and Amanda."

"I think I remember seeing Amanda and Robby in the bakery," Kendra admitted. "But I've never actually met them, or Holt."

They began walking over to the seated couple, but before they reached them, Robby and his border collie raced up to the group.

"Who's your friends, Uncle Dale?"

Dale quickly introduced his nephew to Kendra and Mila.

"Kendra owns Kendra's Cupcakes," Dale told the boy. "Bet you'd like her cupcakes. You should try them. They're yummy."

A thick fringe of brown hair hid the boy's eyebrows as he rolled a pair of blue eyes at his uncle. "Gosh, Uncle Dale, you need to go to town more often. Me and Mom go in the bakery all the time and eat cupcakes."

Dale shot Kendra a helpless look. "I'm always out of the loop. I guess I spend too much time on a horse."

Kendra chuckled, while next to her, Mila let out a squeal of joy as Bentley approached her with a wildly wagging tail.

She looked eagerly at Robby. "Is it okay to pet your dog?"

"Sure. Bentley loves attention," Robby told her. "He won't bite or anything. That why my parents let me bring him to the picnic."

Mila bent down and gave the dog a hug around the neck. In turn, he let out a happy bark and ran excited circles around her.

"I think Bentley has found a new friend," Dale said to Kendra. "Does she like animals?"

"Oh my. *Like* is an understatement. She's been begging me for a dog or cat. And after today my promise to let her have one is going to be even harder to put off much longer."

"When you do decide to get Mila a pet, you might want to consider adopting one from Happy Hearts Animal Sanctuary. Daphne Taylor Cruise owns the place, and she's always looking to find good forever homes for her animals."

Kendra nodded. "That's a nice thought, Dale. I'll do that," she said, then smiled a bit sheepishly. "Whenever I get myself psyched up to take on the added responsibility of caring for an animal."

He flashed her an encouraging smile. "Take it from a man who cares for animals every day of his life. I can promise you, Kendra, the affection they give back to you makes all the extra work worthwhile."

One of her winged eyebrows arched slightly upward. "I'm surprised to hear you say that."

"Why?" he asked wryly. "Didn't you expect me to have pets?"

Since the cool wind had already stung her cheeks with color, it was impossible to tell if the deepening shade of pink was caused by a blush. Either way, she sure was a beauty, Dale thought.

"Coming from South Beach in Florida, I don't know much about ranchers. I understand there are plenty of ranches in the state, but I was never near any. I just assumed you were all about raising livestock. I guess I never thought of you having pets. The image of you cuddling up to a cat or dog never crossed my mind."

"I see. Well, ranchers aren't any different than regular folks. Except we spend most of our time outdoors and do lots of work from the back of a horse."

In spite of the faint smile on her face, Dale got the impression something had flustered her. Him? What had he done? Grinned in a lecherous way? Said a wrong word? He'd not thought so, but women were sensitive creatures. Any little thing could set them off. Or so it seemed to him.

Hell, Dale, why should it matter to you what Kendra is thinking? It's just like Morgan told you. Kendra isn't your type. Trying to do or say the right thing to her isn't going to win you any favors.

Doing his best to dismiss the pessimistic voice in his head, Dale gestured to his relatives. "Come on. My family is right over here."

She glanced over her shoulder at Mila. The girl was a few feet away, running and romping with Robby and his dog.

Dale said, "She's having fun. I wouldn't bother her with stuffy introductions."

She laughed softly and Dale decided it was a sound he'd like to hear every day of his life.

"You consider introductions stuffy?" she asked.

"I did when I was Mila's age. Especially when I had to stand still and behave politely in front of my elders."

The corners of her lips tilted upward impishly. "You must have been quite a little rounder when you were a child."

He let out a short laugh. "All of us Dalton brothers were little rounders."

"All? How many brothers do you have?"

"There are five of us. I'm second from the youngest, and Holt, who you're about to meet, is second from the eldest."

When they neared Holt and Amanda, the couple rose to their feet and eyed Kendra with friendly curiosity.

Dale quickly introduced her. "This is Kendra Humphrey. She runs Kendra's Cupcakes in Bronco Heights."

"Hello, Kendra. Nice to meet you," Holt greeted, while Amanda tacked on another hello.

Turning to Kendra, he said, "This homely guy is my brother, Holt. And his saint of a wife is Amanda. I call her a saint for putting up with him."

Tall with dark wavy hair and brown eyes, Holt and Dale faintly resembled each other. But as far as their personalities, Holt had turned into a real family man, whereas Dale ran from any woman who mentioned the word *marriage*. Still, the two brothers shared a love of horses and making Dalton's Grange the home their mother deserved.

Holt reached out and gave Kendra's hand a friendly shake. "I should warn you not to listen to Dale. He'll have you believing all of us Daltons are wild guys."

Amanda leveled a pointed look at her husband. "Would he be all wrong?" she joked.

Holt groaned and Dale was glad to see Kendra was taking their teasing banter in stride.

Smiling warmly, Amanda reached for Kendra's hand and gave it a friendly squeeze. "I've seen you working behind the counter at the bakery, but you were always so busy I never had a chance to actually meet you. It's nice to see you again."

Kendra returned the woman's smile. "When we ran into Robby a few moments ago, I thought I recognized him from the bakery."

Raising her hand, she let out a guilty laugh. "Yes. We come in far too often," she admitted. "You make everything far too tempting."

"Thanks for the compliment," Kendra told her, then explained, "I see so many faces in the bakery I can't remember them all, but when I saw Robby and then you my memory clicked."

Dale wasn't sure why Kendra had recognized him among the sea of faces here at the park. But he was thrilled that she'd not only recognized him, but had also agreed to spend these few minutes with him.

"Kendra has a daughter—Mila," Dale told Holt and Amanda. "That's her playing with Robby and Bentley."

"Oh, she's a cutie," Amanda said.

"Mila's only problem is that she's terribly bashful," Dale added, unable to help himself.

Kendra shot him a befuddled look before she burst out laughing.

"Dale is pulling your leg," she said. "Mila never meets a stranger. Unfortunately."

"I wouldn't say that. She might grow up to have an important job in communications," Amanda said.

Kendra darted a glance at Dale. "Well, Mila certainly has a knack for talking. But it's usually at the wrong times."

"Robby is our son," Amanda told her. "He'll be starting fifth grade this year."

"Mila will be a second-grader," Kendra replied.

While the two women continued to discuss the children and the coming school year, Dale remained out of the conversation. But once he caught a short lapse in their talk, he gestured to a park bench a few feet away.

"Would you like to go sit down for a few minutes, Kendra? Looks like Mila is still having a good time with Bentley."

She glanced around to see the children playing fetch with the border collie. Judging by Mila's happy squeals, she was having the time of her life.

"I imagine if I tried to pull her away from that dog right now, I'd never hear the end of it." She gave Dale an agreeable nod. "I suppose I could sit for a few minutes. It's not something I often get to do."

Dale cupped a hand beneath her elbow and internally shouted with triumph when she didn't pull away from his touch. And as they strolled over to the bench, he was struck by the warm scent drifting from her hair and the feel of her arm as it brushed against his.

"It turned out to be great weather for a picnic," he commented. "The wind is a little chilly, but the sun makes up for it."

They reached the bench made of slatted wood and Dale quickly brushed off the seat before she sat on one end.

"It's a lovely day," Kendra agreed. "Mila and I don't get to spend much time outdoors, so it's nice for us to visit the park."

He eased down next to her, but was careful to keep a

small space between them. He didn't want to blow this
opportunity by giving her the impression he was a wolf
in cowboy clothing.

"You don't have a yard where you live?" he asked curiously.

She let out a long sigh. "Yes and no. We live in an apartment complex in Bronco Valley. Everyone's back door
opens up to a large courtyard with a lawn. It's better than
having no yard at all. But I'd like it better if we didn't have
to share it with a dozen other renters. Don't get me wrong.
All my neighbors are great people. I like them. But— Well,
privacy can be a great thing."

"Sure," he told her. "I'm not sure I could get used to
having neighbors living right next to me. If me and my
brothers couldn't yell at each other across the ranch yard,
it would drive me crazy."

She laughed softly and then her blue gaze momentarily
locked with his and Dale's breath lodged in his throat.
What was it about this woman that made him feel so connected to her? he wondered. What made being with her
feel as if he'd known her all of his life? It made no sense.
And if he was being honest with himself, it scared the
heck out of him.

She said, "Well, we're fortunate to have any kind of
yard and Mila is thrilled that the complex allows pets."

Today her long golden hair had been let loose of its bun
to fall freely around her shoulders. Presently, the wind
was whipping the silky strands across her face. As Dale
watched her fingers tuck the wayward tendrils behind her
ears, he was once again surprised to see no engagement
or wedding ring.

Morgan had said she was divorced and that was even
more difficult for Dale to imagine. Why or how could any
man have given up this woman? He must have been the

biggest fool to walk the earth, Dale thought. If she was his wife…

Dale's thoughts came to a screeching halt. There was no chance Kendra would ever be his wife! He didn't even want a wife. So why had the idea even entered his head?

"So you're a part of a big family," she said thoughtfully. "I can't imagine having so many siblings. I only have one brother, Sterling. He's a few years younger than me. He lives in South Beach, not far from our parents."

So her parents and brother still lived in Florida, yet she'd chosen to move way out here to Montana. Three thousand miles wasn't a little move, it was a major one. He couldn't imagine her doing such a thing just for a change of scenery. Might her ex have been involved in her decision? he mused.

"You must miss not being around your family."

She shrugged. "I do. But we stay in touch regularly. And like I said, Mila and I love it here. The small town feel of the place is nice and the people are generally friendly and helpful."

"Sound like you've been here in Bronco long enough to make friends and really call the town home," he said.

"A little more than three years. Fortunately, it only took a few days to find the ideal spot for my bakery, so I started the business right after I negotiated the deal for it. And, yes, Bronco is definitely our home now."

He couldn't believe how interested he was in her life. How much he wanted to know every little detail about her. This wasn't his normal MO with an attractive woman. No, he usually skimmed over the personal and got right down to the physical attraction.

"Were you already experienced with bakery work?" he asked. "I'll be honest, other than my mom, I don't know any women who love to bake."

She chuckled. "I've always enjoyed it and always wanted my own business. I had my own bakery in South Beach and it did very well. And so far, Kendra's Cupcakes has been equally successful, for which I'm very grateful. The people around Bronco have been very supportive of my business."

"Hmm. You made quite a change," he remarked. "From the hot sand and the surf to the cool, rugged mountains. I'm glad the move has turned out good for you."

She cast him a curious glance. "Have you always lived in the Bronco area?"

He shook his head. "No. We moved here about five years ago. Another branch of the Dalton family has a ranch over in Rust Creek Falls, about three hundred or so miles from here, but our dad wanted a bigger place to raise cattle and horses. He liked this area, so when he happened to come into a large sum of money, he bought the property that's now Dalton's Grange."

She seemed genuinely interested in his background and the fact gave him a bit hope. Maybe if he got up the nerve to ask her for a date, she wouldn't laugh in his face.

"So you and your brothers were living with your parents back then?" she asked.

He shook his head. "No. We were all kind of scattered around the state, doing our own thing. But when Dad bought Dalton's Grange, he asked for our help and Mom needed us too. So we all decided to move here."

"Do your brothers like living on the ranch?"

Dale let out a wry grunt. "In the beginning we were all a little reluctant to uproot and move here to Bronco. But it didn't take long for the situation to change. See, none of my brothers were married when we first settled on Dalton's Grange. But then Morgan found Erica and they got hitched. And as you've seen, Holt and Amanda are married. Then Boone and Sofia tied the knot. I'd say my brothers are all happy about the move here—now."

Her smile was thoughtful. "What about you and your single brother? You don't have the urge to take a wife?"

Dale very nearly squirmed, but somehow he managed to keep his ankles crossed casually in front of him.

With an awkward chuckle, he said, "I can't speak for Shep. Except that he's twenty-nine and thinks he's way too young to take on a wife."

"And you?"

His laugh this time was worse than awkward. It sounded more like a painful gurgle.

"I guess I never met a woman who'd be willing to take me on a permanent basis," he said, attempting a joke. "You know the old saying about bachelors. It's hard to change a man who's already set in his ways."

"I hope a woman never changes you, Dale," she said gently. "That would be a shame."

Momentarily stunned by her remark, he stared at her. "A shame? Really?"

Her smile deepened, and then to his great surprise, she reached over and softly laid her hand over the back of his. The touch was as soft as a dove's wing and he tried not to think of how it might feel to have her hand gliding over his body.

"I like you just as you are," she said gently.

Dale's chest swelled to the point that he feared the snaps on the front of his shirt were going to pop wide open.

"That's, uh, nice of you, Kendra. And in case you haven't noticed, I like you too."

"Thank you, Dale. A person can't have too many friends."

He was thinking he could sit on this park bench with

her for hours and still not want to move when Mila suddenly came trotting up to them.

Dale couldn't help but notice how the girl's keen gaze went straight to her mother's hand resting atop his.

"Did you get tired of playing with Bentley?" Kendra asked her.

Mila grimaced. "No. But Robby left to go find his friend and Bentley went with him."

Kendra slowly eased her hand from Dale's and he was immediately struck by the loss of connection.

"Well, we'll go look for Louisa in a minute or two," Kendra told her daughter. "She might have brought her dog with her."

Mila sidled closer to her mother's knee and Dale could see she was weighing the situation carefully. Obviously, the girl wasn't accustomed to seeing Kendra sitting next to a man. At least, not as close as she was to Dale's side.

"She won't have Samson with her, 'cause her parents told her she couldn't bring him to the picnic." She purposely clamped her hand around Kendra's wrist. "But we should walk around, Mommy, and talk to some other people. If we see Mr. Drake he might ask you for another date." She looked directly at Dale. "He's one of the nicest teachers at school."

So Mila was trying to make sure Dale knew he had competition. He had to admit the girl was far from bratty, but underneath her polite manners, there was a wily little mind at work.

Kendra let out a groan of frustration.

"This Mr. Drake must not be a cute cowboy," Dale said to the girl.

Mila looked properly offended. "Of course, he's not a cowboy. He's a teacher."

Dale looked at Kendra and winked. "Guess a guy can't be both things at once."

Groaning again, Kendra shook her head. "Mr. Drake is just a casual friend and that's all he'll ever be." She leveled a pointed look at her daughter. "Remember what we talked about this morning while we were getting ready to come to the park?"

Scuffing her toe on the ground, Mila met her mother's disapproving gaze. "Yes. You said we weren't going to the picnic to hunt a boyfriend. And I'm not supposed to ask any man questions about being married or having kids."

Mila hardly sounded apologetic. But Dale figured the girl didn't believe she was doing anything to be sorry about.

Kendra nodded. "You do remember. So why are you saying such things about Mr. Drake?"

Mila glanced innocently at Dale, then back to her mother. "Well, this is a school picnic and Mr. Drake is a teacher. And lots of teachers are here."

With a hopeless sigh, Kendra rose to her feet. "Looks like it's time Mila and I move on," she said to Dale. "I'll go say goodbye to your brother and sister-in-law."

Dale realized he'd been lucky just to garner this much of Kendra's time. But that didn't stop a wave of disappointment from washing over him.

Rising from the bench, he cupped a hand beneath her elbow. "I'll walk you over."

Once she'd said her goodbyes to Holt and Amanda, she turned a faint smile on Dale.

"Goodbye, Dale. Maybe we'll see each other again sometime."

Maybe? Sometime? Dale was so busy wondering how soon he could walk back into Kendra's Cupcakes without looking like an eager fool that his tongue suddenly forgot how to work.

Finally, he managed a reply. "Yeah. See you around, Kendra."

She walked off with Mila in tow. Behind him, Holt chuckled.

"That was some real cool maneuvering, brother. 'See you around?' Was that the best you could do?"

As he glanced at his brother, Dale could feel his face turning red. "Look, Holt, I can't be Mr. Cool all the time. Besides, Kendra is different. She's not the sort to appreciate a glib line."

Holt exchanged a pointed glance with his wife before he turned an amused grin on Dale.

"Yes. We can see Kendra is *very* different."

CHAPTER FOUR

DARKNESS HAD ALREADY fallen when Dale finally parked his truck in the Dalton's Grange ranch yard. After a hard day of fence building in the warm sun, the night had turned cold. Now the brisk wind penetrating his denim shirt drew his eyes up to the chimney on the sprawling rock-and-log structure he called home. With no sign of smoke, he supposed his father had been too busy to build a fire in the fireplace.

Do you and your brothers like living on the ranch?

The question Kendra had posed to him during the school picnic drifted through Dale's mind once again as he slowly walked to the back of the big ranch house.

Dale realized he'd given her a pared-down answer. He hadn't explained that since his three brothers had married, they'd moved into their own houses on Dalton's Grange. Dale and Shep were the only brothers still residing in the ranch house with their parents. Nor had he told her how all five brothers had frowned upon going into the ranching business with their father. Admitting that tidbit of truth would have required him to explain why, and he wasn't quite ready to talk to Kendra about his father's infidelity. He hardly wanted her thinking like father, like son.

Actually, the only reason Dale and his brothers had agreed to move to Bronco and throw their efforts into building Dalton's Grange was because of the deep love they all had for their mother. At that time, Deborah's health had been fragile and, for her sake, Dale and his siblings had felt like they needed to show a united front. As a result, she now had the home she'd always wanted, and thankfully, their father had kept his promise and turned over a new and better leaf.

At the back of the house, Dale crossed the porch and entered a door that led directly into the kitchen. Except for his mother, who was busy at the counter putting leftovers from the evening meal into plastic containers, the room was empty.

She glanced over her at him as he hung his hat on a peg by the door. "I'm glad you're home. I was beginning to worry."

He walked over and planted a kiss on her cheek. "Now why would you worry about me? I'm too mean to get hurt."

"Ha! There isn't a mean bone in your body. Not since you grew past the age of thirteen," she teased, then asked, "Neal said you and Shep were fencing all day. Is that why you were late getting back to the ranch?"

"Yes. We had to finish one section before we could let the cattle back into the pasture. And Dad has decided to replace more cross fence than he'd first planned."

Deborah shook her head. "I told Neal he should hire a fencing crew instead of putting the load on you and Shep. It's very nearly fall roundup time. You two need to be getting ready for that job."

"Fence builders are an expensive luxury," he told her. "It isn't going to hurt me and Shep to work until dark."

He peered over her shoulder at the food she'd put into a large container. "Is that Swiss steak? Smells like it."

She flashed a smile at him. "It is. And since your dad and I are the only ones who've eaten, there's plenty left of everything. Want me to fill a plate for you before I put everything in the fridge?"

In her early sixties, his mother was still an attractive woman with a slender build and blond hair worn in a smooth bob. At one time, before she'd met Neal, she'd had a job in the corporate world. But most of her adult life had been spent as a wife and mother to her five sons. If Dale ever did get the crazy notion to look for a wife, he'd want one as loving and devoted as Deborah had been to Neal. But finding a needle in a haystack would be easier than finding that kind of love and devotion, Dale thought.

"I'd appreciate it, Mom. But I can take care of myself. You go sit down with Dad or whatever you need to do."

"Neal is in his study. Talking on the phone with a cattle broker."

"Oh? Buying or selling?" Dale asked.

Deborah chuckled. "Buying, of course. Your father is always thinking in bigger terms. But he promises not to make any deals without all of you boys involved first." She made a shooing gesture with her hand. "Go on and wash. I'll take care of heating your supper."

Dale went to the mudroom, which was located just off the kitchen. After using the deep double sink to wash his hands and face, he returned to find his mother had already placed the warmed plate of food on the table, along with a long-necked bottle of beer.

"You're an angel, Mom. Thanks."

"Just doing my job." She carried salt and pepper shakers over to the table and took a seat in the chair opposite his.

Even though his mother had once had a promising career in business, Dale supposed being a mother had become the most important thing in Deborah's life. She'd always put all of her energy into caring for her husband and children. As a mother, she'd never been overly strict. But she'd not let any of her boys go unpunished if they crossed the boundaries of right and wrong.

The thought made him wonder about Kendra and the relationship she had with Mila. He supposed if it came right down to it, Kendra would choose her daughter's happiness over her own. Never being a parent himself, Dale was hardly in a position to know whether that was good or bad. But it made him wonder how Kendra could possibly find a man to love if she allowed Mila to dictate her life.

He glanced at his mother. "Speaking of Shep, has he shown up tonight? Earlier this afternoon, he left the area we were fencing to go into town after more supplies."

She said, "He stopped by the house to change his dirty shirt for a clean one and told me he'd grab a burger or something in town. I don't think he's gotten back from Bronco yet."

"Probably ran into a girlfriend." And if that was the case, he most likely wouldn't be back to Dalton's Grange until the wee hours of the morning, but his mother didn't need to be reminded of her sons' carousing ways. At least, not her single sons. Although, Dale had to admit it had been a while since he'd even gone on a date. For some reason, the idea of calling up one of his old girlfriends for a night out on the town just didn't hold any appeal. Not since he'd met Kendra.

Damn. Was he turning into a sap, or what?

Deborah rested her chin on the heel of her palm as she slanted Dale a thoughtful look. "Son, there's something I've been wanting to talk to you about."

He shoveled up a forkful of the smothered steak. "Okay, shoot, Mom."

"It's about all those cupcakes you've been bringing home from town. I think it's extra nice of you to want to save me from baking, but, Dale, we can't possibly eat all of them. I'm going to have to freeze that last bunch you brought in yesterday and save them for later."

Dale felt his cheeks growing warm. Since the picnic in the park, he'd visited the bakery a couple of times. Once on Monday morning, when he'd run an errand in town for his father, and last evening after making a trip to the feed store for vet supplies. And during each visit, he'd purchased two dozen cupcakes in assorted flavors.

"Sorry, Mom. I guess I didn't realize just how many I'd been buying."

She reached over and patted his arm. "Honestly, Dale, I'm surprised that you've been bothering to stop by a bakery. I've never known you to be so into cupcakes."

He downed a few swallows of beer, then gave her a lopsided grin. "Okay, Mom. I need to fess up. I've been stopping by Kendra's Cupcakes. And I had to buy something or I'd look like a jerk or worse. Because—Well, the woman who runs the bakery—she's really special. And I'd like to get to know her better."

Deborah's eyebrows arched with faint surprise. "You mean you'd like to ask her for a date?"

"Exactly. But I'm not sure— Heck, Mom, I'm afraid if I do ask her, she'll turn me down."

Frowning, she studied him for a thoughtful moment. "This isn't like you, Dale. You've never exactly lacked self-confidence."

"No. But Kendra is different. She's been married before and she has a seven-year-old daughter. And the child thinks I'm all wrong for her mother."

Deborah continued to frown. "How do you know the child thinks that about you?"

"Because she told me directly to my face."

She shook her head with wry amusement. "Nothing like the honesty of a child. But, Dale, I wouldn't worry about what the child thinks. If you believe you have a chance with Kendra, then go ahead and ask her for a date. The worst she can do is say no."

Dale reached for his beer. "Yeah, but once she says no that might be the only answer she'll ever give me."

"The way I see things, Dale, if she's not smart enough to see what a great guy you are, then you need to find a gal who does."

"I don't want to find anyone else."

The admission was out of him before he could stop the words, and from the look on his mother's face, he could see she was somewhat surprised.

"I'm curious now," she said. "Is this woman from around here?"

Dale continued to eat. It was easier to keep his eyes on his food than to deal with his mother's searching gaze.

"She moved here a little over three years ago from South Beach, Florida."

"Hmm. Quite a switch from there to here. What made her come to Bronco? Does she have relatives here?"

"No. She just wanted a change, I think. Although, I wonder…well, I wonder if—"

"She's running away from something?" Deborah asked, finishing for him.

He didn't know how his mother managed to do it, but she always seemed to be able to put her finger right on the spot that was itching.

"Sort of," he admitted. "I've only talked to her a couple of times. Mostly when I went to the school picnic with Holt and Amanda. She never mentioned she wanted to get away from her ex or anything. But I keep asking myself why she'd need to move three thousand miles. And maybe none of that should matter."

"You know, I think what you just said makes the most

sense. If you like this woman, then none of that should matter. She'll share things about her life with you eventually."

"You mean, if she agrees to date me?"

Smiling, Deborah gave his arm another pat. "I'd be very surprised if she turned you down. But, Dale, I don't think you should keep buying cupcakes to impress her." She flashed him a smile. "Maybe next time spend your money on a few maple bars or apple fritters for a change."

Dale chuckled. "Good advice, Mom."

THE NEXT EVENING, as closing time was drawing near, Kendra was getting ready to package the unsold cupcakes when the door chimed and she looked up to see Dale entering the bakery.

This was the third visit he'd made to Kendra's Cupcakes this week and she had to admit that each time she saw him she was thrilled just a little more. Now, as she gazed at his smiling face, something snapped inside her and she suddenly felt as soft and gooey as the inside of a chocolate bismarck.

"Hi, Dale. You're out late this evening."

He glanced at the clock hanging on the wall behind the checkout counter. "Oh. Are you about to close?"

"I've sent my barista home and Andrea has left. You're the only customer I've had in the last thirty minutes. In fact, I was about to lock the door and help Jackie with the cleaning."

He looked totally crestfallen and she couldn't help but laugh. "Don't worry. I'll lock you inside and let you out whenever you're ready to leave."

He chuckled. "So in other words I won't be held captive?"

"Not against your will." With a light laugh, she gestured over to the empty tables and chairs. "Would you like to sit

down and have a cup of coffee? I'll make us a fresh cup
and there are plenty of leftover goodies."

A wide grin dimpled his cheeks. "Sounds great.
Thanks."

She grabbed her keys from under the checkout coun-
ter, then went to the front door. As she locked it, she said,
"Sit at any table you'd like. They've all been wiped down.
What would you like to eat? A cupcake?"

His chuckle held a sheepish sound. "No. I think I'll
go for something different. Other than cupcakes, what's
your specialty?"

"Well, I like to think everything I serve tastes good. So
I'll just surprise you," she told him. "Make yourself comfortable and I'll be back in a couple of minutes."

As Dale took a seat, Kendra hurried to the kitchen.
Jackie was already starting her nightly cleaning routine
by washing the empty display trays. She shot Kendra a
puzzled look when she saw her making coffee at the pod
machine they used for their personal use in the kitchen.

"I thought you were going to lock the door."

"The door is locked. But I have one customer I've invited to have coffee."

Jackie's expression turned shrewd. "Dale Dalton?"

Kendra smiled. "How did you guess?"

Jackie rolled her eyes. "Let me see. The cowboy has
been here three times this week. And I don't think he's
showing up because he has a sweet tooth."

Kendra wasn't going to argue Jackie's point. She was
beginning to believe Dale had developed a crush on her
and the notion made her so ridiculously happy, she felt like
laughing and crying at the same time.

"I think you're right, Jackie. And you know what—
it feels good to have a guy like him look at me like I'm
an angel."

Jackie sighed. "Maybe one of these days I'll discover how it feels to have a hunky cowboy look at me like I'm something special. But for now, I'm just glad Mila is at the sitter's. Otherwise, she'd be wedged between the two of you."

Kendra groaned. "Don't remind me."

Carrying the two coffees, she headed out of the kitchen and paused at the display cases long enough to place the cups and several bakery items on a serving tray.

When she approached the table where he was sitting, he immediately rose and pulled out a chair for her. "You're making me feel special, Kendra. Or do you often do this for cowboys you feel sorry for?"

The idea that he thought she probably had lots of suitors was a compliment, she supposed. Yet, the notion of her having the time or inclination to flirt with male customers was laughable.

What do you think you're doing now, Kendra? Aren't you flirting with Dale?

Doing her best to ignore the provocative questions swirling through her mind, she placed the tray on the table.

"Actually, I don't do this sort of thing, period," she told him. "And what makes you think I might feel sorry for a big strong guy like you?"

His low chuckle was more like a purr. "Maybe because I look like a lost and lonely pup," he joked.

He was standing directly behind her with his hands resting on the back of her chair, yet she could easily imagine their warmth curling around her shoulders, drawing her closer.

Her throat suddenly tightened, forcing her to swallow before she spoke. "Are you always so funny?"

He moved around the table and took the chair opposite hers. "Believe it or not, I have my serious moments. But my motto is that life is mostly meant to be enjoyed. I like to laugh and be happy. Don't you?"

She handed one of the coffees to him, then poured a dollop of cream into her own cup and slowly stirred the steaming liquid.

"Sure. Sometimes it's not always easy to put on a happy face, but I try. Especially for Mila's sake." She pushed a brownie topped with chopped walnuts toward him. "If you like chocolate, try a bite of this."

He bit into the brownie and as Kendra watched him chew, she couldn't help but think how different he was from her ex-husband. Bryce considered roughing it in the outdoors to be playing eighteen holes of golf. The man handled little more than an ink pen, a cell phone and the keyboard of a computer. Whereas Dale worked in the harsh elements. His hands were tough and strong from handling ropes and saddle leathers. He nurtured the land and the animals on it, because it was something he loved, instead of a means to make money.

Yes, Dale was different in the best kind of way, Kendra thought. But would he be best for her?

"Mmm. This is delicious," Dale commented after he'd swallowed a couple of bites of the brownie. "Mom was right when she told me I needed to buy more than just cupcakes."

Kendra slanted him a quizzical look. "Your mother told you that?"

His grin was sheepish. "She thought I was overdoing things with all the cupcakes. Guess I'm a little too obvious, huh?"

Kendra couldn't explain the attraction she felt toward Dale. Over the years, she'd been around good-looking men with plenty of sex appeal, but none of them had left an impression on her. Not the way Dale had firmly stuck in her mind.

"To tell you the truth, I'm enjoying you being obvious."

He blew out a heavy breath. "Whew! That's a relief."

She could have told him she was completely endeared by his effort to spend a few minutes with her. She could confess how each day this week, she'd watched for him to walk through the door. And then she'd be the one looking totally obvious.

But suddenly none of that mattered, and before she could analyze what she was about to do, she reached across the table and placed her hand over his. "I think you're very nice, Dale. And I'm wondering if you'd like for us to go out one evening? Maybe have a burger or pizza together?"

His blue eyes stared at her in complete fascination. "Are you serious?"

Her fingers tightened around his hand and just like the day in the park, it felt good to touch him. It felt right to be connected to him even in this simple way.

"Absolutely, I'm serious," she answered. "Why? You don't think you'd like to go out with me?"

He opened his mouth to speak, but when nothing came out, he turned his head to one side and coughed. After clearing his throat a second time, he said, "Sorry. I promise I'm not coming down with the flu. You shocked me, that's all. I was thinking— Well, I've been wanting to get up enough nerve to ask you for a date. But I thought you'd probably turn me down."

At some point since she'd met this man, she'd memorized everything about his features. The stubborn jut to his chin, the faint lines fanning from the corners of his eyes, the deep grooves in his cheeks whenever he smiled and the sparkle in his vivid blue gaze. His was a face to remember.

"Why would you think such a thing? I haven't been cold or distant, have I?"

His short laugh was a sound of disbelief. "Not at all. But I'm just a cowboy. And you're beautiful and successful and, well, Mila doesn't exactly consider me Mr. Right for her mother."

He could never guess just how much his unassuming attitude drew her to him. Yet she wanted him to know he was just as good, or better, than any man she'd ever met.

"Listen, Dale, Mila is a child. She doesn't pick my friends. Furthermore, don't ever call yourself *just a cowboy*. Your job is as admirable and as important as mine, or anyone's." She leaned slightly toward him. "So what's your answer about the date?"

His hand shifted beneath hers and then his fingers were sliding intimately between hers. The contact sent a flood of heat up her arm and straight to her face. The gentle touch also filled her with an odd sense of belonging.

"Would it embarrass you if I stuck my head out the door and let out a happy howl?" he asked.

Smiling, she gestured toward the door. "Be my guest. If anyone happens to be walking by, they'll just think you've eaten one of my special 'happy' cupcakes."

His skeptical expression made her chuckle.

"You make 'happy' cupcakes?" he asked. "What sort of magic ingredient do they have in them? Bourbon? Rum?"

"I was only teasing about the cupcakes," she confessed. "But I'm glad I made you happy."

His blue eyes sparkling, he asked, "So when would you like to go on this date? Is tomorrow night too soon?"

She pretended to ponder his question for a moment before she answered. "Let's see, tomorrow is Saturday. The bakery is closed on Sunday and Mila doesn't have to go to school. I think tomorrow night would be perfect. Will that fit in with your schedule?"

The grin he gave her very nearly melted her bones. And for a split second she wondered if going out with Dale might be worse than playing with fire. On the other hand, why should she be concerned about getting her wings scorched? She wasn't going to allow herself to get close enough to the man to risk getting burned.

"No worries. I'll make it fit." Reaching inside the front of his jacket, he pulled out a cell phone. "I'd better put your address in my phone so I won't forget it."

He punched in her private cell number, along with her address, and was slipping the phone back into his jacket when the sound of the kitchen door opening caught their attention.

"Don't mind me," Jackie sang out. "I'm only going to pack up the leftovers."

Kendra glanced at the clock and was shocked to see she'd been sitting here with Dale much longer than she'd thought.

"I didn't know it was so late," she told Jackie. "But there's no need for you to deal with the leftovers. I'll take care of them later."

Jackie continued to pull out the trays of unpurchased pastries. "Finish your coffee, Kendra, and let me take care of this. The nursing home is expecting me in about thirty minutes. A patient is having a birthday and the staff wants to treat her with special refreshments."

Sizing up the situation, Dale gulped down the last of his coffee, then rose to his feet. "I'm keeping you from your work."

"There's really no need for you to rush off," Kendra told him. "And you haven't finished your brownie."

He winked at her. "I'll take it with me. I have chores

waiting on me at the ranch. And it's past your closing time. We'll talk tomorrow night."

Disappointed, but doing her best not to show it, she stood and gathered what was left of his brownie and the other desserts he'd not yet sampled. "Okay. Give me a minute and I'll put these in a container for you."

Kendra walked behind the display counters and over to a wall of storage cabinets. As she fished a foam box from a shelf, Jackie sidled up to her and silently mouthed, *I'm sorry.*

Shaking her head, Kendra said under her breath, "Don't be."

After Kendra put Dale's treats in the take-out box, she walked over to where he was waiting for her to unlock the door.

When she handed him the container, he said, "This feels too heavy."

"I added a few more brownies—for your mother," she explained.

He gave her a grateful smile. "Thanks. I'll be sure and let her know you sent them to her." He pushed the door partially open with his shoulder, then paused. "I'll see you tomorrow. Six thirty okay?"

The very thought of being alone with Dale sent a silly little thrill rushing through her. "I'll be ready. Goodbye for now."

He lifted a hand in farewell, then slipped out the door. Kendra didn't linger to watch him leave. As soon as she carefully locked the door behind him, she hurried over to where Jackie was still working to clear the trays.

The redhead cast a rueful grin at Kendra. "I'm so sorry, Kendra. I didn't mean to interrupt your coffee date, but I had to come out here and get these things."

"Don't be silly," Kendra told her. "You're only doing what you're supposed to be doing."

Jackie waggled her eyebrows in a suggestive way. "So how did your coffee with the cowboy go? From what I could see, you two were looking extra chummy."

Kendra couldn't stop a smug grin from crossing her face. "We're going on a date tomorrow night."

"Oh. So he finally decided to ask you out," Jackie said as she hurriedly placed the last of the maple bars into a cardboard box. "That's great, Kendra."

"Before you get the wrong idea," Kendra said, "Dale didn't do the asking. I did."

Jackie gasped and whirled around to stare at her. "*You?* Pardon me if I faint! What's come over you, Kendra?"

If anyone knew how hard Kendra worked at the bakery, and how rarely she took time off for any kind of entertainment, it was Jackie. The young woman also knew how Kendra had become gun-shy of dating and how mistrustful she'd grown of men since her divorce from Bryce.

"Honestly, I can't explain it," Kendra told her. "Something about the man gets to me. And when I talk with him, he, uh, well, he seems very sincere."

Jackie tapped a forefinger against her chin. "In other words, you don't think he's faking his niceness?"

She shrugged. "I'll admit I don't know much about him—yet. Mila keeps telling me that Dale isn't my type. And maybe she's right. Heaven knows, she's been right about people before. But I need to find out for myself if he's all wrong for me."

"Sure," Jackie said slyly. "After all, there's nothing wrong in having a little fun while you're getting to know the man."

Kendra wasn't looking for fun with Dale. Nor was she searching for everlasting love from the sexy cowboy. She simply wanted to feel like a desirable woman again without having to worry about commitments or promises.

"I'm not sure I remember how to have fun with a man, Jackie. And there's something else about this date that I'm a bit concerned about."

"Oh? What's that? You're wondering what to wear?"

Kendra rolled her eyes toward the ceiling. "I wish that was my only concern."

Jackie picked up the large box of baked goods she'd gathered for the nursing home, then she turned a knowing look on Kendra.

"Mila?" she asked.

Kendra nodded as she tried to imagine the look on Mila's face when she heard her mother was going on a date with Dale Dalton.

"Yes, Mila." Kendra sighed. "She tells anyone who'll listen that I'm going to get married and give her a daddy. And I keep telling her it's not that easy."

"So? You don't think Dale would make Mila a good daddy?"

Kendra's mouth fell open, and laughing, Jackie hurried out the door.

But later, as Kendra finished closing up and turning off the lights, she thought once again about Jackie's loaded question.

When Dale had talked about his three brothers finding wives and making families of their own, he'd not exactly stated he was against the idea for himself. But he'd implied he was perfectly happy as a bachelor.

Which meant their time together tomorrow night would be nothing more than fun and laughs. But that was just fine with her. In spite of what Mila was broadcasting to all their friends, Kendra wasn't looking for a husband. So she and Dale should make the perfect match.

CHAPTER FIVE

THE NEXT EVENING, Dale was walking across the ranch yard to his truck when Morgan stepped out of the barn and intercepted him.

"Look at you! What sort of fancy shindig is going on in Bronco tonight? Erica hasn't mentioned anything. And you're too dressed up for having a few beers at Doug's bar."

"No fancy shindig. And I'm not headed to Doug's." Dale self-consciously glanced down at his dark jeans and Western-cut leather jacket. "Do I look overly dressed?"

Morgan pushed the brim of his hat back just a fraction as he gave Dale a closer inspection. "You haven't told me where you're going yet."

"Do I have to?"

"No. You don't have to tell me anything." Grinning, he lifted a hand in a wave, then started walking in the direction of the house. "See you later."

Dale trotted after him. "Okay. I might as well tell you. Most likely you'll hear about it, anyway."

Morgan turned and arched his eyebrows. "You've got me curious now."

Dale tapped a finger against the brim of his black hat. It wasn't exactly a new one, but he only pulled it out for special occasions. Now, with Morgan raking him over with a keen eye, he was beginning to feel like a fool.

"You think the hat looks a bit too much for a casual date?" he asked.

"The hat looks like you've never done a day's work in your life. So who's the gal you're trying so hard to impress?"

Dale wanted to puff his chest out, but he didn't. "Kendra Humphrey. You remember, the baker I asked you about?"

Morgan was clearly surprised. "You asked *her* for a date and she accepted? Man, I never would've thought she'd agree to go out with you." He held up a hand before Dale could take offense. "Not that there's anything wrong with you. But she's a city girl. And—"

"Yeah. And I'm hayseed. But maybe she's getting into organic things," Dale joked. "Anyway, you have it all wrong, brother. Kendra is the one who asked me for a date. Not the other way around."

Morgan playfully swatted Dale's arm. "Since when have you started lying to your brother?"

Dale used his finger to make a cross over his heart. "If I'm lyin', I'm dyin'. But I'll tell you, Morgan, I nearly fell out of my chair when she asked me."

Morgan shrugged. "Well, if she's not concerned about dating a confirmed bachelor, then who am I to worry about either one of you. Go and have fun."

"Thanks, Morgan. And for what it's worth, I wouldn't ever want to do anything to hurt Kendra."

"I believe you," he said. "Now, I'd better go say goodnight to Mom and Dad and head on home before Erica gets out of bed and tries to fix supper."

"I haven't had a chance to ask you today, but how is she?"

Morgan made an okay sign with his thumb and forefinger. "So far, so good. Keep her and the baby in your prayers, will you?"

"Always, brother."

Minutes later, after Dale had climbed into his truck and

headed to town, he wasn't just thinking about Morgan and his unborn child, he was also thinking about Kendra. If she was carrying Dale's child and the pregnancy was at risk, he'd be crazy with fear. He'd be worried about the wife he loved. He'd be frantic for the baby. A baby he would very much want to love and nurture and see grow into an adult.

But by the time he was entering Bronco city limits, he realized there wasn't any need for him to be mulling over such serious matters. Especially tonight. He and Kendra were simply going to enjoy each other's company. He'd leave the serious stuff to his married brothers.

KENDRA GAVE HER hair a final brush before she pinned one side back with a tortoiseshell barrette, then stepped back to carefully study her image in the dresser mirror.

Her dress was made of cotton material printed with tiny brown, gold and orange flowers. The bodice was fitted, while a full, tiered skirt floated over her brown suede boots. She'd fastened tiny silver-dove earrings to her ears, but that was the only jewelry she'd chosen to wear. After all, they were only going out for a burger or pizza. She didn't want Dale to think she was overdoing her appearance.

Satisfied that she looked decent, she walked over to the closet and pulled out a jean jacket when the doorbell rang.

Her heart thumping with eager excitement, she tossed the garment over her arm and hurried out to the living room to answer the ring.

After a quick peek through the peephole, she opened the door to find Dale standing on the small portico with his hat in his hand and a wide smile on his face.

"Hi, Dale. Please come in. I'm almost ready. Did you have any trouble finding the apartment complex?"

He stepped across the threshold and stood to one side while she closed the door behind him.

"No trouble at all," he told her. "The navigation system on my truck makes me feel like a genius."

He followed her out of the short foyer and into the living room, where Kendra turned a smile on him. "You should feel like a genius, Dale. I can't figure how to work the system in my vehicle. If I followed its directions, I'd end up in Wyoming or Idaho."

Her admission drew a chuckle out of him, but the amusement quickly fell from his face as his gaze swept over her.

"Wow, Kendra. You look too pretty tonight."

The compliment thrilled her and Kendra wondered if she'd reverted back to her teenage days, when the attention of a cool guy had left her sighing. She was being ridiculous. But just for tonight, it felt oh, so nice to feel young and desirable.

"You look pretty spiffy yourself," she told him.

On all the occasions Kendra had seen Dale, his jeans had been extremely faded and work-worn with frayed hems. Tonight they were dark without any rips or strings, and his black hat, which was normally dusty and sweat-stained, looked so clean it could've been new.

"Thanks," he said. "Mom always told us boys that the best way to impress a girl is to show her you can clean up good. So I tried."

"You've done very well," she told him, then gestured around the living room that was simply furnished with a long burgundy-colored couch, two matching armchairs and a TV. "This is my little home. Would you care to see the rest of it?"

"Sure. From what I can see of this room you're a tidy housekeeper."

"I have you fooled," she said with a wry groan, then

motioned for him to follow her through an open doorway. "Don't swipe your fingers over the coffee or end tables. They're probably dustier than one of your cattle pens."

They crossed a short empty space and through another doorway to the kitchen. The long, narrow room was out-fitted with stainless-steel appliances and a work island in the middle. A large window over the sink revealed a view of the courtyard in back.

"This is where I do more baking. Whenever I'm not at the bakery." She gestured to their left, to the open space beyond a breakfast bar. "That's the dining room over there. But since it's just the two of us. Mila and I usually eat at the breakfast bar."

"This is cozy," he told her. "Mom would love this kitchen. She wouldn't have to walk her legs off to get from the stove to the fridge."

She said, "I've never seen Dalton's Grange, or your parents' ranch house, but compared to it, I imagine this apartment looks like a dollhouse."

"Originally, Dad built the ranch house on Dalton's Grange large enough to house his five sons, so, yeah, it's huge. But you have plenty of space for just you and Mila."

"Yes. But you're not counting the fact that it often feels as though Mila is the same as having three daughters."

He chuckled and she motioned for him to follow her out of the kitchen and into a hallway.

"Two bedrooms and two baths are down that way. I'd show them to you, but they're a bit messy. It's been a hectic week," she explained, then added, "Maybe the next time you're here I'll have them tidy enough for you to see. And when we have more time I'll show you out back. That is, if you—" She broke off as it suddenly dawned on her that she was chattering like a parakeet. She was also assuming that Dale would want a next time with her.

"If I what?" he prompted her to finish.

Her cheeks grew warm as she met his inquisitive gaze. "Sorry, Dale. I was getting a little ahead of myself. Are you ready to go?"

"Whenever you're ready," he replied.

He came to stand by her side and Kendra was reminded of the fact that they were completely alone, and he was looking at her the way a man looked at a woman he found attractive. Or was she imagining the faint glint in his blue eyes? Either way, he was shaking up her senses.

"Is Mila not here? I thought I'd say hello before we left."

"She's at the sitter's house. Which, lucky for me, is only four doors down from mine. I've been friends with Ada since we first moved here, so when Mila is with her, I don't worry."

"Oh, I assumed you probably had a sitter stay here with her." He leveled a rueful look at her. "But I guess it's probably best she isn't here. I don't imagine she was too happy about you going out with me tonight."

"Actually, Mila didn't put up a fuss at all. Probably because I promised her a trip to Happy Hearts in a week or two. Next to having a father in her life, the thing she wants the most is a dog or cat to call her own. And, anyway, she doesn't believe you're anything to worry about."

He let out a short laugh. "She knows how to make a guy feel really important."

They moved back into the living room where Kendra slipped on her jean jacket and picked up her purse from a console table.

As the two of them migrated to the front door, Kendra said, "You'll have to overlook her, Dale. She hasn't seen her father since a little before her fourth birthday and I think her memory of him is somewhat blurred. In her mind, she has the image of a perfect father. But you and I know there isn't such a thing. My father has been a wonderful parent, but even he makes mistakes."

He grimaced. "My dad has been far from perfect. But he tries. And he loves his family. In the end that's what matters the most, I think."

She stifled a snort. She could explain to Dale how Bryce hadn't even acknowledged his shortcomings, much less tried to make amends with his daughter. But this first date with him was hardly the time to spotlight her failed marriage.

Outside, Kendra locked the door to her apartment, and as they walked to his truck, he rested a hand against the small of her back. The night had turned chilly and a canopy of stars stretched above their heads.

She didn't know if it was walking so close to his side, or something about the velvety sky that was making her feel unusually romantic. But for one wild second, Kendra wished he would pull her into his arms and kiss her.

The urge was unlike anything she'd ever felt and caused her to wonder if she could restrain herself around this good-looking cowboy.

Why would you want to, Kendra? Don't you think you've gone long enough without a man's physical affection?

By the time he'd helped her into the truck and he'd driven out of the parking lot, she'd pushed the taunting voice out of her head. But not the desire to be close to him. She wasn't quite sure how she could get rid of that feeling.

AFTER A SHORT discussion about what they wanted to eat, Dale and Kendra ended up choosing Bronco Brick Oven Pizza, a small, family-owned pizza parlor located in Bronco Heights, not far from Kendra's Cupcakes.

After turning in their order, they took a seat at one of the small square tables.

When the owner, who also served as a waiter, arrived with their drinks, he placed a fat white candle in the middle of the table and stuck a burning match to the wick.

"There you go, Kendra. Candlelight for a lovely lady."

"How thoughtful of you, Mr. Leone. Thank you."

The older gentleman with curly salt-and-pepper hair smiled with approval as his gaze encompassed the two of them. "It's nice to see you with a companion, Kendra."

Dale noticed a blush bloom upon her cheeks and he couldn't help thinking how lovely she looked with a soft pink color on her lips and her hair curved gently upon her shoulders.

Smiling at the man, Kendra gestured to Dale. "Mr. Leone, I'd like for you to meet Dale Dalton. His family owns Dalton's Grange."

The barrel-chested man reached out and shook Dale's hand. "Oh, yes, I've heard of the ranch. Maybe you have a brother who comes in to eat quite often. His name is Shep."

Dale nodded. "Shep is my younger brother. In fact, he's the baby of the bunch."

Mr. Leone's tanned face spread into a clever grin. "He comes in with plenty of different ladies."

Dale let out a good-natured groan. "That's my little brother, all right."

The other man laughed knowingly. "Your pizza will be ready in just a few more minutes."

They both thanked Mr. Leone and once he moved away from their table, Dale looked at Kendra and said, "Nice guy. I take it you come here often."

"More often than I should. Mila loves the lasagna they make here." She picked up her drink and sipped through the straw. "Mr. Leone has told me some very interesting stories about his grandparents and some of the horrors and hardships they went through in Italy during World War

Two. Sometimes when I'm thinking I've had a tough day, or life is hard, I think about his grandparents and realize my life is a romp through a flower garden."

"I do the same thing. Only I think of my parents," he admitted. "Things weren't always as good for them as they are now. Dad was— Well, he wasn't always the responsible sort of guy he should've been. And Mom didn't have it easy taking care of five boys on a shoestring budget."

She cast him a curious look. "Clearly, he got things turned around. How did he do it?"

With a slight shake of his head, he said, "I guess you could say two things turned Dad around. Mom had a heart attack. And he won a huge pile of money in Vegas."

"Gambling?"

Nodding, Dale reached for his soda. "Yes. And thankfully he decided to use the money for a good cause—purchasing the property for Dalton's Grange."

"Hmm. Tell me if I'm being too nosy, but your mother's heart attack—was that before he won the jackpot?"

Other than his brothers, Dale didn't discuss his parents' past problems to anyone. But Kendra was different. Now that he was beginning to know her, he didn't think she was the sort to look down on anyone just because they'd made mistakes. Still, he didn't want Kendra thinking he'd ever follow his father's wandering footsteps.

"Yes, her heart attack was before. You see, Mom and Dad were having marital problems." He drew in a bracing breath. "Dad was a serial cheater, until Mom had a heart attack. The fear of losing her opened his eyes to the mistakes he'd made. So when the money came along, he wanted to use it to make a special home for her—for the both of them."

"I'm sorry your mother has gone through so much. But to me she sounds like a woman with a strong constitution.

Otherwise, she wouldn't have survived the heart attack or her husband's betrayal."

He grimaced. "The whole thing is not something I like repeating to anyone. But I, uh, thought you'd see it with an open mind."

A smile suddenly brightened her face. "That's a nice thing to say, Dale. And I do see your parents' problems with an open mind. And there's something else I see."

"What's that?"

"You shouldn't be trying to shoulder the blame of your dad's mistakes."

He stared at her, amazed that she'd so accurately picked up on his feelings. "Okay, I admit I'm guilty of thinking Dad's disreputable behavior puts a blot on me and my brothers."

"That's easy to understand. But it's not your fault. Just like it's not my fault that Mila's father has basically deserted her. I've learned you can't change a person for the better, Dale. He or she has to make the change on their own. Be thankful your father made that choice."

He grinned at her. "I'm glad you asked me out on this date, Kendra."

She laughed and the sound made his heart feel as if it just sprouted wings.

"I'm glad I asked you for a date too."

KENDRA AND DALE were both stuffed with pizza when they finally walked out of the restaurant and down the street to his parked truck.

"I've never eaten pizza that tasted so good. I made a hog of myself," Dale said as he helped her into the truck.

"That's because you were eating the real deal," she told him. "Not the fake stuff."

He climbed into the driver's seat, but didn't immediately

start the engine. Instead, he looked over at her and Kendra was surprised to see a serious expression on his face.

"The real deal is always better than make-believe. But you know something, I'm not having to pretend I'm enjoying this evening with you. It all feels pretty darn nice."

Something inside Kendra melted like warm sugar, and without hesitation, she reached across the console and wrapped her fingers around his.

"I'm enjoying it too, Dale. Very much. It's a little crazy how easy it is for me to talk with you. I don't normally chatter this much to anyone. Not about personal things."

His blue gaze swept gently over her face. "Same thing with me. And according to Mila we're not even each other's type," he added with a wry grin.

Her spirits soared and for the first time since her divorce, Kendra saw a future full of blue skies and warm sunshine. Maybe Dale wouldn't turn out to be her special "forever" guy. But he was making her see that she could want again, that she could still hope and dream for the things she wanted in her future.

"I think we're proving my daughter wrong." She squeezed his hand, then eased back in her seat. "So where are we going now? I still have an hour and a half before I have to collect Mila from Ada's."

"What would you like to do? I'm here to serve."

She bestowed him with a warm smile. "Anything—as long as it doesn't involve a crowd of people. And don't get me wrong, I love people. They make my living. But when I'm away from work it's nice to have some quieter moments."

"Hmm. Well, we could drive to the outskirts of town and look at the mountains. There's a moon out tonight. I think we'll be able to see something."

"If nothing else, we can count a few stars," she told him. "Did you ever do that as a child?"

Chuckling, he started the engine and backed the truck onto the street, then headed in a northerly direction. "No. I was too busying seeing stars from being bucked off a horse or wrestling with my brothers. Did you count stars?"

"Whenever I was out of the city, where I could actually see them," she answered as she settled herself comfortably in the leather bucket seat. "The first time I ever visited a Western state, I was about ten. Dad took us to Arizona for a summer vacation and I was amazed at how the sky seemed to go on forever. And, yes, I had fun counting stars and daydreaming."

He grinned. "About baking cupcakes and running your own bakery?"

No, Kendra thought, her dreams had been about growing up and being a wife to a loving husband, and mother to a houseful of children. But sadly, by the time Mila was a few weeks old, she'd realized her dream of having a big family was not to be. Certainly not with Bryce.

"Well, not quite as early as ten," she said. "But by the time I entered my teens I'd been doing lots of baking. I learned everything I know about my profession from my mother, not from my college studies."

"You went to college?"

"I have a degree in business. Operating a bakery is more than just making sweet treats. In fact, there's a ton of office work that goes with it."

"Hmm. I imagine so. But I took it for granted that you had someone taking care of the business end of things for you," he said.

"So far I've been doing it all myself. But with the bakery getting busier and busier, I'm coming to the conclusion that I'm going to have to give in and hire a person to deal with all the purchasing orders, bills and that sort of thing. I'm also considering hiring another barista. The coffee part of Kendra's Cupcakes has really taken off in the past few months and with cold weather coming on, I expect it will pick up even more. Since Smitty is in college he can only work part-time. The same goes for Andrea."

He cast her a thoughtful glance as he braked the truck to a stop behind a line of vehicles at a red light. "You can't run the bakery all by yourself. But then you have to consider the extra salaries. Good thing you have a business head on your shoulders. I wouldn't know how to decide about such things."

"I'm hardly an expert, Dale. But operating my own bakery in South Beach taught me a lot about the business. And you're right, the extra salaries will cut into my profits. I'm hoping, however, that an increase in sales will make up for the loss." She glanced over at him. "What about you? Did you go to college?"

The light changed and he accelerated the truck as the traffic ahead of them moved forward. "Yes. For ranching and land development. I didn't necessarily like being housed up and taking classes, but in the end I thought it would help me be a better conservator of the land. And it has."

Her gaze traveled over his rugged profile. There was so much more about this man that she wanted to learn. Over dinner, he'd told her he was thirty-one. At that age, most men were usually married; some even had young children. Or they'd tried marriage and ended up divorced. But Dale hadn't experienced either and she wondered if he'd ever been in love and suffered a broken heart. Why else would he be avoiding commitment to a woman?

"So you've always planned on being in the ranching business?"

"Pretty much. Cowboy work is about all I've ever done. I don't think I'd be happy doing anything else."

At least he hadn't had any trouble dedicating himself to a vocation, she thought. "We're blessed to be doing what we like to do. Don't you think?"

"Very much so," he said, then inclined his head to her side of the street. "There's the headquarters of the Bronco Ghost Tours business. Ever go on one of Evan Cruise's spooky tours?"

She laughed lightly. "No. But I think it might be fun. What about you?"

"I haven't taken a tour. There's really no need. We have a real live ghost working on Dalton's Grange now."

Kendra sat straight up in the seat and stared at him. "A live ghost? There isn't such a thing," she argued.

He chuckled. "In this case, there is. You remember seeing all those flyers that Sullivan Grainger hung around town when he was searching for Bobby Stone?"

"Oh, when you said *ghost* I wasn't thinking about Bobby. So *he's* the phantom you have working on Dalton's Grange." She let out a good-natured groan. "Yes, I remember those flyers. They were fastened to every light pole and store window in town and folks were talking about seeing a ghost. Made me wonder what kind of town I'd moved into."

"Yeah, at that time no one in town knew that Sullivan was actually Bobby's twin and had come to Bronco searching for the brother he'd never known he had. So it's understandable why everyone believed a ghost was walking around town. The two men look practically identical," Dale said. "Did you ever hear Bobby's story? About his disappearance?"

"I hear all sorts of gossip through the bakery," she told him. "And the way I heard the story, everyone initially believed Bobby had died because he'd sat on the death seat in Doug's bar." Shaking her head with dismay, she said, "Why some people believe such folklore is beyond me."

Dale nodded. "Well, there are stories from local townsfolk, who insist the death seat has brought grief to more than one person who's dared to sit in it. And in a way, I suppose it did bring a bit of grief to Bobby. He ended up drinking way too much and then decided to go off mountain climbing. So when he disappeared, everyone naturally assumed he'd suffered a fatal fall. The death seat just happened to play into people's suspicions."

"I am acquainted with Bobby," she told him. "He and his fiancée, Tori Hawkins, frequently stop by the bakery. I've heard him mention working on Dalton's Grange."

"Yeah, Bobby's life has turned around and Tori is the main reason he's on a better track. Do you know the other Hawkins Sisters?"

"I do. They often come into the bakery. Back in November of last year, Mila and I went to the Mistletoe Rodeo here in Bronco. And last month we attended the Bronco Summer Family Rodeo. We thoroughly enjoyed both events.

"I'm a bit surprised that Mila liked the rodeo. She seems more like the ballerina sort. If I remember right, she was wearing a tutu when I first came into the bakery. That is what you call those frilly skirts, isn't it?"

She chuckled. "Yes. Mila loves her tutu. But dreaming about dancing in a ballet troupe is just a secondary interest with Mila. She went crazy for the rodeo and is totally starstruck by the Hawkins Sisters. She has a poster of Audrey and Jack Burris hanging on the wall in her bedroom. Now she's convinced she wants to grow up and be a rodeo star just like the Hawkins Sisters."

"Hmm. I wonder why—" He cast her a curious glance. "That evening in the bakery she talked about dancing on a stage, but she didn't mention anything to me about being a rodeo competitor."

Kendra shook her head. "She talks about plenty of things she shouldn't talk about. But I'm guessing she could see that you're a real-deal cowboy and she might have thought you'd laugh at her."

"I'd never laugh at any child's dream. In Mila's case, I would've encouraged her. The Hawkins Sisters are highly successful."

"True. But Mila has no background with horses and livestock and it's doubtful she ever will. But most children are fickle. In a few months she'll probably lose the idea of being a cowgirl."

"Possibly. But I wouldn't burst her bubble and discourage her cowgirl dreams. A person doesn't necessarily have to live on a ranch to be a rodeo competitor. For instance, Tori boards her horse on Dalton's Grange."

Kendra nodded while thinking how much Mila would enjoy seeing Tori's horse and meeting her rodeo idol. But she wasn't going to mention the idea to Dale. He'd think she was hinting for an invite to the ranch. And she didn't want to appear that forward.

Just like asking him for a date hadn't been forward? Who are you trying to fool, Kendra? You've been giving the cowboy all sorts of green lights.

As Dale maneuvered the truck through a few more blocks of town, the mocking voice lingered in her head. But thankfully, by the time he'd driven a few miles from town and parked on a wide pull-off, she'd pushed aside the thoughts.

"Would you like to get out for minute or two?" he asked. "It's a bit chilly tonight, but not exactly freezing."

"I'd love to stretch my legs and look around. I haven't been on this highway before."

"Shame on you," he gently scolded. "You need to get out more. The countryside around Bronco is especially beautiful."

Her soft laugh held a slight tremor, while every nerve in her body felt like she was humming with electrical current. What was this man doing to her?

"You're saying I need to see more than the inside of a bakery?"

"We all need a change of scenery from time to time," he answered.

After climbing out of the truck, he came around to her side of the cab to help her to the ground. His hand felt incredibly warm as it wrapped firmly around hers and once she was standing next to him, she realized she didn't want to let go of him.

"I have another jacket in the back seat if you think you'll be too cold," he told her.

His thoughtfulness touched her. "Thanks. I think I'll take you up on the offer. The wind is sharp tonight."

He fetched a denim jacket lined with sherpa wool from the back seat of the truck and draped it around her shoulders. She was instantly enveloped by his scent, which was a mixture of evergreen and sage, and something else that was undeniably masculine and sexy.

"Better?"

Not bothering to slide her arms into the sleeves, she pulled the front of the jacket together. "Yes. I'm toasty now."

With his arm curved against the back of her waist, they walked several yards away from the truck to where a guardrail separated the parking area from a steep drop-off. Beyond the gorge, the moonlight illuminated a pair of tall mountain peaks covered with dense forest.

"This is lovely," she said. "I imagine it won't be long before the mountains are snowcapped."

"Yes, and in a few short months Bronco will be decked out with holiday decorations. It's a fun time of the year. Has Mila already been talking about what she wants for Christmas?"

"You mean after she adopts a dog or cat?" she asked with a short laugh. "Mila starts her Christmas wish list early. This year she wants a barrel-racing saddle. One that's exactly her size."

"A saddle? Is she expecting Santa to give her a horse to go with it?"

Kendra groaned. "Thankfully, it hasn't occurred to her to ask for the horse yet."

"A horse and saddle. Well, lots of kids wish for those things at Christmas. It's not completely out of the realm of possibility."

Kendra looked up at his shadowed face. How would it be, she wondered, to have this strong man helping her raise Mila? How would it feel to have his love and support?

You need to slow down, Kendra. You're getting way ahead of yourself. Dale isn't in the market for a family.

Shaking away the warning voice in her head, she said, "Mila's wish list doesn't end there. The main thing she wants is a daddy. That will be at the top of the letter she sends to Santa. Just in case she can't find one on her own," she added wryly.

Dale let out a commiserative groan. "Mila's not asking for much, is she?"

"Believe me, I've tried to explain about how she can't go up to a group of men and pick one out. But she doesn't seem to listen." She let out a weary sigh. "We went to Audrey and Jack's wedding and I thought it would be a nice experience for Mila. I wanted her to see all the lovely flowers and dresses and the cake and hear the music. But the whole event has turned my daughter into a— Well, a little wedding monster."

He chuckled. "Wedding monster? I don't think I've heard that term before."

"Mila's probably the first," she said ruefully. "She's obsessed with getting me married. To the man of her choice, of course."

His arm gently squeezed the back of her waist. "I realize some of her talk embarrasses you, but don't let it get to you. People understand she's just a kid. As for her asking Santa for a daddy, you can remind her that Santa doesn't hand out every wish. When I was a little boy, I kept asking for a guitar. I never got it and Mom explained that whenever I was old enough to apply myself to lessons, Santa might deliver one."

"Did he?"

"No. And before long my heart's desire had already moved on to a pair of fringed chaps." Turning to face her, he clasped his hands around her upper arms. "I'm not trying to say Mila will grow out of her desire to have a father. And she shouldn't. Material things can't compare to a parent. But when the time is right, she'll get the father she wants. And not at the expense of your happiness."

She gave him a grateful smile. "Thanks, Dale, for helping me view the whole thing in a sensible way. Actually, Mila's wedding obsession isn't really what bothers me the most. It's feeling like a failure as a mother."

His hands tightened on her arms. "Kendra, you shouldn't be feeling that way. You're a wonderful mother."

The tenderness in his voice brought a mist of tears to her eyes and she bowed her head and swallowed hard. "Sorry, Dale," she said in a choked voice. "I didn't mean to get emotional. We're supposed to be enjoying ourselves."

"I am enjoying myself. Just being close to you like this, Kendra, is a pleasure."

Something in his voice drew her face up toward his and as she stared at him through watery eyes, her heart gave a hard lurch then jumped into a rapid thumping.

"It feels good to be close to you too."

She watched in fascination as his eyelids drooped and his head slowly descended toward hers until the only thing she could see was the hard line of his lips.

"It will feel even better when we get closer," he murmured.

She didn't try to utter a response. Instead, she closed her eyes and waited for his lips to settle over hers. A second later, his lips were lightly brushing against hers, teasing them with what was about to take place. Then, slowly and surely, his mouth took command of hers and a tiny moan vibrated in her throat as she surrendered to the pleasure.

His kiss swept her into a vortex where the two of them were whirling together through the darkness. To steady her dizzying senses, she planted her hands against his chest, and although the thickness of his shirt acted as a barrier between her fingers and his flesh, she could feel the heat of his body. She also felt a sweet hunger in his kiss, like a man supping at something he'd never tasted before.

Eventually, the headlights of a passing car caused them to instinctively step back from each other.

Dale was the first to speak. "Kendra, I should probably apologize for that, but that would make me a hypocrite. I wanted every second of that kiss."

Kendra realized she was breathing hard and her lips felt swollen. "No apologies needed," she said huskily. "The kiss was a nice...shared thing."

"A shared thing," he murmured. "Yes. It was."

The urge to step forward and wrap her arms around

him was so great it left her trembling. Or was her shivering a result of the cold wind? No matter, she thought. This wasn't a time for her to be reckless.

As if he could read her thoughts, he said quietly, "We should probably be heading back to town."

Disappointment weighed on her, but only for a moment. Just because their evening together was coming to an end, it didn't mean their budding relationship was going to fade away. Not if she could help it.

"Right. I have to pick Mila up at Ada's in about a half hour," she told him.

Dale held her hand tightly as they walked back to the truck and just before he handed her up into the cab, Kendra's gaze caught and held his. The look in his blue eyes was both tender and promising, and suddenly she was so overcome with emotion, she found it impossible to speak.

Apparently, he must have felt the same way because he simply looked at her for long, silent moments before he handed her up and into the truck.

It wasn't until they'd reached town and he merged into the traffic that he finally spoke. "I think it would be a shame if we don't go out again. Don't you?"

Her heart thumping a happy rhythm, she glanced over at him and smiled. "A huge shame," she agreed.

With his gaze remaining firmly on the busy street, he asked, "How about Tuesday? Can you get away from the bakery a little early?"

His question put a quizzical frown on her face. "Why Tuesday? Are you doing something special that evening?"

"Tomorrow is Sunday. Your bakery is closed and you need that day to rest. Mondays are usually too hectic as everyone gets back into the swing of their jobs. So Tuesday should be better for what I have in mind," he said and flashed her a clever grin. "If you agree, I thought I'd drive you and Mila out to Happy Hearts so that she could look at the cats and dogs up for adoption."

Kendra was so overwhelmed by his gesture she didn't know whether to laugh or cry. In the end, she swallowed hard and stared out the window at the passing shops and businesses.

"That's very thoughtful of you, Dale."

"I got you fooled. It's really selfish of me. I can spend time with you, while giving you the impression I'm a good guy."

His remark caused her gaze to swing back to him and she was totally surprised to see he wasn't teasing.

"You are a good guy, Dale."

He shrugged. "I try. But I don't want you to expect too much from me. I'm a cowboy. I don't have any experience dealing with kids or ladies like you, Kendra."

Was this a nice way of telling her he wanted to spend time with her, but she shouldn't expect more than a few pleasant kisses and some laughs in between? No. She wanted to believe he simply wanted her to understand him and not compare him to other men.

"For what it's worth, I don't have any experience dating a cowboy, either. So you'll have to overlook my ignorance about ranching."

Smiling now, he reached for her hand and Kendra was very glad he didn't let go until he walked her to the door of her apartment.

"I'd ask you to stay and say hello to Mila," she told him as they stood close together on the small concrete portico. "But it's already past her bedtime. And I think it might be better—"

"For her not to see me tonight," he said, finishing for her. "I imagine you're right. She probably needs a bit more time to process the idea of the two of us together."

She sighed with relief. "Yes. You took the words right out of my mouth. I'll tell her tomorrow about the three of us making a trip out to Happy Hearts. If I told her tonight, she probably wouldn't go to sleep until midnight."

He let out a wry chuckle. "I might not go to sleep until midnight, either."

Holding onto both his hands, she raised up on her toes and pressed a soft kiss to his lips. "Good night, Dale."

"That's not good enough," he whispered.

Before she guessed his intentions, his hands were on her shoulders, pulling her into his arms. And then he was kissing her, and just as before, the searching movement of his lips caused everything around them to fade away.

By the time he finally lifted his head, Kendra was far too dazed to utter a word, much less form a cohesive sentence.

"Good night, Kendra."

He walked off and as Kendra watched him climb into his truck and drive away, she could only wonder if she was making a major mistake by letting herself get close to Dale. Or was she finally on a path to finding the real love she so desperately wanted?

CHAPTER SIX

"SMITTY, WILL YOU be able to handle the bakery plus the coffee tomorrow evening? Say from four o'clock through closing time? If not, I'll see if Andrea can come in and help you," Kendra asked the young man, who'd been serving endless cups of coffee ever since the bakery had opened early this morning. He had to be exhausted and she figured now was not a good time to ask him about working double duty for her tomorrow. Unfortunately, she didn't have any other options.

Smitty said, "Andrea can't come in. I heard her say she has a psychology test tomorrow afternoon. But no worries, Kendra. If you need time off I can handle things."

Kendra wearily pushed at the hair that continued to fall from her bun no matter how often she rearranged the clips. Dale was right when he'd said Mondays were usually hectic. This one had been exceptionally chaotic. She'd been serving her first customer this morning when Jackie had emerged from the kitchen with the frantic announcement that a water line had broken and was flooding the floor.

After shutting off the water supply, it had taken Kendra an hour to finally locate an available plumber willing to take on the job and then another hour for the man to finally show up. And the whole time the line of customers hadn't stopped.

"Thanks, Smitty. I'll tell Jackie to keep an eye out and if you get in a bind, she'll need to come out front and help you. I normally wouldn't ask, but this is sort of a special thing for Mila. She's going to Happy Hearts to pick out a dog or cat."

The young man grinned. "Now that is special. Steer her toward a dog, Kendra. A big one. Those little ones bark too much."

"Mila's babysitter has a dachshund and he rarely barks, but that might be because he's older," Kendra told him.

Jackie walked up to join their conversation. "It's too bad, Kendra, that I accidently let the stray orange cat out of the kitchen. He would've made Mila the perfect pet. Now the feline is probably caged up at the animal shelter and dreaming about his free roaming days."

Kendra shook her head. "Even if we had managed to keep the cat contained, I couldn't have kept him for myself. Morris belongs to someone. He must. Otherwise, why would a person be bothering to hunt him?"

Smitty said, "The way I heard it, the missing orange cat supposedly belonged to the young woman who was in that apartment fire a couple months ago."

"Yes and she died from her injuries," Jackie said sadly. "Morris must've used some of his nine lives to escape the fire."

The doorbell chimed and two middle-aged women entered the bakery and walked straight to the coffee counter. As they studied the menu displayed on the wall, Smitty said, "Duty calls. And I can already tell by looking at those two they're going to want extra caramel and whipped cream."

He moved away to tend to the customers and Jackie rolled her eyes. "Why is it that men seem to think they can read a woman's mind? But then they can't understand a word we actually say? It's infuriating."

Amused by Jackie's theory, Kendra asked, "Man trouble?"

"What man? I haven't been on a date in weeks. I must be doing something wrong. I'm beginning to think I need a complete makeover. Maybe turn my red hair into a cool blond. Or try for an exotic look and dye it black."

Kendra looked at her in horror. "Never! You need to stay just as you are. Sooner or later the perfect guy for you is going to come along."

"Easy for you to say. You have a hunky cowboy gaga over you."

This morning Jackie had overheard Kendra talking on the phone to Dale about their plans to go to Happy Hearts. Naturally, the young woman had leaped to the conclusion that Kendra and Dale were getting seriously chummy. And maybe they were, she thought. Those kisses he'd plastered on her lips had felt anything but casual. But would the attraction between them last?

"Jackie, there are no guarantees Dale will ever be more than just a cute guy who wants a date or two," Kendra told her. "Anyway, I've tried the serious thing before and it didn't work. If I'm meant to have something special with Dale, it will happen."

"It amazes me that you can be so nonchalant about the whole thing, Kendra. I've heard the Daltons are rich. That the old man hit it big in Vegas. Just think. If you married Dale you wouldn't have to worry about money. And tell me, where could you find a cuter guy than Dale?"

Yes, Dale was nice-looking, sexy and not hurting for money. But none of those things was the reason Kendra was drawn to him. To be honest, she didn't know exactly why being with Dale made her happy. It just did.

"I hate to burst your bubble, Jackie, but when it comes to romance, money and looks really have no importance."

Jackie released a short, mocking laugh. "Who says? A

girl can love a rich good-looking guy as easily as she can love a poor homely one."

Kendra walked over and pulled a nearly empty tray of pecan tarts from one of the display cases. "You're getting it all wrong. Sure, it's easy to fall in love with a handsome and successful man. My ex-husband was both. But he didn't love me back. And that's the important point. Love has to be a shared thing, or it isn't any good at all."

"I wouldn't mind giving handsome and successful a try." Jackie walked over and took the tray from Kendra's hands. "But in your case, Kendra, I wouldn't worry about Dale. There's more to him than looks and money. He's different."

Kendra leveled a droll look at the sassy redhead. "How did you reach that conclusion? Studying the dimples in his cheeks."

Chuckling, Jackie said, "No. Woman's intuition."

Kendra groaned. "And this from someone who said a man can't read a woman's mind? You're hilarious, Jackie."

"I know. It's a curse. I just can't help myself." She turned toward the kitchen. "You want more tarts on this tray or something different?"

"The pumpkin cupcakes are ready. Bring those out. The weather is full-blown autumn today—cool and foggy. They'll go quickly."

Jackie nodded. "Right. I'll be back in a jiffy."

Kendra followed the young woman into the kitchen, then entered another door that opened into her office. Every spare inch of the small room was crammed—there was a desk equipped with a computer, two chairs, a file cabinet and a couch piled with throw pillows. While the quiet room was meant for Kendra's office work, Mila often used the space to play with her toys. When she wasn't out front with the customers, cornering men who looked like potential marriage material for her mother.

After sinking into the chair at her desk, Kendra clicked the computer out of snooze mode and scrolled through the order form she'd been trying to finish for the past hour. So far today, each time she'd sat down at the computer something had interrupted her. Hopefully, with a break in the customers, she'd finally get the task completed before she was needed again.

Ten minutes later, Kendra had just finalized the supply order and was about to leave the office when the cell phone in her apron pocket rang. Since only her family and a few close friends, along with Mila's school, had her number, she couldn't ignore the call entirely.

Stifling a sigh, she pulled out the phone and was somewhat surprised to see the call was from her mother, Laura. Although Kendra was close to both parents, she didn't call them on a daily or even weekly basis. Her mother and dad both stayed very busy with their own successful businesses. Laura operated a combined hair salon and day spa, while her father, Weston, was a real-estate agent for the busy South Beach area and beyond. Once Kendra had become an adult, neither of her parents ever tried to run her life. But they'd always been there for her whenever she'd needed love and support. And when she'd decided to make the move to Montana, they'd encouraged her to follow her dreams to a new life.

"Hi, Mom. What's up?"

"Got a minute?" Laura asked. "Or have I caught you with a line of waiting customers?"

Kendra eased comfortably back in the leather swiveling chair. "Actually, I'm in my office right now. Smitty is handling things out front."

"Good. So how are you, honey? Sorry I haven't called

sooner. But it's been a bit crazy here. End of summer hair-cuts and that sort of thing. And then we had a hurricane scare. Thankfully, the storm headed away from Florida."

"Yes, I was relieved when I saw that on the news." She smiled even though her mother couldn't see her. "It seems so crazy. You and Dad down there in the heat and the threat of a hurricane, and Mila and I up here wearing jackets and watching the leaves fall."

"Sounds lovely," Laura said wistfully. "Ready for some company?"

"Sure. Are you and Dad coming up soon? Maybe for Christmas?" Her parents hadn't yet made a trip to Montana, but they were planning to. To keep connected, Kendra was constantly sending them pics of Mila, the bakery and their home in the apartment complex.

"We're throwing around the idea of coming out to see you. Your father and I haven't seen snow in probably ten years and that was when we took the skiing trip to Vermont."

"I'd love for you to come for the holidays," Kendra said. "Then you could help me explain to Mila why she isn't getting a saddle for Christmas."

Laura chuckled. "Oh dear, she still wants to be a rodeo cowgirl?"

I wouldn't burst her bubble and discourage her cowgirl dreams.

Dale's comment suddenly drifted through Kendra's mind and she realized he was right. Mila needed her mother's encouragement, even if her dreams weren't feasible.

"Just as much as ever."

"And what about her quest for finding herself a father? I hope all of that has tapered off."

Kendra's thoughts instantly turned to Dale. He'd been the last man Mila had accosted with personal questions.

And surprisingly, she had to admit her daughter had judged him correctly when she'd announced Dale wasn't the family type. He didn't consider himself daddy or husband material, but Kendra could see he had the makings of both.

"Not at all. Since I last talked with you, Mila has pulled some embarrassing capers. But I'm dealing with it."

Laura didn't immediately reply and Kendra was beginning to wonder if the call had dropped when her mother finally asked, "Honey, have you heard from Bryce lately?"

The unusual question had Kendra's spine straightening to a stiff line. "Bryce? No! Why would he be calling? He had no time for me and Mila while we were still living in Florida. Why would he suddenly want to talk now?"

"I don't know. But he called me yesterday and I'm not sure why. At first, I thought he might have misplaced your phone number and wanted to talk to Mila. But that wasn't the case."

Frowning, she said, "How strange. What did he say he wanted?"

"Nothing. He said he'd been wondering how you and Mila were doing and thought it best to ask me rather than call you directly."

Bitterness boiled on Kendra's tongue. "Naturally. He was probably afraid if he called me, Mila would want to speak with him. And that would've put too much stress on him—the phony creep."

"I got the impression something was on his mind. And when I asked him about Gillian, he muttered something like he didn't know or care. When I asked him to elaborate, he said they were no longer together."

Funny, Kendra thought, how little Bryce's marital status mattered to her. She didn't care how many women the man had in his life just as long as none of them were paraded in front of Mila. Which was another reason Kendra had decided to move so far away from Florida. She wanted her daughter to be shielded from her father's life in the fast lane.

"Somehow that doesn't surprise me, either," she said to her mother. "They were a mismatch from the very beginning. Gillian was hardly more than a teenager when they married."

"And she definitely acted her age," Laura replied. "But there's a good side to this news. The woman is no longer Mila's stepmother."

Kendra snorted. "She couldn't even be a bad stepmother. She wanted nothing to do with Mila and I suppose I should count myself lucky that she didn't."

"Well, I just thought I ought to give you a heads-up about Bryce. Just in case he starts ringing your phone," Laura replied. "So I'll say goodbye and let you get back to work."

Kendra swiped a hand across her furrowed brow. She couldn't allow this news about Bryce to worry her. She had too many important things to focus on besides her ex-husband.

"Wait, Mom. There's something else I'd like to tell you."

"Okay."

Since her divorce five years ago, she'd never once mentioned a man to her parents, or to her brother, Sterling. Mostly because there hadn't been a man worth mentioning. But now she felt a need to inform her mother about Dale.

"I've met a man," Kendra told her. "His name is Dale Dalton and he's a cowboy—a rancher. He lives on the family ranch called Dalton's Grange."

A short stretch of silence came back at her and Kendra figured her news had probably taken her mother by surprise.

"Honey, that's wonderful news. And you like this guy… in a special way, I mean?"

"I do. He's tall and dark and good-looking and comes from a big family. Counting him, there are five sons. They all work together on the ranch. I, uh, I don't know if things will actually go anywhere with him, but I— Oh, Mom's he's the first guy I've met in a long time that interests me."

"Then by all means you should see where this interest you have for the man takes you," she said.

"I've not known him long," Kendra told her. "Only a couple of weeks. But I would like to get to know him better. I just don't want to rush anything and make a mistake."

Laura laughed. "It took me about two hours to fall for your dad. One look at him and I was blind to any other man."

Kendra smiled to herself. "And what if Dad had run from you instead of to you?"

"Then he would've had a long, hard chase on his hands. I wasn't going to give up on catching him."

Obviously her mother had been certain about going after the man she loved. Yet Kendra wasn't even convinced she should be dating Dale, much less hoping he might become the love of her life.

Kendra sighed. "You clearly caught the right man. But, Mom, I've already made one terrible mistake with Bryce. I keep asking myself if I'm headed toward another mistake."

"Kendra, your father and I have told you this before— the biggest mistake you can make now is letting Bryce ruin the rest of your life."

Kendra was about to reply when the door to the office opened and Jackie jerked her thumb in the direction of the bakery front. Kendra acknowledged her with a nod and an okay sign formed with her thumb and forefinger.

"I will, Mom. Right now I have to go. I'm needed out front. I'll call you soon."

The two women exchanged goodbyes and Kendra slipped the phone back into the pocket on her apron, but as she made her way out of the office, unease rippled through her.

Since their divorce, Bryce had never called Kendra's parents and it had been over a year since he'd even bothered to call and check on his daughter. Something was off, she thought.

And suddenly she was very, very glad she was going to see Dale tomorrow. He made everything seem better.

DALE TAMPED DOWN the last shovelful of dirt around the fat cedar post and leaned against the newly set post to catch his breath.

Shortly after daylight this morning, he and his brothers Morgan and Shep had started building cross fence in a back pasture of the ranch. Now that midafternoon had rolled around they were at least five hundred yards away from reaching their final destination. It would take two more days of steady work to finish this particular job.

Dale said, "Sorry, guys, but I have to head back to the house. I have an early date this evening."

Morgan and Shep looked at him as if he'd just spoken in a foreign language.

"Did I hear you right?" Morgan asked. "A date? We still have a few hours of daylight left to work on this fence. What are you doing? Planning on driving the woman to Great Falls or Missoula?"

Dale walked over to a work truck and picked up the denim jacket he'd thrown on the tailgate. "To make it up to you guys, I'll tamp all the dirt around the post tomorrow. And, no, I'm not planning on driving but a few miles out of town. I'm taking Kendra and her daughter to Happy Hearts. The kid wants a pet and that's the best place for her to get one."

"Heck, Dale, that doesn't sound like a date to me," Shep said. "Sounds more like a boring family outing."

Shep could label the outing any way he wanted, Dale thought. But he was the one who was going to be spending time with a beautiful blonde with lips that tasted sweeter than the cupcakes she baked.

"So what? What's wrong with me going on a family outing?" Dale quipped.

Shep's mouth gaped wide, while Morgan chuckled.

"Leave him alone, Shep. The man is falling in love. Can't you see it on his face?"

Dale scowled at the two of them, then, as if he needed to reassure himself, he walked up to the front of the truck and peered at himself in the side mirror. "There's nothing on my face except a day-old beard. Not a thing, except a handsome mug."

"Oh damn, do we have to hear this, Dale?" Shep asked with a good-natured groan.

Morgan leaned against one of the set posts. "Okay, since you're going to use the time off for a good cause, Dale, I say go enjoy your evening. Just be ready to stretch wire tomorrow."

"Don't worry. You guys are going to need extra vitamins to keep up with me," he joked, then walked over to his older brother. "Say, Morgan, before I head back to the ranch house, maybe you can give me a few pointers."

"About women? Bah!" Shep exclaimed with a grin. "I'm the guy you ought to be asking for advice."

Frowning at Shep, he said, "Not about women. About little girls." He turned a helpless look on Morgan. "How do you make JoJo like you?"

Morgan shook his head. "Like me? I'm her daddy. *Like* isn't exactly the thing I want from my daughter. Especially as she gets older. Respect, obedience, trust and admiration. Those are the things I want JoJo to have for me. Of course, I want her to love me too. Does that answer your question?"

Dale tried not to feel like an idiot in front of his brothers, but he did. It was stupid of him to allow a child of Mila's age to erode his self-confidence. But it would be even more foolish of him to dismiss Mila's part in his plans to date her mother. Kendra had told him she wasn't going to allow Mila to dictate her love life. But Dale could clearly see that Kendra would never deliberately do anything to make her daughter unhappy. If Mila started to sulk at having Dale around, he knew his time with Kendra would end quickly and permanently.

"Sort of. I'll try to keep everything you said in mind."

Dismayed, Shep shook his head. "Dale, why don't you wise up? Dating a woman with a kid is not what you need. Not unless you're looking for a major headache. And who wants one of those?"

Dale darted him an annoyed look. "You need a swift kick in the pants, little brother, but I don't have time to give you one right now. I'll see you two tomorrow."

As Dale's truck bounced over the rough pasture leading back to the ranch house, Shep's unsolicited advice continued to roll through his head. Yeah, Shep could be right, he thought ruefully. He could be setting himself up for a catastrophic heartache. But if a man was ever going to have anything worthwhile in his life, he had to take a risk, didn't he?

Hell, just look at his father, Dale thought. Look at Dalton's Grange. If Neal hadn't had the guts to gamble, none of them would even be on this ranch. No, the way Dale saw things, he had to take a chance on Kendra and her little strong-minded daughter.

After a hurried shower and slipping into clean clothes, he managed to arrive at Kendra's apartment at the same time she was driving up from collecting Mila from school.

Leaving his truck, he joined the two of them at the front of her SUV. "Hi, Kendra. Hi, Mila," he greeted.

Mila gave him a polite hello, while Kendra bestowed a sunny smile in his direction. "Hello, Dale. Your timing is perfect. As soon as Mila changes her clothes, we'll be ready."

"Great. I'm ready whenever you two are." Dale looked at the girl and was relieved to see her expression had brightened somewhat. "Mila, are you excited about picking out a pet?"

She nodded emphatically. "Yes! I've been waiting a long time to get a dog or cat."

"Well, your wait is nearly over," Kendra told her, then with a hand on her shoulder urged her toward the door of the apartment. "Now hurry and get changed from your school clothes. I've laid your jeans and sweater on the bed."

As soon as Kendra opened the apartment door, Mila rushed inside. Glancing over her shoulder, she motioned for Dale to follow her.

"Come in and have a seat while Mila changes."

Inside the living room, he eased down on the end cushion of the couch, while Kendra sank onto the arm of one of the stuffed armchairs.

The room appeared just as clean and tidy as it had the evening he'd picked her up for their date. Dale was amazed how she found the time to take care of a child, their home and the bakery, which remained open until eight o'clock through the weekdays and five on Saturdays.

"Would you like something to drink before we go? Water? Soda?" she asked.

"No, thanks. I'm fine."

She said, "I was so glad the weather warmed today. Yesterday was so dreary, but the sun is shining beautifully now. Hopefully that's a good omen for Mila finding the right pet."

The other night when they'd gone out for pizza, Dale had been mesmerized by the image Kendra had made in her gypsy-style dress with her long hair loose upon her shoulders. He'd believed she couldn't possibly get any prettier than she'd been that evening. But now, in a pair of blue jeans and a black turtleneck sweater and her hair pulled into a ponytail, there was something about her that was simply beautiful and totally sexy. Maybe it was the happy light in her blue eyes, or the glow of her fair skin. He didn't know. He only knew he was struggling to keep from staring at her.

"I think Daphne and her staff at Happy Hearts are very good about matching people up with the right pet," he said.

One of her eyebrows lifted slightly. "Do you go out there often?" she asked.

"No. I haven't been out to the farm in quite a while. But I do try to donate regularly to their cause. I'm sure you've already guessed that when it comes to animals, I'm a chump," he added with a guilty grin.

She smiled back at him and Dale thought how looking at her was like gazing at a ray of sunshine. It filled him with hope and a joy he'd never quite felt before. The sensation was an effervescent thing, like bubbles popping and snapping inside him.

"That's a good kind of chump to be. Nowadays, there are so many orphaned animals that need our help. And someone is still hunting for Morris. I don't think he's been located yet."

"Morris?"

"Yes. The orange cat who's pictured on all the flyers around town," she explained. "Maybe you haven't seen any of the posters. There's one on a light pole not far from the entrance to the bakery."

He could explain that whenever he made a trip to the bakery, he had one thing on his mind and that was her. Everything else around him seemed insignificant.

"Sorry," he said with a wry chuckle. "I never was the most observant guy in the classroom."

"Well, I'll put it this way. Morris is sort of Bronco's feline version of Bobby Stone. At first, folks believed the cat perished in an apartment fire, but that theory was soon shot down when he was spotted in different places around town. Did I tell you he ran into the bakery not long ago? Actually, it was the same night you came in to pick up Erica's order."

"No. What happened?"

"It was almost closing time when one of my regular customers—she walks with a cane—was trying to get through the door and the cat dashed between her legs and into the bakery. Mila chased after him and he ended up hiding in the kitchen. I called animal rescue, but by the time they arrived, the cat was gone. Turns out Jackie inadvertently left the back door of the kitchen open and the cat slipped out."

"Aw, that's too bad. The cat needs a home."

"Yes. But I don't think he knows it quite yet. He's been on his own for so long now that he may be thinking being free is the way to go."

Kendra might have been talking about Morris, but it sure as heck came close to the feelings Dale had always held about being hemmed up by someone who professed to love him.

And how would you know the feeling, Dale? You've never had a woman really love you. The kind of love that flowed from her heart. The kind of love that bound you to her with unbreakable bonds.

He was so absorbed in his thoughts, he failed to notice he hadn't made a reply until she spoke again.

"But I have a feeling someone will latch on to Morris sooner or later. I only hope that happens before the really cold weather hits. I hate to think of him roaming the streets out in the ice and snow."

"Yes," Dale finally replied. "He needs to be rescued before that happens."

The sound of footsteps racing through the house had him glancing around to see Mila rushing into the room. She was dressed in jeans and a bright orange sweater with a jack-o'-lantern appliquéd on the front.

"I'm ready!" she announced.

Kendra glanced at Dale. "Give me a minute to get our coats. Just in case it gets cool before this outing is over."

As her mother left the living room, Mila walked over and sidled up to Dale's knee. He could say one thing about the girl—she was far from shy.

"Do you know all about cats and dogs?" she asked.

"A little," he said, while wondering if she was attempting to be friendly or planning to kick him in the shins.

"Do you have cats and dogs on the ranch where you live?"

He nodded. "We have several dogs and cats on Dalton's Grange."

Wide-eyed, she asked, "Do they live in the house with you?"

He smiled to himself as he took in her little features.

How would it feel to have a child who resembled him? A son with the same dark hair and blue eyes? Or another daughter with a perky dimple...

Another daughter? What are you thinking, Dale? Mila won't ever be your daughter. Your daydreams are starting to get dangerously foolish.

Blocking out the voice in his head, he answered Mila's question. "Only two of them stay in the house. A dog and a cat. They belong to my mom. The dog's name is Sam and the cat is Jewel."

He could see she was carefully digesting this information.

"Is your mommy pretty like mine?"

Thankfully, she was asking him easy questions, Dale thought. With any luck, Kendra would rejoin them before Mila could think up some hard ones for him to answer.

"She's very pretty. All mommies are, don't you think?"

She tilted her head to one side as she thoughtfully regarded him. "I guess so. Do you have a daddy?"

That one last word put Dale's attention on high alert. "Yes, I do. He's big and tall and rides horses."

A skeptical look crossed her face. "Your daddy rides horses? Isn't he too old?"

Dale held back a laugh as he imagined how Neal would react to Mila's question. "Neal—that's my daddy's name—isn't old. He rides almost every day. Ranchers ride horses to do their work," he explained. "So lots of times my brothers and I ride with him."

Dale could see wheels churning in her blue eyes, but he could only guess what she was thinking. Probably that she envied him. Not only because he had a father, but also having a father, plus a horse to ride, made Dale's life sound like heaven to her.

She asked, "Do you like your daddy?"

The simple question caused Dale to pause and ponder. Yes, he'd been angry and disappointed with Neal Dalton in the past, but on the other hand, he realized how blessed he and his brothers were to have a father who loved his sons and wanted them near him.

"Yes, I do. He's a pretty good dad."

She lifted her chin to a proud angle. "I have a daddy, but he doesn't live here. He lives in Florida."

Not knowing how to respond, Dale simply said, "I'm glad you have a daddy."

She swiped the heel of her palm against the end of her little nose, then folded her arms across her chest. "His name is Bryce and he's real smart. He works in an office and makes lots of money. Mommy says he can't come to Bronco to see me 'cause he's too busy with his work."

Dale glanced toward the doorway where Kendra had disappeared. She should be returning any minute now and if she walked in and overheard him saying the wrong thing to Mila about her father, it would make for a terribly bad start to their outing. On the other hand, he couldn't treat the whole subject like he was juggling raw eggs.

He said, "Well, adults get very busy with their jobs. And they don't get to do everything they'd like to do."

She nodded as though she understood. "Mommy stays busy all the time, but Smitty is taking her place today. I call him the coffee man because he makes all the coffee. Do you know him?"

"I've seen him at the bakery."

An impish grin turned up the corners of her mouth. "Smitty is cute. But he's too young to be a daddy."

Thank goodness this child didn't know everything about men.

Struggling to keep a straight face, Dale said, "I think

you're probably right. Smitty needs to get a little older before he gets a wife and kids."

"Smitty has a girlfriend, though. Her name is Joni and
she's kinda pretty, but he needs a different one."

"Why? What's wrong with his girlfriend?"

Mila's frown was full of disapproval. "Joni talks mean
to him. That's not good."

Apparently, Mila kept her eye on more than her mother's
romantic life, Dale thought. "No, talking mean is bad," he
said, then pointed to the top of her head. "What happened
to your tiara? Did you lose it? Or have you decided you
don't want to be a princess anymore?"

Her features pinched together as she slapped a hand on
top of her head. "No, I didn't lose it. And I don't want to
be a princess. I want to be a queen. A rodeo queen with a
crown and a banner across here." She swiped her finger
in a slant across her chest. "And it's going to say Bronco
Rodeo Queen."

"Wow! That will really be something to see. But what
about dancing ballet on the stage? Remember you told me
you were taking dancing lessons."

"I am," she said with another proud thrust of her chin.
"I can dance and be a rodeo queen too. Mommy says a
person that can do more than one thing is well-rounded."

"You know, Mila, I have a feeling you're going to be
very well-rounded."

He'd just gotten the words out of his mouth when Kendra hurried into the room with two heavy garments thrown
over her arm.

"I'm sorry it took me so long," she quickly apologized.
"I couldn't find Mila's play coat. And I didn't want her to
wear her school coat out to the farm."

Dale rose to his feet. "No problem. Mila and I were just
having a nice chat."

Kendra's skeptical glance took in the both of them. "I won't ask," she said to Dale.

Chuckling, he slid a hand beneath her elbow. "Don't worry. I can use a few lessons in childcare."

"With Mila it's more like lessons in child psychiatry," Kendra joked.

Mila looked back and forth between Dale and her mother. "What does that mean, Mommy?"

Kendra rolled her eyes. "It means you're too smart. Now come along, or we're never going to get to Happy Hearts."

Out in the parking lot, they quickly transferred Mila's booster seat from Kendra's SUV over to the back seat of Dale's truck.

Once the child was safely buckled in and Kendra had climbed into the passenger seat, Dale set them on their way.

"It feels a bit odd to be out of the bakery at this time of day," Kendra said as she watched the residential area slip behind them. "It's not often I take off."

"I figured as much," he said, then chuckled. "I think my brothers wanted to wring my neck when I told them I was taking off the rest of the day. We're in the middle of building miles of new fence on the ranch. And we're doing it all ourselves—to save on cost."

Kendra looked at him. "Sounds like hard work. Will your brothers be speaking to you tomorrow?"

"Morgan will. Shep will probably be hissing at me instead of talking," he said, then added, "Only kidding. We all get along well. If one of us needs time away from the ranch, the others will step up. And Dad isn't the kind that stands right over us barking out orders."

Apparently listening in on their conversation, Mila spoke up from the back seat. "Dale's daddy's name is Neal and he rides a horse," she told her mother.

Kendra glanced over at Dale and gave him a conspiring wink. "He does? That sounds interesting," she said to Mila. "Maybe one of these days we can go out to Dalton's Grange and see some of the horses. That is, if Dale wouldn't mind having company."

Dale could hardly believe what he was hearing and his first instinct was to lift her hand from the console and smack a happy kiss on the back of it. But with Mila watching the two of them like a hawk, he decided to express his joy by giving Kendra a wink.

"I wouldn't mind at all," he said as casually as he could. "Tori Hawkins boards her horse on our ranch. I imagine she'd be fine with you looking at her. Tori travels a lot, but she might even be there exercising her mare."

Glancing in the mirror, he could see Mila had gone wide-eyed and was leaning up in her seat as far as the safety belt would allow. "Tori Hawkins and her horse! Mommy, did you hear? Oh wow, that would be cool."

Lowering his voice, Dale said to Kendra, "Sorry. I just couldn't resist. After all, we were talking about horses."

Smiling, she reached over and gave his hand a brief squeeze. "It's okay. I think you've made a few points with her."

And maybe, just maybe, he'd made a few points with Kendra. How he'd managed to do it, Dale didn't know. But he was sure of one thing. She was making him a very happy man.

CHAPTER SEVEN

KENDRA HAD ALMOST forgotten what it was like to be strolling outdoors with sun shining on her face, autumn leaves drifting through the air and a man's arm snug around the back of her waist. Or maybe she'd never really known what the experience was like, she thought. Her ex had certainly never invited her on one of his many golfing excursions. And the one vacation they'd taken together had been spent gazing out a hotel window at a mountain full of skiers because Bryce had quickly decided he couldn't deal with getting cold and wet.

Sometimes she wondered how she could have been so blind to Bryce's faults. Or why it had taken her so long to finally see he was all about himself. Now that she was getting to know Dale better, she was beginning to see just how hollow her short marriage had been. Frankly, the more time she spent with Dale, the more she wondered if she'd ever truly been in love with her ex-husband, or if she'd simply married him because she'd thought it had been the right thing to do.

"I like this brown-and-white dog. She's pretty," Mila said as she gazed into the kennel at a collie mix. "And she's friendly too."

Mila's eager voice pulled Kendra from her somber musings and she focused on her daughter, who was giggling as the little dog licked the finger she stuck through the panels of the kennel.

"Yes, she's a beautiful dog," Kendra agreed.

The tall, blond young man who was touring them through the kennels spoke up. "Daisy is a collie mix and is very feisty. She needs lots of exercise and plenty of space to run. Most of the time we leave her out in the big yard so she's not confined. Also, another thing to consider is that she's long-haired dog. She'll require plenty of grooming."

Kendra turned a doubtful look on her daughter. "Mila, I don't think Daisy is the dog for you. Not while we're still living in the apartment. Maybe once we get a house of our own with a yard where the dog can run and play without needing to be on a leash." She glanced up at Dale for added support. "What do you think?"

Kendra watched him study Mila's wistful face, then turn his attention to Daisy. She understood she was putting him on the spot to ask for his opinion. Especially when she knew how hard he was trying to make friends with Mila.

He said, "I think Mila would be responsible enough to care for Daisy. And collies are smart and loyal. My brothers and I had one when we were growing up. He was a loving, family-type dog. But I think Daisy would be a little sad to be mostly cooped up indoors."

Mila looked up at Dale, then back to Daisy, and Kendra could see her daughter was carefully weighing everything he'd said.

While Mila continued to gaze lovingly at the dog, Kendra turned a grateful look on Dale. "Thanks for giving your honest opinion," she told him. "I appreciate it."

He shrugged. "As far as Mila is concerned I probably just drove the last nail in my coffin. But I want you both to be happy with whatever pet you choose. And right now I'm thinking we should go have a look at the cats. You know. Smaller, quieter, easier. At least, most of the time."

"I totally agree," Kendra told him. Then, she stepped

closer to Mila and placed a comforting hand on her shoulder. "What do you think, Mila? Want to go look at the cats? We might see one that looks like Morris."

Mila gave the friendly dog one last wistful glance. "Dale says Daisy would be sad cooped up inside. I don't want her to be sad."

Kendra tenderly patted her cheek, while hoping Mila or the others couldn't spot the mist in her eyes. "I'm very proud of you, honey, for thinking of Daisy before yourself. We'll get a dog like her someday. I promise. And then the two of you can run everywhere together."

Dale must have recognized how much Kendra needed his support because he moved to her side and curled an arm around her shoulders.

A few steps away, the assistant quickly sized up the situation. "If you'll all follow me, I'll show you to the cats' housing. We have all colors and sizes. I'm sure you'll fall in love with one or two of them."

"Yes, we'd like to see the cats," Kendra told the young man.

The four of them started off in the direction of another building and when Mila skipped a few steps ahead of them, Dale lowered his head toward Kendra's ear.

"This is harder than you imagined it would be, right?"

"Very." She cast him a rueful smile. "I think I actually wanted Daisy as much as Mila did. But we can't always have what we want, can we?"

"Unfortunately, no. Sometimes we have to use common sense."

Kendra said, "I'm sorry I put you on the spot back there about the dog. But I'm grateful to you for helping Mila see what's best for her and Daisy. You know, Mila might not approve of you as my future husband, but she does respect your opinion. She understands you have experience with all sorts of animals."

"It's a good thing I don't have a kid of my own. I'd have a hard time telling him or her no. 'Cause it sure as heck wasn't easy discouraging Mila," he admitted. "She's a sweetheart and I want her to be happy. Let's just hope she finds a cat she falls in love with."

"You're a nice guy, Dale Dalton. Has anyone told you that lately?"

He chuckled. "I'm not sure anyone has ever associated me with the word *nice*. But I'm glad you think so. Now I have added pressure on me not to disappoint Mila—or you."

She cast him a clever glance. "Have you stopped to think I might worry about disappointing you?"

He chuckled again and this time Kendra spotted a twinkle in his blue eyes.

"Don't make my head any bigger than it already is," he said.

No. Dale was far from full of himself and Kendra liked that about him. To be honest, she was liking a whole lot of things about him. But where were these feelings going to lead her? Right now, with Dale by her side, his hand wrapped firmly around hers, she wanted to believe they were headed for something special. Yet she was afraid to allow her hopes to go that far.

They walked a few more yards up a gentle slope before they finally entered a building lined with numerous cages filled with cats of all colors and sizes. Along one side of the room, an open space had been fenced off to allow many of the animals to explore, play with their friends or toys, or simply snooze in a shaft of sunlight coming through a skylight in the roof.

"Those must be the lucky cats," Dale said, gesturing

to the open space. "Wonder what a guy or gal has to do to get promoted to the playground?"

Hearing his comment, the assistant chuckled. "The cats are rotated twice a day, so they all get to have some freedom. Unless they have behavioral problems and pose a threat to the other cats. Fortunately, we don't have any troublemakers with us right now."

Mila hurried over to the nearest stack of cages and peered at the assortment of cats. Some of the animals ignored her, while others watched her with wide, curious eyes.

"Mommy, look! These cats are beautiful!"

"Yes, I see," Kendra told her. "You're going to have a hard task trying to find the one you like best."

For the next several minutes, Mila went from cage to cage studying each cat, then over to the play yard to study the lucky ones, as Dale had referred to them. But it wasn't until she spotted a pair of young kittens in a cage at the end of the room that her face lit with joy. The two tabby cats, one orange and the other gray, were rolling and tumbling in a playful fight.

"Those are the ones I want," she said, pointing to the energetic kittens.

The assistant said, "Those are a brother and sister pair. They're four months old and Daphne doesn't want them to be separated. Not unless their adoption drags on for too long and they're forced to go to different homes."

Mila hurried over to their cage and poked a finger though the wire in an effort to gain the cats' attention. When the curious pair finally eased over to sniff at her finger, she laughed and looked over her shoulder at Dale and Kendra.

"They like me! See?"

"We see," Kendra told her, then turned a skeptical look

on Dale. "All at once I go from having no animals in the apartment to two? What do you think?"

Dale chuckled. "Okay, this time I'm not trying to make points with Mila. Daphne is right about not wanting to split them up. At their age they need a feline buddy to be happy and content. While Mila is at school, they'll have each other to play with instead of shredding the furniture or the curtains."

"All right," Kendra told him. "You've convinced me. Besides, it's just one more little mouth to feed. And siblings shouldn't be separated. Right?"

The grin on his face said he was proud of her and Kendra basked in his approval.

"I have a feeling you're going to enjoy these kittens as much as Mila," he said.

She shot him a guilty look. "You're probably right."

When they joined Mila at the cage, she immediately turned a pleading look up at Kendra. "Can I have them, Mommy? They're cute and funny. And I'll take real good care of them, I promise!"

Kendra gave her daughter an indulgent pat on the top of her head. "If Daphne okays the adoption, then you're going to have two kittens," she told her.

Squealing with joy, Mila hopped up and down before finally flinging her arms around Kendra's waist. "Thank you, Mommy!"

Kendra and Dale were exchanging knowing glances when Mila stepped back from her and looked up at Dale.

"And thank you too, Dale. For bringing us out here to Happy Hearts."

Wonder of wonders, Kendra thought. Was her daughter having a change of heart toward Dale? For everyone's sake, she could only hope.

"You're very welcome," he told Mila. "And you picked out the best kittens in the whole barn."

A beaming smile appeared on Mila's face and her daughter's reaction caused Kendra to recognize what a good father Dale would make. Only he didn't want to be a family man. At least, that was his feelings on the matter right now. But time had a way of changing a person, she thought. Eventually, he might decide he would like to be a daddy.

BY THE TIME they'd finished with the adoption process and loaded the pet carrier with the kittens in the back seat beside Mila, the afternoon was rapidly slipping into evening. As Dale drove them back to town, he stopped by Bronco Pets Emporium, and after purchasing food, bowls, a litter box and litter, and last but not least, an assortment of cat toys, drove the last few blocks to Kendra's apartment.

When he finally pulled into the parking slot, darkness had fallen and the streetlamps were creating an eerie glow over the sidewalk leading up to Kendra's front door.

"I'll help you carry everything in," he told Kendra. "And then I should be going."

Surprised, she looked at him. "Going? Why? Don't you want to stay and see how things go with those two little fur balls?"

He felt like Mila when Kendra had told her she could adopt the kittens. Like a kid wanting to jump up and down with joy. Controlling himself, he gave her a lopsided grin instead. "Sure. But I don't want to wear out my welcome."

"Nonsense. I'll call in an order for lasagna from Mr. Leone and have it delivered. After all, this is a special evening for Mila. The kittens are the first pets she's ever had. She—" Her lips parted as though another thought struck her. "I wasn't thinking, Dale. You might have something else planned to do tonight. If you do, I'll understand."

"Unless you count going home and listening to Dad talk about cows and whether fall is a good time to buy or sell, I don't have a thing to do. I'd like to stay."

"Great." She glanced over the seat to see Mila was totally absorbed with the kittens before she turned her attention back to Dale. "I think she's a little preoccupied."

"Yeah. Just a little," he agreed. "It's good to see her so thrilled."

After hauling everything into the apartment, including the carrier with the kittens, Kendra called in the order for the lasagna. While they waited for it to arrive, they found an appropriate spot for the litter box in the laundry room and a place for the food bowls in the kitchen.

When Dale finally opened the carrier to let out the kittens, the two animals peered cautiously out at their surroundings, before the orange one stuck one paw outside the carrier and then another. Once she walked out, her gray brother followed, much to Mila's delight.

Dale asked, "What are you going to name them?"

"The boy cat is George and the girl is Gypsy."

"George and Gypsy. Those are good names."

The kittens suddenly realized they were free and began to explore the kitchen as fast as their little legs could trot across the tiled floor. While Mila took off after them, Dale walked over to where Kendra was getting plates out of a cabinet.

"Is there anything I can do?" he asked.

While he'd been helping Mila deal with the cats, Kendra had cut up a salad and made a pitcher of sweet tea. With those things already on the table, he figured setting the table was all that was left to do before the food arrived.

"You can dig out some silverware if you'd like." She

pointed to a drawer to the right of the double sink. "It's in there."

He opened the drawer and as he began to pull out the utensils, she asked, "Do you ever help your mother in the kitchen?"

"Sometimes I help her with dish washing and cleaning up, but my cooking is limited. Us boys were usually out helping Dad, so we never got any cooking lessons. Now that Erica is on bed rest, Morgan wishes he'd learned how to fry bacon and eggs, at least."

"How is Erica doing? I miss having her and little JoJo stop by the bakery."

"From what Morgan tells me, she and the baby are still doing okay."

Dale glanced over his shoulder to see Mila was on the far side of the room, sitting cross-legged on the floor, while the kittens climbed all over her. He had to admit he'd surprised himself today during their trip to Happy Hearts. When he'd watched her looking at the collie with such longing, he'd wished he could give her everything her heart desired, just as any father wished to give his daughter. But being a father required far more from a man than giving his daughter material things. He'd have to know how to deal with tears, tantrums and tummy aches. He'd have to answer a thousand questions in just the right way. He clearly wasn't equipped for the job.

"That's good news. Still, I'm sure Morgan is stressed out with worry."

He glanced at Kendra. "I'll be happy whenever the baby does finally get here."

"So will I. They—" The remainder of her sentence was left hanging as the sound of the doorbell announced the arrival of their meal. "There's our dinner."

She started out of the room and Dale trailed directly after her.

"Wait, Kendra," he said to her. "I'll get the door."

"I have to pay," she explained.

By the time they entered the living room, Dale managed to catch her by the arm. "Forget it, Kendra. This will be my treat," he insisted.

With a hopeless roll of her eyes, she shook her head. "You are one stubborn man."

"But I'm a nice one. Remember?" he asked impishly.

MUCH LATER, AFTER the lasagna had been consumed, along with a few treats Kendra had brought home from the bakery, she and Dale carried their coffee to the couch in the living room. Mila managed to coax the kittens into following her and now she was stretched out on the floor tossing a toy mouse back and forth to the kittens. The felines' silly antics had her giggling with delight.

"Normally at this time of the evening, Mila would be begging to watch TV or play a video game. I'd much rather see her playing with the kittens than staring at a screen." She looked at Dale, who was sitting close beside her on the couch. "I have to admit, you were absolutely right."

"I was? Which time?"

Chuckling, she said, "About having two cats instead of one."

His grin was nothing but humble. "Shoot, that was an easy deduction. Everything is better in pairs."

As though to prove his point, he reached over and clasped his hand around hers. The touch of his fingers only added to the warm vibes she'd been getting from having his long lanky body so close to her.

She said, "I, uh, used to think in those terms, Dale. I

thought everyone and everything needed a companion. But that was before my marriage ended."

A moment of silence passed before he gave her hand a light squeeze. "I should have said everything is better with the *right* pair."

Her gaze was drawn back to his face, and the tender expression she found on his features melted a few more spots of her frozen heart. These past few days she'd felt herself growing closer and closer to him. Now, sharing things about her life with him felt right and even necessary. If she ever expected their relationship to grow into something meaningful, she had to be brave enough to expose her past mistakes. Otherwise, they'd only be two people spending time together.

She nodded, then glanced at Mila, who was too far away and too preoccupied to hear their conversation. "Bryce and I were the wrong pair right from the start," she told him. "I just didn't realize that until it was too late."

His expression somber, he studied her face. "How long were you married?"

"Two years," she answered, then let out a rueful sigh. "I realize it sounds like I didn't give the marriage enough time. But in the end, it was too much time."

"I'm sorry it wasn't good," he said.

She lifted her gaze to his. "The problem was that I was expecting a traditional marriage like my parents have always had. You know, a typical home where spouses share everything. Before we were married, Bryce promised he would give me those things. But it didn't turn out that way."

His blue gaze continued to delve into hers. "I'm sure you believed he'd carry his promises through."

"I did believe him. He seemed eager for us to get married. Now, when I look back on things, it was his deception along with his indifference to Mila that hurt the most."

His eyes narrowed. "What do you mean?"

She grimaced. "The company he worked for wanted its executives to project the image of a settled family man. I didn't find this out until much later, after we were married, and then it became fairly clear that Bryce had considered his marriage to me as a stepping stone to becoming an executive—a cushy position with lots of perks. See, his main ambition in life was to travel, play golf and hang out with his buddies. That was how he spent his time while I was trying to build a bakery business in South Beach and raise our child."

"In other words he used you for his own gain," he said with disgust. "In my book, Kendra, that's evil."

Her snort was a mocking sound. "Of course, Bryce would never admit such a thing. He'd swear he wanted the higher position to better 'our' lives. He was such a hypocrite. Unfortunately, I didn't really see the full picture until Mila was born."

A thoughtful frown creased his forehead. "Did he want a child?"

"While we were dating, he'd insisted he wanted me to have as many children as I wanted. Even after we were married and I unexpectedly got pregnant, he acted as though it was a good thing, especially for his image. But once she was born—" She glanced over to make sure Mila's attention was still on the kittens, before she turned back to Dale. "He took one look at the baby and that was it. He wouldn't have anything to do with her. To be frank, he considered being with me and Mila boring and a waste of his time."

"The man needed the hell kicked out of him." His thumb gently massaged the skin on the back of her hand as though he wanted to soothe away all the pain she'd ever suffered. "I'll tell you what else I think, Kendra. He didn't deserve the time of day from you. And he sure didn't deserve Mila."

She sighed. "He'd had the audacity to say if she'd been a boy, he might have been interested. As it was, he claimed he didn't have anything in common with a daughter. To hear him say such a thing about his own child was the final straw for me, Dale. I ended our marriage just as fast as the papers could be filed and finalized."

"And that's when you decided to move here to Montana?"

She shook her head. "No. I stayed on in South Beach for a couple of years. I was foolishly hoping if I stayed there Bryce might change and realize he wanted to be a part of his daughter's life. It never happened. He remarried a much younger woman with the maturity of a teenager. She certainly had no desire to be a stepmother. Not that she made any difference. By then it was clear that Mila didn't have a father. Not a real one."

Frowning thoughtfully, he said, "I'm hardly a guy to know what's best for a child. But I'm not so sure I'd want the man around Mila. What kind of influence would he have on her?"

Her sigh was full of regret. "I've always been careful not to say critical things about Bryce in front of Mila. She has this grand idea that he's a great guy and right now I think it's kinder to let her go on believing her father loves her. Later on, when she's older, she can decide for herself if he's someone she wants in her life."

Scooting closer to her side, he enveloped her hand between the two of his. Warmth flooded her and helped to ease the chill in her heart.

His voice low, he said, "Kendra, that first night I walked into the bakery and saw you, I felt certain you were married. But when Mila intercepted me and I figured out she was husband-shopping for you, I was bowled over. I couldn't believe that any man had been fool enough to let you go."

Tears stung her eyes and she desperately tried to blink them away before he could see them. But he did see them and when he groaned with misgivings, she felt like a maudlin fool.

"Aww, Kendra, don't be sorry you told me all of this. I'm glad you explained why your marriage ended and why Mila is so dead set on finding herself a father. I can understand it better now."

Even though her eyes were watery, Kendra could see his expression was full of tenderness. The notion that he cared about her and Mila's feelings caused her voice to turn husky. "I'm glad I could talk to you about this, Dale. And that you understand how things happened."

His expression suddenly turned awkward. "It's obvious I don't have any experience as a husband or father. Heck, I haven't even been serious with a woman. But in my thirty-one years I've learned enough about life to know you and Mila were given a raw deal."

Drawing up one knee, she squared around on the cushion in order to look at him head-on. "You've never been serious, but I'm curious to know—have you ever had your heart broken?"

His lips took on a wry slant. "I've had my pride broken a few times, but not my heart."

Which meant he'd never been in love. Not the deep kind that once it was lost left a wake of tremendous pain. A part of her was glad no woman had ever touched Dale's heart. But it also made Kendra wonder if he was incapable of feeling love to its deepest degree.

The thought had her gaze slipping over his profile and down to the middle of his chest, where diamond-shaped pearl snaps held his gray denim shirt together. She didn't have to touch him to know his chest would be padded with strong muscles-or that lower down, his stomach would be washboard hard. Everything about his lean body screamed masculinity and every part of it called to her. The only thing that was keeping her from wrapping her arms around him and inviting him to kiss her was Mila's presence.

Heaving out a heavy breath, she tried to push aside the erotic thoughts. "To be honest, Dale, I'm the guilty one for my failed marriage. Yes, Bryce was a hypocrite. But in a way I was worse—I was delusional about him, about love and what it really was. Now when I look back on that time when we were dating, I can see I was too young to know the difference between infatuation and love. He was good-looking, charming and already successful at a career in business. I fell for all of it. You know, like a girl goes gaga over the high-school quarterback. It's not real love. It's a euphoric fog and it takes a while for the mist to clear. But eventually it rolls away, and whenever that happens reality slaps you in the face. Believe me, Dale, I'm not going to let infatuation take hold of me again. Not ever."

He said, "I get what you're saying. But I don't believe you should take the majority of the blame for your marriage ending. You tried."

"Hmm. Yes. I tried. But sometimes trying isn't enough." She cast him a wan smile. "Now that you've listened to all my past troubles you're probably even more determined to remain a bachelor. I can't say that I blame you."

Shrugging, his gaze dropped to their entwined hands. "You might be surprised to know that when I was much younger I wanted all those things you talked about. The house and home. A wife to love me and children to carry on my name and eventually help me run a ranch of my own. But..."

More than curious now, she waited for him to continue. When he didn't, she asked, "What's the matter? Are you afraid I'll laugh at you or something?"

She softened her question with an impish smile and he squeezed her hand in a way that made it feel almost as intimate as a kiss.

"No. You're too sweet to poke fun at a person."

She purposely cleared her throat. "Uh, Dale, I should point out that just because I bake sweets, doesn't mean I am sweet."

He smiled at her, then glanced away. "You remember I told you about my dad's infidelity?"

"Sure. I could tell how deeply it affected you and your whole family."

"Well, when the truth exploded and Mom had the heart attack, something turned sick inside me. I saw all the pain she was going through because of Dad's betrayal. It took all the sunshine and happiness out of her life and for a long time she was just a shell of the mother we'd always known. My brothers and I hated Dad and for a while our whole family was split up."

"And your mother? Did she hate her husband?"

"No. I think Mom is incapable of hating anyone. But we all thought their marriage was going to end. That's when I decided I didn't want any part of love and marriage. To me, it wasn't worth the risk of the pain and suffering my parents were going through. And since then, I haven't met any woman who's changed my opinion on the matter. Until—"

His last word hung in the air and so did Kendra's breath as she waited for him to complete his thought. Was he going to say…*until I met you?* Yes, something in his voice made her think so.

Drawing her hand free from his grasp, she wrapped it over his forearm. "Dale?"

He lifted his gaze back to hers and from the dazed look on his face, she decided he must have surprised himself by even thinking the unspoken words.

"I'm sorry, Kendra. I shouldn't be saying this—not tonight. Not in the same room with Mila. But I'd be a liar if I didn't tell you how much I want you. How much you've come to mean to me."

Kendra silently groaned as she was overcome with the urge to fling her arms around his neck and press kisses all over his face. Instead, the most she could do was to glance over to make sure Mila hadn't moved within earshot. But to her amazement, her daughter appeared to be sound asleep with her head pillowed on her arm and the two kittens snuggled in sleeping balls against her chest.

"You don't have to worry about Mila overhearing you, Dale. Look over there. She and the kittens have played themselves to sleep."

He looked across the room to the spot where Mila and the kittens had been playing. "I feel awful now. I've interrupted her bedtime."

"No. The long day and all the excitement have caused her to fall asleep earlier than usual," she said in a hushed voice. Then, rising to her feet, she urged him up. "Come with me."

He followed her out of the living room and down the shadowy hallway. As soon as they reached a spot where they were safely out of sight, she turned and wrapped her arms around him. "Now I can tell you how much I want you too, Dale. So very much."

A look of amazement crossed his face and then a tiny groan sounded in his throat as he lowered his lips down to hers.

This time when he kissed her everything felt different.

There was no hesitancy or set boundaries. There was only him and her giving and taking freely, hungrily.

If the kiss lasted for hours it wouldn't have been long enough. She wanted to keep holding the hard length of his body against hers, to keep the magical maneuvers of his mouth upon hers. But given the circumstances, they couldn't let themselves lose control.

Dale's thoughts must have been running along the same line as hers. After making a few more desperate plunders of her lips, he tore his mouth from hers and looked regrettably down at her.

"We, uh, can't do this now." His hands lingered on her shoulders as he drew in deep, ragged breaths.

Through drowsy eyes, she scanned his face. "No. You're right. We can't. But I'm happy, anyway. So very happy. Are you?"

Groaning, he pulled her head against his chest and stroked a hand over her hair. "Oh darlin', you have me walking on air. Tomorrow my brothers are going to have to tie a lariat around me to keep my feet on the ground."

Suddenly she wanted to laugh and sing. She wanted to dance him down the hallway and straight to her bed. She wanted him lying beside her, holding her, loving her. Not just for tonight. But other nights to come.

She clung to the front of his shirt. "So when are we going to be together again—alone? I'll need some time to figure this out."

His hands were caressing her face and shoulders and sliding down her arms as though he wanted to savor every second of touching her before he said good night.

"We're going to need more fencing supplies from town tomorrow. I'll volunteer for the chore and drop by the bakery," he suggested. "Maybe by then we can figure out something."

"Yes, that will give me a chance to plan." She smiled coyly up at him. "And see you again."

He chuckled knowingly. "Why do you think I'm going to do the volunteering?" he asked, then reluctantly set her back from him. "Now, I'd better get my hat and jacket and get out of here. Mila needs to be in bed."

"She's going to hate that she missed telling you goodbye," Kendra told him.

He cast her a doubtful glance as they headed back to the living room. "I seriously doubt it."

"Trust me. Every time she looks at George and Gypsy she's going to think of you."

"And everywhere I look I'm going to think of you," he murmured.

She reached for his hand and held it until they reached the short foyer leading to the front door, then released him so that he could slip on his jacket and tug his hat over his dark hair.

Once he was finished, she rested a hand on his arm. "Thank you for today, Dale," she whispered. "And tonight."

He pulled her close and placed one last kiss on her lips. "I'll see you tomorrow."

"Yes. Tomorrow."

He slipped out the door and once she'd locked it securely behind him, she leaned against the wooden panel and let out a dreamy sigh.

How much you've come to mean to me.

The moment he'd spoken those words to her everything in her heart had shifted like a dark cavern suddenly bursting open to the bright sunlight.

She might be taking things too quickly and she should probably think harder about getting seriously involved with Dale before she leaped into his arms. But for the past five years she'd been cautious and leery. She'd been skeptical of every man who'd taken a sidelong glance at her. Yes, she'd played it safe and kept her mind focused on raising her daughter and building her business. Yet, at the same time, she'd been very lonely. And now that Dale had walked into her life, she realized she didn't want to be lonely anymore.

CHAPTER EIGHT

THE NEXT AFTERNOON as Dale drove into town for the fencing supplies, he hummed along to a song on the radio while his thoughts continued to whirl around Kendra and everything she'd said to him last night.

He'd not expected her to talk about her failed marriage or explain why Mila didn't have a father in her life. Each time he thought of the man shunning his newborn daughter, his stomach literally churned with loathing. And each time he imagined Kendra being emotionally hurt and humiliated, he wanted to go to Florida and hunt the man down. But Dale had to believe that hurtful part of her life was all in her past now. He had to believe she was ready to start a new life with him.

For how long, Dale? Have you finally decided one woman is all you'll want for the rest of your life? Do you honestly think you can be a father to Mila? And what if Kendra wants another child?

A few days ago, those questions would've shot arrows of icy fear shooting through him. But some sort of upheaval seemed to have taken place inside him. Ever since he'd taken Kendra into his arms and kissed her, his world had turned into a different place. She made everything in his life feel bright and special. He didn't want to give that up, even if it meant he might ultimately get hurt.

When Dale reached town, he went by Bronco Feed and Ranch Supply to pick up the post and wire. After the truck was loaded with the supplies, he drove deeper into the business section of Bronco Heights, where Kendra's Cupcakes was located.

Since it was midafternoon, he expected there to be a lull in business at the bakery, but he was wrong. The nearest parking slot he could find was a block away, and when he finally walked through the front entrance, he found the tables all taken and a line of customers waiting at the display counters. Presently, Andrea, the young brunette server, was taking care of those customers while Smitty was carrying a tray filled with fancy coffees over to the tables.

From the corner of his eye, he spotted a couple waving in his direction and he turned his head to see Tori Hawkins and Bobby Stone sitting at a table near the window. The couple had been gone to Australia on a rodeo tour and had just arrived back in Bronco only a few days ago.

As soon as Dale walked up to their table, Bobby held up both hands. "Okay, you caught me. I plead guilty. I'm eating Kendra's cupcakes instead of back on the ranch training horses."

"Don't worry. I won't tell anybody if you don't," he joked, then shook his head. "I imagine you came into town for a reason other than to see Tori and eat cupcakes."

Tori smiled lovingly at her fiancé. "Bobby tells me he showed up just to see me, of course."

"Of course," Dale said. "The man isn't dumb."

Bobby chuckled. "Actually, your dad wanted me to take Opal to the vet. She's limping again on her front left."

"I hope the vet gets Opal fixed," Dale said. "She's a special mare."

Bobby nodded. "Don't worry. She'll be okay. So what's your excuse for being here in Kendra's Cupcakes instead of building fence with your brothers?"

Dale playfully held a finger up to his lips. "Shhh. Somebody might hear you," he said, then grinned. "I came in for fencing supplies. But I didn't want to beat it right back to the ranch without a brownie."

"A brownie! So that's why you're here!" Kendra said in a teasing voice as she suddenly walked up by Dale's side and looped her arm around his. "And all along I thought it was me."

While Tori and Bobby laughed and exchanged knowing glances, Dale turned to Kendra. In spite of being in the busy bakery, he bent his head and placed a light kiss on her cheek.

"I didn't see you behind the counter so I came to say hello to Tori and Bobby," he told her.

The smile she gave him hit him smack in the middle of his chest. "While Andrea is on duty, I was taking advantage and doing some work in my office. Want to come back with me? You can take a brownie and some coffee with you. Since that's why you're here," she added teasingly.

Dale glanced over at Tori and Bobby. "See you two later. I have an offer I can't refuse."

"Sure, Dale. But I don't know why you're getting such special treatment."

Dale laughed and gave him a wink. "Frankly, I don't, either."

He followed her through the milling customers, then around the display cases and through a door to the kitchen. He barely caught the glimpse of a row of cabinets and several stainless-steel ovens before she opened another door to their right and they entered another small room, which appeared to be an office.

The second she shut the door behind them, he caught her by the shoulders and pulled her into his arms.

"Mmm," he murmured against her lips. "You taste better than anything I could get from one of your display cases."

"Oh, I don't know about that," she said with a provocative growl. "I'm a pretty good baker."

Chuckling under his breath, he moved his hands against her back and drew her even tighter against him. "You're pretty good at making me want you."

He pressed a light kiss on her lips, but before he could lift his head, her hand curled against the back of his neck and urged his mouth back to hers.

This time he knew she wasn't going to settle for a simple little kiss and he was only too eager to fill her request. With her soft body crushed against his and his lips feasting on hers, his senses began to spin and all he could think about was making love to her for hours on end. Nothing in his life would make sense until he could make her his woman.

When the burning in his lungs finally became too much to bear, he lifted his head and stared into her blue eyes.

"I don't know what happens to me, Kendra, but each time I kiss you my mind goes a little haywire."

Smiling gently, she reached up and touched her fingertips to his cheek. "Mine goes a little haywire too. But that's the way it's supposed to be, isn't it? When two people have chemistry, the formula usually creates an explosion."

And he was on the verge of one now, Dale thought, as he eyed the couch pushed against one wall of the cozy room. With the door safely locked, he could make love to her right there, right now. No doubt, the experience would be fast and furious and mind-blowing. But Kendra deserved better than a quick romp on a couch with dozens of people in the next room. And so did he. Whenever he did finally have the chance to make love to her, he wanted their time together to be special.

He released a heavy breath and eased her out of his arms. "Yes, and at this moment my chemistry is boiling."

She chuckled knowingly, then turned her back to him

and made a sweeping gesture with her hand. "In case you haven't noticed yet, this is my office. There's nothing fancy about it, but the space serves the purpose of what I need."

"You don't need fancy to do a good job. And you're definitely doing a superb job of running this bakery. It's the middle of the afternoon and it's jammed with customers. I'm amazed."

Facing him, she eased a hip onto the corner of the wide desk and Dale thought how perfectly cute she looked with a splotched apron tied over her jeans and long tendrils falling from her messy bun. At one point today she must have applied rosy color to her lips. Now, after their heated kisses, the color had faded to a pink that matched her cheeks.

"At this time of the day, the coffee items are what draws the customers in. People are wearing down and need something to perk them up. Poor Smitty is getting a workout."

He closed the short space between them and reached for her hand. "So far today I haven't been much help to my brothers. All I can think about is you and the two of us being together."

"Jackie asked me earlier if I'd taken some sort of sedative. She said I was out of it. Her way of telling me I haven't been making much sense. And I don't make much sense when I'm thinking of you."

He leaned forward and pressed a kiss on her forehead. She smelled like cinnamon and vanilla, and though he'd never considered those scents as being sexy, on her they were amazingly sultry.

"Have you figured out a plan for us to go out again? Alone?" he asked.

"On school nights Mila has to be in bed early. So the best I can do is make our date for Friday night. Mila has a good friend, Louisa, who lives a couple of blocks from us. She often stays overnight with her. And, in turn, Louisa, spends a night with us. I've already spoken to Louisa's mother and she's perfectly fine with having Mila over Friday night."

"Yes, but what about Mila? Does she know you're going on a date with me?"

Kendra nodded. "Yes, I told her."

"And? How did she react?"

Sighing, she pushed at the strands of hair on her forehead. "Well, she certainly didn't argue with me about it. She knows better than to try to give her mother orders. But she did give me another reminder that you weren't my type."

Under different circumstances, Dale might have resented Mila's attitude. Particularly when he'd been nothing but kind to her. But he couldn't be angry at the girl. Especially now that he'd learned how her father had neglected her.

"Hmm. I guess her reaction could've been worse," Dale said with a good-natured shrug. "I'll just have to change her opinion by showing her I *am* your type."

Smiling, Kendra squeezed his hand. "You *are* my type, Dale. She'll eventually figure that out for herself."

"I hope you're right, Kendra. Because I don't want to just make you happy. I want Mila to be happy too."

She kissed his cheek. "Just be yourself and give her time."

He gave her a wry grin. "If you say so. Right now I'd better be heading back to the ranch. What time Friday evening do you want me to pick you up?"

"Six thirty, if you can make it."

"A major earthquake couldn't stop me," he promised. "And if you'd like, I can try to get reservations at DJ's Deluxe."

She thought for one quick moment before she said, "DJ's

Deluxe is a lovely offer, Dale, but let's just have something simple—and closer to home."

He shot her a clever grin. "Something like *fast* food?"

Slipping off the corner of the desk, she rose on the tips of her toes and planted a promising kiss on his lips. "*Really fast* food," she whispered.

Dale cleared his throat and started to the door. "I'd better get out of here while I can."

Kendra followed behind him. "I'll get you a brownie and coffee for the ride back to Dalton's Grange."

"MOMMY, WHY ARE you going out on another date with Dale tonight? You're only wasting your time. He won't ever get married to you. If you'd go out with Mr. Drake again, he'd probably ask you to marry him. And then we could have a big, beautiful wedding with lots of flowers and music. Just like Audrey Hawkins. And you'd have a giant diamond ring on your finger that sparkled when you turned your hand."

Kendra bit back an impatient sigh as she stood at the end of Mila's bed, watching the girl carefully pack her overnight bag. Although she hadn't put up a protest about going to Louisa's tonight for a sleepover, she was hardly exhibiting the excitement she normally displayed whenever she was going to stay with her friend. In fact, Mila had been whining for the past half hour and Kendra was on the verge of losing her patience.

"Listen, Mila, I'm not going to say this again. I am not romantically interested in Mr. Drake. I never will be. So don't mention him again. And just because I'm going out to dinner with Dale, doesn't mean I'm expecting him to marry me."

"You sound mean, Mommy."

Kendra picked up Mila's toothbrush holder and stuffed

it into the overnight case. "I'm not trying to be mean, Mila. I want you to think about these things you're saying. Dale is a nice man and he cares about you. And deep down, I believe you know that."

Though she refused to look at her mother, Mila's lips spread into a smirk. "Yes. He's nice. But he won't ever be my daddy. My daddy is in Florida and one of these days he'll come to see me. I know he will!"

By the time Mila finished the last sentence, her lips were quivering and Kendra struggled not to break down in tears. She didn't want her daughter to hurt for any reason. On the other hand, she'd been looking forward to tonight and eagerly waiting to finally be with Dale again.

Sighing, she walked around the bed and gave Mila's shoulders an affectionate squeeze. "Maybe so. But for now you'll have to do with just a mommy."

Mila finished loading her overnight bag and didn't say any more on the subject. And during the short drive to Louisa's house, she remained quiet. Not a sulky quiet, but a thoughtful silence that told Kendra her daughter's mind was working overtime. Probably on how to turn her mother against Dale. The idea hurt Kendra. But she had to remember that Mila was also hurting because her friends had a daddy and she didn't.

An hour later, after she'd finished donning a short black sweater dress and a pair of brown suede fashion boots that reached her knees, her spirits begin to lift. And by the time she'd done her hair and added a bit of light makeup, she'd convinced herself that time would fix this obsession of Mila's to get her mother a husband. As for her daughter believing Bryce was going to show up in Bronco, she might as well believe she could catch a falling star. It simply wasn't going to happen.

When Dale arrived, Kendra was ready and waiting and

the two of them wasted no time in driving to a fast-food restaurant that specialized in Mexican dishes.

"So how did things go with Mila this evening? Did she want to take the kittens with her when she went to stay with her friend?"

Smiling wanly, Kendra shook her head. "I convinced her the kittens would be traumatized to be moved again so soon after leaving Happy Hearts and she understood. But I— Well, I had to get a little stern with her earlier. She, uh, thinks I'm wasting my time dating you."

He lowered the tortilla chip he was about to put in his mouth and stared at her. "Is that what you're thinking?"

Kendra groaned. "Oh please, Dale. Not you too! Of course, I don't think I'm wasting my time! Would I be here with you if I did?"

He smiled sheepishly at her. "No. I guess not. It's just that I worry Mila will convince you to find a better man than me."

She reached across the table and touched her fingers to his. "Not a chance. I've found the man who makes me feel very special," she told him. "Eventually Mila will understand. I only wish she'd stop all this wedding nonsense. It's really beginning to wear on me."

"She's doing it all because she wants a daddy. Even I can see that. You know, she talked to me a bit about your ex-husband. She believes he's a wonderful man who is eventually going to come after her."

"Yes, well, it's like I told you. I've never bad-mouthed Bryce to her. Maybe it's wrong of me to deceive her. But she's just a little girl. And letting her believe her father is a great guy can't be as bad as her learning he'd turned his back on her."

"Yeah. I understand." He smiled at her. "And who

knows, by the time Mila gets a little older she'll have the father she wants."

Was he implying he might take up the role of Mila's father? No. She wasn't going to let her thoughts go there. Not tonight. She needed more time with him and he needed more with her. Later, she could begin to ask questions.

"Yes, who knows," she repeated quietly, then, purposefully putting a cheery smile on her face, she deliberately changed the subject. "So how did the fence building go today? Are you getting close to being finished?"

"We are. About a mile more to go. After that we have a bunch of new calves to be branded. And with winter coming on, we're beginning to spread hay for the livestock. The hired hands usually take care of that chore, but that means us brothers have to deal with the other jobs they normally do around the ranch yard."

"In other words, the tasks and who does them depends on the weather and the time of the year," she said.

"Exactly."

"Do you like things that way?" she asked. "Or would you rather focus on one thing? Like Bobby does with the horses."

He grinned. "Variety is the spice of life. I enjoy doing different jobs on the ranch. Keeps things interesting." He leaned eagerly toward her. "I'd really love for you and Mila to come out to Dalton's Grange soon. I think you'll love it. And I believe you'll like my parents too."

Surprise widened her eyes. "You want me to meet your parents?"

A crease appeared between his dark eyebrows. "Well, sure. They'd think it mighty strange if you came out to the ranch and I didn't make a point to introduce you."

She forked a bite of burrito, while questions darted

through her mind. "Oh, so they're used to you having a girlfriend visit you on the ranch."

He shot her a puzzled look, then let out a laugh loud enough to pull a few eyes in their direction.

"What's so funny?" she asked.

"These ideas you have about me. Like I'm a regular cowboy lothario or something. Kendra, I haven't had any girlfriend out to the ranch. There's not one I've wanted to show my home to—until you."

There it was again. *Until you.* Only two little words and yet to her it sounded so much like "I'm falling in love with you." But a woman could think most anything when she was gazing into the eyes of a man who made the rhythm of her heart change into a pagan drumbeat.

"I'd love to see your home and meet your parents, Dale. Mila hasn't forgotten your promise to show her the horses."

"And that's a promise I aim to keep."

A few minutes later, when they left the restaurant, the wind had grown cold and clouds were making a hasty trip south as they scudded across the night sky.

Dale flipped up the sherpa collar on his jacket and snuggled Kendra closer to his side. "This is hardly a night to take a stroll in the park," he said.

She slipped an arm across his back as they walked the last few steps to his truck. "Good thing. I wasn't wanting to stroll in the park tonight."

His knowing chuckle was swept away by the wind as he whirled her into his arms and lowered his mouth to hers. "All I want is you...close to me."

After a quick kiss on her lips, he helped her into the truck and drove the short distance back to her apartment without either of them saying a word.

She'd left a small lamp burning in the living room, and as they stood in the pool of light, Kendra quickly shed her coat and the white scarf she'd wrapped loosely around her neck, while Dale removed his coat and hat.

"Would you like for me to hang those up for you?" she asked.

"Don't bother. They'll be fine here."

He tossed the coat over the back of the nearest armchair and laid his hat in the seat. Kendra placed her coat and scarf alongside his.

"So will mine," she said, then rested a hand on his arm. "I'm not going to ask if you want anything else to eat or drink."

"You can ask me that later," he murmured. "Much later."

He pulled her into his arms and as she looked up at him, a clever smile tilted her lips. "Do you hear what I hear?"

"I don't hear a thing."

"Exactly. It's blessedly quiet. And other than two little kittens that must be asleep in their bed, we're completely alone."

His hand lifted to her face and the tip of his forefinger skimmed lightly over her cheekbone, across the bridge of her nose, then down to the hollow indention of her lips. "Alone. With you," he whispered. "This is all I've been thinking about, Kendra. You and me together."

With his hands cradling the sides of her face, his thumbs reached under her chin and lifted it upward. She could feel her lips trembling as they waited for his kiss. But the trembling didn't stop there. It was coursing its way up and down her body and turning her legs into two wobbly sticks.

"Dale. I never thought I'd ever want another man. But here I am, wanting you with every fiber in my body. And I'm not going to ask myself why. It doesn't matter. All that matters is that you want me too."

"Oh yes, darlin'. With everything inside of me."

He lowered his mouth to hers and for the next few moments they were lost in the erotic pleasure of their lips meshing and searching, their tongues curling and locking in a heated dance.

Desire plunged through her, washing her senses of everything but him and the eager caress of his hands sweeping over her breasts, then cupping her bottom.

When he pulled her hips forward, she could feel his hard manhood bulged against the fly of his jeans and the notion that he was already that aroused filled her with a heady sense of power.

Groaning with pleasure, she clutched the front of his shirt, hoping against hope that her legs wouldn't collapse or she'd end up fainting at his feet.

But just as she thought she'd die from lack of oxygen, he pulled back from her. "I think you, uh, need to show me your bedroom."

Unable to do more than nod, she reached for his hand and led him down the dark hallway to her bedroom.

"I cleaned off the bed earlier this evening," she told him in a husky voice. "Otherwise, the room is cluttered so you might want to keep your eyes shut."

He chuckled under his breath. "Don't worry. My eyes are going to be on you and you alone."

Even in the semidarkness of the room she could see he was smiling at her, and suddenly all the emotions that had been building in her these past few days boiled to the surface and slipped from her eyes in a trail of salty tears.

Stepping forward, she wrapped her arms around his waist and rested her cheek against his chest. "Oh Dale. I haven't waited days to be in your arms. I've been waiting years for you—to find someone who makes me feel this much. Thank you for coming into my life."

His cheek rested against the top of her head as his arms circled tightly around her. "You want to know how I feel?

I hate myself for not walking into your bakery three years ago. For wasting all that time we could've been together."

Her chin rested against his chest as she tilted her head back to look at him. "You think so? You think this would've happened back then?"

"You don't?"

"I'm not sure. I wasn't looking for a man."

Her logical reasoning put a smile on his face. "You weren't looking for one when you first saw me. But here we are."

"Yes, here we are. Enough said."

"Mmm. More than enough."

He placed another kiss on her lips, then, catching the folds of her dress with his hands, he began to tug it upward until the fabric bunched around her breasts. She lifted her arms straight up to allow him to slip the garment over her head.

Once he'd tossed it aside, she didn't have time to be embarrassed at standing in front of him with nothing on but a black satin bra and matching panties. He instantly swept her into his arms and began raining kisses over her neck, along the ridge of one shoulder, then down her chest until he reached the cleavage between her breasts. When that happened, he undid for the front clasp and let the garment fall around her waist, exposing her breasts. The exploration of his lips continued over the soft mounds until his mouth settled on one puckered nipple.

Fiery pleasure shot through her, rocking her balance and forcing her hands to find a steadying hold on his arms.

Groaning with need, she whispered his name and he lifted his head to meet her gaze. His eyes were half-closed and drowsy with desire and Kendra knew he was seeing the same sort of longing on her face. Strange, she thought, that for once in her life, it didn't bother her to let a man see her wanton needs. Moreover, she wanted Dale to see the feelings swirling through her and know how much these moments meant to her.

"Kendra. My Kendra."

He kissed his way back to her lips, and this time when his tongue plundered the inner cavity of her mouth, she was engulfed with the need to have his bare skin next to hers.

She lifted her hands to the front of his shirt and managed to pry two snaps apart before he broke the kiss and stepped back from her.

"I'll do this," he murmured. "It'll be faster that way."

While he dealt with removing his clothes, Kendra sat on the side of the bed and unzipped her tall boots. By the time she set them aside and stepped out of her panties, he'd shed all of his clothing, except for a pair of navy blue boxers.

Oh my. His body was a sight to behold and Kendra leaned back on one hand and took immense pleasure in gawking at him.

"You know, you really shouldn't wear clothes," she told him. "You're depriving the women of Bronco."

Chuckling, he joined her on the bed. "It's dark in here and you can't see all of me."

"Hmm. You're wrong. I'm getting a perfect view."

With his hands on her shoulders, he eased her downward until her back was flat against the mattress.

"So am I," he said. "And I don't want to close my eyes. I don't even want to blink. I'm afraid you might disappear."

Lying next to her, he rolled her into him, and as his arms came around her, she was enveloped by the hard heat of his body. As the heady warmth seeped through her, she slid her palms over his arms and shoulders, across his chest, then down to the hard flesh above the waistband of his shorts.

"I'm not going anywhere," she whispered as she pressed light kisses along the ridge of his collarbone. "We have all night."

ALL NIGHT. DALE should have been thrilled with her promise. Instead, he was thinking it wouldn't be enough time with her. Not even close to enough. He wanted days and months of making love to her. No. He wanted a lifetime of making love to her. And until he had her promise of forever, he wouldn't feel complete.

Making love to her for a lifetime. Do you know what that means, Dale? Are you ready to give your heart to this woman?

The voice of reason dashed through his mind as he pushed a curtain of hair away from the side of her neck and dropped his lips to the smooth, velvety skin. But he didn't allow the questions it presented to linger. No, he'd think of them later. When his senses were cleared of this enchantment of having her in his arms.

"Yes. All night," he whispered against her lips. "And we're not going to waste a second of it."

Her arm slipped around his neck and as he drew her even closer, her soft breasts flattened against his chest and her leg settled loosely over his. Instinctively, his hands slid down her back until he reached the flare of her hips, then with his hands on her buttocks, he pulled the lower half of her body next to his aching manhood.

She pressed the juncture of her thighs tight against his arousal, while at the same time her lips traveled across his face until her mouth was on his.

With a groan of surrender, he kissed her until the room around them began to spin and the fire in his loins grew to unbearable proportions.

Beneath his hands, her hair felt like satin, her skin like

warm velvet, and it was all surrounded by the sweet scent of exotic flowers. Touching her was like stepping into paradise. Tasting her was like lapping an endless bowl of sweet cream. And yet, none of the pleasures were enough to ease the ache that had been building in him from the first moment they'd kissed.

Breaking the contact between their lips, he was breathing hard as his gaze met hers. "I need to be inside you, darlin'," he said in a voice rough with desire. "Are you ready for this?"

Her eyelids drooped, while the corners of her mouth tilted up. "I'm more than ready for this—for you."

He didn't need to hear more. Quickly, he climbed off the bed, and after digging a condom from his wallet, he tossed away his shorts and rolled the protection over his hardened shaft. And all the while he could feel her watching him, and the knowledge that her eyes were feasting on his intimate parts aroused him even more.

When he rejoined her on the mattress, he positioned himself over her and she instantly parted her legs. He slipped one hand to the moist folds between her thighs and for a few incredible moments he touched her there. But soon, the unbearable need to connect their bodies overtook his desire to explore.

"I want to touch you everywhere, Kendra. I want to taste every part of you," he whispered. "But that's going to have to come later. Much later."

Planting his hands on either side of her head to support the upper part of his body, he lowered his hips and entered her with a slow, smooth thrust.

Somewhere beyond the roaring in his ears, he heard a tiny moan in her throat and then, as he sunk deeper and deeper in her velvety body, he didn't hear anything. He couldn't think anything, except that he was drowning in a pleasure so intense it was nearly impossible to breathe.

"Dale. Oh Dale."

She whispered his name and then with her hands clamped onto his shoulders, she arched her hips up to meet his.

Hot, searing desire gripped his body as he began to thrust slowly, then faster. And all at once they settled into a perfect rhythm of give and take. Back and forth. Up and down. She was like a soft marshmallow in his arms and he wanted to fill himself with her and nothing but her.

"This is how it should be for us, darlin'. So good—so perfect."

"Yes. Perfect." Lifting her head off the mattress, she slid her open lips over his chest, around each nipple and on to the middle of his breastbone. "Don't stop loving me. Don't stop."

The raw desire in her voice acted on his senses as much as the hungry thrust of her hips, and the need to please her drove him onward. And just when he thought his heart was going to beat out of his chest, he felt her fingers digging into his back and her hips made one desperate arch against him.

He tried to hang on and extend their erotic trip a few more moments, but when a cry of release rushed out of her, the fragile thread holding the last of his control snapped. Suddenly he was flung into an empty space, where tiny pinpoints of lights were showering him, blinding him with their brilliance and pricking every nerve in his body with sizzling waves of ecstasy.

By the time his upper body collapsed over hers, he wasn't sure he was still alive. His heartbeat was thrumming in his ears and his lungs were so starved for oxygen that he figured they were too damaged to work.

He gulped in several ragged breaths before he found enough strength to roll his weight to one side of her, and even then he was too drained to lift his head from the mattress.

When she finally rolled toward him and smoothed a hand over his damp chest, he groaned and opened his eyes to see her face was close to his and her eyes were soft and full of wonder.

"Are you okay?" she asked softly.

He wanted to laugh, but he didn't have the strength.

No. He wasn't okay. He was somebody else. Some guy he didn't know. What had happened to him? And why didn't he want to go back to the old Dale? The Dale that had always considered sex a purely physical thing?

He managed to grunt with amusement. "Shouldn't I be the one asking you that question instead of the other way around?"

"There's no need to ask me. You can see for yourself how wonderful I am."

Twisting his head in order to have a closer look at her face, he saw she was smiling at him as if she adored him. Could that be? Or was he only seeing something he wanted to see?

He grunted again. "Does that mean my condition looks questionable?"

Laughing softly, she scooted close enough to kiss his cheek. "No. I just want to know that you're happy."

Rolling onto his back, he pulled the top part of her body into his arms and nuzzled his nose in the curve of her neck. "Happy doesn't begin to describe how I feel right now. I'm pretty much on a cloud. And you know the best part about it? You're right here on the cloud with me."

"Together. Yes, that's the best part." Her fingers thrust

into his hair and combed it back from his forehead. "Because I never thought—"

He eased his head back far enough to look at her. "You never thought what?"

The corners of her mouth dipped downward. "Oh, that I'd ever find a man that I would want to be this close to. I was actually afraid I had grown incapable of feeling anything for a man. And then you—" A sly grin suddenly replaced the dour expression on her lips. "Why the heck did you have to be so sexy? Before I even knew it, you'd turned my head."

"I find that hard to believe."

Her hand slid up and down his arm as though she was trying to memorize the shape of the flesh and bone. Or maybe she was trying to make sure the hot coals in his loins didn't cool anytime soon.

"Why?" she asked, then frowned. "Sometimes I get the feeling you thought I was too— Well, that maybe I'd be a snob."

He frowned. "I never thought you could be a snob to anyone. I just think—I'm just a simple cowboy. I'm not suave or sophisticated or comfortable at fancy events. Give me a horse and a saddle and a range to ride on and that's about all I want—along with you, that is."

Her chuckle was a sexy sound that slithered right down his spine and had his hands drawing her closer to him.

"I don't need or want suave or sophisticated. And I certainly don't need fancy. All I want is for you to be genuine and honest with me."

Pushing his fingers into her hair, he drew her face close enough to place a long, lingering kiss on her lips. "I'll never make promises to you that I don't intend to keep, Kendra. That's not the way I work."

Her soft sigh brushed against his cheek. "I believe you. Otherwise, you wouldn't be here in my bed."

"Mmm. Speaking of being in bed, don't you think we need to make the most of our time here?"

Lifting her head, she gave him a coy grin. "I was just thinking I should go to the kitchen and make a pot of coffee? You need to replenish your strength."

Chuckling under his breath, he flipped her onto her back, then climbed over her. "I'll show you how much strength I have—without the coffee."

Snaking an arm around the back of his neck, she drew him downward until his chest was pressed close to hers. "Come here, cowboy."

With their lips bonded together and her hands making exploratory circles upon his back, the desire that had momentarily cooled was rapidly rising to a boiling point.

"I can't believe I already want to be inside of you again," he whispered. "I can't believe my body is telling me it has to have you."

With a needy sigh, she smoothed a hand against the side of his face. "And my body is telling me the same thing. I think you've cast a love spell on me."

"If it's a love spell, I don't want anything to break it."

He lowered his mouth to hers again and just as he was losing himself in her kiss, the phone on her nightstand rang.

The unexpected sound jarred the quietness of the room and he lifted his head to look at the offensive instrument.

"Are you expecting a call?"

"Not at all. I rarely get calls on the landline. I'll check the ID. It's probably a spam call."

She scooted out from beneath him and over to the edge of the bed. As soon as she spotted the identity of the caller, she quickly picked up the receiver.

"Hello, Bev. Is anything wrong?"

Sensing the call might be important, Dale sat up and waited uneasily for her to finish the conversation.

"Oh. That's not like her. No," Kendra continued. "Yes, and it's no problem. I'm just sorry to put you through this. I'll be there in just a few minutes."

She hung up the phone, then turned a look of utter disappointment on him.

"What's wrong?" he asked.

"That was Bev. Louisa's mother. She called to let me know Mila isn't feeling well and wants to come home."

The image of Mila sick and calling for her mother popped into his mind, and the anxious concern that followed it wasn't a typical boyfriend reaction. It was the sort of unease a parent would experience.

"Do you think it's anything serious?" Dale asked.

"Without seeing her, I honestly can't say. But I—"

When she didn't finish, Dale prompted her to explain. "But what? Is Mila throwing up? Running a fever or something?"

She shook her head. "Nothing so bad as that. Bev said Mila is complaining of a headache. She never has a headache. I can't say for certain, but I'm thinking my daughter is having an I-don't-want-Mommy-and-Dale-to-have-a nice-long-date-tonight kind of illness."

Only a few minutes ago, Dale's spirits couldn't have soared any higher. Now they were free-falling to rock bottom. If her suspicions were correct, then he'd have to fight extra hard for Kendra's love. And, yes, he did want that much from her. Tonight had opened his eyes to his feelings about her and the two of them being together. Not just for tonight, but for always.

"Damn, Kendra. Surely she wouldn't pull such a trick.

Mila isn't a mean child. She wouldn't want to hurt you in such a manipulative way. Would she?"

Sighing heavily, she stood and gathered her underclothes from the floor. "In her mind, she doesn't think breaking up our night together is hurting me. She believes she's doing me a favor. According to her, you're all wrong for me. And she's trying to save me from making a mistake."

He stood and took her into his arms. "I think we just proved we aren't a mistake."

"No. We're not a mistake." She gave him a tight hug and then turned away to dress.

He raked a hand through his hair while his mind spun. What was he supposed to think? Do? Up until a couple of minutes ago, their night together had been perfect. Now he was torn with the notion of Mila actually being ill, or faking it in order to keep him separated from Kendra. Either was a miserable thought.

"I'd be glad to go with you to pick up Mila...if you'd like."

She stepped into her panties, then quickly donned her bra, and as Dale watched her hurried movements he wanted to circle his hands around her wrists and draw her back into his arms. A part of him wanted to tell her that if Mila was putting on an act, it would be a mistake to give in to her whims. But *if* was a mighty big word and he didn't have any right to interfere in her parenting decisions. Besides, he had to remember there was always a chance the child wasn't faking it and truly did need her mother's attention.

"Thank you, Dale. But I think it would be better if I handle this myself. Seeing you with me might make the situation worse."

She was trying to view the problem with rational reasoning. Even so, the fact that she didn't want the two of them to deal with Mila's problem together felt like a hard slap to his face.

"Okay."

He hadn't meant for the word to sound terse, but apparently she'd heard the disappointment in his voice.

Her dress bunched in her hands, she looked at him, her expression tinged with disbelief. "Are you angry with me?"

Groaning, he reached down and picked up his shirt. "No. I understand you didn't want this thing with Mila to happen any more than I did."

"So you're angry with Mila?"

Frowning now, he shoved his arms into the shirt and began to snap the front of it together. "Of course not. She's a young child. I'm not angry with either of you. I'm disappointed and worried, that's all."

She stepped closer and as she placed her hand on his forearm, Dale could see a torn look in her eyes.

"I'm sorry about this, Dale. Believe me, I'm just as disappointed as you are. And if you're thinking I'm trying to shut you out, I'm not. I just want to handle this with as little drama as possible."

He stifled a groan. "I get what you're saying, Kendra. And, yes, I'm sure you can handle this problem with Mila tonight, but I'm looking ahead to the future. What are you going to do the next time something like this happens?"

Her lips parted as though his question had caught her off guard. Surely, she wasn't thinking the issue with Mila would be resolved with a snap of her fingers.

"Honestly, Dale, I don't know. I'm not even sure how I'm going to handle the situation tonight. First, I want to make sure she isn't really sick. If she isn't, then I'm going to let her know that I'm not going to accept such behavior."

"Well, her health is the important thing," he said, then turned his back to her and quickly finished dressing.

A few short minutes later, they left the apartment together. Dale waited on the small porch, while she locked the door behind them.

When she turned to him, he gathered her into his arms and she tilted her face up to his. "This isn't the way I wanted our night to end. But the time we had together was pretty wonderful," she said.

She was using the word *wonderful*, yet her troubled face was a picture of sadness, he thought.

"Short or not, this night has been amazing for me, Kendra." He touched his fingertips to her cheek and did his best to ignore the desperate urge to make love to her again. "I'll call you tomorrow. And if you can, would you send me a text to let me know about Mila's headache?"

"I will."

He planted a swift kiss on her lips, then quickly walked to his truck before he could say or do something that might wreck their budding relationship. But why should he worry about making a misstep with Kendra? It looked as though Mila was in the driver's seat. And until he earned the child's approval, he didn't have a chance of winning Kendra's love.

CHAPTER NINE

NORMALLY, KENDRA SPENT her Saturdays working at the bakery, but this morning she'd asked Jackie to fill in for her. After Mila's unexpected complaint with a headache, she'd decided to stay home with her daughter just in case there was an ultra-slim chance that Mila had actually been sick.

Usually when Kendra took a day off, she used the spare time to do something special with Mila. More often than not, she'd take her daughter shopping, while making sure she kept the spending to a small amount. Sometimes, if there was a child-appropriate movie being shown, she'd take her to the theater, or there was always the park to enjoy the outdoors. But today Kendra was doing none of those things. Instead, she was using her time away from the bakery to clean house and catch up on her laundry.

This morning, when Kendra had informed Mila they wouldn't be going out for the day, the girl had been shocked and then she'd wanted to argue. But Kendra had quickly pointed out that a person with a bad headache needed to rest and get well. After that, Mila realized she didn't have leg to stand on, and thankfully, she'd been pleasant and obedient so far.

Perhaps she was being too hard on her daughter, Kendra thought, as she stuffed wet clothes into the dryer. But she couldn't let the stunt she'd pulled last night go unpunished. And it had been a stunt. As soon as Kendra had picked Mila up at Louisa's house and she'd learned that Dale had already gone home to Dalton's Grange, she'd been all cheerful smiles and insisted her headache had quit almost instantly.

Kendra had been so aggravated and disappointed, she'd come close to bursting into tears, but somehow she'd managed to clamp down on her emotions. Once they'd arrived back at the apartment, Kendra had decided to go along with Mila's fake illness and she'd made a big deal of checking her temperature and tucking her into bed. But she'd also decided her daughter had to learn there were consequences to telling fibs, especially when those fibs hurt other people.

With the clothes drying, she walked out to the kitchen and made herself a cup of coffee in a pod-cup machine. For the past hour, Mila had been perched on a seat at the table, entertaining herself with crayons and a coloring book. But now that the kittens had woken from a nap, she was sitting cross-legged on the floor, tempting them to chase a feather attached to the end of a plastic wand.

"Look, Mommy! Gypsy can go faster than George. She catches the feather first and then George takes it away from her. That's not fair."

"Gypsy doesn't care if her brother gets the feather. They're having fun," Kendra said as she sat on one of the stools at the breakfast bar.

Mila glanced at her. "Did you have fun last night with Dale, Mommy?"

This was the first time her daughter had even mentioned Kendra's date with Dale and she wondered if the punishment of staying home today was causing her to think hard on the matter.

"Yes, we had fun," Kendra told her. "We ate Mexican food and enjoyed talking to each other."

As for the rest of the evening, Kendra was still walking

on a cloud. Making love to Dale hadn't just been a plea-
surable experience. Being intimately connected to him
had affected her deeply and touched her heart in places
she hadn't known existed. There had been moments she'd
wanted to cry out as she'd suddenly and surely realized
how much she loved him, how much she never wanted
him to let her go. But she'd held back, afraid it would be
too much, too soon, for him.

And maybe Dale would never want to hear those words
from her, she thought ruefully. He'd not exactly been happy
when he'd left her apartment. And she couldn't blame him.
She'd promised him they'd have a whole night together and
if the call about Mila hadn't interrupted them, they would
have been well on their way to making love a second time.

Last night she'd sent him a brief text to let him know
Mila was fine and he'd responded with one word—*good*.
And today she'd foolishly carried her cell phone around in
anticipation of his call. But now the afternoon was beginning to stretch into evening, and with no text or call from
him, doubts were starting to creep into her thoughts. Had
he decided dating a woman with a precocious child wasn't
worth the headache?

"I'm glad you had fun, Mommy."

Was this Mila's way of apologizing? Kendra wondered.

"That's nice, honey. Thank you."

Mila climbed to her feet and walked over to Kendra.

"Mommy, do you think Dale is going to propose to
you?"

Any other time, Kendra would have considered her
daughter's question as just another one of her many wedding inquiries. But last night had Kendra wondering if
Dale might change his mind about hanging on to his single
status. She could easily imagine herself spending the rest
of her life with him. But would he ever forget the marital

struggles his parents had gone through? Would he ever put away the fears of heartbreak and divorce? Maybe, if he loved her. But so far, she'd not heard anything close to the word *love* pass his lips.

"I don't know, Mila. Dale and I need to know each other a lot longer before something like that happens. Why are you asking?"

She shrugged and glanced sheepishly to the opposite side of the room. "Because I can tell you really like him and he really likes you."

How had the child reached such a conclusion? Mila hadn't spent enough time with the two of them to know how they felt about each other. But sometimes it was easier for children to see things that adults could never see.

Kendra thoughtfully regarded her daughter. "Are you thinking Dale will propose to me?"

She shook her head. "Nope. He just wants to have fun."

Mila could be right. But last night, when Dale had made love to her, she'd seen more than fun in his eyes. She'd seen something raw and real and tender. It might be a long leap from her bed to a marriage proposal, but it was a start.

Kendra was searching for the right words to counter Mila's emphatic statement when the phone lying a few inches from her coffee mug rang.

Seeing Dale's name light up on the screen, she eagerly snatched it up and swiped to answer.

"Hi, Dale!"

"Hello, Kendra. Did I catch you at a bad time?"

The sound of his voice was like a steadying hand against her back, and without even knowing it, her lips spread into a wide smile.

"No, you called at a perfect time. Actually, I just sat down with coffee," she said cheerfully, while from the corner of her eye, she could see Mila watching her like a hawk. "I've been house cleaning most of the day, so I'm taking a little break."

"Same thing here. We've been stretching the last of the barbed wire today and we decided to stop for a little break. Your text last night said Mila was fine, so I thought I'd call and check on her today. No more headaches?"

With Mila still standing nearby, Kendra was forced to carefully choose her next words. "Oh, that little problem quickly resolved itself last night. Everything is fine today."

He paused and she could easily picture the image of his strong face, his blue eyes. Now that she'd made love to him and discovered the wonder of touching him and holding his strong body next to hers, it was impossible to think of her future without him in it.

"I'm glad to hear it," he said, then added in a lowered voice, "After I got home to Dalton's Grange last night, all I could think about was you and the two of us together. I'm missing you."

Her sigh was laced with longing. "I'm missing you too. Will you be coming back to town anytime soon?"

"Uh, I'm not sure about that, but I thought— Well, the main reason I'm calling is to ask if you and Mila would like to come out and look at the horses tomorrow. With it being Sunday, we only take care of the essential chores and put off any major work until the weekend is over. So I'll have a bit of free time."

Even though the sky was gray with gloomy clouds, Kendra felt as if a bright ray of sunshine had just slanted through the kitchen window. "I'd love to, Dale." She looked at Mila and purposely raised her voice. "But give me just a minute to check with Mila. If her head is hurting there's no way she could walk around the ranch and look at horses."

Before Kendra could present the question to Mila, her

daughter was jumping up and down. "Yes, Mommy! Yes! My head doesn't hurt at all!"

"Okay, Dale. Mila has made a miraculous recovery," she said shrewdly. "She can't wait to see the horses. What time should we be there?"

"Good to hear Mila is feeling well again. One or one thirty should be fine. Do you know where the ranch is located?"

"I've driven by the entrance before."

"The house isn't far from there. Just stay on that road and you'll find it."

"We'll be there," she told him. "Is there anything I need to bring with us?"

"No. I'll—" He broke off as a male voice yelled in the background. "Sorry, Kendra. My brothers are waiting for me. I'll be watching for you."

He ended the call and as Kendra placed her phone aside, Mila asked in a skeptical voice, "Are you sure Dale invited me to Dalton's Grange too?"

Kendra frowned. "Of course. He wants to show you the horses. Why are you asking?"

Her expression turned sheepish. "I thought he only wanted to be with you and not have me around."

Kendra studied Mila's glum face. Was this part of the reason she'd pulled the headache stunt last night? Because she thought Dale didn't want to include her in their plans?

Wrapping a hand around Mila's little chin, she tilted her face upward. "Mila, listen carefully to me. Dale isn't trying to take me away from you. And even if he was, I wouldn't allow that to happen. Not ever. Do you understand what I'm telling you?"

Mila flashed her a grin. "Yes! It means you'll always be my mommy. No matter what."

"You're right." She gave Mila's shoulders an affectionate squeeze. "Now, are you happy about going to Dalton's Grange?"

"Oh this is supercool! I'm going to go find my boots and hat so I'll be ready tomorrow!"

Kendra smiled as she watched her daughter race out of the kitchen. Tomorrow the three of them would be together, and hopefully Mila would begin to see Dale in a better light.

THE NEXT AFTERNOON, when Dale spotted Kendra's SUV driving up the circular driveway that led to the front of the ranch house, he quickly strode out to greet them. After she'd parked the vehicle a respectable distance from the yard fence, he went to the driver's door to help her out.

"Hello, Kendra. I see you made the drive okay."

"No problems," she said as she stood beside him. "Mila sang to me most of the way."

Dale stuck his head into the open door to see the girl was in the process of unfastening her seat belt. A pink cowboy hat with white lacing around the brim was perched over her blond waves, while matching pink boots were on her feet. She looked far too adorable to be capable of using manipulative tactics on her mother, he thought.

"Hi, Mila. Need some help?"

"I can do it," she told him.

Dale gave Kendra a wink before he walked around the vehicle and opened the door where Mila was sitting.

"All cowgirls appreciate a helping hand," he told her. "And now that you're on Dalton's Grange, you're going to start turning into a cowgirl."

He helped her out of the vehicle and once she was standing on the ground, she stared at him in awe.

"I'm going to be a real cowgirl? Today? Really?"

"Well, sure. You're already looking like a cowgirl in your hat and boots. All you need now is a crown."

She shook her head at him. "I'm not old enough or big enough to be a rodeo queen yet. I have to grow before I can have a crown."

Dale shared a quick grin with Kendra before he turned back to Mila. "You don't have to grow that much. You can get in the Junior Queen contest."

Mila turned a doubtful look on her mother. "Is Dale telling me the truth?"

Kendra nodded. "I recall a rodeo queen contest for the younger girls going on back in the summer. When the time comes, we'll look into it. But like Dale says, first you have to learn to ride."

"And I'm going to give you your first lesson today," Dale told her. "What do you think?"

Mila clapped her hands and jumped up and down. "This is going to be fun, fun!"

Dale turned to Kendra. "One of the ranch hands is saddling a pair of horses for us now. But I'd like to take you both inside to meet my parents before we do any riding. Is that okay with you?"

"It's perfectly okay," she said, then motioned to Mila. "Get your coat from the car, honey. We're going into the house for a few minutes and then we'll go see the horses."

Once Mila had pulled on her coat, the three of them headed across the yard to the porch. As they walked, Dale could see Kendra looking around with interest.

"The ranch is beautiful, Dale. And I love the log exterior of the house. It fits in perfectly with the rugged landscape," she told him. "It's no wonder your dad fell in love with this place."

Her praise made him realize just how proud he was of

Dalton's Grange and all the hard work that he and his family poured into the land.

"I'm glad you like it." He glanced over at Mila, who was busy gawking at everything. "What do you think about the place, Mila?"

"Everything is big! And it's pretty!"

Kendra chuckled. "Coming from my little critic, that means it *really* is pretty."

Dale pretended to wipe sweat from his brow. "Whew. At least Dalton's Grange has passed her test."

Inside the house, Dale led them to a large great room with a high ceiling built with exposed wood beams. A huge fireplace separated the comfortably furnished area from an equally large kitchen.

His parents were sitting on a couch, drinking coffee, but as soon as they spotted their son and visitors entering the room, the pair quickly put aside their cups and stood.

"Mom, Dad, I'd like you to meet Kendra and her daughter, Mila," he told them, then to Kendra and Mila, he said, "These are my parents, Deborah and Neal."

Kendra stepped forward and offered her hand to both of them. "It's very nice to meet both of you. Your ranch is magnificent."

Neal slanted a grin at Dale. "This young woman has good taste."

Dale chuckled. "That's why she's with me."

"Then you'd better hang on to her," Neal told him.

"Well, I want more than a handshake. I want a hug." Deborah gathered Kendra in a warm hug, then turned to Mila, who was watching her with wide eyes. "Can I have a hug from you too?"

Mila nodded and Dale was surprised to see the girl actually returned his mother's hug.

"You're just as pretty as your mother," Deborah told Mila. "Do lots of people tell you that?"

Mila nodded and grinned. "Lots of them."

Deborah laughed, then cast her husband an adoring look. "Why didn't we have a little girl before we stopped having babies?"

Neal cleared his throat. "Probably because we already had a house full of boys. She wouldn't have stood a chance."

"Not with you spoiling her rotten," Deborah joked.

"Kendra is the lady who baked all the cupcakes," Dale proudly informed his parents. "She owns and operates Kendra's Cupcakes."

Neal groaned and patted his midsection. "Now I know who to blame for these extra two pounds I've put on. I like the vanilla ones with the sprinkles."

"Those are my favorites too," Kendra told him.

Neal looked at Dale and winked. "See, I told you. The girl has good taste."

"Where did you learn to make all those pastries? And the brownies! Oh, they were scrumptious!" Deborah exclaimed.

"Thank you," Kendra told her. "My mother taught me how to bake. And I've had years of practice."

Before Deborah could begin asking more baking questions, Neal spoke up. "Sorry, Kendra, we've forgotten our manners. You and your daughter have a seat and Dale can get you something to drink."

"It's nice of you to offer, Mr. Dalton, but we just finished lunch before we drove out. I think Mila is itching to go see the horses. But we might take you up on the drink later."

"We'd love that," Deborah told her.

"I'm going to give Mila a riding lesson," Dale told them. "She's going to be a first-rate cowgirl."

"Hey, that's good to know," Neal said and leveled a kindly smile at Mila. "We have too many cowboys around here. We need some cowgirls on the ranch. Especially one with a pink hat."

Mila giggled. "You're funnier than Dale," she told him.

Neal laughed. "That's only because I'm older, sweetie."

Dale reached for Kendra's arm. "I think we need to exit on that one." To his parents, he said, "We'll be back later."

OUTSIDE, AS THE three of them walked toward a huge barn located at the far end of the ranch yard, Kendra said, "I like your parents. They're down-to-earth and clearly crazy about each other."

"They are now," he replied.

After watching Deborah and Neal interact with each other, Kendra found it hard to imagine their marriage had ever been in jeopardy.

"I expect they always were, Dale. Things just happen."

"Yeah. Things just happen." He gave her a faint smile. "And today they're all going to be good."

Mila skipped slightly ahead of them and Kendra looped her arm through his.

"You're talking my language now," she told him.

They entered a long barn with horse stalls lining both sides and a dirt walkway running between. Skylights in the tin roof allowed shafts of golden light to slant in intervals down the length of the building.

As soon as they reached the first stall, where a gray horse was lying on a bed of clean wood shavings, Mila let out a happy squeal.

"Mommy, look how big he is! And how pretty!" She looked up at Dale. "Why is he lying down? Does he feel bad?"

Smiling, Dale patted the top of her head. "No. He's fine. He's just resting. Horses get sleepy just like you and me."

"Oh. But what if he got sleepy at the rodeo? That would be bad."

Mila's question had him casting a look of amusement over at Kendra. "There's too much excitement going on at a rodeo for a horse to get sleepy," he explained.

As they moved on to the next stall, Kendra couldn't help but notice the soft music coming from overhead speakers.

"Is the music for the benefit of the ranch hands? Or the horses?" Kendra asked.

Dale chuckled. "The horses. It helps keep them soothed and content."

"So that explains the classical music. The horses have highbrow taste," Kendra said as she recognized a familiar symphony. "I would've expected country or soft rock."

"The classical stuff is Shep's doing. He heard you were going to be visiting today and thought he'd impress you. Otherwise, we'd be hearing songs about truck driving and beer drinking. Whether the horses can tell the difference, I couldn't say."

She laughed. "Well, you'll have to thank him for me. I always did want to tour a horse barn with Chopin playing in the background."

"I'll be sure and let Shep know you liked his music loop," he said with a chuckle.

Standing between the two adults, Mila's attention was glued to a coal-black horse with a long wavy mane and tail. "Why do the horses have to be in the barn? I bet this one would like to be outside eating grass."

Kendra said, "I've been wondering the same thing. Why are these horses stalled? On our drive in to the ranch house, we saw several horses grazing in the pasture."

"Those horses are part of the ranch's working remuda. They're usually always outside. Unless there's a blizzard going on. Then we run all the horse stock into pens with loafing sheds for shelter. Most of the horses in here are in training. And a couple of them are being doctored for various issues."

"I see. Different horses for specific jobs," Kendra replied.

He flashed her a grin. "Right. Like the people who work for you in the bakery. Each one has a certain purpose."

His example pulled a laugh from her. "Most of the time we do. But when the bakery is overrun with customers we all end up doing a bit of everything."

Mila turned away from the stall and Kendra was somewhat surprised to see her reach for Dale's hand and give it a tug.

"When are we gonna see Tori's horse?" Mila asked. "Is he in the barn?"

Dale gave the girl an indulgent grin. "Tori's horse is a girl. In horse language that means she's a mare. And you're going to see her right now. Ready?"

"Yeah!"

Dale led the girl over to the next stall, where a brown-and-white quarter horse was chomping on alfalfa hay swinging in a net that hung from a rafter.

Mila tilted her head one way and then the other as she tried to peep through the stall gate. "I can't see all of her!"

"Here. I'll help you get a better look." Dale reached down and lifted her into his arms so she could peer directly into the stall. "Now you can get a full view of Bluebell. Pretty, isn't she?"

While Mila stared in fascination at the mare, Kendra's eyes misted over at the image of Dale carefully holding her daughter in the crook of one arm.

"Oh, Bluebell is really, really beautiful! And Tori makes her go really fast!" Mila exclaimed, then looked directly at Dale. "I want a mare just like Bluebell! And when I get old enough to work and make money, I'm going to get one!"

Smiling wryly, Dale glanced at Kendra. "Money," he repeated. "That one nasty issue has a habit of getting in the way of things."

"Unfortunately," Kendra replied, while thinking Bryce had made plenty of money, but it hadn't given them a solid, loving marriage. "But it can't buy the best of things, Dale. I learned that long ago."

He turned a thoughtful gaze on Mila. "No," he said gently. "The best things in life aren't for sale."

After allowing Mila a few more minutes to admire Bluebell, Dale set her back on her feet and announced it was time for her first riding lesson.

"What do you think, Mommy? Are you ready for a ride?" he asked Kendra.

Chuckling, she said, "I'm fairly sure you're going to need to give both of us a riding lesson. I haven't been on a horse in several years."

"Have you ridden much?" he asked.

"Only horses that you rent at a riding stable. You know. The kind that has one gait—super-slow."

He flashed her a grin. "I promise I have a nice quiet mount for you. And Mila is going to ride with me. Until she gets the feel of things. Don't worry—I'll take baby steps with her."

As usual, Mila had been carefully listening in on their conversation and she let out a loud protest. "I'm not a baby, Dale! I'm seven!"

He gave Kendra a subtle wink. "Seven! Gosh, I'd practically forgotten you were that old," he told the girl. "But when I said baby steps I was talking about my mare. She needs to stretch her legs slowly before she goes fast."

Somewhat mollified by his explanation, Mila asked, "Your horse is a girl too?"

"Sure. Her name is Moonpie. 'Cause she's sweet like your mommy's cupcakes."

Mila wrinkled her nose at him. "Do you give her kisses?"

Kendra could see his eyes covertly roll in her direction.

"Whenever I can," he answered.

BEFORE THEY STARTED the ride, Dale had feared he might have trouble with Mila being a little bossy and refusing to listen to his instructions. Instead, he'd been pleasantly surprised when the girl had carefully followed every command he'd given her. By the time the three of them had returned from a long ride in a nearby pasture, he felt comfortable enough to dismount and allow Mila to sit alone in the saddle.

When he'd led Moonpie at a slow walk around the ranch yard, Mila had been beaming from ear to ear and waving at the ranch hands.

"She's getting her queen wave mastered," Dale told Kendra, who was walking at his side.

Kendra laughed softly, something she'd done quite a bit this afternoon. The happy sound reassured him that she was enjoying her time here on the ranch.

"She'll be prepared when she wins Miss Junior Rodeo Queen of Bronco. I'm not sure there is such a thing, but she's having fun imagining herself in the role."

Lowering his head toward hers, he said, "Just between you and me, I'm not all that certain that Bronco has a junior queen contest, either. But like you said, it's something she can have fun dreaming about. Until she grows into big-queen age."

Touching her hand to his arm, she looked up at him. "Dale, you've been so wonderful with Mila," she said gently. "You can't know how much that means to me. And to her."

Her praise poured into him like warm, sweet wine. "And you can't know how much it means to me to have the two of you here, enjoying my home."

Her gaze caught his and the dark smoky look in her eyes told him she was thinking about the two of them being alone and making love...again and again. The idea caused the pit of his belly to clench with longing.

"I haven't enjoyed anything so much. Not in a long, long time," she told him, then after a quick glance to make sure Mila couldn't overhear them, she added in a lower tone, "I only wish you and I could have a few minutes together—without an audience."

"I do too. But in the long run I think that the three of us being together like this will help matters. You know, maybe a change of opinion about my 'type,'" he added with quirky waggle of his eyebrows.

She squeezed his forearm. "Like I told you, you're definitely my type."

As it turned out, Dale and Kendra didn't get an opportunity to be alone together before she and Mila left the ranch much later that evening.

As soon as they'd finished riding the horses, the three of them had gone back into the house with the plan of having a brief visit with his parents. But the chat turned into a long conversation over cups of coffee for the adults and hot chocolate for Mila. Then Deborah had introduced Mila to her dog, Sam, and cat, Jewel. The girl had fallen instantly in love with the friendly pets, and by the time Kendra had managed to pry her away from the animals, the day was growing late and a purple twilight darkened the sky.

Dale had escorted the two of them to Kendra's SUV and after giving her a chaste peck on the cheek, he waved them off.

It wasn't until much later that night, when Dale was about to climb into bed, that his cell phone rang.

As soon as he spotted Kendra's name on the screen he snatched the phone off the nightstand and hurriedly punched the accept button.

"Kendra, I wasn't expecting to hear from you again tonight."

He picked up her soft sigh before she spoke. "I apologize for calling so late. Were you about to go to bed?"

"Not yet," he said. "I still need to jump in the shower. Is anything wrong?"

"Not a thing. I've been waiting for Mila to go to sleep and she was so wired from all the excitement of the day that it took her a while to settle down. I wanted to be able to talk with you and not have to worry about her walking in and overhearing part of our conversation."

Her voice was low and husky and the sound of it had him closing his eyes and remembering the taste of her lips, the way her soft, naked body had yielded to his.

"I'm glad you called. We didn't have much of an opportunity today to talk about me and you. Mila and my parents kept us occupied."

"Yes, but I adore your parents and enjoyed talking with them. And Mila— Well, it's like you said, we needed to share the day with her. I think you really made an impression on her today. After we got home, she made some positive remarks about you. I didn't make a big deal out of it. I want her to realize for herself what a great guy you are."

He smiled even though she couldn't see him. "I don't know about the *great* part. But I hope she can see I'm going to do my best to make her mother happy. At least, I'm going to try."

She sighed. "I've been trying to think of a way we can be alone together and all I can come up with is taking Mila to the sitter. We couldn't make it a whole night, but at least we could be together."

Dale was yearning to make love to Kendra and yet the instant she'd said the word *sitter* he was put off. "As much as I want to be with you, darlin', I don't think that would be a good idea."

"Why? What else am I supposed to do? I don't have relatives around here to watch her. And now that I've found you, I deserve to have a social life, don't I?"

"Sure you deserve it. But I don't want her to resent me."

"So you think we should just cater to her wishes?"

Frustration laced her voice and Dale could've told her that he was feeling just as vexed. "No. I think we just need to have a bit more patience and give her time to get used to the two of us being a couple."

There was a long stretch of silence and then she said, "Dale, for such a diehard bachelor, you have all the makings of a wonderful father."

Diehard bachelor. He wasn't one of those men. The kind that wanted to flit from one woman to the next for the rest of his life. No. Since Kendra and Mila had come into his life, he was thinking in totally different terms. He was beginning to imagine himself as a husband and father. Whether he'd be wonderful in those roles, he couldn't say. But he knew he'd be a damn sight better than Kendra's ex.

"It would be nice if Mila saw me as you do. But for now, what about us getting together for dinner in a day or two? We could grab some fast food and Mila could bring a friend. That way the two of us might have a chance to be together without her hanging on to our every word."

There was a slight pause and then she said, "Sounds good to me. I'll tell Mila to invite Louisa. I'm sure her mother will agree to let her join us. Let's make it Wednesday night. Tomorrow and Tuesday I'm going to be working later than usual. Some extra cleaning on the ovens."

Wednesday sounded like an eon away, but he'd settle for whatever time he could get with her.

"Sounds good. If I happen to come to town before then, I'll stop by the bakery. To say hello," he added in a low, suggestive voice.

A soft chuckle sounded in his ear. "To say hello. Of course," she said, then her voice dropped to a murmur. "Dale, I want you to know how wonderful today was for me. And for Mila. She'll never forget it. Neither will I."

He breathed deeply as the ache to hold her practically overwhelmed him. "It was special to me too, Kendra. I'll show you just how special whenever I see you again."

"I can't wait. Good night, Dale."

She ended the call and in spite of his dusty clothes, Dale lied back on the bed and stared thoughtfully up at the ceiling.

When he'd walked into Kendra's Cupcakes for the first time and spotted Kendra behind the counter, he'd dreamed about having a date with the beautiful blonde. Now, a few weeks later, he was imagining himself as a family man.

Had he lost his senses? Or had Kendra opened his eyes to the fact that love and marriage didn't necessarily mean suffering and loss? Was he finally beginning to believe he could have the same sort of happiness his brothers enjoyed now that they were married?

Dale couldn't answer the self-imposed questions, much

less understand the rapid changes he'd undergone. He only knew that common sense couldn't compete with the feelings in his heart.

CHAPTER TEN

BY TUESDAY, KENDRA was so desperate to be with Dale again that she could hardly serve her customers for watching the door and hoping to see his tall, rugged figure step into the bakery.

When she glanced up and spotted him walking down the sidewalk, she quickly informed Jackie she needed to leave for a half hour and to cover the front for her, then hurried to intercept him before he could enter the bakery.

"Well, when did you start greeting your customers on the outside?" he teased.

Grinning slyly, she grabbed his hand and hustled him back down the sidewalk. "Are you in a hurry?"

"No."

"Good. I am. I have thirty...forty minutes at the most. Would you like to drive us to my apartment?"

He looked at her as though she'd just handed him a pot of gold coins. "Seriously?"

"Yes, seriously. Why do you think I'm herding you to your truck?"

"Because for some reason today, you want to keep me out of the bakery?"

She laughed. "Exactly. Because I'd much rather have you in my bedroom."

Less than five minutes later, she was opening the door of her apartment with a key she kept hidden beneath a holly shrub.

"Are you sure this isn't going to cause problems back at the bakery?" he asked as they stepped into the house and she carefully locked the door behind them.

"Jackie is watching the front for me. She can handle things. Sometimes it's necessary to have a few minutes leave of absence, and you are a *very* necessary reason."

She turned away from the door and he quickly snatched her into his arms. "I don't know why or how this idea entered your mind, but I like it—a whole lot."

"It entered my mind because I couldn't keep waiting, hoping for a time to make love to you again. I know we don't have much time, but—"

"Who's worried about time?" he interrupted. "We're not going to waste one second, my darlin'."

He fastened his mouth over hers and they kissed deeply and hungrily for long moments until the need for air forced them apart.

Still gasping for air, she grabbed his hand and led him down the hallway to her bedroom. She said, "I left for work in a rush this morning and didn't straighten the bedclothes."

He took off his hat and tossed it toward a dressing bench at the foot of her bed, then popped the snaps down the front of his shirt. "The only clothes I care about are yours and mine and how fast we can get out of them."

Desperately eager to be in his arms, Kendra pulled the sashes on her apron, then quickly shed her jeans and sweater. By the time she'd removed her undergarments, he was stripped down to nothing, and judging from the sight of his hard erection, there wouldn't be much time for foreplay.

She reached for him at the same time his hands wrapped around her waist. Locked in each other's arms, they fell sideways onto the bed. His lips fastened over hers once again, while his hands began a wild exploration of her body.

"Kendra, Kendra. I've been aching for you. For this. We were meant to be together."

The passionate words were spoken against her lips and she wanted to swallow them up and store them for later—whenever it would be impossible to touch him like this.

"Yes, Dale. Together."

He used another minute to kiss her and then he eased to a sitting position. "I need to find a condom," he said hoarsely.

Reaching for his arm, she tugged him back down on the mattress. "I didn't explain the other night that I'm on the pill. I thought you might not trust just one type of birth control."

His eyebrows arched. "Are you trying to tell me that I don't need a condom?"

She nodded. "Not unless you're worried."

"Worried? Hell, I'm ecstatic!" Laughing and groaning at the same time, he rolled her onto her back, then poised himself above her. "Do we have much time left?"

She smiled up at him. "We have enough."

WHEN KENDRA ARRIVED back at the bakery, she was relieved to see the few customers standing in line were waiting for coffee, a job that Smitty handled by himself.

Tightening the sashes on her apron, she walked behind the counter and waited for Jackie to check out a customer.

"Did you have any problems while I was gone?" Kendra asked.

Jackie's expression was sly as she studied Kendra's swollen lips and messier-than-usual bun. "No. Did you?"

Kendra rolled her eyes. "No. And since you're dying

to ask, yes, that was Dale that I left with. We had a few things to talk over."

Jackie chuckled knowingly. "Talk? With a guy like Dale I'd be doing more than talking, Kendra! Are you thirty or eighty?"

Turning her back to Jackie, she pulled a tray of half-empty cupcakes from one of the display shelves and hoped her assistant didn't see the blush on her cheeks. Her time with Dale might have been short, but the passion between them had been hot and incredible, and just as earth-shaking as the first time they'd made love.

"Don't worry, Jackie. I'm aware of my age."

"I hope so. Because you need to latch on to Dale," Jackie said, then reached to take the tray from her. "I'll take care of this. Why don't you go sit down and collect yourself?"

Kendra smirked at the redhead. "Collect myself? I've never felt better."

"I'll bet you do." Laughing, Jackie started toward the kitchen, then suddenly turned back to Kendra. "Oh, I almost forgot. There was guy in here earlier who was looking for you. I'd never seen him before."

"Hmm. What did he want? To sell us some new coffee or frozen desserts? Which I'd never serve my customers."

Jackie shook her head. "If he was trying to sell something, he didn't mention it. He was only interested in talking with you."

Kendra frowned. "That's odd. Did he leave a message or his name?"

"No. But I got the impression he'll be back," Jackie said.

Puzzled now, Kendra asked, "What did he look like?"

"Thirtyish. Blond. Kind of good-looking, but a little too smooth for my taste. You know the sort. Soft hands, creased slacks and Italian loafers. Give me a guy with boots and manure splattered on his jeans. Then you know he's not lazy."

Oh God, could it be? No! Surely Bryce wouldn't come all the way to Montana! Especially when he hadn't bothered to come around when Kendra and Mila had lived in Florida, only a few miles away from him.

Pressing a hand to her forehead, she tried not to panic. But she couldn't help but wonder if her past had come to Bronco to mess up her future.

"Kendra, what's wrong? Are you getting sick?"

Drawing in a bracing breath, she did her best to smile at Jackie. "I'm okay. It's just that I have a lot of things on my mind and a bunch of work in my office to finish."

"You go on," Jackie told her. "I'll take care of things here in the front for you."

Yes, but who was going to take care of her ex-husband if he showed up and tried to mess with her and Mila's lives?

You, Kendra. You're a strong, successful woman now. You're not going to make the same mistakes you made years ago.

THE NEXT DAY Dale and his brothers were finishing up a job in the branding pen, when his cell phone buzzed. Stepping over to the corral fence, he pulled the phone from his shirt pocket and glanced at the ID.

Smiling at the sight of Kendra's name, he said, "Hello, beautiful."

"Dale," she said in a rush. "Do you have a minute to talk?"

The quiver in her voice instantly set off alarm bells in Dale's head. "Sure, I have time. We just finished branding a pen of calves."

A moment of silence passed and then she asked, "Do you have manure splattered on your jeans?"

Frowning quizzically, he glanced down at his nasty jeans. "I do."

He heard a short breath ease out of her, while at the same time he noticed there were no sounds of the busy bakery in the background. Instead, he could hear the wind and the rumble of traffic. Which told him she must be standing outside on the sidewalk.

"I'm glad," she said. "That means you're my kind of guy."

Had she been drinking something stronger than the bakery's coffee? Her voice sounded odd and she wasn't making a whole lot of sense, but for the moment he decided to go along with her.

"Oh. I thought you might've been afraid I'd show up at your apartment this evening wearing my dirty work clothes."

"No. I— Oh Dale, I don't know what to do! I'm scared!"

She was crying now and his first instinct was to jump in the truck and get to her as fast as possible.

"Sweetheart, what's happened? Is Mila okay?"

"She's at school. She's fine. But I don't know— Dale, I'm sorry, but we're going to have to postpone our little dinner this evening."

Confused, Dale stared across the ranch yard to where Bobby was working with a red roan yearling. Only a few weeks ago, Dale had told his friend not to feel pressured into getting married just because others expected him to be a family man. Now, here he was hanging anxiously on a woman's every word.

"What's wrong?" he asked. "I can hear you're upset."

She didn't answer immediately and Dale got the impression she was trying to compose herself.

Finally, she said, "I'm trying not to cry. It's just that I

don't need this happening in my life right now. But Mila does and—"

When she didn't continue, he asked, "So this is about Mila?"

"Mostly." She drew in a deep breath. "Bryce has come to Bronco. He showed up here at the bakery yesterday and again today, right in the middle of the morning rush."

Dale went stock-still as he struggled to absorb what she was saying. "Bryce? Your ex?"

"Yes. I was knocked sideways, Dale. We've been living here in Montana for more than three years and other than a card on Mila's birthday, he hasn't bothered to contact us. Now he's suddenly decided he wants to be a father."

The bastard. Where did he come off playing with other people's lives? "Uh, what about his wife? Was she with him?" Dale asked.

She snorted. "They've divorced."

The cogs in Dale's head began to spin faster. How was this going to affect their budding romance? These past several days they'd both been so happy. And yesterday, after their brief, but incredible session of lovemaking, they'd clung to each other, hating to part, even for one evening. Now...

"What a jerk," he muttered.

Her groan was a sound of frustration. "Bryce wants to see his daughter this evening and I'm afraid if I try to put him off, he'll just pester me more. And— Well, I don't have to tell you how she's longed for her father to be in her life. She's talked to you about him and how much she wants a daddy."

Oh yes, she'd made it very clear how much she wants a father and how she definitely didn't want Dale in the role, he thought.

"Does Mila know her father is in town?"

"No. I plan to tell her when she gets out of school this afternoon."

A sick feeling hit the pit of his stomach. "She's going to be very excited."

His voice must have sounded hollow because she let out another exasperated groan.

"I understand this is hard for you."

Hard? That didn't begin to describe what this news was doing to him. "Don't worry about me. Just take care of Mila. She doesn't deserve to be hurt a second time," he said crisply, then, closing his eyes, he wearily pinched the bridge of his nose. "What about the little dinner we'd planned? Are you canceling it completely?"

There was long pause and then… "Of course, I'm not canceling it, Dale. I thought— If you can, that is, we'd get together tomorrow night. By then maybe I'll know what Bryce's intentions are."

"So you don't know how long he's planning to hang around?"

"No. And whatever he tells me I'm not going to put much stock in. He's good at telling people what they want to hear. Not necessarily the truth."

"All right. Unless something comes up, I'll be at your apartment about six thirty tomorrow evening."

Her sigh of relief caused the frown on his face to deepen. What had she been thinking? That he'd turned his back on her now that Bryce had shown up in her life? Or was she simply worried about the whole situation?

"Okay. I'll see you then. And, Dale, thank you for understanding."

He didn't understand. Not completely. She was postponing their date because her ex-husband was in town. That didn't make a heck of a lot of sense to him. But she was already distraught enough without him adding to the problem.

"We'll talk when I see you." He told her goodbye, then hung up before something rolled out of his mouth that would do more harm than good.

He was slipping the phone back into his pocket when Shep walked up to him.

"What's wrong? You look like you could eat a handful of nails."

Dale grimaced at his brother. "Just a handful? I could eat a bucketful and not even flinch."

Shep chuckled. "Feeling tough today, are we?"

"No! I'm feeling like a fool."

"You mean, more so than usual?" Shep teased.

Dale's frown turned into an outright glare. "Kendra just broke our date for tonight. Her ex-husband is in town. How would you handle that kind of news?"

Shep let out a short laugh. "I'd probably hunt the guy up and give him a not-so-gentle persuasion to leave town."

Oh sure, Dale thought miserably. Mila would really love him if he beat up her father. "Shep, violence is not the solution."

"Then I'd say you'd better step back and take a deeper look at the whole situation. This setup with Kendra sounds pretty sticky to me." He slapped a hand on Dale's shoulder. "Come on, forget about it for now. Let's go to the house and have a beer before we have to jump on the rest of that fence."

Sounds pretty sticky. Yeah, Shep was sure right when he'd spoken those words. It was going to be as awkward as hell if the man came around while Dale was with Kendra. But there was no use in him worrying about that possibility...until it happened.

By THE NEXT AFTERNOON, Dale was so anxious to see Kendra and hear about Mila's meeting with her father, he decided to drive into Bronco early and stop by the bakery. If the place wasn't overrun with customers, they might be able to talk a few minutes without Mila around to overhear their conversation.

He had just parked his truck and was walking down the sidewalk to the bakery when he saw a sleek black car pull into a nearby parking slot. His steps slowed as he watched a tall blond man dressed in slacks and a pale blue shirt emerge from the driver's side and walk around to the back door of the luxury sedan.

Dale wasn't surprised when he lifted Mila out to the ground. Something about the vehicle and the man had told Dale he wasn't a native of Bronco and he'd been right.

Trying not to stare at the man who'd caused Kendra and her daughter so much anguish, Dale walked on toward the bakery. He'd made it almost to the door, when Mila spotted him and called out.

"Dale! Dale!"

Turning slightly, he saw she'd left Bryce and was tearing down the sidewalk to intercept him. Dale stopped and gave her the cheeriest smile he could manage.

"Hi, Mila. Did you just get out of school?"

Her face beaming, she grabbed his hand. "Yes! My daddy came to pick me up! Remember, I told you he'd come to see me!" She turned and proudly pointed at Bryce, who was slowly walking toward them. "That's him! I want you to say hello, Dale. Will you?"

How could he resist the child? He couldn't. It was no fault of Mila's that the man had ignored the fact that he had a child...until now. Now that Dale had fallen in love with both mother and daughter, he thought miserably.

"Hello," Bryce said. "I hope my daughter isn't pestering you."

My daughter. Just hearing the man say the words made Dale physically ill.

"No. Mila is, uh, we're buddies."

The man's eyes narrowed as they scanned Dale's face. "I see. Well, I'm Bryce Humphrey—Mila's father."

Like hell you are. "I'm Dale Dalton. Kendra's boyfriend," he added with a meaningful look.

Mila tugged on Bryce's sleeve and Dale could see he wasn't enjoying having the child's hand touching his clothing.

"Dale is a cowboy, Daddy. He rides horses and ropes cows. And he makes Mommy laugh a lot," Mila explained.

Bryce glanced down at her. "That's nice, honey. But now I think we should let Mr. Dalton be on his way. And I need to let Kendra know you're here."

Dale considered turning around and heading back to his truck, but why should he give this guy a break? Dale had more business here at the bakery than this phony.

"'Bye, Dale. See ya later."

Mila and Bryce entered the bakery and Dale waited until they were well inside the bakery before he followed.

Kendra was behind the counter tending to a customer, but she looked up when the door chime sounded and immediately spotted him. She looked utterly frazzled and Dale desperately wished he could sweep her out of here and away from all the customers and work and, most of all, her ex-husband.

As he stood to one side and waited for Kendra to have a pause in customers, he glanced to his left and saw that Bryce and Mila had taken a seat at one of the tables. Seeing the girl with her biological father should be making him happy, Dale thought. But it didn't. Mila needed a real father, not one who was trying to fake the role of a parent.

Don't you think you're doing a bit of faking yourself, Dale? Since when have you become such an expert at child-rearing and what a seven-year-old girl needs?

The goading voice in his head had Dale turning away from the pair and he edged a few steps closer toward the counter, where Kendra was counting change back to a young woman.

As soon as she finished the transaction, she skirted around the counter and wrapped her hand lightly over his forearm. "Come on," she said. "Let's go back to the office. I'll get Jackie to watch the front."

Dale gladly followed her into the private room and as soon as she shut the door behind them, she practically fell into his arms and buried her face against his chest.

"Oh, Dale, I'm so glad you here. Hold me. Just hold me."

Her words were muffled against his shirt, but he could hear the angst in her voice and he instantly wrapped his arms around her and held her tightly.

"Has that jerk been giving you trouble?"

"Not exactly. It's just a strain having him around. I saw the three of you out on the sidewalk and I could only imagine what Mila must have been saying to him and you."

"Don't worry. She didn't say anything out of line. I told Bryce that I was your boyfriend. He didn't look too pleased with the information."

Her hands clutched his back. "Too bad. Our relationship has nothing to do with him."

"Do you mean that, Kendra? Truly?"

Tilting her head back from his chest, she looked up at him, and the wounded shadows he saw in her eyes made him feel like a heel for asking the question. But damn it, he had a right to know where they stood.

"Do you have to ask, Dale? You are the guy in my life now. Not him."

"Yes, but he's Mila's father. And he's divorced."

"I can't change either of those facts. I want to think you care enough about me to handle this awkward situation until he goes back to Florida."

"And when will that be? Has he mentioned how long he plans to stay?"

"He hasn't and I haven't asked. I didn't want to give him the impression I was interested."

"You think that's why he's really here in Bronco? Because he's interested in you? And using Mila as an excuse?"

She shook her head. "I honestly don't know, Dale. But whatever his motive, I can't trust him."

His gaze probed hers. "You're worried about Mila, aren't you?"

Her nod was stiff. "Dale, I wasted years staying in South Beach and hoping Bryce would decide to be a father. At that time I believed it would be a good thing for Mila to have him in her life. Now, I'm far from sure. He puts on a sincere front, but I have a feeling the facade will eventually drop. Mila isn't a baby anymore. She isn't fooled. Once she figures him out, she'll be hurt. Not to mention disillusioned."

The thought sickened Dale and yet he felt like an outsider looking in. He had no right to interfere. A fact that left him feeling more helpless than he could ever remember.

—"Maybe it's best that Mila figures out now that he's a phony," he said. "At least, she'd be saved a worse heartache later on. However, there's one thing you haven't considered, Kendra."

Her eyes widened. "What's that?"

"The possibility that the guy has changed."

After all, Dale had gone through an inner transformation since he'd met Kendra. No one else might have noticed the change in him, but he was becoming a different man. Whether this new side of him was good or bad, he couldn't yet decide.

Groaning, she pulled out of his arms and walked over to her desk. With her back to Dale, she absently drummed her fingers on the desktop. "The fact that he's here in Bronco proves his life has taken a different turn, but as for his character…that's questionable."

Walking over to her, he gave her shoulders a gentle squeeze. "I'm going to get out of here and let you finish work. I'll be at your apartment at six thirty. That is, if you still want us to have a date," he added.

Her lips formed a perfect *O* as she whirled around to face him. "Of course, I want to keep our date! Why wouldn't I?"

He shrugged. "You're stressing over all of this. Later on might be better for you."

Grabbing both his hands, she held them tightly as though he was a lifeline, and Dale could only wonder if she thought of him more as her protector than as her lover.

"I need you, Dale. And whether you realize it or not, Mila needs you too."

Bending his head, he placed a soft kiss on her lips. "I'll see you at the apartment."

WITH TIME ON his hands, Dale's first instinct when he left the bakery was to drive straight to Doug's bar and down several beers, but numbing his senses with alcohol wasn't the answer. Besides, he wasn't about to drink and then drive across town to Kendra's apartment.

Eventually, he decided to use the remainder of the afternoon to pick up a few items he needed from Bronco Feed and Ranch Supply. While he was there, he ran into a couple of cowboys who worked on a ranch that bordered Dalton's Grange, and by the time he'd shaken loose of their company and driven to Kendra's apartment, he was only a few minutes early.

Mila answered the door and on their way to the living room, she informed Dale that her mother was running late and was still getting ready.

"She had some extra stuff to do at the bakery," Mila explained as she watched Dale take a seat on the couch. "Jackie got sick and was throwing up so she had to go home."

From what Dale had gathered from Kendra, Jackie was her extra right hand. No doubt, the woman leaving work early put an even bigger strain on Kendra's day.

"That's too bad," Dale told the girl.

Mila was wearing jeans with a blue tutu fluffed over the hips and the rhinestone tiara on her head. She looked almost as she had that first night he'd walked into the bakery. So much had happened since then, he thought. The mother and daughter had become an integral part of his life.

She twirled her way across the living room until she was standing in front of Dale. "Mommy says it was just something she ate and not the flu."

"That's good to know," he said, while thinking what he really wanted from this child was her thoughts about her father. Had she found him as wonderful as she'd professed him to be? But Dale wasn't about to pump her for such information. On the other hand, if she offered it freely, he wasn't about to shut his ears.

As though she could read his thoughts, she plopped down on the cushion next to him and said, "I was super-duper happy when I saw my daddy yesterday. And he was happy to see me too."

Mila was smiling from ear to ear and the expression revealed more than any words she could have told him.

"I'm glad you were happy. Were you surprised to see him?"

"No. I've been thinking he was going to come soon and he did. Now I can see him all the time. 'Cause he won't be in Florida."

Her remark sent a sense of dread spiraling through him. "He's not going to be living in Florida?"

Grinning, she lifted her chin. "No. He's gonna stay here in Bronco—so he can see me."

Dale wondered if Bryce had actually told Mila such a thing or if this was the girl's wishful thinking. Either way, the idea left him uneasy. "Uh, that will be nice for you."

"Oh yes! And it will be nice for Mommy too. 'Cause him and her are going to get back together and we're going to be a whole big family again!" She let out a sigh of contentment. "But first they'll have a big wedding with flowers and music and all that fancy stuff. And I'll get to be the flower girl and wear a wreath of roses in my hair."

"You already know the wreath will be made of roses?" he asked cautiously.

"Sure I do. Because I'm going to tell Mommy to have roses for her flowers. They're the prettiest and they smell the best."

And that was the most important thing when a woman was remarrying her ex, Dale thought sourly, then silently muttered a few curse words.

Actually none of what Mila was saying sounded like Kendra, but he wasn't about to point this out to the child. Her mother would have to set her straight. Unless Kendra did decide she wanted to give Bryce one more try.

Oh God, he wasn't going to think about that possibility tonight.

The sound of footsteps caught his attention and he turned his head to see Kendra entering the room. She was wearing another flounced dress that was cinched in at the waist with a silver concho belt and a pair of tall black cowboy boots. And although there were faint shadows of fatigue beneath her eyes, the warm smile on her lips made her face glow. She looked so lovely it made him ache with longing.

Rising quickly, he walked over and kissed her cheek. "You look far too beautiful tonight to be eating fast food," he told her. "I think we should go to a nice restaurant—wherever you'd like."

"Sounds good. But it's not really necessary. We can eat whatever."

Dale glanced over at Mila. He'd been so busy listening to the girl talk about her father, he'd not thought to inquire about her little friend.

"What about Louisa?" he asked. "Is she still planning to go with us?"

"Yes. I told her we'd pick her up on the way." To Mila, she said, "Go get your coat, honey. It's going to be chilly tonight."

Mila skipped out of the room and once she was out of sight, Kendra raised up on tiptoes and placed a hurried kiss on his lips.

Smiling slyly, he asked in a low voice, "Was that kiss a teaser of better things to come?"

"That was a promise for better things to come," she whispered. "As soon as I can make arrangements."

She handed him her coat and as he helped her into the sleeves and smoothed the fabric across her shoulders, he tried to reassure himself that he had nothing to worry

about. Kendra might not love him yet, but she wanted him
and that had to be enough for now.

As for her ex-husband, Dale could only hope that whenever Kendra was around him, she would only remember
the suffering and heartache the man had caused her.

CHAPTER ELEVEN

THAT NIGHT ON their way home from dinner, while Mila and Louisa had been chattering nonstop in the back seat, Kendra had made plans with Dale to meet again on Friday night. Mila could have another sleepover with Louisa and hopefully she and Dale would have an uninterrupted night together.

However, by the time Friday rolled around, their carefully made plans were foiled when Bryce called and invited Mila to a children's animated movie showing at a theater in Bronco Heights. Once the girl was given a choice between a sleepover with Louisa or going to the movies with her father, she'd not hesitated to choose the outing with Bryce.

Kendra had been devastated, but when she'd called Dale to give him the disappointing news, she'd insisted they could still salvage a big part of the evening.

"Bryce and Mila shouldn't be home from the movies before nine thirty or ten. That would give us two or three hours together," she told him.

"I don't mind telling you, Kendra, this whole setup is making me feel cheap."

She gripped the phone as she stared at the wall of her office. "It didn't make you feel cheap before. If it did, you didn't mention feeling that way."

"Before was different. Bryce wasn't in the picture," he said.

He sounded more than perturbed and Kendra could understand up to a point. But she was dealing with the situation as best as she could.

"He isn't in the picture now!" she said, unable to stop her voice from rising. "He has nothing to do with you and I being together."

"The hell he doesn't! He's the reason our plans have blown up in our faces."

"Is that my fault?" She shot the question back at him. "Am I supposed to keep Mila away from her father just so you won't be offended?"

The line went deathly quiet and then he said in a tight voice, "No. Heaven forbid that I should ever come between Mila and her real father. She and Bryce should go to the movie. In fact, now that I think about it, you should probably go with them. The three of you together—a family back together. Mila would love it. As far as that goes, Bryce would probably love it too."

Kendra's back teeth snapped together as anger poured over her. "You're sounding like a jealous idiot! And frankly, I don't have the time or desire to listen to such crap."

Her hand shaking, she punched the end-call button on the face of her phone, then dropped it onto the mouse pad on her desk.

Dropping her head into her hands, she closed her eyes and tried to calm her breathing when a knock sounded on the door. She looked up just in time to see Jackie stepping into the office.

"Am I needed out front?" she asked.

"At the moment, the only customers out there are coffee drinkers, and Smitty is handling those." Her eyes narrowed as she walked over to Kendra's desk. "Why are your cheeks fire-engine red? Let me guess, your ex is causing problems."

Kendra rolled her eyes toward the ceiling. "It's probably awful of me to say, but I'll be shouting hallelujah whenever he leaves."

Jackie perched a hip on the corner of the desk. "You used to tell me how much you wished he would come to see Mila. Now he's here and you're already wanting him to leave. You've made a quick turnaround."

She sighed. "Yes, I guess I have. Because deep down, I'm not sure he's sincere about being a father. Not for the long haul. Besides, I'm getting vibes from Bryce that he'd like to strike things up with me again. And that just isn't going to happen. Not ever."

"It's none of my business, Kendra, but was that Bryce on the phone just now?"

Kendra ran a hand over her burning eyes. She'd slept very little last night and this morning she'd had to hurry around in a groggy daze to get ready for work. Unfortunately, her day wasn't getting any better.

"No. It was Dale."

Jackie's mouth gaped open. "You were angry at Dale? Why?"

Good question, Kendra thought. Why was she angry? Because he resented the constant interruptions of their plans? Because he wanted her to consider his feelings as important as Mila's?

Groaning, she shook her head. "Everything is closing in on me, Jackie. Trying to deal with Mila, Dale and Bryce all at the same time. Trying to make them all happy. It's becoming too much for me. But me getting angry with Dale— I was wrong and I feel terrible about it."

Jackie shook her head. "Kendra, when are you ever going to try to make yourself happy?"

The question caused Kendra to pause. *Make herself happy?* The night she and Dale had made love for the first time, she'd actually believed she was on her way to a life of contentment. Now, the days ahead of her looked shaky at best.

She said, "Jackie, a woman can't just *make* herself happy. It's something that has to occur naturally."

Jackie lifted her arms in a gesture of frustration. "You're hopeless, Kendra. You can't sit around and wait and hope. You got to go after whatever you want—and that means Dale!"

Kendra was trying to decide how to counter her assistant's advice, when the door suddenly cracked open and Andrea peeped inside.

"Sorry to interrupt, but I need help," she said. "Customers are backed up to the door."

Jackie hurried out of the office and Kendra rose to go join them.

Halfway across the room, her cell phone rang and she paused to check the ID. If it wasn't important, she'd let voice mail pick up the call.

Dale!

Her hands trembling, she punched the accept button. "Dale, are you—"

"Don't say anything," he interrupted. "I need to apologize, Kendra. I was out of line and I'm sorry. The things I said— I was frustrated. I want to be with you and—"

"I want to be with you," she said, finishing his sentence before he could say more. "And I'm sorry too, Dale, for losing my cool and practically shouting at you. This is all just as frustrating for me. I want us to be together. Terribly so."

He released a long sigh of resignation and the sound sent a chill rushing through her. Clearly the strength of their bond was being stretched to the limit and Kendra wasn't sure how much longer he was going to hang on.

"I feel the same way. So I—I'll be there tonight. As long as I'm still invited, that is."

She fell back against the closed door and realized she was close to bursting into tears. "You're still *very* invited, Dale. I'll be waiting for you."

"'Bye, Kendra."

He ended the call without giving her a chance to say goodbye, but Kendra wasn't going to worry about that trivial detail. She'd be in his arms tonight and that was all that mattered.

SATURDAY NIGHT, DALE was in the tack room, going through the motions of oiling a saddle he'd cleaned only two days ago, when from the corner of his eye he saw Shep walk by the open doorway, then slowly back up.

"Hey, brother, what are you doing in there?" he called to Dale. "It's Saturday night. Aren't you going into town?"

Dale glanced in his direction. "Aren't you?"

"Sure. I have a hot date with a cute little nurse. Black hair and caramel-brown eyes and a little turned-up nose. Mmm. She says she wants to check my temperature."

Dale shot him a droll look. "Where did you meet her? Doug's?"

Shep chuckled. "No. At the gas pumps. She needed fuel and so did I. Our eyes met and— Well, you know how it is."

Yeah, Dale knew exactly. The moment his eyes had met Kendra's something inside him had clicked. Like a button being pushed or a light switching on. Now he was paying the price.

"Yeah, brother, gasoline fumes have a way of sparking a romance. Lucky for you. I'm not so sure about the nurse."

Chuckling again, Shep stepped into the tack room and walked over to where Dale was sitting on an overturned feed bucket. "After tonight, she'll count herself lucky," he joked, then asked in a more serious tone, "So why are you out here instead of getting ready to go see Kendra?"

"I saw her last night."

Shep's expression was one of disbelief. "And that's enough? Man, I thought you were gaga over the woman."

Grimacing, Dale began to rub a spot on the saddle he'd already polished a dozen times. "I am gaga over the woman," Dale admitted. "But I'm beginning to see my feelings for Kendra don't really matter."

Last night, Dale and Kendra had spent a whole two and a half hours in her bed. After that he'd hurriedly dressed and left the apartment before Mila and Bryce returned from the movie. Kendra had practically begged him to stay. As long as the two of them weren't in bed, there was nothing wrong with Bryce and Mila finding him there, she'd argued. But Dale had felt awkward about the whole setup and left, anyway.

To be honest, he'd not wanted to have another face-to-face with Bryce again. The urge to punch the guy was so intense he could hardly control himself. But there had been more pushing him to grab his hat and jacket and walking out the door. It was a feeling that he was falling into a hopeless pit. They'd made sweet, passionate love last night and yet she'd not spoken one word to him about the future or how he'd become a permanent fixture in her heart. Maybe she didn't understand that he wanted more from her than sex. He wanted her love.

Shep had remained silent while Dale's dour thoughts had been circling his brain, but now his younger brother snorted.

"Dale, that has to be one of the stupidest remarks I've ever heard you make. Why wouldn't your feelings about Kendra matter?"

A ball of raw emotion was suddenly clogging his throat. "Because with her and Mila I'm standing on the outside looking in." His eyes narrowed as he turned his gaze on his brother. "You know, if I remember right, I think you warned me about dating a woman with a child. But I didn't pay you much mind. I thought I could deal with Kendra having a daughter, but it's not— Well, things haven't turned out like I thought they could. How I wanted them to."

Shep frowned. "I thought you loved Mila. The three of you certainly seemed happy together when they visited the ranch."

"I do love Mila. That's not the problem." Dale tossed aside the cloth he'd been using on the saddle. "The problem is her real father has shown up in Bronco. She and Kendra haven't seen him in more than three years. Mila is over the moon with having her dad show her attention. And Kendra is—"

When he broke off, Shep cursed. "Hell, Dale, nowadays a man is fortunate if a woman gives him one chance in life to make her happy. She damned well isn't going to give a loser a second chance. Kendra doesn't want him, if that's what you're thinking."

Ever since he'd driven away from Kendra's apartment last night, he'd been swimming in the miserable thoughts of Bryce worming his way back into Kendra's life. Maybe he was a fool for thinking in those terms, but he couldn't help himself.

When Dale failed to say anything, Shep went on, "I'll tell you one thing, brother. If I loved Kendra, I wouldn't sit around and give her ex the chance to win her back. And, anyway, who says the guy is going to stay around Bronco?"

"Mila. She says her dad is going to buy a place in town.

But Kendra hasn't mentioned the possibility. She says she doesn't know anything about his plans."

"If the guy is planning to hang around, Dale, that's all the more reason you need to get a firm hold on Kendra's affections. And you can't do that by polishing a saddle until you wear a hole in the leather." Shep started toward the door, then glanced over his shoulder at Dale. "If you're not going to go see Kendra tonight, just make sure you stay away from Doug's."

"Why? A miserable man isn't supposed to drink beer?"

Shep grinned. "Sure, you can drink beer. But if you're at Doug's you might unintentionally end up sitting in the death seat and I don't want you ending up like Bobby Stone."

On that last bit of advice, his brother disappeared through the door and Dale thoughtfully screwed the cap back on the jug of neat's-foot oil sitting between his feet.

Why should he mind ending up like Bobby? Yeah, the guy had gone through some misery. But his life had taken a turn for the better. He had a good woman's love now and that was a hell of a lot more than Dale had.

Something was wrong with Dale. Kendra hadn't seen him in several days. Not since the night Mila had gone to the movies with Bryce. Her calls to him had ended up in his voice-mail box and her text messages hadn't fared much better.

Been very busy on the ranch.

Those were the only words she'd received from him and with each passing day, she was growing more hurt and perplexed. Sure, a rancher's work was never done. But this wasn't about work monopolizing his time.

No, she thought, as she pulled a tray of peanut-butter cupcakes from the hot oven. Dale was obviously avoiding her. Oh yes, the last time he'd been at the apartment, he'd made love to her. But even as he'd held her close, she'd sensed his thoughts were far away. Since then, she'd been trying to tell herself he'd soon get back to the sweet understanding Dale she'd fallen in love with. But now she was beginning to doubt she'd ever see that Dale again.

"Kendra, the timer hasn't gone off yet, but these cinnamon rolls look ready to come out. You should probably have a look."

Kendra glanced over to Andrea, who was peeping into an industrial-size oven. "If they're brown, pull them. Do you have the glaze mixed?"

"It's ready. I'll take care of the rolls. You go ahead and finish the cupcakes."

Andrea had only started helping Kendra with the actual baking about six weeks ago, but thankfully, the young woman was catching on very quickly.

Glancing at her watch, Kendra saw she had an hour to go before she dropped Mila off at Ada's and unlocked the door at five thirty, but there was still much to do in the kitchen before opening the front to the public.

"You have enough time, Kendra. But do you have enough energy?" Jackie asked as she paused at Kendra's side. "You look awful."

Kendra walked over to a worktable, where two dozen cupcakes were waiting to be frosted. Jackie followed on her heels.

"Thanks, Jackie. I always look forward to your cheery words to start the day," Kendra said dryly. "And I have a good excuse for looking awful. I got about three hours of sleep last night."

Bending her head close to Kendra's, Jackie whispered, "I hope it was Dale keeping you awake."

"Not in the way you're thinking," she snapped, then grabbed up an icing gun and began to squeeze white buttercream on the cupcakes. "Dale has been missing in action. He doesn't come around to see me. He won't answer my calls. Any sensible woman would tell him to go jump in the lake. But I—"

"Care too much to do that," Jackie said, finishing for her.

Kendra nodded miserably. "I swore I'd never make a fool of myself over a man again. But I have."

Jackie picked up a second icing gun and went to work helping Kendra top the cupcakes. "Look, Kendra. You don't actually know what's going on with Dale. You need to find out before you start making assumptions," she said. "And here's something else you might need to know. Maryann, the real-estate agent who works down the street, was in the bakery yesterday and she told me that Bryce had been in her office inquiring about houses for sale."

Kendra frowned as her cloudy day was already growing cloudier. "How would Maryann know Bryce?"

"She ran into Mila at the bakery and your chatty daughter introduced him to her," Jackie explained.

"Mila's proud to finally have a father to introduce."

"Yeah, but is he a real father?" Jackie shook her head. "Don't bother answering that. Just tell me you're going to drive out to Dalton's Grange and have it out with Dale face-to-face."

Kendra glanced at her assistant. Jackie might be flighty at times, but right now she was making sense.

"If you can take over for me here, I'll drive out to the ranch this afternoon. Ada is picking up Mila at school and keeping her until I finish work tonight, so it's a good time for me to go."

Forgetting the icing for a moment, Jackie slung an arm around Kendra's shoulders and squeezed. "I'll take care of everything here. You take care of Dale," she said.

IF KENDRA HADN'T alerted Dale with a text message that she was coming to the ranch, he would've already ridden out with his brothers to round up a herd of heifers. Now, as he waited for her to arrive, he wished he'd left with his brothers, anyway.

These past few days he'd been trying to forget her face, the touch of her hand, her soft sighs and gentle smiles. He'd been trying to convince himself that stepping out of her life would be better for everyone. Now he had to convince her.

The sound of an approaching vehicle had him glancing toward the road leading into the ranch yard. When Kendra's white SUV came into view, he left the porch and walked out to meet her.

This time when she climbed out of the vehicle, Dale didn't greet her with a kiss. Those days were over with, he thought sickly. But, oh, she looked so lovely in a long black skirt and her blond hair flowing loosely over a white sweater. And how could she even smile at him after the way he'd been ignoring her?

A lump suddenly formed in his throat, making it painful to speak. "Hello, Kendra."

"Hi, Dale. I apologize for interrupting your work. I, uh, needed to take advantage of Mila being with the sitter. Otherwise, she would've had a fit to come with me."

He slanted her a skeptical glance. "I'm sure you could've gotten Bryce to watch her. Mila would choose him over Dalton's Grange any day."

The corners of her lips turned downward, but she didn't

bother contradicting his remark. Probably because she knew he was speaking the truth.

What the hell is wrong with you, Dale? You're behaving like a child and sounding like a brat.

"Sorry, Kendra. That was a cheap shot. I want Mila to be happy. And she deserves to have her father in her life."

"Does she? I'm glad you're sure about that," Kendra said. "I'm still trying to make up my mind about the situation."

What did she mean by that? he wondered, then quickly doused his curiosity. Kendra and Mila were no longer his business.

Slipping a hand under her elbow, he said, "Let's go in. The house is quiet right now. Mom and Dad have gone to town and my brothers are out on the range."

She nodded and the two of them didn't speak until they were in the great room and he suggested she take a seat.

"I don't think I should bother sitting down."

"Why?" he asked.

Her features crumpled and it was all Dale could do not to sweep her into his arms and smother her with kisses. Had he gone crazy? He wanted this woman more than he'd ever wanted anything in his life. But sometime in these past few days, he'd come to the conclusion that it was time for him to be generous, to consider the needs of others before himself.

"I can see that you—" Turning her back to him, she bowed her head. "I came out here, Dale, to find out what has happened with you—why you haven't called or come to see me. I didn't understand. But now I can see for myself that you've quit caring."

Quit caring. Oh God, help him get through this, he prayed.

"Kendra, I think you're a wonderful person and Mila

is a sweetheart. But since— Well, I've been doing a lot of thinking and I can see that I'm just not the settling down kind."

She turned to face him and her eyes were brimming with tears. "In other words, you've decided dealing with me, a child and an ex-husband is too much for you."

"If you want to put it that way, yes. I'll admit that once your ex showed up, it opened my eyes to what being married and having a child is all about. And I—I'm just not cracked up for that kind of life." He'd never been much of a liar, but he was doing a bang-up job of it now, he realized.

"I haven't tried to rope you into anything," she said.

"Be honest, Kendra—you want a husband, a family. And that's what you need to focus on, instead of wasting your time on me."

Her blue eyes clouded with confusion as she stepped close enough to place her hand on his forearm. "Then those times we, uh, were together was just sex for you?"

Was it possible for a man's heart to burst into a thousand pieces, Dale wondered. Because his felt on the verge of exploding with pain.

"I— Yeah, I guess it was."

He couldn't look her in the eye, not while every word coming out of his mouth was a lie. But he was doing this for her sake and Mila's, he told himself. One day she'd be glad and thank him for it.

A breath shuddered out of her and she quickly turned her head away. "Well, there's not much use in me saying anything else, is there?"

"No. No use at all."

She started toward the door and somehow he managed to follow, even though the walls and the floor seemed to be tilting to a drunken degree. Maybe he was about to pass out, he thought, and when he woke up he'd find out this was all just a nightmare.

"Goodbye, Dale. I hope you won't avoid the bakery just because there is no *us* anymore. I'll still be glad to see you."

"That's nice of you, Kendra."

Dale, can you be any more of a bastard? She ought to be slapping your face and calling you what you really are.

"Please tell your parents hello for me."

"Sure."

He walked with her as far as the steps of the porch, but that was as far as he could go. Otherwise, she was going to see what a cowboy looked like when he cried.

WITH ONLY A week of September left on the calendar, the hours of sunlight were growing shorter, forcing Dale and his brothers to begin and end their workdays in the dark. However, this morning as Dale and Morgan finished saddling their horses, the sun was already peeping over the ridge of the mountains, but the weak rays were hardly enough to counter the cold wind blasting them in the face.

"This weather is miserable," Dale muttered as he buttoned his sherpa-lined jacket tightly at his throat. "I should have pulled on my duster. It cuts the wind better."

"Go to the house and fetch it," Morgan told him. "We have plenty of time to make the ride out to check the bulls and get back by midafternoon."

Dale tugged the brim of his hat farther down on his forehead. "I don't want to bother. I'll be warm enough when the sun gets a little higher."

"Suit yourself." He nodded his head in the direction of the door directly behind them. "Let's go in the barn and drink a little coffee before we go."

Shrugging, Dale said, "Let's go."

Inside the barn, Morgan filled two foam cups from a thermos and the brothers sat down together on a wooden bench. An overhead heater was blowing air in their direction, but Dale felt little warmth.

It's not the weather making you feel cold and empty inside, Dale. You'll never feel warm again. Not without Kendra.

Dale couldn't deny the mocking voice in his head. A little over a week had passed since he'd told Kendra they were finished and he was just as crushed now as he'd been when she'd driven away.

"This isn't like you to dawdle around when we have work to do," Dale said. "Taking care of Erica must be wearing you out."

"No way. She's carrying my baby. It's an honor to do things for her," Morgan told him. "I only wish I could do more to make this time easier for her."

Dale studied his brother's profile. "You love her very much, don't you?"

"This will probably sound corny to you, Dale, but sometimes I feel like I'm full up to here with love for her." Smiling, he used a finger to measure a spot at the base of his throat.

Dale's gaze drifted down the barn to where a ranch hand was already busy mucking out one of the horse stalls. But he didn't really see the cowboy. All Dale could see was the crushed look on Kendra's face when they'd parted.

"Must be nice to feel that way about a woman and have her feel that way about you."

"You ought to know."

Grimacing, Dale said, "If you're talking about Kendra, then you're barking up the wrong tree. I'm not seeing her anymore."

Morgan muttered a curse. "You think that's news? The

whole family can see you've been moping around like a calf with shipping fever."

"I don't need your sarcasm, Morgan. Not today or any day."

"Right. You need help and in the worst kind of way." He took a sip of coffee, then said, "Tell me why she broke up with you."

Dale stared into his cup. "She didn't. I'm the one who ended things."

Morgan's expression turned to disbelief. "I thought you were smarter than that, Dale. I thought you realized that Kendra was the kind of woman who wanted a family. Not an affair. What happened? You started getting cold feet?"

"Not exactly. I realized I was fighting a losing battle. Her ex-husband is in Bronco now."

Morgan didn't so much as flinch. "And that made you tuck your tail and run? When have you ever backed away from a fight? When has any Dalton held up a flag of surrender?"

Dale said, "Believe me, it was all I could do not to tell him exactly what I thought of him and then show him a one-way road out of town. But that would've only made matters worse. You see, Mila is crazy about the guy. He's never been a part of her life before now. He never bothered to be a father. But that makes no difference to her."

"So you think the man is unworthy of Mila's adoration?"

Dale tried to wash the bitterness from his mouth with a swig of coffee. "Morgan, you and I both know we weren't raised to serve judgment on another person."

Morgan studied him for a long, thoughtful moment. "So you're trying to be fair and noble about this whole situation. Is that it?"

The pain in Dale's chest was rapidly spreading to his

stomach and beyond. "Isn't that what a decent man is supposed to do? I figure in the end Mila needs her two parents
together again. Families are better off together, not apart.
Just look at us, Morgan. Think how awful it would be if
Mom and Dad were divorced."

"Mom has always loved Dad unconditionally. That kind
of love doesn't end. You think that's how Kendra feels
about her ex?" Morgan snorted. "I doubt it. And who gave
you the right to decide she should be back with a man
who'd obviously wronged her? Are you trying to sentence
her to a life of unhappiness? Or are you just afraid of love
and marriage and being a father?"

Without him even knowing it, Dale's spine stiffened.
"I'm not afraid! I mean, once I might've been afraid, but
not anymore. And Kendra—I want her to be happy."

"Don't you believe you can make her happy?"

Groaning, Dale's gaze dropped to the toes of his boots.
"At first I'd hoped I could. But now… I don't know if she
loves me, Morgan. She's never spoken the words to me."

"Have you spoken them to her? Did you ever think she
might be waiting on you? You need to remember she's been
hurt by a man before. It's only natural she'd be cautious
about handing out those words to another fellow…unless
she knew for certain that he really cared."

Dale looked at him and as his brother's words of advice
slowly sunk into his breaking heart, he felt a spark of hope
try to flicker beneath the pain.

"You really think she might be waiting on me?" he
asked in wonder. "If she knew how much I loved her, do
you think she might forgive me?"

Grinning now, Morgan clamped a hand on his shoulder
and gave it an affectionate shake. "You'll never find out
until you try, little brother."

LATER THAT NIGHT, Kendra was curled up on the end of the couch, trying to reassure her mother that she was surviving, in spite of her breakup with Dale, but Laura wasn't buying in to her daughter's phony cheerfulness.

"If this was a FaceTime call, I know I'd see tears in your eyes," she told Kendra. "So drop the pretense. What you need to be doing is figuring out what went wrong with you and Dale and try to fix it."

Kendra pressed fingertips against her furrowed forehead. For the past week and a half she'd been walking around like a zombie, so numb with pain that getting through each hour was a struggle.

"It's an unfixable problem. Dale wants to keep his freedom. He's decided there's too much drama in dating a woman with a child and an ex-husband."

Kendra's reply was met with a long stretch of silence, then her mother said, "From everything you've told me about the man, none of that sounds like it fits his character."

I can see that I'm just not the settling-down kind.

When Kendra had first met Dale, he'd told her he wasn't looking to get married. Even Mila had warned her over and over that Dale wasn't her type, or the marrying kind. It was humiliating to discover a seven-year-old girl had a better judgment of men than Kendra.

"Dale explained it in a different way, but the end results are the same. Let's face it, Mom. It's not meant for me to have a real family."

"You're talking nonsense, honey. If you love him—"

"There's no *if* about it, Mom," she interrupted. "In spite of him treating me like a disposable dishcloth, I still love him deeply. I realize there's no logic to my feelings, but that's the way it is for me."

"Darling daughter, there is no logic to love. And all I was going to say is don't count everything over yet. Not until you've explained to Dale how you really feel about him."

Kendra frowned. "You think he doesn't know? How—" The chime of the doorbell caused her to pause. "Someone is at the door, Mom. I'll have to call you back."

Glancing at her watch, she decided it was a bit early for Mila to return from her playdate with Louisa. Besides, Mila knew where the outside key was hidden. And she didn't think the caller was Bryce. Several days ago, she'd made it brutally clear to him that she had zero interest in getting romantically involved with him again. Since their frank conversation, he'd kept a cool distance, only coming around whenever he had plans to see Mila.

When Kendra reached the door and peeked through the peephole, she was stunned to see Dale standing on her porch. What was he doing here?

Her hands trembling, she quickly unlocked the door and swung it wide.

"Hello, Kendra. May I come in?"

Realizing her mouth was gaped, she quickly snapped it shut and gestured for him to enter. "Certainly."

Cold wind followed him over the threshold and Kendra wasted no time in shutting the door and fastening the lock.

"I should've called," he said as she moved alongside him. "But I was afraid you, uh, would refuse to see me."

She couldn't refuse this man anything. At least, not while he was standing this close and she was aching to throw herself into his arms.

What a little fool you are, Kendra.

Ignoring the taunt in her head, she said, "Whatever you might think, I'm not a vengeful person, Dale."

"I'm relieved to hear it."

Gesturing ahead of her, she said, "Let's go to the living room. It's much warmer in there."

Once there, he pulled off his hat and, holding it with both hands, he looked at her with an expression she could only describe as humble. Which didn't make much sense. But his being here didn't make sense, either.

"You might as well sit down, Dale."

"Am I interrupting anything?"

"No. I was just talking with my mother." She walked over to the couch and sat down. Otherwise, her legs were likely to betray her and she'd end up collapsing right in front of him. "Mom is already thinking ahead to December. She and Dad are considering flying out for the Christmas holidays. But you're not here to talk about my parents or Christmas."

He pulled off his denim ranch jacket and placed it and his hat on an armchair, then walked over and took a seat on the cushion next to hers.

"I'm here to talk about you and me," he said frankly.

Everything inside Kendra began to tremble. "I don't understand. You made it clear we were no longer a couple."

He closed his eyes and drew in a sharp breath. "I know. I said a lot of damned stupid things to you that day on Dalton's Grange. I didn't mean any of them. I—I was— Well, in the words of my brother Morgan, I was trying to be fair and noble."

The pain she'd been going through these past several days had done something to her brain. It didn't seem to be able to process what he was saying.

Frowning, she asked, "What do you mean 'fair and noble'? All I heard was that you're not a settling-down man and everything between us was just sex."

Grimacing, he reached for her hands. "I'll never forgive myself for saying those things to you, Kendra. But

I thought— I believed in the long run I was doing the right thing."

"For yourself? Because you don't want a wife and child hanging around your neck?" she asked, unable to stop bitterness from tinging her voice.

"No! Because I thought Mila has needed her father for so long and she'd be much better off if she had her parents back together—the three of you as a family again. I was in the way of that, Kendra. I guess I still am."

Disbelief furrowed her brow. "Dale, how could you think I'd ever want such a thing? Bryce is no good. Not for me. And whether he ends up being a good father to Mila is something he has yet to prove. But I've already made it very clear to him that I want nothing to do with him romantically or any other way."

He let out a sigh of relief. "I'm glad to hear it, Kendra, because I've decided I'm not so noble after all. I love you too much to let Bryce have you."

Kendra stared at him in wonder. "You...love me? Is that what you said?"

His expression sheepish, he nodded. "I thought you knew how I felt. But I thought— Well, that you didn't feel the same way. So I kept my feelings to myself. But now I have to know, Kendra. Do you care enough for me to give us another chance?"

Like a thousand exploding stars, joy flashed through her and she flung her arms around him and smacked hurried kisses all over his face. "Oh, Dale, you darling fool! I've been in love with you ever since that night Mila had her headache! Even when you said all those things to me at Dalton's Grange I still loved you. I'll never stop loving you."

His arms came around her and as his face buried in

the curve of her neck, she thought the sound he made was something like a sob.

"Kendra, sweetheart, I've never been good at expressing my feelings. And I'm probably not saying anything right tonight. But I want you to know I'll always love you too. I want you to be my wife. I want us to have children and a home and be a real family. I desperately hope you want the same thing."

She eased his head up far enough from her shoulder to look into his deep blue eyes. "Yes, Dale! Yes, I want to be your wife. I want us to have children and a home and all the things that go with it." Pressing her cheek to his, she whispered, "Good or bad, we'll deal with all of it together."

His arms tightened around her. "I don't expect the idea of you marrying me instead of Bryce is going to go over very well with Mila. I figure I've got a lot of work ahead of me to try to win her approval."

Leaning her head back, Kendra gave him a clever smile. "Oh, I wouldn't say that. This will probably surprise you, but Mila has been missing you. She told me so herself. I guess you'd started to grow on her. And I also think that she's beginning to figure out for herself that Bryce isn't turning out to be the perfect father she imagined him to be. This past week, on two different occasions, he found excuses not to see her as he'd promised. I could tell she didn't believe him."

"She's a smart girl. She's going to figure out a lot of things. Especially how much I love her mother."

Kendra moved her lips to his and he captured them in a long, promising kiss that was still going on when Mila's voice suddenly shattered the silence.

"Yay! Looks like we're finally going to have a wedding!"

Laughing, Dale held his arm out to Mila and as the

three of them hugged, Dale said, "That's right, sweetie. A big wedding with a pretty little flower girl with a rose wreath in her hair and sparkly cowgirl boots on her feet. How does that sound?"

Tears of joy misted Kendra's eyes as she watched Mila circle her arms around Dale's neck and kiss his cheek.

"It sounds like we're going to have the best wedding ever!" Mila happily exclaimed.

Kendra squeezed Dale's hand and as he looked at her, she could see forever in his eyes.

EPILOGUE

Two WEEKS LATER, on the front porch of the Dalton's Grange ranch house, Kendra held out her left hand to allow Tori Hawkins, and her two cousins, Audrey Hawkins, who was married to Jack Burris and Corinne Hawkins, to get a closer look at the engagement ring Dale had slipped on her finger a few days earlier. The autumn afternoon sun glinted on the large square diamond flanked on both sides by a row of smaller round diamonds.

"Kendra, this is exquisite!" Tori exclaimed, then smiled suggestively at Dale, who was sitting close to his fiancée's side. "Looks like you mean to have Kendra for keeps."

Smiling smugly, Dale slipped his arm around Kendra's shoulders. "She's stuck with me from now on."

Audrey spoke up in a teasing voice. "It looks to me like Kendra is enjoying being stuck."

The three cowgirls had agreed to come out to the ranch this Sunday in order for Mila to meet her rodeo idols, and so far, the child had been happily monopolizing their attention. As for Dale, he didn't know the first thing about weddings or anything they entailed, but as long as he was sitting close to Kendra, feeling the warmth of her side pressed to his and seeing her smiles, he was a contented man. Later tonight, when they were alone in bed, he'd get her complete attention.

Besides, this afternoon get-together was mostly for Mila and worth it to Dale to see the girl thoroughly enjoying herself. The past two weeks, she'd gone through some major changes in her life. Her mother had gotten engaged and she'd had to say goodbye to her father, who'd gone back to Florida only a few days ago.

For a while Bryce had implied he might remain in Bronco permanently and Mila had even been telling everyone her daddy was here to stay. But shortly after Dale and Kendra had become engaged, the man had admitted that Montana just wasn't his style and he was going back to Florida. Even so, he'd insisted that he'd learned his lesson and vowed to be a father to Mila on a more regular basis. So he and Kendra had been talking to their former divorce attorney about renegotiating their custody agreement, to create a new visitation schedule. And Kendra had agreed to allow Mila to visit her father on designated dates in Florida, and Dale could only hope Bryce kept his promises.

Well, he thought to himself, at least he'd get some Florida sunshine himself out of the bargain, since he and Kendra planned to take Mila back and forth on her visits. He'd grudgingly talked to Bryce about a family trip to Disney, too, perhaps next summer—if things worked out.

"I already have a dress picked out for Mommy's wedding. It's in the Ever After wedding boutique in town," Mila declared as she carried a stack of magazines and wedding brochures over to where the Hawkins women were seated in cushioned lawn chairs.

After opening one of the brochures, Mila held the page up for the women to view. "This will be her dress. See, it has lots of lace and tiny pearls and a veil with a train that goes a long way behind her. So long that someone will have to carry it."

Tori winked at Kendra and Dale. "You mean, someone like you?" she asked Mila.

Mila's blond ponytail swished back and forth as she

shook her head. "Oh no! I can't carry the bridal train. I'm going to be the flower girl. I have to toss out the rose petals."

Audrey exchanged an amused glance with Corinne, before posing another question to Mila. "You already know your mommy is going to have roses as her wedding flowers?"

Mila glanced at her mother. "Well, sure. 'Cause she loves roses. They're her favorite flower. And mine too."

"Roses. Hmm. I'll have to remember that," Dale whispered in Kendra's ear. "Maybe by the time we get married, I'll have memorized a few more of your favorite things."

She smiled dreamily at him. "My favorite thing is you, darling. We're going to have a wonderful life together. You, me and our children living here on the ranch. I never thought I could be this happy."

Dale leaned over and pressed a kiss to her forehead. "And I'm going to do my best to make sure you stay that way."

"So have you two fixed a wedding date yet?" Tori asked Dale and Kendra.

Dale looked questioningly at Kendra and she smiled coyly at Tori. "Not yet. But we're thinking about when we might like to have the ceremony. Right now we're just celebrating being engaged, aren't we?"

Dale's smile for his fiancée was full of love and promise. "We're thrilled, and so are our families."

Still clutching her armload of wedding magazines, Mila sidled up to Corinne's chair. "When are you and cowboy Mike going to get married, Corinne? I bet you want a big fancy wedding like my mommy is going to have. Would you like to look at my books for a dress?"

Hearing Mila's question, Dale glanced over at Corinne just in time to see a tight grimace pass over her face. Mike

Burris was a brother to Jack and brother-in-law to Audrey. Like his famous brothers and the Hawkins Sisters, he was a rodeo cowboy, too, and for a while now he'd had an on-again, off-again relationship with Corinne. Judging by the agitated expression on her face, she wasn't exactly happy with Mike at the present.

Smiling wanly at Mila, Corinne said, "I'm not planning a wedding, sweetie. Mike and I are just friends."

Mila looked disappointed, while Dale gave Kendra a conspiring wink and murmured close to her ear, "I have a feeling that relationship might soon change."

With a knowing smile, Kendra squeezed his hand and whispered back to him. "No doubt about it. Cowboys are hard to resist."

* * * * *

Don't miss the stories in this mini series!

MONTANA MAVERICKS: LASSOING LOVE

Welcome to Big Sky Country, home of the Montana Mavericks! Where free-spirited men and women discover love on the range.

MILLS & BOON

Her Hometown Cowboy

LeAnne Bristow

MILLS & BOON

LeAnne Bristow writes sweet and inspirational romance set in small towns. When she isn't arguing with characters in her head, she enjoys hunting, camping and fishing with her family. Her day job is reading specialist, but her most important job is teaching her grandkids how to catch lizards and love the Arizona desert as much as she does.

Dear Reader,

I am so thrilled for the opportunity to take you back to Coronado. I knew Stacy's story wouldn't be complete until she found her sister. I felt a special connection with Abbie. I understood her desire to find out as much as she could about her birth family while wanting to remain loyal to her adopted family. I am blessed to have family members on both sides of the adoption story. I have cousins who were adopted into our family, and I have connected with cousins who had been given up for adoption. While the circumstances surrounding their stories are all different, I am proud to be able to be part of their journey.

In this story, I hope to introduce you to some of the beauty surrounding the area where I have based my Coronado series. My hope is that you will find it as beautiful as I do.

I love connecting with readers. You can find me at leannebristow.com, Facebook.com/authorleannebristow and Instagram.com/leannebristow1 or send me an email at leanne@leannebristow.com.

Blessings,

LeAnne

DEDICATION

A special thanks to my husband, Jeff,
who puts up with all my ramblings, cold dinners
and long weekends, so I can chase my dream.

CHAPTER ONE

COLD AIR SLAPPED Noah Sterling in the face as he stepped onto the porch of the ranch house. Technically, it was still summer, but nights in the White Mountains were chilly all year long. Now that fall was almost here, the brisk air had icy fingers. Noah sucked in the chill, letting it wake him up. He'd had less than four hours of sleep but getting up before dawn was so ingrained, he couldn't change it if he wanted to. Besides, he didn't have time to sleep. Not if he wanted to save his ranch.

He paused on the porch and gazed into the darkness. It was too quiet. No cattle lowed for their breakfast. No rooster warned that the sun would be up soon. No coyotes yipped in the distance. The only sound was the crunch of gravel beneath his boots as he made his way to the barn.

At the entrance to the stables, he flicked on the lights. Two heads poked over the fence to gaze at him. He fed them and checked their water. Jasper, his brother's palomino filly, started eating, but the roan gelding nudged him with his head, almost knocking Noah into the wall behind him. "Knock it off, Paddy."

The horse stomped his foot and nudged him again.

Paddy was a ranch horse, through and through. Every day of his life had been spent on the range, and he was antsy to get back to work.

Noah rubbed the velvet soft nose. "I hate this as much as

you do. This truck-driving gig is just temporary. As soon as I get the bank off our back, I'll build the herd back."

He patted the horse one more time and headed back to the house. Coffee. He needed coffee and lots of it. The rich smell drifted out the screen door and met him on the porch.

Something nudged his leg and he glanced down. A large yellow tomcat weaved in between Noah's legs, seeming to purr louder than any rooster could crow. He bent down and scratched the cat behind the ears. "Morning, Tom."

The cat butted Noah's hand and sat on his haunches, looking at him expectantly.

"Go catch your own breakfast."

Tom responded with a hoarse meow and went to stand by the door.

"Fine." Noah opened the door. "Stubborn cat."

He went to the kitchen and poured some food into Tom's dish before pouring himself a cup of coffee. Sitting down at the dining room table, he flipped through the mail, stacking the bills into their appropriate pile. Pay now. Pay later. Pay never. The first and last piles were empty.

Opening his planner, he stared at one number with a large red circle around it. Ten thousand was written in the box. He'd already sold off all his cattle and had two jobs, but he was still five thousand dollars short. Unless he won the lottery or robbed a bank, it was unlikely he'd come up with the money in the next eight days.

His cell phone lay on the table, next to his planner. He picked it up and stared at the screen. That was one bill he could do away with. After all, the only places he could get service were around towns. Out here in the mountains, it was useless. There was one voice mail message on his phone, but he didn't need service to know what it said. He'd listened to it so many times, he'd memorized it.

Hi, Noah. Sorry to do this on such short notice, but we

have to cancel your truck runs for the rest of the month.
We're all on hold until the Forest Service gets those wild
horses rounded up.

For the last six months, he'd been hauling logs to the
sawmill in Nutrioso. He needed that income to rebuild his
herd after he paid off the bank. Guilt pinched his chest. If
he couldn't haul logs to Reed's Mill, Stanley Reed couldn't
run his business either. They were both in a tough spot,
but Stanley's was worse because he had a wife and four
kids to support. Noah had no one.

A postcard with a picture of the Grand Ole Opry lay on
the table and he picked it up. On the back was his brother
Luke's scrawled handwriting.

Loving Nashville. Things are really starting to happen here. Meeting with a record exec next week.

Noah stared at the postcard. Without giving himself
time to think, he went to the phone on the kitchen wall and
punched in the number to call Luke. It rang a half dozen
times, and he was about to disconnect the call when Luke
answered.

"'Lo?"

"Were you asleep?" Noah glanced at the clock.

"Yeah. Late night." Luke had never been an early riser
like Noah was. "What's up? Everything okay?"

Noah took a deep breath. "No, not really. The ranch is
in trouble."

"What kind of trouble?"

How many kinds of trouble could there be? He swallowed the sarcastic remark. "I have to come up with five
thousand dollars or we lose the ranch."

"Sell some cattle. That's always good for a few thousand."

He huffed. "Already did."

"Oh." Luke's voice was quiet. Before Luke left for Nashville, he'd sold off his half of the cattle to finance his dream. "How much time do we have?"

The concern in his brother's voice was touching. Luke had no interest in the ranch. From the time he'd picked up a guitar, the ranch was at the bottom of his priority list.

Noah read the postcard again and guilt pressed on his chest. He couldn't ask his brother to put his dream on hold. "I'm sorry I bothered you. This isn't your problem. I'll figure it out."

He could still hear his brother's argument as he hung up the receiver. He knew Luke would call right back, so he waited a second and lifted the receiver off the cradle. After a while, he'd get tired of getting a busy signal and give up. Calling his cell phone would be useless since there was no signal in this part of the mountains.

Two hours, one shower and five cups of coffee later, Noah still didn't have a clue how he was going to save his ranch. If only he'd accepted the contract to clear logs from the burned area for the Department of Forestry and Fire Management six months ago. His brow furrowed. Maybe it wasn't too late. He opened a small box and rummaged through it for the business card he'd been given.

A flicker of hope filled him when he found it. The kitchen phone was still off the hook, so he replaced it on the cradle and waited a second before dialing the number.

The office line rang twice and went to voice mail. While Noah was leaving his name and number, someone banged on the front door. He frowned. No one ever came out to the ranch. His chest tightened. Probably someone from the bank, wanting to serve him with papers about the loan.

If he didn't answer the door, they couldn't serve the papers. How much time would that buy him? The pounding got louder.

Standing in the kitchen, he felt like a coward hiding from the school bully. He hadn't backed down then and he wasn't going to back down now. Stomping across the living room, he threw the door open so hard it bounced off the wall next to him. "What?"

The woman on the porch jumped at the sound.

"Stacy." Noah sucked in his breath. "I'm sorry. I thought you were someone else."

She grinned. "I feel sorry for that guy."

He leaned against the door frame. "Luke's not here."

"We're not looking for Luke." Stacy glanced over her shoulder and a redheaded man emerged from the pickup truck in the driveway. She waved him over.

The man stepped up on the porch and stopped next to Stacy. He held out one hand. "I'm Caden Murphy, Stacy's husband."

Noah shook his hand. "I heard Stacy got hitched. Congratulations."

Stacy wrapped one arm around Caden's waist. "We've come to ask you a favor."

Alarm bells went off in Noah's head. He didn't do favors for other people. He didn't have the time or the resources to help anyone. Right now, he couldn't even help himself.

He shook his head. "I'm sorry, Stacy. I can't."

She raised one eyebrow. "You haven't even heard what we want yet."

Noah shook his head. Unless she was offering him money in the next thirty seconds, the answer was no. It had to be.

"What Stacy should have said, is that we came to offer you a job. You would be doing us a favor if you take the job, but we're not asking you to do something for nothing."

Noah's chin lifted. "I'm listening."

"Stacy says you're good with horses."

"Yes." He grew up on a ranch, which meant he could ride before he could walk.

"Summer is almost over, and we want to take a few weeks off," Caden said. "Kind of a delayed honeymoon."

Noah frowned. "You want someone to work at your store?"

"No," Stacy said. "I've got plenty of help with the market. We need someone to manage Whispering Pines for us."

Whispering Pines was the campground Luke worked at before he disappeared and left everyone high and dry. It was a small campsite with only ten cabins. Even if they paid him, it wouldn't be much. "Not many campers this time of year."

"We offer more than cabin rentals, now. We have stables, and ten horses on-site. Some campers bring their own, but we offer lessons and trail rides to those that don't." Caden pulled a folded brochure out of his back pocket and handed it to him. "Which is why I need someone I can trust with the horses."

Getting paid to care for horses and take a few city slickers out on rides seemed like a cushy job. He doubted it would even put a dent in what he owed the bank. Still, every little bit helped.

But could he fit it in? He already worked at Bear's Garage during the weekdays and the Watering Hole tavern on Thursday, Friday and Saturday nights. Daytime on the weekends was reserved for making truck runs. Or at least that was how it had been.

How long would it take to find another trucking job? If he agreed to working at the campground, he might get the bank off his back for a while. "How long you planning to be gone?"

"At least a month. Maybe more."

He whistled. "That's a long honeymoon."

"Truth is, it's more than a honeymoon." Stacy gave her husband a warm smile. "We're going to Georgia to look for my sister."

"I didn't know you had a sister," Noah said. "Can't you find her on Facebook?"

She shook her head. "Not Georgia, the state. Georgia the country. And we aren't sure how much information the orphanage we were adopted from is willing to share. It may take a while to work through all the red tape."

A month was a little longer than he'd anticipated. But it might be better in the long run. "How much you paying and what are the hours?"

"The pay is negotiable. Besides taking care of the horses, you would be on call twenty-four hours a day for maintenance issues in the cabins, so room and board are included, of course. You're welcome to board your horses with ours if you need to."

Noah rubbed the back of his neck. He needed the money too much to turn down an opportunity. Problem was, he needed it fast. "I have some conditions."

"Like what?"

"I'm not giving up my other jobs."

Caden cocked his head. "The busy season is almost over, so as long as the cabins don't get neglected and the horses are cared for, I don't have a problem with that."

"And—" Noah took a deep breath "—I want five thousand dollars up front. By Friday."

ABBIE HOUGHTON ROLLED down the windows of her Porsche 911 to let the mountain air fill the car. After driving through miles of New Mexico desert, the White Mountains of Arizona were a welcome sight. She took a deep breath of the pine-infused air.

Too bad she hadn't been able to convince her father she needed a convertible for her college graduation. The weather was perfect for riding with the top down. He had a long list of reasons why a convertible wasn't practical. Or safe. The man was consistent, at least.

Thinking about her father sent a sharp pang of regret through her middle. Their last conversation hadn't been pleasant. He told her driving over two thousand miles across the country was a foolish thing to do. And if she insisted on traveling that far away from home, she needed to get over her fear of flying and get on an airplane. Most of all, he couldn't understand why she felt such a strong urge to seek out her biological sister. A sister whom, until six months ago, she never even knew about. Her hand reached up to touch the tiny locket on her necklace.

Her parents had never hidden the fact that she was adopted, but they also hadn't been in favor of her searching for information about her birth family and Abbie couldn't understand why. She had spent much of her childhood in and out of hospitals, and doctors speculated it was due to poor nutrition in the first year of her life. But could it have been genetic? Getting information about her birth parents seemed like a logical place to look for answers.

Against her parents' wishes, she'd written Saint George's Orphanage in the former Soviet republic of Georgia, requesting any information they could give her regarding her birth parents. Two months later, she received a package in the mail containing the locket, copies of her records and her sister's adoption records.

Her sister. Abbie still couldn't believe she had a sister. Anastasia had been adopted by Vince and Melissa Tedford from Coronado, Arizona. An internet search revealed that Melissa Tedford had died last summer, and according to the obituary, Anastasia still lived there.

Abbie glanced at the navigation screen on the dashboard of her car and her chest swelled with excitement. In fifteen minutes, she would be in Coronado. What would she find? Would she be able to find her sister? Would Anastasia even want to know her?

A swarm of butterflies suddenly invaded her stomach. What if Anastasia didn't appreciate Abbie showing up out of the blue? She pushed a button on her steering wheel to activate voice control. "Call Mom."

The call failed. That was odd, but come to think of it, she hadn't received a text message from her mother in several hours. One glance at the display screen explained why. No signal. She picked her phone up from the passenger seat to double-check. When her gaze returned to the road, a streak of brown shot in front of her. She stomped her foot on the brake and jerked the steering wheel to the right to avoid the large animal.

The smell of burning rubber filled the air, and the world outside of the car became a blur. Abbie screamed as the car spun around before slamming into something that made it stop.

Her breath came in gasps, and she opened her eyes. The passenger side of her car had slammed into a tree. The door was caved in, and pine branches stuck through the window. Dust swirled in the air, mixed with smoke from skidding tires, making it hard to breathe.

Abbie's hands shook so hard she could barely open the door. Once she did, she tried to slide out, but something gripped her. Panic clawed her chest before she realized it was just the seat belt. She fumbled for the button. It took her a few seconds to press the button hard enough to release the seat belt and she tumbled from the car.

She tried to run away from the smoke-filled air, but her feet slipped on the embankment of the ditch, and she fell to her knees. Twice more she tried to stand, but she couldn't. Her chest tightened and she began to cough. She knelt on the grass and inhaled between coughs, forcing herself to calm down.

The coughing didn't stop, and her lungs wheezed with each breath. No. She couldn't be having an asthma attack now. The tightness in her chest increased. She hadn't packed an inhaler. It had been years since she'd had an attack. So much for outgrowing it.

Her gaze went to her car. Could there be an old inhaler in her glovebox? She tried to stand again, but light-headedness threatened to overtake her. Closing her eyes, she concentrated on taking slow, steady breaths. She lifted her arms as high over her head as she could.

Her father warned her about driving across the country by herself. Anything could happen on the road, and she would have no idea how to handle it. No. She would not prove him right by dying by herself in the middle of nowhere. First, she needed to get away from the overpowering smells of her wrecked vehicle. Maybe then she could get her breathing under control.

She started to crawl away from the car as fast as she could.

"Ma'am." A hand touched her shoulder. "Are you okay?"

Someone had stopped. Relief flooded through her. Abbie grasped the arm that was touching her and pulled herself up. She started to cough again.

"Are you having an asthma attack?"

Unable to speak, she patted her chest and nodded.

"Where's your inhaler?" There was something soothing about the masculine voice, but she couldn't respond.

He guided her to the edge of the road and sat her on the grass. A moment later, she heard her car door open and things getting tossed around inside the vehicle. She wanted to tell him not to waste time looking for an inhaler. He needed to get her to a hospital. A second later, the man was back at her side.

"Here." He held something to her mouth. "Breathe."

She sucked a puff of medicine. Where did he find an inhaler?

"Again," the voice repeated. His hand cupped the back of her head, supporting her while she fought for air.

After a few minutes and many more puffs, the foggy haze started to lift from her brain. The coughing stopped and although the tightness in her chest relaxed a little, she was still wheezing. She knew the danger wasn't over yet. She scanned the area, looking for her rescuer.

She didn't hear the man move away, but he wasn't kneeling on the ground next to her anymore. Dark boots graced the bottom of long, denim-clad legs. She had no idea what the rest of him looked like, since he was leaning inside her car, digging through it again. She tried to call out to him, to tell him there wasn't another inhaler, but her voice was little more than a squeak.

A second later, he emerged from the car. He looked over at her with eyes so brown they were almost black. He lifted his cowboy hat and pushed his long hair back before replacing the hat. Except for his long hair and scruffy beard, he looked like a cowboy straight out of the Wild West.

She frowned at the inhaler in her hand. "This is empty."

"Do you have another one?"

She shook her head. "I didn't know I had this one. Where was it?"

He cocked his head. "In your console."

"I don't—" a fit of coughing stopped her midsentence "—have another one."

She rubbed her chest as the tightness began to build again. The man let out a groan and scooped her off the ground as if she were no bigger than a doll. He cradled her in his arms and was across the road in two strides.

It dawned on her that she was being carted away by a strange man, but she wasn't afraid. He opened the door to a large pickup truck that looked like it hadn't seen a car wash in years and deposited her in the passenger seat. He shut the door and disappeared.

A second later, the driver's-side door opened, and he climbed into the seat. The engine roared to life and the truck started to move. Abbie leaned her head against the seat and focused on getting air into her lungs while the man fiddled with something on the dashboard.

Static blared through the speakers, followed by a couple of clicks. Then she heard the man's voice. "Breaker breaker, Big Mac, come in."

"This is Big Mac, over."

"Contact Springerville Hospital. Let 'em know I'm bringing in a teenage girl having an asthma attack. Then contact Sheriff Tedford and tell him there was a single car accident just past 2150."

"Copy that," the voice on the radio responded. "Keep me posted."

Teenage girl? Abbie looked at him and smacked his arm lightly to get his attention. He turned his gaze from the road ahead and gave her an alarmed look.

"I'm not—" she stopped to catch her breath "—a teen." Another fit of coughing overtook her.

"Don't try to talk," he said. "I'll have you at a hospital in twenty minutes. Relax."

She held up her hands, one with two fingers up and the other with three.

His brow crinkled. Suddenly his eyes widened. "Oh. I get it. You're twenty-three."

She nodded and rubbed her chest, even though she knew it was useless to relieve the pressure in her chest.

The man turned his attention back to the road. "Then you're old enough to know better than to travel without your inhaler."

He sounded like her father. Only this man had no right to judge her. As soon as she could breathe enough to talk again, she would give him a piece of her mind.

CHAPTER TWO

NOAH GLANCED AT the woman in the seat next to him. She wasn't coughing as much now, but the wheezing in her lungs continued. The sound brought back memories of lying awake at night listening to his grandfather. Of course, his grandfather's coughing was caused by fifty years of smoking, and no inhaler could help that. Noah was sixteen the last time he rushed his grandfather to the hospital because he couldn't breathe. The old man never left.

The woman in the cab leaned her head back, closed her eyes and seemed to be concentrating on her breathing. What would have happened if he hadn't come along and found her? And what was a woman, from New York, according to her license plate, doing in this part of the country? Alone. Without an inhaler. The town of Springerville came into sight and the tension in his shoulders relaxed a little. Until she was safely inside, she wasn't out of the woods.

The cattle trailer he was towing wouldn't fit in the hospital parking lot, so he got as close to the emergency room entrance as he could. When he stopped the truck, she opened her eyes and peered around. Confusion clouded her green eyes.

"I'm sorry," Noah said. "I can't pull my trailer through the parking lot."

She nodded and reached for the door handle. He jumped

out of the truck and was by her door before she could get out. As soon as she stepped away from the vehicle, he picked her up in his arms. No way was he letting her walk all the way to the entrance.

The woman tried to lower herself to the ground. "Relax," he murmured close to her ear. "It's a long walk. Longer when you can't breathe." Noah took off walking as fast as he could.

After a moment, she relaxed and let her head rest against his chest. The sweet, clean scent of her shampoo, mixed with something else, tickled his nose. He fought the urge to lean his head closer to her so he could place the scent.

When they entered the emergency room, a nurse saw them and pushed a wheelchair over to him. "Is this our asthma patient?" The nurse clicked the end of a pen and held up a clipboard.

"Yes," he said.

"What's her name?"

Noah frowned. "I don't know."

The woman in the wheelchair began coughing again. Between breaths she managed to say, "Abbie Houghton."

The nurse handed him the clipboard. "Here. Fill this out. I'm going to take her back."

He stared at the papers in his hand. At least he knew her name. And her age. Beyond that, he had no idea.

He took the clipboard to the front desk. The woman behind the counter scanned the papers. "Does she have insurance?"

Noah shrugged. "I picked her up on the side of the road after she wrecked her car. You know as much about her as I do."

The woman pressed her lips together and circled something on the clipboard. "I see."

FROM THE FANCY car that was mangled on the side of the road, she came from money, so he was pretty sure she had insurance.

The lady turned back to her computer. "They will call you back when the doctor is finished."

Now what? He paced around the waiting room. He was supposed to be halfway to Albuquerque by now, but until he knew she was okay, he couldn't leave. He pulled his cell phone out of the breast pocket of his shirt and turned it on. It wouldn't do much good to call Sheriff Tedford. There were very few places in the White Mountains where cell phones worked outside of city limits. Chances were the sheriff was still at the scene of the accident, or headed here.

He glanced at the clock. The Maxwell Ranch moved a lot of cattle. One of their truck drivers couldn't make it today, so Becky Maxwell asked him to fill in. It was an opportunity too good to pass up because it could lead to more work. Not only from the Maxwells; word of mouth among ranchers spread fast. He couldn't afford to miss this. Scrolling through his phone, he found Becky's name. She didn't answer. Most likely, she was headed to her father's ranch and didn't have service either. He waited for the beep. "Hey, Becky. This is Noah. I'm running a little behind schedule, but I'll be there as soon as I can."

For almost an hour, he continued pacing around the waiting area. It was almost one o'clock. Why hadn't they let him know anything? He could understand if they didn't want to give him personal information about her, but since he'd brought her in, wouldn't they at least let him know she was all right? And where was Frank? Surely, the hospital would give the sheriff an update.

He called Freddy Macias's landline. Surely, Freddy— Big Mac—would have let him know if he hadn't been able to get in touch with the sheriff.

"Hey, it's me," he said when Freddy answered. "Did you get hold of Frank?"

"Yeah. He's having the car towed into the garage, and then he was going to meet you at the hospital."

Noah's gaze drifted to the entrance. Lo and behold, Frank was coming through the doors. "Actually, he just walked in. Thanks."

He ended the call and waved the sheriff over. "Hey, Frank. How bad is the car?"

The sheriff reached out with one beefy hand and shook Noah's. "Not too bad. Just some bodywork and new windows. I don't think the engine is damaged. How's Miss Houghton?"

Of course, the sheriff would already know her name. "Don't know. She was having a pretty bad asthma attack when I found her." He shuddered to think what would have happened if he hadn't come along when he did.

"I brought her purse and her cell phone from the vehicle."

The double doors leading back to the patient area opened and the nurse who had taken Abbie back walked through. Her gaze fell on Noah. "She's asking to see you."

Frank stood up. "I'm coming, too. I need to get her statement."

Noah followed the nurse past several rows of beds. She pulled the curtain back to reveal Abbie, lying on a bed with an oxygen mask over her nose and mouth. Her face was pale, but she wasn't coughing or fighting for every breath.

Her eyes lit up when she saw him, and she pulled the mask off her face. "You're still here."

Noah laughed. "Was I supposed to dump you at the door and leave?"

She shrugged. "Most people would. I'm glad you didn't. Thank you."

"You're welcome." He clasped the hand she offered him. Her fingers were ice cold. He covered the tiny hand with his, trying to warm it up.

Frank cleared his throat. "I'm Sheriff Frank Tedford. I need to ask you a few questions."

Her head snapped around to look at him. "I'm sorry. What was your name again?"

"Frank Tedford."

Her brow furrowed. "Tedford?" The words were almost a whisper.

Frank was flipping through the pages of his notepad and wasn't looking at her, but Noah didn't miss the apprehension on her face. "Do you know the Tedfords?"

Abbie's face turned red. "No." She replaced the oxygen mask on her face and leaned back against the pillows.

Frank removed a pen from his front shirt pocket and clicked it. "Can you tell me what happened?"

Abbie removed the mask again. "Something ran in front of me, and I swerved to miss it. My car hit the slope of the ditch and spun. That's it."

"Something?" Frank frowned. "You don't know what it was?"

She bit her bottom lip. "It was big. At first, I thought it was a horse, but that's impossible."

"Probably an elk." Frank scribbled in the notebook.

Noah disagreed. "Could've been a horse." Wild horses wandered off the reservation all the time. A few herds had been causing a lot of trouble for local ranchers. They'd caused him enough trouble.

Frank nodded. "Were you distracted? Playing with your phone?"

Guilt flickered across her face. "I did glance down to see if I had a signal."

"Around these parts, the only place you'll get a signal is inside city limits," Frank told her. "Where were you heading?"

"Coronado."

Noah straightened up. The town was a popular attraction for outdoor enthusiasts, but a young woman traveling alone from New York was a different story. "Why?"

She lifted her chin. "Vacation."

Frank handed her the purse and cell phone he'd recovered from her car. "As soon as they release you, you're probably going to want to give someone a call. Your phone rang at least three times since I got close enough to town to get service."

"My mother." She shook her head.

The sliding curtain opened and a doctor appeared. He frowned at Frank. "Hello, Sheriff. What are you doing here? Is there a problem?"

"No," Frank said. "Her car had a little run-in with our local wildlife, so I was just following up."

Frank pulled a card from his shirt pocket and handed it to her. "This is the garage where your car was towed. You can call Harry to get a quote on the repairs."

Abbie nodded. "Thank you. I will."

Frank turned his attention to Noah. "I have to get back. Can you make sure she gets to Coronado?"

Noah hesitated. He was supposed to be in Albuquerque by three o'clock. How long would Becky's father be able to wait?

Before he could answer, she spoke up. "That's okay. I can call an Uber."

Noah laughed. "We don't have Ubers here."

She bit her bottom lip. "I don't suppose there is a rental car place around here?"

"Sure," Noah said. "Four hours away."

Her face fell. "In that case, I guess the only way to Coronado is with you."

"Thanks." Noah couldn't keep the sarcasm from his voice.

She let out a soft gasp. Words began to tumble out. "No, I didn't mean it the way it came out. It's just that you've already done so much for me and you were traveling down the mountain with a trailer, not up, so you were obviously going somewhere for a reason and now I've put you behind and I just don't want to cause you any more trouble."

If she wasn't so flustered, he would have laughed at the way she stumbled over her words, but he didn't want to make it worse. Instead, he turned to Frank. "I'll make sure she gets to Coronado safely."

Frank shook his hand before tipping his hat to Abbie. "I hope the rest of your stay in Coronado is less eventful."

The doctor handed Abbie some papers. "Miss Houghton, you're free to go. But I would get this prescription filled as soon as you can. The change in elevation may have contributed to your asthma attack, so if you plan on staying in the White Mountains for any length of time, keep your inhaler with you at all times."

"Thank you." She swung her feet to the side of the bed and looked at Noah. "Can you hand me my shoes?"

Noah followed the direction she was pointing and spotted a pair of sandals underneath a chair. He handed her the shoes.

"Let's get out of here." She slipped the sandals on and stood up.

Nodding, he followed her toward the lobby. As they approached the entrance, she showed no signs of stopping. "Did you give them your insurance information?"

She halted. "Oh. Of course," she said, and made her way over to the intake desk.

His phone vibrated in his pocket. He glanced at the message from Becky.

Got your message. How late will you be?

Stacy and Caden had paid him enough to stop the foreclosure proceedings, but if he didn't find a way to make more money soon, he wouldn't be able to hold the bank at bay for long. How much longer would he be able to hold on?

He glanced at Abbie standing at the counter and stepped outside.

On my way. Be there by 4:30.

ABBIE STOOD JUST outside the entry of the emergency room. Her rescuer was scowling at his phone.

Without her asthma-induced haze confusing her senses, he looked different. Rougher. She'd always pictured cowboys as clean-shaven, with short, neat haircuts, wearing pressed shirts and jeans. This man's hair hung past his shoulders, and he looked like he hadn't shaved in days. His jeans were faded, and the bottom hems were worn and tattered. His Western shirt was so thin she could see the T-shirt he wore underneath. Even his boots were dull and scuffed.

Still, no one could doubt he was a true cowboy. It was in the way he moved. The way he spoke. It was hard to explain, but Abbie knew this man was the real deal.

He turned around and saw her. Slipping the phone onto the clip on his belt, he nodded. "Did you get the bill taken care of?"

She gave him a half smile. "I gave them my insurance information. They're supposed to bill me once it goes through."

A flicker of relief crossed his face. "You ready?"

"The nurse said there's no pharmacy in Coronado, so I should get my prescription filled here in Springerville. Is that going to be a problem?"

"I've got someplace I need to be soon."

She nodded. "Okay. I'm sure I can get it tomorrow."

"You didn't let me finish." His brows drew together. "I don't mind stopping by the pharmacy, but I'm late picking up a load of cattle. Do you mind if we do that before heading to Coronado?"

As anxious as she was to get to Coronado, she'd already put this man out enough. The least she could do would be to let him take care of his responsibilities first. She smiled. "Sure. I've never seen cattle up close. It'll be an adventure."

His shoulders slumped in relief, and he smiled back at her. "Wait here. I'll try to get the truck a little closer."

"It's okay. I don't mind walking." At least now that she could breathe, she didn't.

He didn't respond, just turned and started walking, leaving her no choice except to follow. She spotted the pickup parked on the side of the road, just outside the hospital's parking lot. The trailer attached to the bed of the truck had seen better days. The paint was almost gone, and dried mud clung to the sides.

They walked toward the truck at a snail's pace. She was certain he was going slow on her behalf. "I guess I messed up your day and I don't even know your name."

"Noah," he said.

She smiled. "Nice to meet you, Noah."

They arrived at the truck, and Noah opened the passenger's-side door for her. "Don't you lock your truck?"

"Nothing in it worth stealing," he mumbled, and waited for her to get into the cab before closing the door.

She looked around the vehicle. The dashboard was faded and cracked. From the condition of the mats on the floorboard, she suspected the seat underneath the brown-and-red Navajo blanket would be cracked and faded as well. The cab smelled of tobacco and dirt, but it wasn't unpleasant.

When he got into the driver's seat, she asked him a question that had been in her head since the sheriff left. "Sheriff Tedford seems to know you pretty well. Are you related?"

"No." Noah inserted the key into the ignition and started the engine.

She waited for him to elaborate, but he didn't. All she knew about her biological sister was that she owned the Coronado Market and the names of her adopted parents. Was Frank Tedford kin to her sister? She was desperate to find out information about Anastasia, and this man probably had some of the answers she needed. "How do you know him?"

He gave her a serious look. "Are you trying to find out if I've had run-ins with the law?"

"No." Heat rushed to her face. "I was just curious."

"If you must know, Frank's son used to be best friends with my younger brother. I've known the Tedfords all my life."

That wasn't helpful. Time to try another approach. "I did some research on the area before I came up here and one of the stores is owned by a Tedford."

He nodded. "Frank's niece owns the Coronado Market."

Her heart leaped. Now they were getting somewhere. "What's she like? I mean, the store. What's the store like?"

Noah stopped the truck and shut the engine off. "The pharmacy." He nodded toward the building.

"Oh. Be right back." She grabbed her purse from the seat and hurried into the building.

The pharmacist assured her it would just take a few minutes. While she waited, she scrolled through her phone. Her mother had left at least a dozen messages and several voice mails. Nothing from her father. She tapped out a message to her mother.

I'm fine. Made it to Arizona. Not much service in the mountains. Will call you tomorrow.

She ignored the pinch of guilt she felt. She'd been in a car accident, had an asthma attack and was rushed to the hospital. Was she really fine? If she told her mother what happened, the woman would be on the first plane to Arizona despite her phobia of planes.

Seconds later, her phone rang. With a sigh, she answered. "Hi, Mother."

By the time she'd convinced her mother she was okay, her prescription was ready. Clutching the paper bag, she hurried back out to the truck.

"Talk to your mother?" Noah asked. "I saw you on the phone through the window."

"You know how mothers are. They worry too much."

He shrugged. "Actually, I don't. Mine doesn't worry about anyone but herself."

Abbie waited for a clue that he was joking. None came. Was he serious?

"You have your inhaler?" His voice held the tone of someone talking to a small child.

"Yes," she said. "And by the way, I haven't had an asthma attack in two years."

Confusion muddled his face.

She let out a huff of air. "That's why I didn't have another inhaler. Not because I'm irresponsible."

"Oh." He pulled the truck onto the road and headed toward Coronado.

When he didn't argue with her, Abbie relaxed against
the seat.

She must have nodded off, because when she opened her
eyes, Springerville was no longer in sight. Neither were the
mountains surrounding Coronado. The road looked very
much like the one she'd been on this morning.

Her pulse thundered in her ears, and a slight sense of
fear crept up her spine. Her father's warnings about being
too naive and trusting echoed in her head. Was she being
kidnapped? "Where are we?"

She glanced at Noah, and the fear left as quickly as it
came. She could trust him.

Noah didn't take his eyes off the road. "About an hour
and a half from Albuquerque."

"What?" She jerked up straight. "Why?"

"I told you I had to pick up some cattle."

She bit the inside of her cheek. "I thought you meant
somewhere close."

"You didn't ask." He cast her a sideways glance. "But
I should've told you. I'm sorry. I just can't afford to lose
this job."

Abbie slumped back in the seat. She was so close to
seeing her sister today. "Will we be in Coronado today?"

Before he could answer her, his cell phone rang. He
slipped it out of the front pocket of his shirt. "Hi, Becky.
I'm almost there."

Abbie stared at him. Who was Becky? His girlfriend?
Her gaze went to his left hand. No ring. But that didn't always mean anything.

Noah swallowed. "Of course. I understand."

Abbie could tell the phone call upset him, but she didn't say anything. A moment later, he pulled to the side of the road and made a U-turn. She pressed her lips together, wondering if she should say something.

He glanced at her. "Change of plans. We're heading for Coronado."

They rode in silence. Abbie didn't want to irritate him further with small talk, and she certainly wasn't going to ask him about the phone call.

Noah was the one who broke the silence just before they got back to Springerville. "Is this the first time you've been to Arizona?"

She nodded.

He cast a sideways glance at her. "Are you going to tell me why you're really here?"

Abbie wasn't going to lie, but she didn't want to reveal too much yet, either. She tucked a strand of hair behind her ear. "My sister lives here."

"Who is she? Coronado isn't that big. I probably know her. I can drop you off at her house."

Her heart raced. She was certain Noah knew Anastasia. After all, he knew her uncle. But she didn't know if her sister wanted to be found. If she did, why hadn't she tried to contact her before now? No. She wanted a chance to meet her face-to-face, with no pressure.

She fingered the locket again. "She doesn't know I'm here yet, and to be honest, I'm not sure if she'll want to see me. I'd rather not drop by unannounced."

"Ah." Noah nodded. "Family drama. I can understand that."

"Do you have a large family?"

"Just a younger brother," he said.

Silence filled the cab again, but this time it was a comfortable silence. Abbie watched the landscape change from desert plants to pine trees. A few hours ago, she had been too anxious about meeting her sister to really enjoy the view.

"I never thought Arizona would have so many trees and mountains."

"Most people don't know how diverse Arizona really is." Noah shifted gears as the road began to climb. "All most people know is what they see in old Westerns or on the weather when Phoenix hits one hundred and twenty degrees."

"Guilty." She laughed.

He gave her an odd look. "If you're not going to your sister's tonight, where do you plan to stay?"

She opened her purse to search for the piece of paper on which she'd written the name of the campground. "I found a place on the internet that looks good. Whispering Pines."

It wasn't exactly a lie. She did see it on the internet, and it did look nice. But that wasn't why she chose it. She chose it because her sister owned it.

"I think Beaverhead Lodge is more your style."

Her eyes narrowed as she stared at him. "What's that supposed to mean?"

"No offense, but you don't look like the type of person accustomed to roughing it. The lodge has a full-service restaurant, Wi-Fi and all the amenities you could want. All Whispering Pines offers is a cabin. Besides, Coronado Market will be closed, and you wouldn't be able to check in."

"Oh." She swallowed the lump of anxiety in her throat. "But it's owned by the same Tedford that owns Coronado Market, and you know the owner, right? You could call her."

"Stacy is out of the country right now on her honeymoon," he said.

Honeymoon? Her sister had gotten married since the obituary in the paper. "Will she be gone long?"

"They just left a couple of days ago, so it'll be a while."

Abbie's heart dropped. She just missed her. Would her sister be back by the time her car was repaired? What had he called her? Stacy. Short for Anastasia.

They rode in silence for a few moments. The road got steeper and although it was still daytime, the sun was low enough in the sky that the trees cast long shadows over the road. As they passed a meadow, Abbie caught sight of horses grazing on the thick grass.

Noah pointed at the small herd. "There's your most likely culprit. One of them probably ran out in front of you."

"It happened so fast, I wasn't sure what it was, but my first impression was a horse. What about their owner? Why aren't they fenced in?"

"For one, Arizona is mostly open range, so livestock can roam freely. For two, those are wild horses, so they don't have an owner."

"Oh," she breathed, watching the horses. "They're beautiful, too."

Noah grunted.

"You don't like them?"

He shrugged. "Like all animals, they have a place and purpose. Unfortunately, some ranchers don't agree."

The truck slowed down and he turned onto a dirt road. A few minutes later, they pulled in front of the main lodge. Abbie grasped the door handle. "Oh, no… I don't have my suitcases." Except for her purse, which the sheriff had brought for her, she didn't have any of her belongings.

"I'll swing by Bear's Garage and get it out of your car and bring it back."

She shook her head. "I can't ask you to do that. I've put you through enough trouble already."

"It's fine. It might take a while, though. I need to feed the horses first, but I'll come back as soon as I get it done."

The thought of seeing him again that evening sent a thrill down her spine. "That would be very nice, thank you."

"I'll wait until you get checked in. That way, I can find you if the front desk is already closed for the evening."

"Okay." She swung the door open. "I'll be right back."

She hurried into the lodge.

The lady behind the desk smiled. "Hello. Do you have a reservation?"

"No, I don't. Do you have any rooms available?"

The woman glanced at the screen. "We do. Would you like a single with a king-size bed, or something smaller?"

She pulled her wallet out of her purse. "What's the difference in price?"

The woman handed her a flyer with prices on it. Quickly, she calculated in her head how much it would cost to stay for two weeks. The cost of the room alone would wipe out her checking account. Plus she still had to eat. There was also the matter of car repairs.

"This is a little more expensive than I expected." She waited to see if the woman would offer her a discount. When she didn't, Abbie handed the flyer back. "Thank you. I'll look for something in town."

CHAPTER THREE

OUTSIDE THE LODGE, Abbie scanned the parking lot. The sun hadn't set, but the trees and mountains obscured the light, casting long shadows over the land. Stars were beginning to twinkle in the sky above the trees, but even in the growing darkness, she should be able to spot Noah's truck. It was nowhere to be seen. Her pulse pounded in her ears. He was her only hope for getting a ride into town. Not that going into town would change her situation.

She squeezed the phone in her hand. Her chest tightened. What were her options? She was stuck more than halfway across the country with no car, no cell phone service and no source of income. What little money she had would have to last until her car was ready, which likely would take a while. Her sister should be back by that time.

Her father's words echoed in her head. She was too trusting. Too naive. She knew nothing about the real world and wouldn't make it without him. She needed someone to take care of her. She was helpless. All the things he had said weighed her down until she could barely breathe. He was probably staring at the phone, waiting for her to call him, so he could tell her he was right.

After the argument with her father, she'd made the bold and dramatic move of cutting up all the credit cards he had given her and depositing the pieces on his desk, declaring herself financially independent. Was he right?

Standing up straight, she turned to go back inside the

lodge and talk to the manager. One night. She would pay for one night and figure the rest out tomorrow.

Just before opening the door, the crunch of gravel drew her attention to the road winding past the lodge and toward the cabins that dotted the hillside. Headlights almost blinded her as Noah's truck pulled into the main parking lot.

Leaning across the seat of the vehicle, he hand-cranked the window down.

"There you are," she blurted out. Even to her own ears, she sounded desperate and whiny. Not at all how she wanted to come across. She gathered her composure. "I mean, I thought you left me."

He gave her a puzzled look. "I had to find a place to turn the trailer around."

Seeing him renewed her determination to stay. If she called her father, he'd try to coerce her into coming home. She wasn't ready yet. One thing was certain, though: her resources were now limited and she had to be smart with her money.

When she yanked the door open and plopped down on the seat, his puzzled look turned into concern. "What are you doing? I said I'd bring your stuff back."

"I'm not staying here." She faced the road. "Can you take me into town, please?"

He slammed the truck into Park. Anger flitted across his face. "What happened? Did someone do something—"

"What?" No one had ever reacted so strongly to something she said. He seemed ready to jump out of the truck. She touched his arm. "This place is a little out of my budget, that's all."

He gazed at her through narrowed eyes, as if he didn't quite believe her. "You didn't strike me as the kind that has a budget."

"Why's that?" She had the feeling he wasn't handing her a compliment.

He gave her a long look. "Fancy car. Name-brand purse. Manicured nails. If I had to guess, I'd say you were born with a silver spoon in your mouth."

She pressed her lips together. "Well, I wasn't." It was true. Technically. She was almost a year old before the "silver spoon" made its way to her.

He put the vehicle back into gear and started heading toward the main road. "Where do you want me to take you?"

The darkness grew outside the windows of the truck, and she crossed her arms over her chest. "If Whispering Pines is closed, take me to the next cheapest place."

He merely nodded, but she could tell by the look he gave her that he didn't approve of her answer. They rode in silence for the next ten minutes. She watched the road, anxious for her first glimpse of the town in which her sister had grown up.

She peered through the window, searching for some clue that they were close to town, but she saw nothing but trees and fields. Finally, she spotted a single lit-up building, with nothing around it. "Odd place for a gas station."

"What do you mean?"

"I would think it would be closer to town."

He laughed. A deep, throaty sound that tickled her ears. He put on his blinker and pulled into the turning lane. "We're right in the middle of town."

"What?" She leaned forward to look at her surroundings.

No traffic. No streetlights. Nothing to indicate a town. Dark buildings sat on the edge of the road, but behind them, she could make out the glow of lights from houses.

"You're kidding," she said, paying closer attention now. Straight ahead, one sign caught her eye: Coronado Market. A shiver danced down her spine. Her sister's store. She was so close. She wiped her sweaty palms on the rough fabric of her denim jeans.

He turned off the main road onto a dirt road, and a little farther along, he turned into a small parking lot and stopped in front of a tall chain-link gate. He got out of the truck and pulled a key ring from his pocket. The gate slid open, and they drove into a large yard. Banged-up vehicles were parked in odd places, reminding Abbie of junkyards she'd seen in horror movies.

"Bear's Garage," he said before she asked. "Might as well get your suitcases while we're in town."

Relief flooded through her. "You have a key to the garage?"

"I work here."

Her brow furrowed. "I thought you were a rancher."

"I am." His words were clipped. "But right now I also work here."

She glanced back at the trailer behind them.

"What about the cattle you were supposed to pick up?"

"I was late, so they hired someone else."

"Oh." No wonder the phone call upset him. "You were late because of me. I'm sorry."

"Yeah, I am, too." He opened the passenger door to the truck for her.

Abbie stiffened at the harshness in his voice. It wasn't like she'd wrecked her car on purpose.

Noah's face fell. "Sorry. I didn't mean it like that. It's just…that job might have led to a better job."

She had never known anyone to have more than one job. "So you're a rancher, you work here and you drive a truck. Don't you ever sleep?"

He didn't answer. Instead, he nodded in front of the vehicle. Abbie followed his gaze. The headlights were aimed directly at her car. Wow. She'd really done a number on it. She exited the truck and inspected the damage.

She ran her hand along the bright red hood. The passenger side was dented in. The windows were shattered, and tree branches still clung to the frame. One tire seemed to be twisted at an odd angle and was flat. "How long do you think it will take to fix it?"

Noah shrugged. "Bear's not real busy right now, so it depends on how long it takes to get parts in. If you're lucky, two weeks, but since this is a foreign car, it'll probably take longer."

She sighed. Did she have enough money to stay that long? Would her sister be back by then? Leaning inside the car, she pushed a button on the dash and popped the trunk open. Noah beat her to the suitcases. With one in each hand, he carried them to his truck and held the door open for her.

"Is that all you need from the car? I need to stop and feed the horses before getting you settled, if that's okay."

Abbie nodded and slid into the passenger seat. She wanted to ask him more about his jobs, but she sensed that now wasn't a good time. Instead, she peered out the window, trying to get a better sense of the town her sister grew up in.

With no streetlights, it was difficult to tell which dark shapes were houses and which ones were businesses. Then, there were no more shapes. Just trees. A little farther and Noah slowed down to turn onto a rough dirt road.

Abbie relaxed as they bumped down the road. She'd never been on a ranch before, but judging from the shape of his truck and trailer, she needed to put the images of a big fancy ranch house and thousands of cattle out of her mind.

A large sign arched over the road. Again, her heart

sang with recognition. "Whispering Pines Campground. I thought we were going to feed your horses."

"Never said they were mine." Noah shrugged.

"You said the campground was closed."

"No. I said the market was closed. To get a cabin, you have to register and pay at the market. I'm taking care of the horses and managing the campground while Stacy's gone."

Abbie pressed her lips together. He'd told her she couldn't stay at Whispering Pines because the store was closed. If he was managing the campground, it didn't matter if the store was closed or not. She drew in a sharp breath. There was only one explanation: he didn't want her there. She turned her head to stare out at the darkness.

A floodlight came on as they approached a large barn. The truck twisted and turned as Noah guided it into the barnyard and then backed it up, using only the side mirrors for guidance. He got out of the vehicle and disappeared. A few seconds later, she heard the scraping sound of metal and the truck rocked a few times as he unhooked the trailer.

He opened her door. "Are you getting out?"

Abbie's jaw clenched. "No, thank you. I'll stay out of your way until you're done. The sooner you're done, the sooner I can find a place to stay and be out of your hair."

He gave her a puzzled look. "You're staying here."

The pressure in her chest continued to build. "But you don't want me to."

"I never said that." Noah gave her a pointed look. "I was giving you a chance to change your mind and call your sister. Since you didn't, I will put you in Cabin Three. You can register and pay in the morning."

NOAH DIDN'T WAIT to see if she would get out of the truck. Her feelings had obviously been hurt, but he wasn't going to apologize. He understood family drama, but she needed to let her sister know she was here. It was the right thing to do.

He wasn't going to coddle her either. He turned and headed toward the barn. "You coming or not?"

He glanced over his shoulder just as she scrambled out of the truck and followed. The smell of hay and horses drifted in the breezeway of the barn. Noah stopped only long enough to flip on an inside light switch that bathed the inside of the barn with light. A dozen horses were waiting for their dinner. Many of them stamped their feet at him. The ears on a large roan were pinned back, and he snapped at Noah. Abbie's eyes widened, and she stepped away from the fence.

Noah patted the horse affectionately. "Behave yourself, Paddy. We have a guest."

The horse shook his head. Noah laughed. "You might as well get used to it. You're going to be here a while."

Abbie leaned against the wall, watching from a distance. He finished feeding the horses and went back to Paddy's stall to give him extra attention. Out of the corner of his eye, he saw Abbie jump.

Tom sat on his haunches and glared at her. She bent down to scratch behind his ears, but he hissed at her. She jerked her hand back.

"Don't mind Tom," Noah said. "He misses his barn, and he's determined to be miserable."

"His barn?"

Noah scooped the cat up and rubbed his head. The cat melted into him and purred loudly. "I couldn't leave him alone at the ranch while I was staying here. He's just homesick."

"Why are you staying here if you have a ranch close by?"

"Caden, Stacy's husband, wanted someone on-site in

case there was an emergency, either with the horses, or with the campground."

Abbie nodded and tentatively reached a hand out to stroke the cat. Tom allowed it for a moment before batting her hand away with a large, hairy paw.

Noah dropped him on the ground. "Go away until you learn some manners."

Tom obliged by disappearing under the gate.

Noah looked at his watch. "I have to be at work in less than an hour. Let's get you settled."

Abbie cocked her head. "You work at the garage this late at night?"

"No. I work at the garage in the afternoons. I'm going to my night job."

She followed him back to the truck and got into the passenger seat. "How many jobs do you have?"

Not enough. "Depends on the day. Right now, I have three steady jobs, one that is unreliable and one that doesn't pay anything."

Abbie's brow furrowed. "Why would you work at a job that doesn't pay?"

Good question. Why was he fighting so hard to hold on to something that caused him so much grief? For a split second, he tried to imagine life without his ranch and immediately he knew. "Because that's the one I love the most."

It only took a few minutes to drive back out to the campground. Almost all of the cabins were empty right now, so he could put her in any of them, but he chose the one closest to his own cabin. He parked the truck in between the two cabins and got out. "That cabin there is mine if you need anything. I'm kind of acting as the maintenance man, too."

How disappointed would she be? The cabins were a far

cry from the accommodations at the lodge. While the cabins were spacious and clean, the decorations were sparse, and the amenities were minimal. No TV. No cell service. No Wi-Fi. And certainly, no dining lodge where breakfast, lunch and dinner were served. At least not yet anyway. According to Caden, Stacy had big plans for the future.

Abbie had taken only a couple of steps toward her cabin when she stopped dead in her tracks.

"What's wrong?"

She tilted her head back and gazed at the sky. "I've never seen so many stars in my life."

Noah followed her gaze. It had been a long time since he'd really appreciated the beauty of the western sky. A million diamonds sparkled on a blanket of gray and black.

"It's so beautiful." Her voice was little more than a whisper. "And you get to see this every night."

Melancholy settled in on him. His mother had often begged him to sit on the porch and watch the stars with her. He was always too busy to stop and enjoy the view. There were two kinds of people: those who lay around enjoying the view and those who worked to get what they wanted. His mother wanted the view without the work. Was Abbie the same way?

He unlocked the door and pushed it open, waiting to see the look of disappointment flood her face when he flipped the light on. "Oh." She let out a soft gasp.

Noah stiffened, waiting for her comment. He wasn't going to apologize if it wasn't up to her standards. He searched the room. The main floor was spacious enough. A fireplace was situated in the center of the wall, with a sofa in front of it. A counter bar separated the kitchen and dining area. "This cabin has two bedrooms that share a bathroom down here and one bedroom upstairs in the loft."

"This is beautiful!" She dropped the small suitcase she

was carrying on the sofa and walked over to the fireplace. She ran her hands along the mantel. "Look at the craftsmanship! Do all the cabins have these?"

Noah stepped closer to see what she was talking about. On the face of the mantel, an elk, bugling next to a mountain stream, was etched into the wood.

"To tell you the truth, this is the first time I've seen the inside of any cabin except my own. I just started this job three days ago."

She explored the rest of the cabin while he went back to the truck to get the rest of her luggage.

He didn't see her when he returned. "Where do you want your stuff?"

Footsteps echoed through the cabin as she came down the stairs from the loft. "I can put them away, thank you."

Noah set the cases on the floor next to the sofa. "If you're all set, I need to get going."

"I'll be fine. Thank you." Abbie wandered into the kitchen and opened the refrigerator.

"Are you hungry?"

She gave him a sheepish smile. "A little."

"Come on." He opened the door, and she followed him to his cabin.

His own cabin had the same layout as hers. Normally, the maintenance man stayed in a smaller cabin on the far end of the campground, but he'd elected to stay closer to the horses.

Dirty dishes were stacked in the sink, but otherwise it was clean. He hadn't been there long enough to make a mess.

"I've only been here a few days, so I haven't done a lot of grocery shopping. But there are sandwich fixings in the fridge. Bread is on the counter, and there are a few frozen dinners in the freezer. Help yourself to whatever you want."

That was the best he could do for her. She would have to take care of herself now. He turned to leave.

"When will you be back?"

"Not until after midnight, so let yourself out when you're done. Don't worry about locking the door."

She frowned. "Where's this one?"

"The Watering Hole."

Confusion clouded her face.

"It's a tavern," he told her. "I don't usually work there on Monday nights, but Freddy's wife is having surgery, so I'm covering for him for a few weeks."

Why did he say that? It wasn't like he cared what she thought. Or at least he wasn't supposed to.

CHAPTER FOUR

ABBIE HAD BEEN awake long before her alarm went off. The bed was comfortable enough, but she'd tossed and turned all night. Partly because it was hard to sleep in an unfamiliar place and partly because she had gotten so cold. She tossed the covers off and rolled out of bed. When her bare feet hit the wood floor, a shock wave of cold danced up her legs. Wasn't Arizona supposed to be hot? Hugging herself, she padded into the living room.

Her suitcases were still on the floor where Noah had set them. She'd been so exhausted that she fell right into bed and hadn't bothered unpacking. She lugged the largest case into the bedroom and heaved it on top of the bed. Goose bumps covered her arms and legs by the time she found the soft flannel pajamas she almost didn't pack. Instead of slippers, which she hadn't packed, she opted for a pair of thick socks.

Now that she could feel her toes again, she could see what her cabin looked like in the daylight. The delicate carvings on the mantel were even more beautiful. A picture of a field of sunflowers brightened the room while forest green curtains swayed in the slight breeze coming in from the open window.

Her stomach growled, and she turned her attention to the kitchen. What were the chances her refrigerator had filled itself with food during the night? First on her list: grocery shopping. She frowned. Make that the second thing. The first thing she needed to do was pay for the cabin. Which meant she needed a ride to town. Which meant she needed to find Noah.

Would her cowboy rescuer be as handsome this morning as he was yesterday evening? A flutter of excitement ran through her. She peered out the window toward Noah's cabin. His beat-up truck was nowhere in sight. Where could he be? It wasn't even seven o'clock in the morning and he didn't get home until well after midnight. She knew because she heard his truck pull in. Maybe he was at the barn taking care of the horses.

She opened the door and stepped onto the porch. The wood creaked beneath her feet. She searched the direction of the barn, but trees obscured the view. Her gaze flickered back to linger on his cabin. Would it be presumptuous of her to make herself another sandwich? Probably. But she was hungry, and she had no idea where he was or when he'd return.

She turned toward the steps and saw a piece of paper taped to her door. Could it be the bill already? She removed the note.

Coffee is made if you want some and there's a breakfast burro in the fridge. Help yourself.

A tiny thrill shot through her. Noah had thought about her this morning. She grinned. She wasn't sure what a breakfast burro was—did he mean a burrito?—but she couldn't wait to find out.

Inside her cabin, she paused only for a moment to grab some clothes out of the open suitcase on her bed and rushed into the bathroom. It was much smaller than her bathroom at home. Actually, it was smaller than her closet at home. The bathroom had a sink, but no counter space, so she sat her folded clothes on the closed lid of the toilet. At least there were clean towels and washcloths in the cabinet under the sink.

She pinned up her long hair then jumped under the spray of the tiny shower before the water had time to get hot. Normally, she lingered in the shower, often listening to a podcast, but not this morning. Driven to speed as much by her desire to see Noah again as she was by hunger, she wasted no time. Although, when she unwrapped the small bar of soap provided for guests, she did regret not taking the time to get her favorite body wash from the toiletry bag still sitting on the sofa.

Less than ten minutes after hopping in the shower, Abbie was at Noah's front door. There was still no sign of his pickup, but she rapped lightly on the door for good measure before pushing it open.

The rich aroma of strong coffee filled the kitchen, reminding her of the coffee shop near her home. Every morning she stopped by for a cappuccino and a pastry. A clean mug sat on the counter, next to the coffeepot. She poured herself a cup and scanned the kitchen for sugar.

When she didn't see a canister, she opened the cabinet above the coffeepot and rummaged through the sparse items. Salt. Pepper. Garlic powder. Flour. But no sugar. She sighed and wrinkled her nose at the cup of dark black liquid. Lots of people drank plain black coffee, her father included. How bad could it be?

Picking up the cup, she took a small sip. Ugh. How did anyone drink that? Maybe cream would help. Then again, if Noah didn't have sugar, he probably didn't have cream either. She set the cup down and moved to the refrigerator. It was as empty as the cupboard had been. At least he had milk. She poured a little into her brew.

It didn't help. With a sigh, she dumped the bitter liquid

in the sink and went back to the refrigerator to claim her breakfast. On the top shelf, a foil-wrapped item sat by itself. She pulled it out and careful unwrapped a large burrito. Mystery solved. Either Noah was bad at spelling, or "burro" was some kind of regional term.

A microwave was on the counter, next to the coffeepot, so she placed the burrito inside and waited for her breakfast to heat up. She glanced around the kitchen and saw another piece of paper on the cabinet with her name on it, although he'd spelled it wrong.

Abby, the market is a short walk over the ridge. The trail starts at the back of the common area and goes straight to it. I let Vince know you would be there this morning to register. Noah

Below the note was a roughly drawn map of the campground with an arrow pointing to the trail. She sighed. He must not intend to be around this morning. The microwave dinged, and she carefully removed the stuffed tortilla. She could barely wait for it to cool down before she took a bite.

She'd only chewed a couple of times when her mouth caught fire. Dropping the burrito on the counter, she grabbed the coffee cup, rinsed it out and filled it with water. She gulped it down as quickly as she could, but it didn't help much. Her tongue still burned.

With a scowl, she picked up the burrito and looked inside. Flecks of green chili peppers were mixed in with the eggs. She carefully wrapped the food up to take back to her cabin. She didn't want to insult him by throwing it in his trash can.

At least the heat from the peppers had taken the edge off her hunger. She would have to get something at Coronado Market.

The market. Her heart fluttered. The business her sister owned. Abbie couldn't wait to see it. She picked up the map and headed back to her own cabin. She went inside just long enough to toss the burrito into the trash can and get her purse from her bedroom.

The map was easy enough to follow. The common area was a short walk down the dirt road in front of her cabin. She passed other cabins, similar in size and style to her own. A couple of cabins had vehicles parked in front, but no one outside. The road met a larger road. This one was wider and smoother than the one she'd been walking on.

Directly across the intersection where the two roads met, a flat, open area was surrounded by a split-rail fence. Abbie glanced at the map. This must be the common area. Several barbecue grills were scattered around the vicinity, each one with a picnic table close by. Firewood stood in neat stacks next to a firepit close to the center of the area.

Abbie imagined the place filled with the smell of hamburgers and the laughter of children running around. It would be a wonderful spot to spend time with family. Her heart swelled with longing. Would she be coming back here someday? Would she bring her future husband and children here to celebrate a special occasion with her sister and her family?

She pushed the feelings down and turned her attention back to the map. At the back of the common area, she found the trail Noah had marked. The well-worn footpath disappeared into the forest, shadowed by the tall pine and aspen trees that surrounded the campground.

Her pace quickened as she began walking up the trail. By the time she reached the top of the ridge, her chest burned. She stopped to catch her breath and check that her inhaler was in her purse. She leaned forward with her hands resting on her knees and waited until she could breathe easily. She frowned at her dusty feet. Sandals were not made for hiking trails. She would need to go shopping if she planned to make this walk very often. A few moments later, she was satisfied that the lack of air was more due to the high altitude than another asthma attack.

She started off again, this time at a slower pace. Up ahead, the trail curved and the trees weren't as thick, giving the illusion of light at the end of a tunnel. The trail widened and buildings appeared as she rounded the curve.

She could see the street ahead. It was the same one she was on last night when she'd seen the store for the first time. An empty dirt lot stretched between the end of the trail and the store. Abbie's heart pounded. If only her sister wasn't out of town. At the back of the building, a door was marked with a small sign: Private Entrance. All Deliveries Should Be Made at the Service Entrance.

Did Anastasia live at the back of the store? Bright pink curtains could be seen hanging in the windows on either side of the door, seeming to confirm her suspicion that the entrance was to an apartment and not part of the store. Abbie fought the urge to go peek in the window and continued to the entrance of the store.

The door swung open, and a man came out carrying a gallon of milk. She caught the door before it closed and stepped inside. There was a counter on either side of the entryway. The one on her right stretched forward and then curved to surround a deli area. A soda fountain machine and two commercial coffee makers were at the far end. The counter on her left held two cash registers.

A man behind the counter nodded. "Good morning."

"Morning." Butterflies invaded her stomach. "Are you Vince?"

"Yes, ma'am. How can I help you?"

Vince Tedford. Her breath caught in her throat. She tried

not to stare at the man who had raised her sister, but she couldn't help it. He was one of the tallest men she'd ever seen. When he was in his prime, he was probably a force to be reckoned with, maybe still was. Her gaze strayed to arms that were the size of small trees. His dark hair was peppered with gray, and fine lines crinkled around the corner of dark brown eyes. She liked him immediately.

She cleared her throat, willing her heart rate to slow down. "Noah let me stay in one of the cabins last night. He told me I could register with you this morning."

"Oh, yes. You're the young lady who had an unfortunate encounter with some of our local wildlife. You weren't hurt, were you?"

"I guess Noah told you about the accident."

Vince shook his head. "No. That boy don't talk about anyone's business but his own. My brother told me." He reached under the counter and pulled out a clipboard with papers attached to it.

Abbie frowned. "Your brother?"

"Frank. He's the sheriff around here." He placed the clipboard on the counter and handed her a pen. "I usually ask people how long they plan to stay, but with your car in the shop, you may not know yet."

Of course. She recognized the family resemblance now. The sheriff was a big man, too. "I was planning on staying a couple of weeks at least, anyway."

She picked up the clipboard and began filling out the information. "What are your rates?"

Vince handed her a sheet with prices. "You get a discount if you pay in advance and another discount if you stay for two weeks or longer."

Relief filled her when she looked at the price. It was less than half of what the other place cost. She could pay for her cabin and have enough left over to buy food. "I'd like to pay for two weeks. I need to pick up some groceries as well. Can I pay for them together?"

Vince handed her another clipboard, this one with registration information. "Unfortunately, no. The campground and the store are separate businesses, so I can't do them together."

"I understand." Abbie picked up the clipboard and filled it out.

If she was going to be stuck in Coronado for a while, she would need to keep busy. Her go-to activity when she was bored was baking bread. She glanced around the store. Could she find everything she needed? She gave Vince her paperwork and paid for the cabins before shopping.

The store didn't have a big variety of products, but it had all the basics. Flour, sugar, milk and eggs were first on her list. Yeast, essential for making homemade bread, was a little harder to find.

As she made her way back to the campground, she kept an eye out for Noah's truck. Maybe she would make him a loaf of homemade bread. Her heart fluttered at the thought.

DIRT AND SWEAT clung to Noah's back. He pulled his truck into the empty space next to his cabin and shut off the engine. Had Abbie found the note about the coffee and breakfast he left for her this morning? He wasn't sure why he felt an urge to look out for her, but he wouldn't give in to it again. She didn't need him to take care of her.

He picked up the paperwork from Bear's Garage from the seat of his truck and got out to take it to her cabin. The door flew open before he even reached the porch.

Abbie beamed at him. "Hi, stranger."

Her smile twisted his stomach into knots, but he kept a blank face. Why did she have to look so happy to see him? "Hey."

Yesterday, her hair had been pulled back into a ponytail. Today her golden brown hair fell in gentle waves past her shoulders. The dark green tank top she wore matched the color of her eyes. Funny, he hadn't noticed how green her eyes were on the ride back from Springerville.

"Thanks for breakfast this morning," she said. "When I read your note, I was confused because I couldn't figure out what a 'burro' was."

He cocked his head. "What do you call them in New York City?"

"I don't know what they're called in the city, but in Upstate New York where I'm from we just call them burritos."

His neck flushed with heat. "Not sure why I assumed you were from New York City."

She shrugged one shoulder. "Probably the same reason I thought Arizona was nothing but cactus and rattlesnakes."

He couldn't help but smile at her. She was so easygoing, it wasn't hard to like her. Because she had money, he assumed she would be a difficult person. His brow furrowed. There he went assuming again. Just because she drove a car that cost more than he made in two years didn't necessarily mean she had a lot of money.

"Bear wanted me to give you the estimate for your car." He handed her the papers in his hand.

"Oh." Her happy face disappeared as she scrutinized the paper, her pursed lips bordering on a frown.

Noah raised one eyebrow. "Is there a problem?"

"No." Her response was too quick to be convincing.

Maybe she didn't think a small-town auto shop could do a proper job on a fancy car like hers. "If you don't agree with the estimate, you're welcome to get a second opinion."

"And where would I do that?" she asked wryly.

"Springerville, Phoenix, Tucson. Take your pick." Noah

cast her a pointed look. "But just so you know, you won't find a better mechanic anywhere than Harry Littlebear."

Her face turned red. "It's not that. I'm sure he does fine work."

"Then what's the problem?"

She stepped closer to him and pointed to the number at the bottom of the page. "Is this what I owe?"

She was close enough that he could smell her shampoo. Which meant she could probably smell him, too. Only gas and car grease didn't smell nearly as good as the vanilla scent surrounding her. He took a step backward. "That's the total, yes, but all you have to pay is your insurance deductible."

"Okay." She searched the document.

He raised one eyebrow. "Don't you know what the deductible is on your insurance?"

Her face turned red, and she shook her head. "No. My father took care of all that when he bought the car."

"Is it his car or yours?" If the car wasn't hers, Harry would need to get permission from him before doing any work on it.

"It's mine," she said. "It was a graduation present."

He'd already guessed she came from money. Now he was sure of it. All his brother had gotten when he graduated from high school were a couple of Amazon gift cards and a little cash. He didn't know anyone who'd been given a car as a gift. Especially not a brand-new one. "I thought you were twenty-three."

"College graduation."

Oh. Heat crept up his neck. He didn't know anyone who'd gone to college, either. Rich and probably spoiled. "Let me guess, all you know about cars is how to put gas in and go."

Abbie pressed her lips together. "I also know how to check the oil and change a tire."

"That's something, at least," he murmured under his breath.

Her brows furrowed as she stared at the paper again. "I'll call my insurance and find out what the deductible is."

"It's right here." He pointed to the number at the bottom of the paper.

"Oh." Her eyes widened slightly. "How long will it take?"

"About four weeks." He stifled a yawn and glanced at his watch. If he was lucky, he could take a nap before feeding the horses and going to the Watering Hole. "Well, I'd better get moving. See ya."

"Wait!" She stopped him before he managed to get off the porch.

He turned back to her, trying not to let her see how irritated he was. It wasn't her fault that she'd had everything given to her while he had to work twice as hard for everything he ever got.

She worried her bottom lip and played with her necklace. "What happens if I can't pay the deductible?"

Noah stiffened. *Can't or won't?* She didn't seem like the type to skip out on a bill, but it wouldn't be the first time something like that happened. He lifted his chin. "Then you don't get your car back until you can."

Abbie didn't say anything, as she slid the tiny locket on her necklace back and forth on the chain. What was she so worried about? Clearly, money wasn't an issue for her. Or maybe she didn't think she needed to pay for it herself.

He sighed. "Do you want Bear to send the bill to your father?"

"No." Her response was swift and loud.

He cocked his head. "Is there a problem?"

"Not yet."

The response was so soft, Noah barely heard her, but the worry in her voice was evident. "Are you expecting a problem?"

She took a deep breath. "I'm a little short on money right now."

He almost laughed. But one look at her face and he realized she was serious. "Just how short?"

"All of it." She looked up at him with wide eyes.

"You father won't pay the deductible?"

"I wouldn't ask him to." There was a hard edge in her voice.

"Why not?"

She straightened herself up. "He seems to think I'm incapable of taking care of myself."

Noah was inclined to agree with him, but he didn't say so. "He must have some faith in you if he let you drive across the country."

"No, actually. He forbid me from going."

Noah recognized the stubborn tilt of her head. He and his brother both had a stubborn streak that could beat a mule. On one hand, Noah could sympathize with her. He didn't like to be told what to do, either. On the other hand, he couldn't blame her father for not wanting her to travel across the country by herself. Still, he had a hard time believing the man would completely abandon her. "You went against his wishes, so he cut you off?"

"No." Her voice was stern. "I cut myself off."

"What do you mean?"

She crossed her arms. "I tossed all his credit cards on his desk and left the next morning."

Alarm bells rang in his ears. "Does he know you're in Arizona?"

What kind of trouble would her father cause when he

found out where she was? Instead of rescuing a damsel in distress, it seemed he might have poked a sleeping bear. His stomach quivered. But her mother knew. Or at least Noah assumed she did. Abbie talked to her on the phone after the accident.

She lifted her chin. "Of course he does. He's just not happy about it."

"You had enough money to get out here, so you have to have some type of income."

"I did. During school, I worked part-time at my father's accounting firm." The line between her eyebrows deepened. "It was the only job I was allowed to have."

Allowed to have? His throat tightened. He was fourteen when he got his first job. By the time he was seventeen, he had to quit high school to take a second job. He'd worked more in his life than she would in four lifetimes.

Her face tightened. "I know you think I'm a spoiled brat, but—"

"I didn't say that."

She arched one eyebrow at him. "You didn't have to. I'm not a spoiled brat. A sheltered, overprotected one, maybe."

He didn't want to hear any more. He was just starting to like her, and she would ruin that if she started whining about how hard her life had been.

"I was really sick when I was a baby." She leaned against the door frame. "My earliest memories are of being in a hospital. When I started school, I started getting sick again. I was never allowed to play sports, or go to slumber parties, or do anything normal kids get to do."

He stiffened. His childhood hadn't been normal either, but for an entirely different reason. At least he and his brother had always been healthy. "I'm sure it was difficult for your parents, too."

"I think they thought if they could just control everything around me, I wouldn't get sick." She shrugged. "As I got older, they relaxed a little, but it's hard for them to admit I'm an adult and capable of making my own choices."

Noah had been making his own decisions most of his life. No one was around to make decisions for him. If they had been, maybe he wouldn't be in the situation he was in now. "At least you know they care."

She smiled. "I know. And it's my own fault. I never questioned their judgment and always just did what they said. Until they told me I couldn't come to Arizona to visit my sister."

There must be a reason her parents wanted to protect Abbie from her sister. His mind raced as he wondered who her sister might be; some of the women in town had reputations as troublemakers. He wanted to ask her, but she had evaded his question the last time he asked and he didn't want to be nosy. "Have you talked to her yet?"

Abbie's face grew somber. "She's not here."

"I'm sorry." It was probably for the best that her sister was gone.

He could feel sorry for her, but it didn't change the fact that she still owed his friend and boss money. "So what are you going to do?"

"I'm going to get a job and work until I make enough money to pay for my car."

"Around here?" Noah shook his head. "You won't find a job in Coronado."

She looked him in the eye and lifted her chin. "Why not? You have three of them."

CHAPTER FIVE

SUNLIGHT STREAMED THROUGH the window, but Abbie pulled the blanket over her head and snuggled deeper into the down-filled pillow, trying to ignore the chirping noise that had woken her up. She'd slept much better her second night in the cabin than her first. Finding extra blankets in the closet didn't hurt either. She covered her ears with the pillow, but the noise got louder. When loud chattering joined the first sound, Abbie gave up on sleep.

She pulled the covers from her face and let her eyes adjust to the light. The chilly air made her reluctant to emerge from the warmth of the quilts that cocooned her, so she lay on the bed and listened to the chorus of sounds outside. When the chattering noises became shriller and more frenzied, she rolled over to peer out the window.

The grumpy tomcat she'd met at the barn sat under a pine tree directly outside Abbie's window. His tail flicked as he stared at the tree. A gray squirrel scampered up and down the trunk, clearly irritated by the presence of the cat. Another squirrel screeched from a nearby pine, drawing the cat's attention. The squirrel ran in circles around the tree, teasing the approaching animal. When the cat got close, the squirrel at the first tree barked to get his attention.

Abbie laughed. The poor cat didn't know which way to go, and the squirrels had the upper hand. She would've watched their game all morning, but she couldn't. Anticipation thrummed through her veins. This morning, she was going to do something she'd never done before: she was going to look for a job.

She had only paid for two weeks at the cabin. Now she needed to stay an additional two weeks and pay for the repairs on the car. She either had to find a way to make the money she needed or call her dad and ask him for help. If she did that, he would insist on her coming home right away.

It wasn't a hard decision. There was no way she was going home before she met her sister. Surely Stacy would be home before four weeks were up. She tossed off the covers and rolled out of bed. She walked over to the closet and scanned her clothes. If she was at home, she would know exactly what to wear, but job hunting wasn't on her agenda when she left New York.

She wanted something business casual, but she hadn't packed any skirts. Fortunately, she had brought some pants. She selected a cream-colored pair that could go with anything. Her fingers flipped through the hangers until she found the blouse she was looking for. The simple navy blue blouse had a scoop neck and a tailored waist. It was perfect.

She showered and washed her hair, taking the time to secure the long locks in a single French braid. She'd only brought a pair of sneakers and two pairs of sandals. Sneakers wouldn't do at all, and one pair of sandals were bright red. She picked up her only viable option. They didn't match her cream pants, but the gray straps were neutral enough that they wouldn't be noticed. She hoped. How many people really looked at feet?

The faint smell of bread still hung in the kitchen. Baking helped her think, so after Noah left last night, she'd made two loaves of bread. Abbie took a deep breath.

Maybe there was a bakery in town. A thrill ran through her at the thought.

She made herself a piece of toast and headed out the door. Her gaze drifted to the cabin next to hers. Noah's truck was gone, of course. He was always gone.

He had a reason for working three jobs. She wished she knew him well enough to ask him what it was. In college, she had friends who got an extra job so they could buy a new dress, or a fancy piece of jewelry. That wasn't Noah. Whatever his reasons, she was certain it wasn't for something shallow like clothes or jewelry.

As she topped the ridge, she paused to get a better view of Coronado. It was hard to see the town because of all the trees, but she could see several buildings on the same street as the market. She glanced at her phone. No service yet, but as soon as she got closer to the main street, there would be.

In front of the market, she stopped to scan the flyers covering the community bulletin board. Free kittens. A horse trailer for sale. Square dancing classes at the community center. Abbie smiled. She'd always wanted to try square dancing. She took her phone out of her purse and snapped a picture of the flyer. A metal rack below the bulletin board held several different brochures and magazines. There were a couple of real estate magazines and something resembling a newspaper called the *Thrifty Nickel*.

She sat on a bench that was nestled against the side of the building and did a search on her phone for accounting firms in town. There weren't any. Even if there had been, who would want to hire a new accountant for just a few weeks? She searched for bookkeeping jobs. Nothing. Finally, she found the website for the town of Coronado and was able to look at all the businesses. It wasn't a very long list. She took a screenshot in case she lost service again.

What if she couldn't come up with enough money to pay for the deductible on her car? Worse, what if she couldn't afford to stay in Coronado until her sister returned? She opened her banking app and checked her account. Yes, she definitely needed a job. Standing up, she smoothed the front of her pants and drew a breath. What better place to start than right here, at her sister's store?

A bell hanging on the entrance chimed as she pushed the door open and entered the market. It wasn't Vince behind the counter, but a young girl with fiery red hair.

"Can I help you?" As soon as the girl spoke, Abbie realized she wasn't as young as she thought. The "girl" was probably close to her own age.

"Hi." Abbie fought back her nerves. "I was just wondering…uh…is there any chance that you're hiring?"

"Not right now." The young woman cocked her head. "You're new around here, aren't you?"

Abbie tucked a strand of hair behind her ear. "Yes. I've only been in town a couple of days. My name is Abbie Houghton."

"Welcome." She gave Abbie a bright smile. "I'm Millie. Where are you from?"

"Upstate New York." She let her gaze sweep around the store. "This is a nice place. Is it the only store in town?"

"For now. Stacy wants to put another store at the campground, but that won't be for a while."

Her breath hitched at the mention of her sister's name. She feigned ignorance. "Stacy?"

"Stacy Tedford—I mean, Murphy," Millie said. "She's the owner."

"Do you know anyone in town who might be hiring?"

"Not off the top of my head." Millie frowned. "Summer is almost over, so things get really slow around here this time of year. You can check the *Thrifty Nickel*. Sometimes people post help wanted ads in there."

"Is there a bakery in town?" She hadn't seen one on the website, but it didn't hurt to ask.

Millie's eyes narrowed as she appeared to think. Finally, she shook her head. "The Candy Shoppe next door sells cookies and fudge and things like that. Paisley's Tea Garden has pastries. Is that what you mean?"

"I was thinking of a bakery that sells bread, but I can try both of those. Thanks for your help."

"Good luck." Millie gave her a sad smile.

Abbie's steps were heavy as she went back outside. She glanced up and down the street. The Candy Shoppe was on one side of the store. On the other side of the market was a log cabin-style building. The sign in front of the building read Coronado Hardware. Across the street a giant wooden bear stood in front of the Bear's Den Café.

She could apply for a job as a waitress. Back home, diners were always looking for waitresses. She'd never been a waitress before, but she was good with people. It might be fun. She was about to step off the sidewalk to cross the street when she heard a voice hollering at her from behind. She looked around.

An elderly man stood under the awning of the hardware store, waving with a giant motion.

Was he waving at her? She glanced up and down the street again. There was no one else in sight. She hurried over to the man. "Are you okay?"

"No." The old man's voice was gruff. "I can't find my glasses. Without 'em, I can't see nothing up close. I can't find the right key. You're a young'un. I bet your eyes are still working."

He shoved a large ring at her that held at least a dozen

keys. They all looked similar. No wonder the man couldn't find the right key.

She inspected each one. "Is there a marking on the key you need?"

The man's bushy gray eyebrows drew together. "Nah. Never needed one."

It took her six tries to find the right key. After opening the door for him, she held on to the key. "Do you want to take this key off the ring and put it somewhere separate?"

"Then I'd just lose it." He snorted.

He motioned for her to come inside, and shuffled down the center aisle of the hardware store. She took her time following him. The store held a faint musty smell. As she got close to the back of the store, she spotted a carousel at the end of an aisle with customizable keys. She turned the display and found a package of silicone key covers.

"Here." She placed the package on the counter, still holding the correct key in one hand.

He picked up the package. "What's this for?"

Abbie pointed to the rings. "If you put one of these on the key, you'll always be able to find it."

"Okay." He handed the package back to her. "Put a yellow one on it."

She opened the plastic and removed a yellow key cap cover. To put it on, she had to remove the key from the cluster of other keys. "Is yellow your favorite color?"

"No, but it was Opal's. And I can still see yellow. Some of those other colors get mixed up. Can't tell the difference between blue and green anymore."

She put the key back on the ring. "Was Opal your wife?"

He nodded. "She passed away six years ago."

The sadness in his voice stirred her. "I'm sorry."

"I am, too." He sighed. "So, what brings you to Coronado?"

"Just visiting." She handed the keys back to him. "Here you are. Now you can always find the key to the store."

"Thank you, little lady. I'm Denny Morgan." He extended a gnarled and bent hand toward her.

She shook his hand. "Nice to meet you, Mr. Morgan. I'm Abbie Houghton."

"If you're not too pressed for time, Ms. Houghton, you think you could help an old man out for a bit?"

Her heart skipped. Had she found a job already?

NOAH HAD BEEN at the campground for a week and a half. He wasn't happy about leaving his ranch, but he had to admit, it was more convenient. With two jobs in town, he was spending a lot of money on gas. And with no one home, the electric bill for the ranch would be practically nothing.

His paycheck from the garage, combined with what he was saving in gas and electricity, could get him far enough ahead to make it to the end of the year. After that, he didn't know. Maybe by then, he'd be able to find a steady truck-driving job.

Without any livestock, he didn't need to be at the ranch all the time. The cattle had been sold months ago, the chickens had been gone over a year and the pigs went before that. Paddy and Jasper were the only animals left, and he'd brought them with him.

Jasper, his brother's horse, was content grazing in the pasture with the other horses, but Paddy was used to working every day and needed to escape the confines of the corrals and pasture. Every morning, Noah rode Paddy around the campgrounds. It wasn't the same as riding at the ranch, but it would do for now.

This was Labor Day weekend and marked the end of the summer tourist season. The campground was almost full. By this afternoon, every cabin would be occupied, and the barn would be bustling with activity tomorrow. One of the main attractions of Whispering Pines was the trail rides. Some campers brought their own horses, but most would use the horses on-site. Noah had been exploring the various trails all week. He had two trail rides booked tomorrow, and he wanted to make sure he knew where he was going.

The last two days, when he was on his way back to the barn, he saw Abbie walking through the common area on her way to town, but he didn't see her this morning. Yesterday, she didn't return until after five o'clock, so she must have found a job. The real question was, would she stick it out long enough to pay for the deductible on her car, or would she end up calling her father for the money?

Instead of circling the outskirts of the campground, he went through the middle. The path he was on would take him right in front of Abbie's cabin.

One man waved at him as he was loading his fishing gear into the back of his pickup. At another cabin, a young couple sat on the porch, curled up next to each other on the love seat, drinking coffee. They were too busy looking at one another to notice him as he passed by. They must be the newlywed couple Vince told him to expect, and were signed up for the afternoon trail ride. Noah hoped they could pay attention to their horses.

As he approached Abbie's cabin, he could see her on the front porch. Her feet were curled up underneath her on one of the chairs, as she clutched a coffee cup between her hands. She was wearing pajama pants.

He turned the horse toward her cabin. "Morning." He tipped his hat to her. "Not going to work today?"

She peered at him over the rim of her cup. "You're funny. Did you stop by to say 'I told you so'?"

The sarcasm in her tone took him by surprise. "You didn't find a job?"

"No."

Noah frowned. "Where did you go the last two days?"

"I'm helping Mr. Morgan at the hardware store."

Noah had known Denny Morgan his entire life. The man was getting on in age, but was too proud to ask for help. "Help him with what?"

She took a sip of her coffee. "I'm entering his sales receipts into his ledger. I didn't even know people did that anymore. Most places have everything on computers."

"He can't do that himself?"

"He lost his glasses and can't see up close, so I'm helping him until his new glasses come in. Then I'm going to teach him how to use his computer."

"Is he paying you?"

"He offered." She ran one hand through her hair, then stopped at the end of a strand of hair to wrap it around her fingers. "But I've seen his paperwork. He's barely making it as it is. He can't afford to pay me."

It didn't surprise him to hear the hardware store was struggling. Nowadays, most people ordered everything online instead of waiting for Mr. Morgan to order what they needed. Noah had been guilty of doing that more than once. He'd never considered what his actions were doing to Mr. Morgan's store.

Paddy stirred underneath him, so he leaned down to pat the horse's neck. "Since you're here, I assume Mr. Morgan got his glasses back."

She took a long drink from her coffee. "He has a doctor appointment in Springerville and isn't opening the store today."

"And you're helping him for free?" Who spent all day long helping someone for free when they were in financial trouble themselves?

"I would feel guilty taking money for doing something so simple."

"Did you give up on looking for a job?" So much for all her talk about paying her own way. She'd probably called her dad despite being so adamant that she would never.

"I've called every number in the *Thrifty Nickel* wanted ads and talked to every business in town. You were right, no one is hiring."

"Sounds like you're going to have to call your dad."

"Nope, not doing that." She clenched her jaw and looked down at the ground. After a few seconds, she lifted her eyes to his. "I'll sell my car."

Noah's eyes widened. "Who would you sell it to?"

"The garage." The tension left her shoulders and her eyes glinted with hope. "If I can sell it to Harry, it should give me enough money to stay here for a while."

"If you sell your car, how will you get home?"

"I'll use whatever money is left over and buy a used car," she said matter-of-factly. "I don't need something that fancy, anyway. I'll find something I can afford."

He frowned. "If you sell your car, you don't have to stay until it's repaired. You can leave whenever you want."

"No." She shook her head. "I can't go back yet."

"Why?"

She stared at her coffee mug.

"I love my parents, I really do. But my whole life, I've done everything they wanted. If I go back now, it will just prove that they were right. I need for them to know I can make it on my own. *I* need to know I can make it on my own."

"Hmm." He shook his head. "You think you can make it on your own, but you have no idea what life is like without the silver spoon you've been born with."

Her nostrils flared and she stood up. "If you'll excuse me, I need to get ready to go into town. I have a car to sell."

She walked across the porch. Noah waited until she opened the door to her cabin before he stopped her. "It won't do any good. Harry won't buy your car."

"Why not?" Anger flashed in her eyes.

The leather beneath him creaked as he shifted in the saddle. "For one, Harry doesn't have the money to pay the car's value, wrecked or not. For two, he wouldn't want anyone to think he was taking advantage of you."

Her chin lifted. "Fine. I have two weeks to sell it. I'll list it online. Or call a dealership."

The door slammed behind her as she went inside. Noah grinned. She was as stubborn as she was beautiful. Too bad she was also a little naive in the ways of the world. The thought of someone trying to take advantage of her situation bothered him.

He sighed and lifted his leg over the saddle to step to the ground. He'd see if she was as serious about finding work as she claimed. He knocked on the door.

She opened it, one hand on the doorknob, the other on her hip.

"You really want a job?"

"Are you making fun of me?"

"No," he said. "It's hard work, but if you can stick it out, I'll cover your repair bill."

Relief flooded her face. "I'll do it."

"You don't even know what it is yet."

She shrugged. "I don't care what it is. I'll do it."

"Okay, meet me at the barn at six o'clock tomorrow morning."

"Thank you." She reached out and squeezed him in a tight hug.

Thrown off guard, Noah wasn't sure what to do. He

couldn't remember anyone ever hugging him before. He patted the back of her shoulder with one hand until she let go of him and stepped back.

"Um… I gotta go to work." His heart did a two-step as he headed back to his horse.

He glanced at her as he settled back into the saddle. She was still there with a grin as big as the Grand Canyon. He tipped his hat and rode away.

So far, she'd broken every preconceived notion he had about how a spoiled rich girl was supposed to act. Tomorrow might be a different story. Tomorrow she might go running back to her father. Tomorrow might be the day he could get her out of his mind.

CHAPTER SIX

ABBIE WATCHED NOAH until he disappeared into the trees. All the tension that had been weighing down on her for the last two days disappeared, and she felt as if she could float.

When Noah had told her that her car wouldn't be ready until almost the end of September, she'd sat down and looked at her account. She had enough money to cover her lodging for the two additional weeks, but not enough to cover the cost of the deductible, too.

Nothing had gone as planned so far. All she wanted to do was meet her biological sister. When she left New York, she thought she'd be gone for two weeks at the most. She thought she could come to Arizona, meet her sister, establish a relationship with her and go home. She hadn't counted on Anastasia—Stacy—not being home when she got here...or wrecking her car.

But her trip hadn't been a total disaster; some good things had happened. When she called her father to apologize for acting like the child he accused her of being, he told her he admired that she was finally willing to stand up to him. He also told her about a job opening at his firm and to hurry home so she could apply. As much as she loved her father, she didn't want to work with him every day, but she hated conflict so she hadn't told him that she wasn't going to submit her résumé.

And there was Noah. The scruffy cowboy who first rescued her from the side of the road and now rescued her from having to ask her dad for money. She wanted to do something to show him how much she appreciated his help. How long had it been since he'd had a really good home-cooked meal?

She checked the refrigerator to see what she had and quickly made a shopping list. As long as she was going to town, she would take the opportunity to look around. She had walked all over Coronado, but she hadn't had a chance to enjoy the town. Wednesday, she got no farther than the hardware store, but yesterday afternoon she'd walked around town, stopping at the local businesses and inquiring about jobs.

Her chest swelled with excitement. She had the entire morning to learn as much about her sister's town as she could. Judging from how long it took her to visit every business yesterday, it shouldn't take long to see all the sights. As she was about to go back to the bedroom to change, a movement on the porch caught her eye. She stepped closer to the screen door and saw Noah's cat sitting on the porch. "Back for more, are you?"

He still hadn't let her pet him, but he was getting close. He wanted to like her; Abbie could tell. He was just too grumpy to admit it. Like his owner. She poured some milk into a bowl and sat it outside, next to the door.

Abbie bent down and waited for the cat to come to the bowl, but he just stared at her. "No?" She straightened up. "You might as well give up. We're going to be friends, whether you like it or not."

The cat meowed but didn't move. She laughed, but left him alone. She'd only taken a few steps into the cabin when the yellow tabby cat moved to the bowl.

The bowl was empty by the time she changed clothes and wrapped her hair into a messy bun. There was no sign of the cat anywhere around. Country music streamed from an SUV parked in front of the cabin next to hers. A woman unloaded suitcases from the back seat. She smiled and said hello. Abbie returned the greeting as she walked onto the road.

Tuesday morning, she hadn't noticed more than one or two families in the entire campground. Now, almost every cabin had a vehicle in front of it. It made sense that the campground would be busier on the weekend, especially since it was a holiday weekend.

In the common area, two young boys chased each other around the grass. A girl sat on the picnic table with a coloring book. The girl smiled and waved at her.

Abbie passed a couple walking on the path between the store and the campgrounds. As she topped the ridge, she could see that the market was busy, too. Vehicles, mostly pickup trucks and SUVs, filled the parking lot. So much for the busy season being over.

Millie had promised to keep an ear out for anyone needing help, so she needed to let her know she'd found a job.

Inside the store, Millie was working at the deli. "Hey," she nodded at Abbie. "Any luck?"

"Yes, actually." There was a line of people waiting to order sandwiches, so Abbie didn't want to bother her with the details. She grabbed a soda from the cooler and strolled up and down the aisles. In the farthest corner, a section was dedicated to souvenirs. She flipped through a box of postcards. The pictures on the front were breathtaking and were all supposed to be of local places. If she'd had a vehicle, she would have loved to visit them. She picked out a postcard with Zane Grey's cabin on it. Her father was a fan of his novels, so she would send that to him. For her mother, she selected a photograph of Big Lake with a herd of elk drinking from the water.

"Good morning," Vince greeted her when it was her turn to check out.

"Hi," she said. "Busy morning."

"Yeah." He scanned her soda and postcards. "We usually get one last hurrah from city folks wanting a getaway just before the fall season starts."

She smiled. "Well, it sure is a nice place to visit. Can you tell me where the post office is?" She'd walked all over town and hadn't seen it.

Vince handed her a small bag with her items. "Go to the stop sign and hang a right. You can't miss it. It's only a few blocks."

"I'm going there right now, if you'd like me to show you the way."

Abbie turned to the voice speaking behind her. The woman looked close to her own age. She had short blond hair that stood up from her head in messy curls. She balanced a baby on her hip. Although she was smiling, Abbie could see a hint of sadness behind her blue eyes.

"Thank you, I appreciate that," she said.

She paid for her things and waited for the woman to check out as well. They walked out the front door together. The baby grinned at her, displaying dimples on his chubby cheeks. Abbie couldn't help but smile.

"I'm Emily and this is my son, Wyatt," the woman said as soon as they exited the market. "You're new in town."

"Abbie," she said, introducing herself. "I'm just visiting for a few weeks. I live in Upstate New York."

"New York." Emily's voice held a sense of awe. "That's a long way."

Abbie just nodded.

"You have family here? Who are you visiting?"

"No one," Abbie said. "I'm just exploring the west." The urge to declare herself Stacy's sister was strong, but until she met Stacy face-to-face, until she knew that Stacy wanted to be part of her life, she would continue to keep her secret.

Emily's eyes widened. "You came here from New York by yourself? Weren't you scared?"

"Not until a large animal ran out in front of me on the highway and I hit a tree," she said.

Emily gasped. "Where did that happen?"

"Just outside of town. My car is sitting in Bear's Garage as we speak."

They followed the main street, passing by the Candy Shoppe and a craft store that looked like it hadn't been open for years. The sidewalk ended at a stop sign where the street met a highway, forming a T-intersection. The road signs claimed it was a highway. Except for the fact that it was wider, it looked no different from the street they'd just turned off.

Directly across the street was a real estate office. They weren't hiring anyone to help in the office, and she wasn't a licensed Realtor, so that was as far as she'd come during her job search. Other than a forest ranger station next door, it was the only business on the highway.

She paused to look around, but Emily kept walking along the edge of the highway. Abbie hurried to catch up with her. "How old is your son?"

Before Emily could answer, a green bus pulled into the ranger station across the street. Big black letters below the windows read: MOGOLLAN RIM HOTSHOTS. The bus doors opened, and men and women—all dressed in black T-shirts and tan pants—exited the vehicle. Some of them unloaded equipment from the back of the bus. Others went into the large building.

"Hotshots?" Abbie had heard of the elite firefighting

crew that fought forest fires on the ground. "Is there a fire somewhere close by?"

"No." Emily stopped to wait with her. "It's monsoon season, so the fire risk isn't high right now. That crew is from Flagstaff. They're here for training."

"You know them?" Abbie watched the team move together without saying a word. The danger inherent in their chosen profession left her feeling awestruck. Some of them were younger than she was.

"A few of them come into the bar on the weekends."

"The bar?" Was it the same tavern that Noah worked at? "The Watering Hole?"

"Yep." Emily pointed to a log cabin-style building tucked behind the real estate office. "It's right there."

Abbie hadn't noticed the building when she was job hunting, and she couldn't remember seeing it on the town's website, either.

One of the men with the hotshot crew noticed them pointing. He smiled and gave them an exaggerated wave.

Another man, this one older, noticed. "Stop flirting and get that gear moved," he said in an authoritative voice.

Immediately the younger man went back to business.

Emily started walking again. "The guy who waved is Shane. He thinks he's a real ladies' man."

"He's a good-looking guy," Abbie acknowledged.

"Those are the ones to watch out for," Emily grumbled. "They're nothing but trouble."

They arrived at the post office, and she followed Emily inside. The bells on the door jingled and two older women, obviously sisters, were chatting behind the counter. Both women were dressed the same, except one had bright pink hair and the other's hair was blue.

"Good morning," they greeted them in unison.

ЦЦ

"Who's your friend, Emily?" the woman with pink hair asked.

"This is Abbie. She's from New York," Emily said. "Abbie, this is Margaret and Edith Reed."

"Nice to meet you," Abbie said. She wasn't sure which sister was which.

There was a table against the back wall with mailing supplies stacked on it. Abbie searched her purse for a pen and moved to the table to write a quick note to each of her parents on the backs of the postcards.

"Edith," Emily said, addressing the blue-haired woman, "have they posted that job yet?"

The elderly woman gave her a sad smile. "No, I'm sorry."

Emily's face fell slightly, but she covered it up with a smile. "Okay. I'll check again later."

"Why do you want to apply here, anyway?" Edith asked her. "Why aren't you working at the store?"

"Grandpa says he doesn't need anyone." Emily's face pinched.

"Nonsense." Edith reached across the counter and squeezed Emily's hand. "He can't hold that baby against you forever. You march to that store and tell that grumpy old man to—"

"It's fine. Really." Emily cut her off and cast a quick glance at Abbie.

The pink-haired sister—Margaret, apparently—made a face at the baby. "You're getting to be such a big handsome boy!"

The baby giggled and buried his face in his mother's shoulder.

Margaret patted his chubby cheek then gave Emily a pointed look. "Why don't you let Edith and I find you a nice young man at church?"

"No, thank you." Emily's face turned red and she smiled politely as she stepped back from the counter. "Your turn," she said to Abbie.

Abbie placed the two postcards on the counter.

Both women's gazes zeroed in on her. "Did you just move to town?"

"No, I'm just visiting." She placed a five-dollar bill on the counter.

Edith picked up the money and handed her some change. "Oh. You have family here, then?"

She couldn't tell the truth, but it wasn't in her nature to lie. She picked her words carefully. "Not right now, no."

"Are you sure? You look very familiar."

Margaret scrunched her face and leaned forward. "She does, doesn't she?"

Abbie's heart leaped a little. Was there a resemblance between her and her sister? Since Stacy didn't post any pictures of herself on social media, Abbie had no idea what she looked like. Her hand touched the locket again. Was there more connecting them than just an old necklace?

Margaret straightened up. "I hope you enjoy your visit to Coronado."

Edith elbowed her sister. "Don't forget to invite her to tea."

"Wonderful idea." Margaret smiled. "You'll bring her, won't you, Emily?"

"Yes, ma'am, if she's not too busy." Emily took Abbie's elbow and ushered her outside.

As soon as they were out the door, Emily apologized. "I'm sorry. They can be a little much."

Abbie laughed. "It's okay. They're cute. You have tea with them often?"

Emily let out a huff of air. "Too often. I love them, but

they are always trying to set me up with someone. They think they're the matchmakers of Coronado."

"Sounds like an interesting affair," Abbie said.

Emily shook her head. "You don't have to go. I'm kind of obligated since my grandmother grew up with them."

"Have you ever gone out with anyone they found for you?"

Emily swallowed hard, pain radiating in her blue eyes. "It didn't work out too well."

"I'm sorry." Her heart ached for the obvious pain her new acquaintance was feeling. She longed to ask Emily if the man was Wyatt's father, but she didn't want to be too intrusive.

She feigned a smile. "Well, there's no danger for me. I'm only here for a few more weeks."

"Lucky you," Emily said.

The sisters might be a little eccentric, but Abbie thought they seemed harmless enough. "If they host a tea while I'm here, I'll go with you—if you want me to, that is. Maybe I can help you fend them off."

Emily's smile was genuine. "That would be great."

"What store does your grandfather own?"

"The hardware store next to the market." Emily's voice was quiet.

Abbie frowned. "I had the impression Mr. Morgan didn't have any family close by."

"He'd probably prefer it that way," Emily murmured.

Emily's relationship with her grandfather was none of Abbie's business, but she'd really started to like Mr. Morgan. "Did you know he lost his glasses and couldn't even open his store?"

"No." Emily shrugged. "I'm afraid he doesn't talk to me much."

"Why?" Abbie nodded toward Wyatt. "Because you had a baby out of wedlock?"

"No. Because I wouldn't tell him who the father was, so he's decided I must not know." Emily's voice had a hard edge to it.

Abbie could tell that it was a sensitive topic, so she didn't press any further. They walked silently back to the main street. When they got to the market, she said goodbye to her new companion and headed to the campground.

The trail was quiet, but Abbie's thoughts weren't. There might be a way to help both Mr. Morgan and his granddaughter. But would either of them be open to her idea? Maybe she'd talk to Noah about it tonight.

As she got closer to her cabin, she remembered what Emily said about the Reed sisters being matchmakers. Had they ever tried to set Noah up with someone?

NOAH'S FEET WERE heavy as he walked from the truck to his cabin. Working three jobs was starting to take its toll, but he couldn't slow down. Not when his head was almost above water. Talk in town was that the White Mountain Wild Horse Management Program had finally been called in to investigate the damage the herds were causing. If the herds were moved, Stanley Reed would have access to the land again and could get his sawmill back up and running. And if that happened, he could start hauling logs again. With a steady source of income, he'd be able to pay off his loan.

Tom was waiting for him by the door. Noah reached down and scratched his ears before opening the door. Once inside, he peeled off his greasy T-shirt and tossed it in the laundry basket on the floor next to his bed before getting clean clothes out of the dresser.

He turned the water on in the shower and allowed it

to heat up while he brushed his teeth. His hair was long enough that it got in his way while working on cars, but barely long enough to be pulled back and secured by an elastic band at the nape of his neck. He took the ponytail out and shook his head.

He stepped in the shower. For several minutes, he didn't move, he just let the hot water melt away the tension in his back and shoulders. He grabbed a bar of soap and went to work on the grease stains on his hands and arms. His skin was almost raw by the time he scrubbed the residue away, but at least he smelled like a human again.

By the time he dried off and emerged from the steamy bathroom, nothing looked more inviting than the queen-size bed in his room. He closed the blinds, set his alarm and crawled under the covers.

He'd barely closed his eyes when a pounding noise jerked him from his sleep. As much as he wanted to ignore whoever was at the door, he didn't dare. His job was not only to take care of the horses, but to be available if there was an issue with any of the cabins or other facilities. He pulled a T-shirt over his head and grabbed a pair of jeans from the closet before heading for the door.

He opened it to find Abbie standing on the small porch, staring at him with wide eyes. "Were you asleep?"

He pushed his hair away from his face. "No."

She raised an eyebrow and gave him a skeptical look.

"Yes." He fought back a yawn and leaned against the door frame. All he wanted to do was crawl back into bed. "Do you need something?"

"Don't you usually feed the horses at six?"

How did she know that? "Yes."

"You're late."

He started to argue with her, but glanced over his shoulder at the time on the microwave. Six thirty. What happened to his alarm? "I must have forgotten to turn my alarm on."

He left the door open and went to put his boots on. His phone was on the nightstand next to his bed. The words *Missed alarm* blinked on the screen. Seriously? He'd never slept through an alarm before. When he came out of the bedroom, Abbie was standing in his kitchen.

"Want some help?"

"It would take me longer to explain what and how much to feed each horse than to just do it myself." He ran both hands through his hair, pushing it out of his face before putting his cowboy hat on. He picked up his truck keys from the counter and headed for the door.

Abbie hadn't moved. He paused at the door. "Thanks for waking me up."

"I made dinner."

He scrubbed his face with his hand. Why was she telling him that?

She let out a sigh. "Are you working at the Watering Hole tonight?"

"Yes."

"What time?" Her voice held a hint of impatience.

"Eight."

"Oh, okay," she said. "I thought you might like to eat before you go to work."

Was she inviting him to dinner? "I usually eat at the tavern."

She crossed her arms. "Is the food any good?"

"Not really."

"Then I'll see you at my cabin when you're finished feeding the horses."

He raised his eyebrows. "Is your food any good?"

She laughed. "I guess you'll find out."

Less than an hour later, he was back.

He hesitated before walking to Abbie's cabin. His heart raced, and he rubbed his hands down the front of his pants. Why did he feel like a teenager going on his first date? It wasn't like they were starting a relationship. Sure, she was beautiful, and kind, and different from anyone he'd ever met. But even if her home wasn't all the way across the country, she would never be interested in someone like him. Other than the fact that she was also almost ten years younger, she was a college graduate from an affluent family. He was a high-school dropout on the verge of losing the only thing that ever mattered to him.

He shoved his hands into the front pockets of his jeans and stepped onto the porch. She only invited him over because she was grateful for a job. No other reason. As long as he remembered that, he could keep the butterflies out of his stomach. The door opened before he had a chance to knock.

She cocked her head. "You showed up."

He took off his hat as he walked through the doorway. "I didn't think you gave me much choice."

"True." She nodded. "I was fully prepared to drag you over here if I had to."

The image she painted in his head made him laugh. She couldn't be more than five foot two. The image of her trying to haul his six-foot-four frame to the cabin was comical. One look at her stern face said she would try, anyway.

"Smells good," he said. "What are we having?"

"Tuscan chicken." She motioned for him to sit at the table. "Except the market didn't have fettuccine, so I'm using spaghetti noodles instead."

Noah frowned. He'd heard of fettuccine, but he wasn't certain what it was. Besides spaghetti, the only kind of pasta he'd ever had was macaroni and cheese. "I'm sure it'll be fine."

Abbie pulled a pan out of the oven and brought it over to the table. The smell made his mouth water. She set the dish on a towel before going back to the oven to get the rolls. Strips of chicken were nestled in a bed of noodles with a creamy white sauce. Bits of something green added a little color to the dish. She removed a salad from the refrigerator and placed it on the table.

He stared at the food. "You got all this at the market?"

"Yes." She sat across from him and put a heaping pile of salad on her plate.

"I've never seen rolls at the market." Noah couldn't resist the hot bread. He pulled one apart, letting the steam escape for a moment before popping the piece into his mouth.

"They don't sell rolls." Abbie handed him the bowl of salad. "But they have flour and yeast."

He paused midchew. "You made these? Like, from scratch?"

She nodded. "When I get bored, I bake."

He took another bite of bread before adding salad to his plate. "You must get bored a lot. These are fantastic."

"Thank you." She beamed. "I enjoy cooking, but baking is my favorite thing to do. When I was younger, I wanted to open my own bakery."

Noah reached for her plate and scooped some of the chicken and noodle combination onto it before filling his own. He still wasn't sure what the green stuff in the dish was, but it didn't stop him from taking a large bite.

"This is delicious." He wiped his mouth with the napkin next to his plate. "You missed your calling. So what did you go to college for?"

"Accounting." Her voice was devoid of any emotion.

"You don't like accounting?" If he'd gone to college, accounting was something he might have wanted to major in. He was good with numbers. If he hadn't been, he would have lost the ranch years ago. As it was, he'd been able to squeak by. Of course, to go to college, he would have had to finish high school first.

She pursed her lips and shrugged. "I like it fine. I'm good at it."

"But?" He raised one eyebrow.

She took a deep breath. "I never had a choice. Or at least I never felt like I did. All my dad ever talked about was me taking over his accounting firm. I never even considered doing anything else because I didn't want to let him down."

"I can understand that." His grandfather had been the same way with him. The difference was, he wanted his life to be the ranch, too. "What do you want?"

Abbie's face pinched and she sighed. "I wish I knew. I went to the college my dad wanted me to go to. I joined the clubs my mom suggested. Now my dad has a job for me when I return."

"Is that a bad thing, though?" Was he supposed to feel sorry for her? On one hand, he could sympathize with her for wanting to make her own choices. On the other hand, she didn't seem to appreciate how fortunate she was. He'd fought tooth and nail for every opportunity he'd ever had.

"Yes." Her voice rose an octave. She toyed with her necklace. "No... I don't know."

"So that's why you really came to Coronado. To get away from your parents?" The pieces were coming together now. "Do you even have a sister?"

Abbie furrowed her brow. "Oh, of course I do. I wouldn't lie about something like that."

"Since you're from New York and she's here, I take it she was better at standing up to your dad than you are."

Abbie glanced down at her plate as she swirled her spaghetti with her fork. "We grew up with different dads."

Now it made more sense. Her voice held a hint of sadness. "How long has it been since you've seen your sister?" he asked.

"A very long time." Abbie took a bite of her food. "I wasn't sure if you liked spinach, so I only added a little."

Spinach. Noah stared at the green bits on his plate. One mystery solved. "I've never tried it before, but I like it."

The answer seemed to please her. She smiled. "I'm glad I was able to expand your food horizons."

The second mystery was why she tried to change the subject every time her sister was mentioned.

CHAPTER SEVEN

IT WAS STILL dark when Noah walked out of his cabin the next morning. He'd told Abbie to meet him at the barn at six o'clock, but her windows were dark. He shook his head. She was probably still asleep. If the lights in her cabin were on, he'd offer to give her a ride to the barn, but he wasn't going to wake her up. He'd offered her a way to earn the money she needed; it was up to her to use it.

Tom followed him to the truck and jumped into the cab when Noah opened the door. As soon as he got in, the cat curled up next to him.

The road between the cabins and the barn was rough, but Tom didn't seem to mind. Noah rubbed what was left of Tom's right ear as they bounced along. A light inside the barn put Noah on high alert. Someone was there.

His truck was loud enough that whoever it was would know he was on his way. He scanned the area, waiting for someone to come running out of the barn, or a vehicle to come flying out from around back as the intruder tried to flee from him, but there was no movement. Instead of pulling close to the building, he parked on the road. If someone decided to make a run for it, he wouldn't have to back up to give chase.

He turned the engine off and listened. The horses didn't sound alarmed. Paddy, especially, didn't like strangers, so if someone was in there, they weren't bothering the animals. He slipped out of the truck and moved up the path to the barn.

Light poured through the open doors. He heard a noise from inside. Every nerve in his body tingled. He pressed himself against the outside wall of the barn and listened again. The squeak of a door, followed by the soft rustle of oats being poured made Noah pause. It didn't sound like a thief rummaging around in there.

It couldn't be. He peeked around the corner and his body relaxed. *It was.* In the corner of the tack room, Abbie studied the white board on the wall. Right behind her, a couple of buckets sat on the ground, two of them filled with oats. She ran one finger along the board, reading the instructions Stacy had written for each horse.

His heart rate began to slow down, and he stepped into the barn. "What are you doing?"

She whirled around. "You scared me."

He pointed to the buckets. "You haven't fed any of the horses yet, have you?"

Her face turned pink. "Not yet. I was just trying to get it ready for you."

Noah picked a bucket up in each hand and walked over to the fifty-gallon drum in which the oats were stored. He poured the oats back into it and pressed the lid down tight.

"What did I do wrong? I was following the directions."

"Nothing," he said. "But that list is for the evening feeding. In the mornings, they each get a flake of hay, and then I turn them out in the pasture."

She nodded. "Sounds easy enough."

"It is. But that's not your job." He looked her over and frowned. "You can't work in the barn dressed like that."

She looked down at her clothes. "What's wrong with how I'm dressed?"

Where did he start? Her light pink shirt would be covered in dirt, manure and horse hair. The tan shorts she was wearing would probably get just as dirty, but the worst part was her shoes—or lack of shoes. He pointed at her gray sandals. "Those shoes might be okay for walking around town, but they're not going to protect your feet from getting stepped on."

A flicker of fear danced across her face. "Will I be close enough to them to get stepped on?"

Noah cocked his head. "Are you scared of horses?"

"No." Once again, her reply was too fast to be believable. She scrunched her nose. "I've just never really been around them before."

"You don't have to work with the horses, but sometimes you'll need to walk by them." He motioned her to follow him.

As soon as he started walking down the center of the barn, the horses poked their noses over the fence to greet him. Paddy tossed his head and nickered, but the palomino mare in the stall next to him waited patiently. He stopped to rub her nose. "Good morning, Maze. Are you keeping Paddy in check?"

Abbie stood at a distance and he waved her forward. He nodded at the mare. "This is Maze. She's as gentle as a lamb."

She stepped forward until she was within arm's length of him. Maze lifted her nose and sniffed.

"What is she doing?"

"Probably sniffing to see if you have any treats for her." Noah stroked the mare's velvet-soft neck. "This is Stacy's horse, so she's a little spoiled."

A little like you, he thought, but kept that thought to himself.

She raised one hand and stroked her forehead. Maze leaned in and lowered her head until Abbie could scratch her ears. A smile slowly spread across her face. "She's so soft."

Paddy tossed his head and whinnied. Noah laughed. "Are you jealous, Paddy?"

Abbie cast a glance at the much larger horse but didn't move away. "What do you want me to do?"

"After I feed the horses and put them out to pasture, you muck out the stalls."

"How do I do that?"

He led her to the far end of the barn. A variety of tools hung from hooks on the wall. He removed a pitchfork and shovel and laid them in a wheelbarrow that was sitting close by. Then he slid the rear barn doors open. "See that big mound back there?"

She nodded.

"Whenever the wheelbarrow gets full, you can dump everything there."

Her face scrunched for a moment. "When you say muck out the stalls, you mean shovel the horse manure?"

"Don't use the shovel, use the pitchfork to scoop up the dung. Most of the horses urinate in the same area of their stall, so use the shovel for that area. Then sweep it out with that wide broom and put fresh straw down when you're done." He waited for her to run screaming from the barn.

She took a deep breath and scanned the barn. "Where do I get the straw?"

"There's a stack of it outside, next to the hay barn."

The horses were getting anxious for their breakfast and started to nicker. Noah lifted a bale of hay and put it in a different wheelbarrow. Lifting the handles, he pushed it down the center aisle of the barn. By the time he'd tossed a flake of hay to every horse, most of the bale was gone. He pushed the wheelbarrow to the back wall and left it.

Abbie watched him but didn't say anything. She was

probably trying to figure out how to get out of there. While he worked, she walked around the barn. She stopped at the wall next to the tack room where several picture frames hung from nails. She stared at the photographs for a long time.

Normally, he would take the horses to the pasture to graze for the day. But this morning a trail ride was scheduled, so every horse needed to be saddled. He walked past her to get a bridle from the tack room.

"Who are these people?"

He sighed and stepped closer. Most of the pictures were from rodeos that Coy had competed in. Abbie wasn't the first girl to admire Coy's good looks. It didn't do them any good. The man only had eyes for Becky. "That's Coy Tedford. His dad's the sheriff."

Her eyes weren't focused on Coy, though. "Who are the girls in the pictures?"

"That's his girlfriend, Becky. She travels the rodeo circuit, too. And that's Stacy."

Her breath hitched. She was still staring at the pictures when he walked away.

He opened Paddy's stall, and slid the bridle over the horse's head before leading him to the tack room. Noah groomed him carefully before saddling him. He moved the saddled horse to the hitching post just outside the barn, next to the corrals, but didn't need to tie him. Paddy wouldn't move until Noah picked up the reins or called for him. The rest of the horses weren't trained to be ground tied, so he would use a hitching post for them.

When he came inside to get the next horse, Abbie was working in the first stall. It impressed him that she didn't wait for him to tell her to get started. He paused outside the stall to watch her struggle to scoop up a few pieces of horse dung with the pitchfork.

DUST AND HAY floated in the air. The morning sun glinted off the particles like diamonds. Already, her light-colored shirt bore a layer of dirt.

He wore a T-shirt under his western shirt, so he unbuttoned his shirt and took it off. "Here." He handed it to her. "Put this on over your shirt so it doesn't get too dirty."

"Thanks." She slipped it on and tied the sides together in a knot at her slender waist. "You do this every morning?"

"Yes."

She picked up the shovel. "How long does it take you?"

"About two and a half hours to do all twelve stalls."

She gave him a curt nod and dumped the manure into the wheelbarrow. At this rate, it would take her all day. When he was done, he'd offer to help her…if she didn't quit first.

Abbie was barely starting the second stall by the time he had the next three horses ready to go.

Her face looked strained, but she only nodded. He was grooming the next horse when she started coughing. The sound was all too familiar. "Are you having another asthma attack?"

"No." She shook her head. "It's just the dust."

"Dust can cause asthma attacks," he said. "Where's your inhaler?"

She rubbed her chest. "At the cabin. I'm okay. I don't need it right now."

He opened the stall and stopped her from trying to scoop anything else up. "Just to be on the safe side, let's go get your inhaler."

A coughing fit interrupted whatever argument she was about to make. He took the shovel out of her hand and leaned it against the wall before letting out a shrill whistle.

Paddy trotted down the center aisle of the barn and

stopped next to the stall. Noah took Abbie's arm and led her out.

"What are you doing?"

"This is the fastest way to get to the cabin."

Panic laced her voice. "I don't know how to ride."

He put one foot in the stirrup and stepped up, throwing his leg over the saddle. He reached down. "Just put your foot in the stirrup and take my hand."

She coughed again but did what he told her, and he pulled her up to sit behind him. She wrapped her arms so tightly around his waist that he could barely breathe.

"Relax," he told her. "Paddy's not going to hurt you, but he can sense your fear and you make him nervous."

Her grip loosened slightly. By the time they got on the road, she'd started wheezing. "Hang on tight." He urged Paddy into a canter.

As soon as he stopped in front of Abbie's cabin, he took her hand and helped her slide down. She disappeared into her cabin, leaving the door open. Noah dismounted and followed her.

Abbie took a puff of her inhaler and faced him. "I guess you were right."

"I usually am," he said, only half-joking.

She looked down at her feet. Her sandals were covered in dirt and grime. "You were right about the shoes, too."

Guilt pricked him. He had ulterior motives for offering the job. He wanted her to know what hard work really was. He wanted her to understand that not everything came so easily. "I guess cleaning stalls wasn't such a good idea."

She tucked her inhaler into the front pocket of her shorts. "I have this with me now. Let's go."

"No," he said. "You're done."

She pressed her lips together and glared at him. "Are you firing me?"

"Is cleaning the stalls worth you having an asthma attack every day?"

Her face flushed. "I won't have another attack. You can't fire me. I need to do this."

"Fine," he said. "You can try again tomorrow. But I don't want you in there alone. You go with me in the morning."

Her face lit up and she smiled. "Thanks."

Noah nodded and went back to his horse. Instead of staying on the gravel road that circled the campground, he cut through the pine trees behind the cabins.

A meadow stretched between the trees and the barn. The grass waved in the breeze, making the ground appear soft and flat. Noah knew better. Sharp rocks and holes hidden under the grass made it dangerous for anything—man, beast or motorized vehicle—to cross quickly.

Appearances could be deceiving. He had learned the hard way. On his first cattle drive, he'd been desperate to show his grandfather that he was a good cowhand, so he'd tried to beat the other cowboys to the corrals by driving his small group of cattle through a meadow just like this one. Instead of making his grandfather proud, all he'd had to show for it was a cow with a broken leg, a horse with cuts all over its body, and a broken arm.

He let Paddy set his own pace through the meadow. Like him, his horse had enough experience with the terrain to know how to navigate it. Too bad he didn't know how to navigate around Abbie.

She was another case of looks being deceiving. When he'd met her, his first impression had been of a young, naive, spoiled rich girl. But he was coming to find out that there was more to her. She had the backbone to stand up to her father, and the determination to make her own way. Denny Morgan would probably add that she had a heart of gold, too. The way she smiled at Noah was unsettling. If they'd met anywhere else, she probably wouldn't even notice him. And what bothered Noah the most was that that bothered him.

Whether he wanted to admit it or not, Abbie intrigued him, and even though he knew she wouldn't be around for very long, he still looked forward to finding out who the real Abigail Houghton was.

ABBIE TOOK ANOTHER puff from her inhaler as she watched Noah ride off on Paddy, then set the inhaler on the counter and paced around the kitchen. Frustration replaced the tightness in her chest. Why did Noah always see her at her worst? He probably thought she was as incompetent as her dad did.

Noah said she could go back tomorrow, but she had a bad feeling he was going to change his mind when tomorrow morning came around. She slapped her hand on the counter. Why hadn't she taken her inhaler with her? If she had, Noah wouldn't have made her leave. What would she do if he decided he didn't want her to risk having another attack? Calling her father still wasn't an option. Especially not now that she'd seen a picture of her sister—she was staying put until Anastasia returned.

The photographs in the barn were old and faded, but Abbie could see the family resemblance. They had the same eye shape, although Abbie couldn't tell what color Stacy's eyes were. They also had the same rounded chin and a mouth that was just a little too wide. Her heart drummed at the memory of seeing her sister's picture for the first time.

No. She couldn't go back now. First, she would take a shower. Then she would figure out what she needed to do to prove to Noah that she wasn't going to quit. She also had to figure out how to do her job faster. It had taken her almost half an hour to clean one stall.

She blamed her shoes. Several times she'd had to stop because long pieces of straw had gotten caught in them. Not to mention the acrobatics she was doing inside the stall to keep from stepping on dung. She looked down at the sandals, now caked with gunk and mud from the stable.

A foul odor drifted to her nose. "Ugh." She slipped her sandals off and dropped them in the trash can.

The smell of horse manure clung to her hands, too. She looked down. Her legs were almost as filthy as her sandals were, and her shorts had a layer of dust that might never come out.

She untied the shirt Noah had loaned her. When he first handed it to her, it smelled like him: a mixture of soap, pine and a hint of leather. Now it smelled like manure. She dropped it on the floor, followed by the rest of her clothes.

She lingered in the shower for almost half an hour. Her skin was rubbed raw by the time she was satisfied that the smell was gone. Most of her clothes were in the pile on the floor waiting to go to the laundromat. She managed to find a shirt that was presentable, but she had to dig through the pile on the floor to find a pair of shorts to wear.

Earlier in the week, she'd noticed a thrift store near the library. Other than the souvenir T-shirts sold in the market, Coronado didn't have a clothing store. She slipped her purse over her shoulder and headed out the door. Her mother would be appalled if she knew her daughter was planning to buy used clothes, but she didn't think she had a choice. She looked down at her sneakers. Hopefully, she could find some shoes in her size that Noah wouldn't frown on.

It was still early and a chill hung in the air. It would take the sun until almost noon to warm up the area. Already, the town was bustling with activity. Just like yesterday, the market was surrounded by cars. When she got to the street, she turned left and walked past the hardware store and on down the main road.

A couple of blocks past the hardware store, a Victorian-style building stood on the corner. The steep, gabled roof was stone gray, and the siding was a muted blue color. There was something about wraparound porches and tall turrets that appealed to her. The building, which had probably been a private residence at one time, was now the home of Paisley's Tea Garden. The sign in front of the building stated that they didn't open until ten. Maybe she would stop by when she was done at the thrift store.

Just past Paisley's was an empty field with an old baseball diamond. Rickety-looking bleachers stood on either side of the field, which was covered in dead grass. Portable toilets were lined up against the fence. It was a far cry from the baseball stadiums she'd visited with her dad.

At the corner, she walked across the street. The community center only had a few cars in front of it. Tonight they were holding a square dance. What were the chances she could get Noah to go with her? She laughed to herself. Even if he wasn't working at the tavern, he would never go with her. If she really wanted to go dancing, she'd have to go by herself.

Behind the community center was an old stucco building that housed the Coronado Thrift Store. A large donation bin sat next to the road. A handwritten sign taped to the front of it proclaimed, This Is Not a Trash Can.

She walked up the sidewalk to the entrance. Her palms were damp with sweat. It was silly to be nervous, but she'd never been in this type of store before and had no idea what to expect. Inside, the store was bright and clean. Racks of clothes stretched across the middle of the building. Each row had a sign identifying what types of clothes were on each rack. The far back wall held shoes, and on the other side of the room an open door led to another section of the store dedicated to furniture and housewares.

"Hello, again."

Abbie looked up and was surprised to see the young woman she had walked to the post office with yesterday. "Hi, Emily! What are you doing here?"

Emily held up a couple of onesies. "Wyatt grows out of things so fast, I'm becoming a regular customer. What about you?"

Abbie took a deep breath. "I need to find some clothes suitable for mucking horse stalls."

Emily raised one eyebrow. "Why are you cleaning stalls?"

Normally, she would refrain from telling people about her problems, but she was long past worrying what anyone would think of her. "I didn't budget for lodging and a wrecked car. So I'm cleaning the stables at the campground to pay the deductible on my insurance."

Instead of reacting with shock or disgust, Emily let out a whistle. "That's a hard job. I helped my boyfriend—well, ex-boyfriend—with that a few times."

"Any advice?"

"Yeah." Emily grinned "Don't do it."

She looped her arm through Abbie's and led her to a rack of denim jeans. "Here. You'll need a couple pairs of jeans. What size are you?"

Together, they flipped through the clothes hangers looking for the right size. Abbie had never seen such a wide variety of clothing. Most of the retail stores she shopped at with her mother carried a very limited selection of the latest styles from high-end brands.

"Look at these." Abbie held up a pair of dark western

jeans. Rhinestones decorated the back pockets. "Aren't they beautiful?"

"They are nice..." Emily's voice trailed off. "But not exactly what you want to wear to the barn."

Abbie's shoulders dropped. "Oh. I almost forgot what I was looking for." She traced her fingers over the rhinestones. Before hanging the pants back on the rack, she peeked at the price tag and gasped.

"What?" Emily stopped browsing through the clothes to look at her.

"These jeans are ten dollars."

"Don't worry," Emily said. "We'll find some cheaper ones."

Cheaper? There were cheaper ones? If they were cheaper, she could afford work pants and these. She tossed the jeans over one shoulder and kept looking.

Emily held up a pair of jeans that were faded but still in good shape. "Here you go. Three dollars. Not fancy and perfect for mucking stalls."

A few minutes later, Abbie found another similar pair of three-dollar jeans.

Emily led her to the shirt aisle. "You need long sleeves to work in the barn."

"Won't I get too hot?" The mornings were nice and cool, but it hadn't taken her long to work up a sweat.

"Better to be hot than stinky. All the dirt flying in the air will stick to your sweaty arms. Also, horseflies bite." Emily picked two long-sleeved button-up shirts. "Now, the most important thing—boots."

"Boots?" Abbie had never owned a pair of boots that didn't have a four-inch heel. "I was thinking more along the lines of a good pair of sneakers."

Emily shook her head. "No. The dirt and muck will soak into the cloth. You need a pair of boots. Come on."

She took Abbie's hand and pulled her to the shoe section. Again, Abbie was amazed at the selection. She picked up a pair of strappy high heels. She didn't recognize the brand name, but they looked as nice as some of her Alexander Wangs. She tried to picture them with the rhinestone jeans.

"You definitely can't wear those to a barn." Emily took them out of her hand and held up a pair of lace-up work boots. "You're in luck."

She tried not to look too disappointed. "They don't have any cowboy boots?"

"Sure, lots of them," Emily said. "But they're too nice for working in the barn."

Abbie took the work boots from her and tried them on. They were a little big, but Emily assured her they would be fine if she wore two pairs of socks.

She tucked them under her arm and walked over to the western boots. Emily gave her a puzzled look. Abbie smiled. "I've never had a pair of cowboy boots before."

"Well, then—" Emily's blue eyes twinkled "—we'd better find you some."

A little while later, Abbie walked out of the store with three pairs of jeans, two shirts, work boots and western boots. All for *way* less than she'd pay for one pair of jeans back home.

Emily offered to give her a ride back to the cabins.

"Thank you, I appreciate that." She followed Emily to her car, a beat-up sedan that might have been cobalt blue at one time. Now, the paint was faded and peeling away.

She tossed her bags in the back seat, next to the car seat. "Where's your son?"

"He was taking a nap, so my aunt volunteered to stay with him for a little while." Emily opened the driver's-side door and got behind the wheel.

It took two tries for the engine to start, but soon they were on the road and headed to the cabin. Abbie stuck one hand out the window and let the wind catch it. Excitement swelled in her chest. Tomorrow, she would be back at the barn, dressed and ready to work. And Noah wouldn't have a reason to stop her.

CHAPTER EIGHT

NOAH TOOK ONE last drink of his coffee and dumped the rest down the sink. He'd be surprised if Abbie was ready to go this morning. A half hour of work yesterday gave her an asthma attack and ruined her clothes. She would quit, he was pretty sure of it.

He opened the door to the cabin and stepped outside to see Abbie waiting by his truck. At least, he thought it was Abbie. The woman in front of him looked nothing like the one he'd seen around the last few days. She was wearing jeans instead of shorts, and a long-sleeved flannel shirt instead of a blouse...and work boots instead of sandals, at that. He stepped off the porch. "Where did you get those clothes?"

Abbie looked down at herself and back up at him. "I went shopping."

"Shopping? Here in Coronado?"

She smiled. "Yes. At the thrift store behind the library. Have you ever been there?"

His eyebrows lifted. She went to a thrift store?

"You really should go." Abbie chattered away. "I found a really nice pair of jeans for only ten dollars. Ten dollars... can you believe that?"

Noah walked around to the driver's side of the truck and opened the door. He paused, waiting for Tom to jump in first.

"Hello, Tom." Abbie reached out to pet him.

Tom hissed, turned around and jumped back out of the truck. Noah almost laughed at Abbie's crestfallen face. "Don't take it personally." He slid into the cab and slammed the truck door.

She crossed her arms. "I don't know how else I'm supposed to take it. Every morning, he uses me for free milk, but he won't ride in the truck with me."

Noah shook his head. "Stop giving him milk. Didn't your mama every tell you not to give your milk away for free?"

"Huh?" Her brow furrowed. "Why would she tell me that?"

"Never mind." He laughed. "It's a saying from before your time."

"Well, when I get home, that cat and I are going to have a long chat."

He put the truck in gear and turned to her. "Do you have your inhaler?"

"Right here." She patted her front pocket.

The back road between the cabins and the barn wasn't used very often. Deep ruts and potholes caused the truck to bounce around. Noah glanced at Abbie, who was holding on to the hand grip on the roof. One large rut jarred her from the passenger side and threw her across the cab and into him.

"Sorry," he mumbled. "Now you know why I took you home on the horse yesterday instead of in the truck. Horseback was much faster."

Even after she moved back to her side of the cab, the smell of her shampoo stayed. She smelled like the jasmine vines his mother planted around the house.

The road got smoother as they neared the barn.

When he turned off the truck, Abbie asked, "Why do you do all this?"

He got out of the truck and started walking toward the barn. "Do what?"

She waved her hand toward the barn. "You do this. Then you go to work at the garage. Then you go to work at the tavern. All you do is work."

Noah stopped at the tack room to get some buckets. She followed him, waiting for an answer. "I took a chance on something and I lost almost everything. I'm trying to hold on to the only thing that's left."

And that was the worst part of it: He had gotten himself into this mess. He knew taking out a loan and using the ranch as collateral was risky, but he hadn't realized just how risky it was.

"What do you mean?" Her eyes widened. "Did you gamble your life savings away, or something?"

"No." He didn't want to talk about it, but the truth was probably better than whatever she imagined. He unlocked the back door and slid open the barn door. "A few years ago, we had a bad drought. All of us ranchers were scrambling to look for hay to feed our cattle and a way to haul water in. I found a few farms that were willing to sell hay really cheap if I bought it in bulk and if I hauled it myself. I saw an opportunity to help out the local ranchers and make some money to boot. I had my CDL license so—"

Abbie interrupted him. "What's CDL?"

"A commercial driver's license. You have to have one to drive a semitruck," he explained. "I could have leased a truck, but I didn't want to do that. I used my ranch as collateral and took out a loan to purchase a truck and two trailers. One for feed and one for water."

"Sounds like a solid plan." She took the large broom, pitchfork and shovel off the hooks on the wall and placed them in her wheelbarrow.

Noah loaded a bale of hay onto his wheelbarrow and started down the center aisle.

Abbie followed him. "What happened?"

"Then wildfires hit and wiped out everything the drought had left. Organizations donated tons of hay to us and hauled in water. Which was great. But I now had a huge loan on a truck I couldn't use. Instead of trying to get rid of it, I thought I should hang on to it and eventually, it would make me money. So I sold off a few cattle each year in order to make the payment."

"How many do you have left?" She pulled off a flake of hay from his wheelbarrow. "Is this big enough?"

He nodded and moved to the next stall while she dropped the hay into the feed trough. "None. I hung on to as many as I could. Then the wild horses wiped out all the grazing areas, and I couldn't afford to buy feed. Half the herd belonged to my brother, and he sold all his to finance his move to Nashville."

"Why don't you just sell the truck?"

"I did. And the trailers, too. But by that time, I was upside down on the loan, so I still owe money. That's why I work three jobs. If I can't make the payments, I lose my ranch."

"What about—"

He stopped her. "Please don't. I've heard every piece of advice there is. I've tried everything I can. It is what it is. Let's talk about something else."

She nodded and turned her attention back to her work. After a few minutes, it was clear that she wasn't going to push it, and the tension in his shoulders lightened up enough that he could go back to concentrating on what he was doing.

So far, Abbie's work ethic impressed him. The fact that she jumped in and started helping without waiting to be told surprised him. Over the years, he'd worked with a lot of ranch hands. Some knew instinctively what needed to be done and did it without question; others hung back and waited for every instruction.

Abbie fell somewhere in between. He couldn't expect her to know what to do when she'd never done it before. Still, it was nice to see that she didn't wait around for him. Working together, they got all the horses fed in no time at all.

"Now what?" she asked when the last flake of hay had been delivered.

"We check their water. If it's dirty, we dump it out and clean it. If it's low, we fill it."

He helped her with the first one; after that, he let her do one on her own while he did another one. By the time they were done with the water, the horses were ready to go to the pasture.

When he came back into the barn, Abbie was cleaning the first stall. He stopped to check on her. She had a red bandanna tied around her neck and pulled up over her nose and mouth. A bucket sat on the floor inside the stall and she scooped up horse dung, shook out the good hay and dropped the dung into the bucket instead of carrying it to the wheelbarrow outside the stall.

"How did you know to do that? I didn't have time to tell you yesterday."

She glanced up from her work. "I googled it."

"You looked it up on the internet?"

"Yep. It's amazing what you can learn from YouTube."

He'd never heard of anyone learning to clean a stall by watching YouTube videos before, but he had to admit that she was moving much faster than yesterday. And even though more dust was floating in the air, she wasn't coughing, thanks to the bandanna masking her face. She must have googled that, too.

She was still slow. With each stall, she got a little slower. A couple of times, she stopped to stretch her arms and back. Would she admit that it was too hard for her? He almost offered to help by cleaning a few stalls for her, but he stopped himself. She wanted a job; she needed to earn it. Especially since he was the one who was paying for her car.

Once Abbie was able to do the job on her own, Noah could go to the garage earlier than he usually did. The money from the extra hours he could work would go straight toward the cost of repairing Abbie's car.

It had been a moment of weakness that compelled him to talk to Bear about Abbie's situation. While Bear would never agree to let an outsider make payments on their deductible, he had no qualms about allowing Noah to do so.

His gaze strayed across the barn to watch her dumping her bucket into the wheelbarrow. She hadn't complained once. She hadn't asked for help. Maybe she would help lighten his load a little after all. If she did, it would be worth the money Bear was taking out of his paychecks to cover her deductible.

Abbie glanced up and saw him watching her. Even with the bandanna covering half her face, Noah knew that she was smiling at him. He had her shoveling up manure, and she seemed happy about it. His heart fluttered. If that woman wasn't careful, he was going to start liking her.

ABBIE STOOD ON the porch until Noah drove away. As soon as he was out of sight, she limped to the front door. Every muscle in her body ached. And Emily was wrong. Wearing two pairs of socks did not keep her slightly too big work boots from rubbing blisters on her feet.

The moment she closed the cabin door, she sank to the floor and unlaced her boots. She pulled her socks off and examined the raw skin on her heels and the balls of her feet. What she wouldn't give for her giant whirlpool bathtub right now. She leaned back against the door and closed her eyes.

Her day was only half over. The last thing she wanted to do was go to town, but now that Mr. Morgan had his glasses, she'd promised to catch him up on his ledger. The store was closed, so they would have lots of peace and quiet to work uninterrupted. And lots of time for her to convince Mr. Morgan that she could train Emily to use the store's computer. She groaned. Noah did this every day.

She needed to go take a shower, but she didn't think she could stand on her feet long enough to do so. She pushed herself off the floor and walked to the sofa using only the outsides of her feet. As soon as she reached the sofa, she flopped down and closed her eyes.

A loud knock at the door caused her to sit up. She didn't remember falling asleep, but she must have. She rubbed her eyes and stood up as the knocking started again. "I'm coming!" she yelled.

She opened the door and saw Emily on the porch.

"You look awful," Emily said. "Are you sick? Is that why you didn't go to the hardware store today?"

"No, not sick, just sore and tired and…" Abbie stopped midsentence as Emily's second question sank in. "What time is it?"

"Two o'clock."

Abbie gasped. "Oh my goodness. I must have fallen asleep. Mr. Morgan was expecting me an hour ago."

"I know. I saw Granddad at the store, so I stopped to see if something was wrong. He told me he was waiting for you." Emily wrinkled her nose. "Please don't take this the wrong way, but you stink."

Abbie burst out laughing. "I know. I'm sorry. When I got home from the barn, I was too exhausted to do anything but sit on the couch. I must have fallen asleep. Tell Mr. Morgan I'll be there as soon as I shower."

"I better get Wyatt out of the car, then. I'll wait and give you a ride to town. If you're not too sore to walk that far now, you will be by the end of the day."

"Deal." Abbie hobbled toward the bathroom as quickly as her aching body allowed.

"Why are you limping?"

Abbie scrunched her face. "I wore two pairs of socks, just like you said, but I still got blisters."

Emily bent down and picked up one of the socks Abbie had discarded on the kitchen floor. "Two of these socks? No wonder you have blisters. You need real socks, girl."

"Now you tell me." Abbie walked into her bedroom.

Despite being tired and sore, she felt good. If Noah had a problem with the work she did at the barn, he hadn't said anything. For the first time in her life, she felt as if she had earned her own way.

She took her shower and dressed as quickly as she could. Emily was sitting on the living room floor playing with Wyatt.

"You look much better." Emily stood up, bouncing the baby on her hip.

"I feel much better."

She followed Emily out to her car and waited for her to buckle her son into his car seat. "Does this mean your grandfather is speaking to you again?"

Emily frowned. "Not really, but I promised my grandmother I would keep an eye on him, so he tolerates me when he has to."

Abbie frowned. "That's sad. I mean, to think that someone has to tolerate you."

"Granddad and I have a complicated relationship."

When they arrived at the hardware store, Abbie nodded toward the pickup truck in the parking lot. "I thought the store was closed on Sundays."

"It is." Emily frowned at the shiny gray Ford. "I hope Mr. Evans isn't trying to start trouble again."

Abbie didn't wait for Emily to get the baby from the car seat. She hurried into the store and scanned the area, looking for Mr. Morgan. He was standing at the end of one aisle, talking with another man. She slipped down the center aisle and sat on a stool next to the counter.

"Something's got to be done." The man's voice carried throughout the store. "They're destroying everything. At this rate, I'm either going to have to haul in more feed or sell off cattle."

Mr. Morgan nodded. "You're not the first rancher I've heard that from. Between the drought and the wild horses, things are tough."

"Nothing can be done about drought, but they could do something about the wild horses. If they don't do something soon, some of the ranchers will start taking matters into their own hands."

Mr. Morgan huffed. "I hope you aren't one of them. You don't need the kind of trouble that'll bring."

"No. But don't think I haven't thought about it."

"I'll reach out to a few people and see what I can find out," Mr. Morgan said.

"I appreciate that."

The two men shook hands and the man left.

Mr. Morgan looked up and saw Abbie at the counter. "Where ya been, girl? I was starting to think you'd skipped town."

"I'm sorry. I fell asleep." Abbie nodded toward the door. "What was that about?"

Mr. Morgan shrugged. "Ranchers always have something to complain about."

He didn't elaborate. What was behind the man's veiled threat? Abbie's curiosity got the best of her. "What did he mean by taking matters into his own hands?"

His eyes grew somber and he leaned closer. "I don't mean to be rude, but it's best you don't know. You're not from around here, so you wouldn't understand."

His words were soft and low, but it didn't lessen the message. She was an outsider, and it was none of her business. She swallowed hard, and one hand moved to her neck to touch the tiny locket.

Mr. Morgan's face softened. "I'm sorry. I wasn't trying to hurt your feelings. It's for his protection as well as yours."

Protection from what? Were the two men discussing something illegal? She nodded. "I understand. And you're right. I don't live around here, so it's really none of my business."

His brow furrowed as if contemplating what to say next.

Emily cleared her throat, breaking the awkward silence. "I just came in to make sure Mr. Evans was behaving. I'll see you later, Abbie. Bye, Granddad."

"Wait." Abbie stopped her.

She pointed to the computer sitting on the counter. "How long have you had that?"

"I don't know," Mr. Morgan grumbled.

"Three years," Emily answered. "My mother got it for him for Christmas."

Abbie nodded. "Has it ever been turned on?"

Mr. Morgan shrugged. Again, Emily was the one to respond. "At least once. I set it up when he got it."

That answered Abbie's first question. Emily knew a little something about computers. She walked behind the counter and pulled Mr. Morgan's giant ledger book from a shelf underneath.

She put it on the counter with a thump. "If you let me, I can set up your computer to keep track of your inventory, update your books and even take care of your taxes. All in half the time it takes you to enter everything into that ledger by hand."

Mr. Morgan shook his head. "I don't know nothing 'bout computers."

"Not yet." Abbie nodded at his granddaughter. "But she does. I can teach her and she can teach you."

He shook his head. "I need to know what my ledger says all the time. It'd take too long to learn all that."

It was Emily that spoke up. "You can still enter things into your ledger. I can print reports on the computer every day and you can double check them until you learn how to use the computer yourself."

Abbie cocked her head. It sounded like Emily knew more than just a little about computers. "You know how to do that already?"

Emily pulled herself up straight. "My grandmother had me take a lot of accounting and bookkeeping classes at the community college in Springerville while I was in high school. I've taken a few more since. Just in case he ever wanted me to help."

Mr. Morgan's scowl softened as he stared at his granddaughter. "I didn't know that."

Abbie's chest swelled and she grinned. "Well, what do you say, Mr. Morgan? Can I start training Emily?"

He nodded. "Might as well. Don't want the money Opal spent on all that to go to waste."

A grin broke out on Emily's face. "Let me run home and get Wyatt's playpen really fast. I'll be right back."

"No need," the old man barked. "I got one in the office."

Emily's eyes glistened. "Since when?"

"No matter." He shrugged. "Just go get it set up so we can get started."

Abbie fought back a grin as she stared at Mr. Morgan. "You're a lot softer than Noah said you were."

"Hmph," he said. "That's 'cause Noah's never cared about anyone else before."

He gave Abbie a long look. "Maybe you can change that, too."

CHAPTER NINE

NOAH LOCKED UP the tavern and went to his truck. He usually didn't work until closing, but he had been the one in charge tonight. The holiday weekend crowd cleared out early, so he sent Emily home around ten.

When things got slow, Emily was always the first person Freddy let go home early, and when Noah was in charge, he did the same thing. Emily's aunt babysat Wyatt when she worked at the tavern, and Emily didn't want to pick him up too late.

He liked Emily a lot. She was a good kid, despite getting into some trouble in high school. She was fifteen when her parents shipped her to Coronado because they didn't want to deal with her. She skipped school a few times, but it didn't take her long to settle down. He even tried to convince his brother to go out with her in high school, but Luke wasn't interested. When Emily started working at the bar, she and Luke became friends, but it never went any further. Noah suspected that Emily had a crush on Luke because after he left town, he got a weird vibe from her for a while. She started dating some guy from out of town shortly after that, but he split when she got pregnant. Noah offered to go find the guy and pound some sense into him, but Emily refused to tell him…or anyone…what his name was.

He climbed into his truck, ignoring the pile of mail on the seat. There was a letter from the bank, but he didn't want to look at it. Not yet. The last couple of weeks had been nice. No phone calls to avoid. No watching over his shoulder to see if someone was coming to evict him from his home.

For two wonderful weeks, he'd been able to relax a little. The envelope on the seat next to him was a reminder that he still had a long way to go.

He took the back way to the cabin, swinging past the barn and corrals instead of driving straight through the campground. Almost every cabin was full, and he didn't want his loud truck to wake anyone up.

The lights in Abbie's cabin were on. His senses went on high alert. Was something wrong? It was almost one o'clock in the morning. He parked and shut off the engine. Abbie was sitting on the wicker love seat outside, wrapped up in a blanket. He gathered his mail and got out of the truck.

He could feel her eyes on him, even before he stepped into the light from her porch. "Everything okay?"

Both hands were wrapped around the coffee mug she was holding in front of her. She nodded. "Want some coffee?"

He shook his head. "You planning on staying up all night?"

"It's decaf," she said. "How was work?"

"Fine." He stepped up on the porch. "Why are you sitting out here?"

"Waiting for you." She moved over, making room for him to sit down.

Noah sat down next to her, catching a portion of the blanket under him. A low growl erupted from under the blanket.

Abbie laughed. "Now you've woken him up."

Noah pulled the cover back to reveal his big, yellow,

formerly mean and grumpy tomcat, curled up like a kitten on her lap. "What have you done to my cat?"

"Nothing." She gave him a solemn stare. "We've come to an understanding. Why are you so late?"

Was she keeping track of him? His heart stuttered at the thought. "The tavern doesn't close until midnight on Sundays."

"Yes, but you're usually home by ten thirty. Eleven at the latest."

He arched one eyebrow. "You're usually in bed asleep by the time I get home."

"In bed," she said, "not asleep."

"Does my truck wake you up?" Funny, he avoided driving on the main road at night, for fear of waking people up, but he hadn't worried about it when it was just Abbie.

"No. I can't really go to sleep until I know you're home. When you weren't home by eleven thirty, I gave up and decided to wait out here."

He wasn't sure what to say. No one had ever waited up for him, much less been worried about him. "Freddy's still off, and the guy who usually closes up had the day off, so it was my turn to lock up for him."

"Where is Freddy again?"

"His wife just had hip surgery, so he's been staying home to help her out. He's coming back tomorrow, though." Noah stood up and tucked the mail under his arm. "I better let you get back to bed."

"Can I ask you a question?"

He stopped at the edge of the porch. "What's on your mind?"

She pressed her lips together and frowned before she spoke. "This afternoon, at the hardware store, a rancher was talking to Mr. Morgan. He was complaining about the wild horses, I think. Why don't the ranchers like them?"

Noah rubbed the back of his neck with one hand. It was a loaded question, so he needed to be careful how he answered. "It's complicated."

"So explain it to me."

"Okay. Remember the wildfires I talked about? Most of the ranchers were able to save their houses, but the land was completely burned. Usually, the land recovers pretty quickly from a fire, because the grass often comes back thicker and richer."

That part was easy to explain. It was the next part where he had to pick his words carefully. He didn't want to sound like he was passing judgment on either side of the debate. "When the wild horses moved in, it caused a lot of problems for the local ranchers. They ate all the grass, leaving nothing for the cattle. They destroyed fences and broke water pipes. And there is nothing the ranchers can do about it."

Abbie frowned. "This rancher told Mr. Morgan that if things didn't get taken care of, they would start taking matters into their own hands. What did he mean by that?"

Noah bristled. It was a sentiment he'd heard before. The outcome of such talk was never good. "Wild horses are protected, but there have been cases where ranchers would have them exterminated."

She gasped. "You mean, killed?"

"Ranchers will do whatever it takes to protect their way of life."

"You're a rancher." Her gaze zeroed in on him. "Would you ever do that?"

"No." He swallowed. "But I don't have anything to protect anymore."

THE PAIN IN his voice was so raw it made Abbie flinch. She didn't know what to say. She had no words of wisdom or advice to give. Nothing she'd ever been through compared to what he'd faced.

He took another step closer to the edge of the porch. She leaned forward. "Sit back down. Talk to me for a while."

"Aren't you tired?"

She shook her head. The moment her head hit the pillow, she'd be asleep, but right now, she wanted to spend more time with him. He moved the corner of the blanket out of his way and sat down. For a while, they just sat together. Abbie had never known how nice it was just to sit with someone. They both stared up at the night sky.

"Look," she gasped. "A shooting star."

Noah nudged her. "Make a wish."

She closed her eyes. *I wish for Noah to get back everything he lost.*

"What did you wish for?" he asked.

"Nope. Can't tell you or it won't come true." She settled back on the love seat, enjoying the heat radiating from Noah's body.

He pointed at the sky. "There's another one."

"Your turn to make a wish."

He shook his head. "I gave up on wishes a long time ago."

She gave him a sad smile before taking a deep breath. "In that case, I'm taking your wish."

"You can't do that."

"Why not? You don't want it. It's a shame to let a perfectly good wish go to waste. Especially since they're so rare."

Tom crawled out from under the blanket on her lap. He placed his front paws on Noah and butted his owner's chin with his head. Noah scratched the cat's ears, and Tom began to purr loudly.

"They aren't that rare around here," Noah said. "The

Perseids. The Orionids. The Geminids. My mom used to wake us up to come outside and watch meteor showers with her."

It was the first time she'd heard him refer to his mother in a pleasant way. "Where's your mom now?"

"Who knows?" He shrugged. "She calls every few months. A couple of times a year she shows up at the ranch. Usually, to recover from a broken heart or when she needs money."

It was impossible to miss the disgust in his voice. "She gets a broken heart often?"

He snorted. "You could say that. She had more boy-friends by the time I was eighteen than we had cattle on the ranch."

Abbie felt sorry for her, a sentiment Noah obviously did not share. "She was looking for something."

"Yeah. An easy life." He crossed his arms across his chest. "We were never enough for her. She always thought she needed a man to solve her problems."

She was probably treading on thin ice, but she had to ask. "What happened to your dad?"

"My father left when I was twelve. We moved in with my grandpa shortly after that. He was the one that raised me."

His voice was monotone. Almost as if he was making an effort not to show any emotion. Abbie knew there was much more to his story. "Just your grandpa? What about your grandmother?"

"I never knew her," he said. "She died when my mom was still in high school."

She rearranged the blanket to cover both of them. "When did your grandpa pass away?"

"When I was sixteen."

"That must have been tough. How did he die?"

He laced his fingers together in his lap. His thumbs made circles around each other. "Emphysema. That's how I recognized your asthma attack."

"Ah, so your grandpa was the smoker." She remembered the faint smell of tobacco the first time she rode in Noah's truck, but she'd never seen him smoke.

"Yes. For fifty years," he said, then paused and looked at her quizzically. "How did you…"

"Your truck. It used to belong to your grandpa, right?"

He half smiled in acknowledgment as it dawned on him what she meant. "It did," he said. "I used to smoke, too, but I stopped the day he died and threw every pack of cigarettes I found in the trash."

Her mouth dropped open. "You smoked? But you were only sixteen."

He shrugged. "I thought it made me look cool. Look older. But I didn't want to die that way, and I certainly didn't want Luke to die that way."

"Luke. That's your brother? Where is he again?"

"Nashville." He lifted up the blanket and tucked the corner around them. "He says he wants to be a country music star."

Something in his voice told her he wasn't as sure about his brother's ambitions. "You don't think that's what he wants?"

"No. He's good, but he's not good enough to make it in Nashville, and he knows that. What he really wants is something of his own."

Abbie had never heard so many words from him at a time. She was afraid to break the spell by asking the wrong question. But she couldn't help herself. "What about you? What do you want?"

"The ranch." His dark brown eyes met hers. "All I've

ever wanted was the ranch. Grandpa left it to both of us, but Luke doesn't want it. He never liked ranch life."

Abbie's heart lodged in her throat. She couldn't imagine wanting something that much. "You miss it, don't you?"

His voice was little more than a whisper. "So much it hurts. But I won't stop fighting to keep my ranch, no matter what the cost."

"I'm glad. You can do it. I know you can." A shiver ran through her as the cold started to seep through the blanket, but she didn't want to get up and go inside. She wanted to stay with Noah as long as he was willing.

He nudged her. "It's getting cold. You better get inside."

She shook her head and fought back a yawn. "I'm okay. I like sitting out here with you."

"Go to bed, Abbie." His voice was as smooth as silk. "We can watch the stars again tomorrow night."

"Promise?"

He stood up, and she immediately missed his warmth. Looking over his shoulder, he gave her a little salute. "Good night."

CHAPTER TEN

ABBIE HUMMED TO herself as she cleaned the stalls. It seemed that after a couple of days, her body had finally adjusted to the rigors of physical labor. Her soreness had worked itself out, and she could move without pain. Emily had given her "real" socks, so her feet didn't hurt anymore. All in all, things were going well.

Noah didn't hover over like he did the first couple of days. This morning, he'd even left her there alone while he went to town to pick up something from the market. Her only complaint now was that her hands were getting raw. Blisters were starting to form on her hands where she gripped the pitchfork the hardest.

As she was giving her hands a rest, she heard Noah's truck in the distance and she picked up the tool again. The last thing she wanted was for him to catch her slacking on the job.

By the time he walked inside, she was back at work. He carried two large boxes stacked on top of each other into the tack room. Abbie was paying more attention to him than to what she was doing, and the edge of her pitchfork hit the wall and stopped. Her hands did not. They slid down the handle and suddenly her hands were on fire.

She dropped the handle with a loud cry. Lifting her hands in front of her, she blew on them. It didn't help much, but it was the only thing she could think of to do.

Noah appeared at her side. "What's wrong?"

Heat rushed to her face and neck, and she dropped her hands. "Nothing. I just tried to lift up part of the wall."

She bent down to pick up the handle, but Noah stopped her. He turned her hands over and ran his fingers around the blisters, now broken and bleeding.

"Come with me," he said.

Abbie followed him out of the stall. Instead of the tack room, he walked to a doorway on the opposite side of the center aisle of the barn. He opened the door and ushered her inside.

She hadn't been inside this room before. It was much smaller than the tack room. A wooden desk and filing cabinets were pushed up against the far wall. A bookcase and storage cabinets covered the entire side of the inside wall, while a large picture window took up most of the space on the wall across. More pictures decorated the room.

Noah opened one of the storage cabinets and started to rummage through it, but Abbie's eyes were drawn to the pictures. The black-and-white photographs were old and faded. A young man stood next to a smiling woman outside the barn. The same couple appeared in many of the pictures. One was of them surrounded by three children: two boys and a girl. Other pictures were just of the man, sometimes with the children at various ages.

It wasn't until she got to the last picture that she realized who he was. The man, much older, stood with a smiling couple on their wedding day. Abbie looked closer and recognized the groom. Vince had his arms wrapped around a beautiful young woman who beamed with happiness. Abbie's heart pounded. She reached up to touch the frame holding her sister's parents.

"Abbie."

She jumped and covered her heart with her hand. "You scared me."

He frowned. "You were studying those pictures pretty hard. You're always stopping to look at pictures. Why?"

She avoided his gaze. "I don't have a big family, so I guess other people's fascinate me."

"Sometimes family isn't all it's cracked up to be," he grumbled. He found a first-aid kit in the cabinet and sat it on the desk.

Another door, one that Abbie hadn't noticed, was almost hidden behind the cabinets. He opened it, revealing a small bathroom, and washed his hands. When he was done, he moved away from the door and told her to wash her hands, too.

When she came out, the contents of the kit were spread out on the desk. "Give me your hand," he said.

"Didn't you ever want a big family?"

He held her hand in the palm of his and used the other hand to smear a smelly ointment over the blisters. "My brother was enough to keep me on my toes."

Abbie tried to ignore the tingles running up her arm when he ran his fingers over her hand and wrist. She swallowed. "What about aunts and uncles? Cousins?"

Noah's eyes stayed on her hand as he wrapped it with gauze. "Is that what you want? A big family?"

"I begged my parents for a brother or sister. That's why I wanted to come to Arizona so badly. To finally have one." She stopped herself and cast a wary glance at Noah. Did he notice that she just admitted to not knowing her sister?

Noah wrapped a bandage over the gauze and secured it with tape. He dropped her hand and picked up the other one. "This one's not as bad. I think we can make do with a couple of Band-Aids."

She sighed. He was paying more attention to her hands than he was to what she was saying. He applied more ointment to the blisters on her left hand.

"Why don't you get blisters?"

Noah took the backing off a Band-Aid and applied it to her hand. "I used to get them. But if you do a movement long enough, you get calluses. Then you don't get any more blisters."

He held one hand out to show her. She ran her fingers over the rough, hardened skin on his palms. "Will my hands feel like that soon?"

He placed the items back into the first-aid kit. "The world isn't always butterflies and rainbows on this side of the tracks, princess." Although he was teasing, a hint of sarcasm laced his voice.

She straightened up. "Please don't call me that."

"What? Princess?" He frowned. "I think it's pretty fitting."

Abbie scowled at him. "Have I acted like a princess at all? Demanded any special favors? No! Just because my parents have money, you think you know me, but you don't. You don't know anything about me."

Noah's eyes opened wide. "You're right. I don't. But I know you have opportunities that most people can only dream of having, and you're throwing it all away because you think you need to prove something to your parents."

She gasped. "I thought you were the one person who understood. You probably think I should go back home and work for my father, regardless of what I want."

He let out a huff of air. "I think you need to grow up and tell him what you want. Stop hiding from him."

"I'm not hiding! My car is in the shop so I can't go anywhere."

Noah shook his head. "You came to Coronado to see your sister, but she doesn't live here anymore. Your car is just an excuse."

She stomped out of the office, stopping at the pictures on the wall. "I said my sister wasn't here. I didn't say she moved."

He eyed her suspiciously. "Where is she then?"

She took a deep breath. "Apparently, she's on her honeymoon."

His mouth dropped open. "You're Stacy's baby sister?"

Her brow creased. "You don't seem surprised that she has a sister."

"It's not public knowledge, but she told me before she left." He rubbed the back of his neck and shook his head. "Just you? Why?"

"When she hired me to look after the campground, she wanted to let me know they might be gone a while and she wasn't sure when she'd be back…"

His voice trailed off in a way that she knew something more was coming. Her heart began to race.

He gave her a one-sided smile. "She went to Georgia, looking for you."

A choked sound escaped her mouth, and her breath came in ragged gasps as emotions flooded through her. Her limbs suddenly felt weak and, instinctively, she threw herself into his arms and held on to him. He wrapped his arms around her waist and held her while she got herself together.

"She's looking for me? She wants to know me?"

"What are the chances that two sisters had the same idea at the same time?" Noah said, as he held her—albeit a bit stiffly—and didn't let go.

"Last year, I wrote to the orphanage I was adopted from. I was hoping to find out about my parents' medical history. I had no idea I had a sister or I would've looked for her sooner. When did Stacy find out about me?"

He shook his head. "I don't know. I just know that she

wanted to find you. Why didn't you tell me who you really were?"

Her hands were still shaking when she let go of his waist and stepped back. "I wanted to tell Stacy first. That way, she could choose if she wanted me in her life or not. If she didn't, I could go back to New York and not interrupt her life."

"She wants you in her life." He nodded toward the horses. "Let me finish the stalls, then you and I are going to the market. You can talk to Vince. He can answer more questions than I can. He'll also know the fastest way to get in contact with Stacy. We need to let her know you're here, so she can come home."

TOGETHER, THEY WENT to the market. Noah waited for a lull in customers before he pulled Vince aside.

"What's up?" Vince's eyes darted back and forth between Noah and Abbie. "You look very serious. Is something wrong?"

"Abbie has something she needs to tell you." Noah urged her forward.

She rubbed her palms on her jeans. "I haven't been telling you the complete truth about why I'm here. Last year, I decided to find out as much about my birth parents as I could. So I wrote a letter to—"

"Saint George's Orphanage." Vince finished her sentence. He wrapped his arms around Abbie. "Stacy has looked for you for years. She's going to be so happy."

"Really?" she breathed. "I was so scared to come. I was afraid she wouldn't want to see me."

Noah gave them as much privacy as he could, but he stayed close enough that Abbie could see him. Every few moments, her eyes caught his and she smiled.

Vince called Millie and asked her to come in and cover

the store for him. It only took a few minutes, and when she arrived, he escorted Noah and Abbie to Stacy's apartment, at the back of the store.

Noah stood to the side while Vince and Abbie pored through photo albums. He wasn't sure what to do, but it was fun just to watch Abbie. She asked so many questions, Vince could barely keep up. While Abbie knew a little about how she ended up in the orphanage, Vince knew more.

Vince was able to tell her that her birth mother and brother had died from tuberculosis and that social services removed Abbie from the home because she was so sick. Their father dropped Stacy off at the orphanage a few weeks later, saying he couldn't take care of her anymore. He was killed in a factory accident not long after that.

"I had a brother, too?" Abbie stared at the documents from the photo album.

Then she told Vince that the orphanage was afraid that she wouldn't make it without the proper treatment, so a few weeks after her arrival, they found a family willing to adopt her and provide the care she needed.

She was in the hospital for six months after arriving in the States. Throughout her childhood, she suffered bouts of illness that doctors suspected were caused by an auto-immune disease. They later decided the weaknesses in her immune system were related to the malnutrition she'd had as an infant. Despite what Noah thought about her initially, her early life hadn't been easy. No wonder her adoptive parents were overprotective.

He had excused himself from the apartment to give Abbie some time alone with Vince, and he did what he always did when his thoughts were in a jumble: he saddled Paddy up and went for a ride.

The trail he chose was one that wasn't used very often.

It was certainly one he wouldn't take new riders on. He weaved in and out of trees, occasionally avoiding limbs that hung over the trail.

A couple of miles in, it opened up to a large meadow. The Black River rolled through the middle. A steep rock face rose up from the edge of the meadow.

Noah closed his eyes and inhaled the fresh, clean air. Paddy stopped at the edge of the stream, and Noah slid off. He dropped the reins while he explored the area.

Technically, it was still summer, but already, the leaves on the aspen trees were starting to turn; the edges were a bright yellow. It wouldn't be long before the entire mountainside would explode in hues of deep gold, red and brown.

At least, the parts of the mountain that still had trees. He turned around to view the mountains on the other side of the meadow. Instead of evergreen trees and aspens, he saw charred sticks, a stark reminder of the devastation that burned through the area ten years before.

Paddy let out a soft nicker. Noah turned to see the horse shuffling nervously. Paddy was too well trained to move from the spot Noah left him, but he was alerting Noah that something was wrong.

Noah's senses went on high alert. He moved closer to his horse and picked up the reins. Paddy immediately relaxed, but his eyes were focused downstream.

Noah didn't see anything, but he climbed into the saddle and reached behind him to slip his rifle out of the saddle scabbard. The meadow was quiet. Even the birds stopped singing and the squirrels ceased chattering to each other. He slid the bolt of the rifle back and loaded a bullet in the chamber.

He signaled for Paddy to back up but didn't take his eyes off the area his horse had been watching. The tops of the bushes swayed and twigs cracked as something made its way through the brush. Noah relaxed at the amount of noise being made. An animal hunting for prey would never be heard. A few moments later, a black bear lumbered out of the bushes and sauntered to the edge of the water. Paddy remained alert, but Noah put his rifle back into the scabbard.

He pointed Paddy toward the trail and headed back to the stables. The horse was happy to set off in the opposite direction from the bear.

Once Noah got to the barn, he brushed Paddy for a while before putting him in his stall. By the time he called the rest of the horses in from the pasture, it was time to feed them before getting ready to go to work at the Watering Hole.

He glanced over at Abbie's cabin when he got to his own. She wasn't there. Most likely, she was still talking to Vince about Stacy's childhood. Would anything change now that Abbie's secret was out? He couldn't imagine Vince charging her for the cabin. Knowing Vince, he'd refund every penny she'd already paid. With enough money to pay the deductible herself, she wouldn't need to help at the barn anymore.

Would she still wait up for him? Ever since she started waiting up for him when he got home from the tavern, he looked forward to coming home.

The thought plagued him while he showered and changed. When he opened the door to leave for the tavern, she still wasn't back. What if Vince had offered to let her stay in Stacy's apartment and she'd already moved her stuff out of the cabin? Abbie would have told him, wouldn't she?

He got in the truck and slammed the door harder than he needed to. He was moping around like a lovestruck teenager. What did he care if Abbie stayed at the cabin or in town? It was none of his business. Besides, once Stacy got back, Abbie would forget all about him.

CHAPTER ELEVEN

ABBIE MET EMILY at the Watering Hole right after dinner Thursday night. Her new friend met her at the door with a bear hug. "Thank you for doing this. If it turns out to be too much, let me know."

"No problem. You're helping me out a lot, too."

She was thrilled at a chance to make a little extra money. And working with Noah was a plus. Emily had talked to her about the job when she gave Abbie a ride home from the hardware store on Sunday. Now that Emily was working at her grandfather's hardware store, she wanted to quit working at the tavern. Abbie had agreed to work until Freddy found a replacement, or until she went home, whichever came first.

She hadn't said anything to Noah. Last night, while the two of them had been watching stars on her porch, she almost told him. Now she was glad she didn't. She couldn't wait to see the look on his face when he came in and saw her working there.

Emily introduced her to Freddy Macias, the owner.

"Thank you so much for letting me work here." Abbie shook his hand. "I hope your wife is doing better."

"She is, thanks," the man said. "And I'm so glad that you were able to step in at such short notice."

After Freddy gave her the rundown on the basics, how to ring up items in the register, where to put the empty bottles and things like that, Emily started schooling Abbie on everything from how to keep from spilling a tray full of drinks, to what to do with drunk customers.

Abbie knew the moment Noah walked into the tavern. His presence seemed to dominate the room. Maybe it was only because she was so aware of him. She was accustomed to seeing him in western wear and a cowboy hat, but he'd shed the button-up shirt for a plain black T-shirt that stretched across his broad chest. His hair hung to his shoulders. Without his cowboy hat on, he looked less like the Marlboro Man and more like Brad Pitt in *The Legends of the Fall*.

He did a double take when he saw her. She smiled and waved at him. He took a couple of steps toward her, but Freddy called him over behind the bar.

Emily's gaze darted back and forth between the two of them. "What was that?"

Heat flooded her face. "I don't know what you're talking about."

"Yes, you do," Emily said. "Is there something going on between you and Noah?"

"No." Did she want there to be? That was an entirely different question.

Emily's eyes narrowed. "Good. Keep it that way."

Abbie's pulse quickened. "What do you have against Noah?"

"Nothing. But he lives, eats, sleeps and breathes that ranch. That's hard to compete with."

She shrugged. "Don't worry. I'm not interested in competing."

Emily shook her head. "The ranch was never enough for Colleen. Anytime someone came along and dangled something better in front of her, she took off after it. I don't know how many times she begged Noah to sell it.

Maybe that's why he's so determined to keep it. Just to prove her wrong."

"Colleen?"

"His mother."

It seemed she and Noah had more in common than she realized. They both wanted to prove someone wrong.

"I guess that's it." Emily took off her apron. "Thanks again."

Abbie gave her a quick hug. "Don't worry. I got this."

"I hope so," Emily said. She looked over Abbie's shoulder. "Do you remember what I said about handling belligerent customers?"

"Yes." Abbie nodded. "Hold your ground and don't let them intimidate you. Why?"

"'Cause here comes one now, and he looks madder than a wet hen."

She looked over her shoulder and followed Emily's gaze. Noah stood behind her, his arms crossed over his chest. She gave him a bright smile. "Hi. Would you like a drink?"

If steam could actually come out of people's ears, she would have seen it then. Noah took her by the arm and led her to the far side of the tavern.

"What are you doing here?"

Abbie pulled her arm from his grip. "Emily is training me for my new job."

His brown eyes were almost black. "You don't need a job now."

She glared at him. "Why? My finances haven't changed just because I told you who my sister was."

"Didn't Vince refund your money?"

"He tried." She crossed her arms. "I wouldn't let him."

"Why not?"

She met his hard gaze with her own. "If I wouldn't

call my father and ask for help, why would I accept help from Vince?"

"That's different. He's not giving you money."

"No. He's just not charging me money that should be going toward my sister's business." She tucked a long strand of hair behind her ear.

He said something under his breath, but Abbie couldn't hear it. She wasn't sure she wanted to.

He sucked in a deep breath and ran one hand through his hair. "Okay. Keep working at the barn, then. Just not here."

She gave him a long stare. What was his problem? They'd gotten along so well the last couple of days. She thought working with him might be fun. Apparently, she was wrong. "Don't worry. I'll stay out of your way and try not to embarrass you. You can even pretend you don't know me if you want."

"That's not what I'm worried about," he said through gritted teeth.

"Then what?"

"This is a bar." He shook his head. "Sometimes people do stupid things. Men do stupid things around beautiful women when they drink, and I'm going to have to rescue you."

Something inside her snapped. "I'm tired of people wanting to rescue me. Just stay out of my way, and I'll stay out of yours."

She stormed across the room when his words hit her. She whipped around and walked back to him. "You think I'm beautiful?" she asked, a small smirk tugging at a corner of her mouth.

He laughed for a moment, then his eyes turned somber. His fingers touched a lock of hair that was hanging in front of her shoulder. "You're beautiful inside and out."

Her heart leaped in her chest. "I thought you didn't like me."

His brows drew together. "Why do you think that?"

"Because I'm a spoiled brat who was born with a silver spoon in her mouth." She threw his own words back at him.

He gave her a lopsided smile. "You are. Don't forget stubborn, independent and naive."

"With adjectives like that, what's not to like?" She tried to keep her voice as light and teasing as his, but inside, her pulse roared like an ocean storm.

"Just don't let it go to your head." He ran one finger down the length of her arm, sending shock waves through her body. Then his face grew serious. "If anyone gives you a hard time, let me know. Don't try to play it off."

She shook her head. "I'm pretty sure I can handle myself, but I'll let you know when I can't."

He stepped closer to her, his gaze fixed on her mouth.

The ocean storm inside her turned into a full-fledged hurricane. *What was going on?* Her lips parted and she licked her lips.

His head bent toward her. "Thank you." He turned around and walked behind the bar.

THE MORNING AFTER Abbie's first shift at the tavern, Noah wasn't surprised to find Abbie standing by his truck when he came out to go to the barn. She had proven her point: she wasn't kidding around when it came to work. She wasn't going to slack off or skip one day of mucking out the stalls.

"Tired this morning?" he asked when she tried to stifle a yawn on the drive to the barn.

She folded her arms across her chest, tucking her hands underneath her arms. "A little, but I'm not quitting."

He shook his head. "You really want *stubborn* to move up to your number one adjective, don't you?"

"What's my number one right now?" Her cheeks turned a light shade of pink.

"I already told you," he said.

She pressed her lips together and raised one eyebrow, but the twinkle in her eyes said she was enjoying this new level of their relationship as much as he was.

Noah had never been this comfortable with a woman before. Abbie was easy to be around. She didn't judge him or look down on him because he wasn't as educated as she was.

"Can I ask you something?" she said as they pulled up in front of the barn.

He put the truck into Park and turned to look at her. "If I say no, are you going to ask anyway?"

"Yes."

"Then go for it." He got out of the vehicle and walked around to open her door.

"Who's the father of Emily's son?"

He raised his eyebrows. "I was kind of hoping she would confide in you, since you two are becoming such good friends."

"She hasn't volunteered the information, and I don't want to be rude and ask." She got a thoughtful look on her face. "But I get the impression she really loved him."

Noah laced his fingers together and turned his palms outward, cracking his knuckles. "If you find out who it is, let me know. I'd like to pound some sense into him."

Abbie stared at him for a moment, her eyes narrowing. "Did you ever date her?"

If he didn't know better, he'd think she was jealous. He held back a smile. "I like her a lot, but no, she's too young for me. I tried to get my brother to go out with her, but he wouldn't do it."

One look at her crestfallen face, and he knew he'd said something wrong. "What?"

Her brow puckered. "Emily's older than I am."

He reached out and took her hand in his. "I know that. But we didn't grow up together. Somehow that makes it less weird."

She squeezed his hand. "Did you date a lot of girls?"

This time, Noah definitely saw a spark of jealousy. He kind of liked it. "No. I dated a few girls, but it was never anything serious." This was the closest to a relationship he'd ever been in. And it didn't really count because they both knew it could never go beyond flirtation.

"I find that hard to believe."

"Well, surprisingly, there aren't a lot of women interested in a thirty-two-year-old high-school dropout on the verge of losing his ranch."

She laughed. "They don't know what they're missing."

He kept her hand in his as they walked into the barn. It wasn't until they'd finished feeding the horses that he remembered her gift.

"I got you something." He opened the door to the office and went to the desk.

"What is it?" She followed on his heels.

He opened the top desk drawer and pulled out a pair of gloves. "These should keep you from getting any more blisters and protect your hands from calluses."

She smiled like he'd just given her a brand-new car. She slipped on the gloves and held up her hands. "What do you think? They'll be all the rage this winter."

"Looks good," he said. "Now get to work."

"Aye-aye." She gave him a mock salute and stepped back out into the barn.

Already Abbie was much faster at mucking out the stalls. Pretty soon, she'd be able to beat him. But not yet.

She had two more stalls to do when he finished his inspection of the horses' hooves. He walked over to the stall and put his elbows on the edge of the gate. "Are you going to the hardware store this afternoon?"

"Yes." She stopped scooping to look at him. "Emily's really good with the software. She'll have that place running like clockwork soon."

He nodded. "Do you want me to pick you up on my way home from the garage?"

"No. I'll be done early today. I'll see you when it's time to go to the Watering Hole?"

"Oh, yeah. Freddy told me to give you a message."

She rolled her eyes. "If you're going to tell me he said I'm fired, you can forget it. Go to work."

He was still laughing as he pulled away. As much as he teased her about quitting the tavern, he had to admit that working with her hadn't been too bad. During the week, the tavern wasn't too busy. Mostly it was retired people who gathered to have a few drinks and gossip, but weekends would be different. He was concerned that Abbie wouldn't be ready for the Friday-and Saturday-night crowds. And he was even more concerned that he wasn't ready.

At six thirty on Friday, Noah knocked on her cabin door and waited.

"Come in!" a voice yelled from inside.

He pushed the door open and went inside, but stopped in the kitchen. "Abbie? You ready to go?"

"Just a second!" she hollered from the bathroom. "Finishing up my hair."

It wasn't like her not to be ready. She was usually waiting on him. A few minutes later, she swept into the room and Noah's mouth dropped. Her long hair was curled and hung in waves down her back. She wore denim jeans with bling on the back pockets and a pale blue tank top. Both the jeans and the shirt seemed a little too tight. She was even wearing makeup. Not much, but just enough to bring out the green in her eyes.

"What do you think?" She twirled around.

His first thought was that he was going to end up in a fight tonight. She was beautiful. He swallowed. "Why are you so dressed up?"

"Emily told me to dress up a little on Fridays and Saturdays because there would be more people from out of town." Abbie walked to the door. "She also said I would get better tips if I looked nice."

He might have to wring Emily's neck. His gaze swept over her. "Where did you get boots?"

"From the thrift store," she said. "I also got my jeans and this top there. I'm surprised at how comfortable the boots are, actually. I thought they would be heavy, but they're not."

Noah walked out behind her. He held the passenger door open for her. "You need to be careful tonight."

"What do you mean?"

He got in and started the engine.

"I mean that every unattached male in the tavern will be after you. Don't take any crap from anyone. And don't flirt too much."

She gave him a hard look. "I don't flirt. I don't even know how to."

He raised one eyebrow. "Looking like that, all you have to do is smile."

"Why, Noah Sterling," she said, "did you just give me a compliment?"

"Just remember what I said."

When they reached the end of the dirt road, Abbie clapped her hands. "I almost forgot."

He put his foot on the brake. "Do you need to go back and get something?"

"No. I wanted to tell you that a man came into the hardware store this afternoon to talk to Mr. Morgan. He was with some wild horse management program."

Noah frowned. There were several different organizations that were supposed to help with herds when they got out of control. "It's about time they decided to do something."

Abbie's eyes glinted. "The man was looking for a rancher who would be willing to take in some of the horses until they could arrange to either transport them somewhere else or sell them."

"He's not going to find a rancher around here that will volunteer to give up some of his land for that."

"That's what Mr. Morgan said." Abbie took a deep breath. "But what about you?"

"Oh, no." He shook his head. "I've got enough on my plate now. I need something that pays."

"It does." Abbie opened her purse and began rummaging through it. "The man said they pay for the feed and any repairs necessary to take them on."

She tried to hand him a business card, but he waved it away. Abbie didn't understand what was at stake.

"That's kind of a standard procedure to offset the additional costs of the herd. And it would be a great deal if I had a working ranch that pulled in a steady income. But, I don't."

A V-shaped line formed between her brows. "So, it wouldn't be a source of income?"

"No. It only covers the cost of having the horses. And

wild horses are experts at destroying fences, so it would be a full-time job keeping them in."

Understanding dawned on her face. "I see. You still need an income to make the bank payments."

"Exactly." He wanted to drop this subject. Trying to figure out how to keep his head above water was a full-time occupation, and right now he didn't want to think about it anymore.

Abbie handed him the business card anyway. "It wouldn't hurt to talk to him. Maybe he'll have some other options."

He took the card from her and dropped it into the side compartment on the door as he pulled into the parking lot of the tavern. Once they were out of the truck, Noah reminded Abbie of what he had said.

She rolled her eyes. "I'm almost twenty-four years old— I've had men make unwanted advances before. I'm pretty sure I can handle it."

His chest constricted at the thought of someone making advances on her, unwanted or not. While he knew nothing could ever happen between them, it wouldn't stop him from punching the first guy who stepped out of line.

He tried to tell himself he thought of her as a little sister, but as he watched her walk into the bar ahead of him, he knew his feelings for her were far from brotherly.

CHAPTER TWELVE

ABBIE WALKED INTO the bar ahead of Noah. He wasn't kidding, the Friday atmosphere was different from what it had been during the rest of the week. Already there were three tables with more than four people sitting at them.

"Good evening," Freddy greeted her. "I hope you're ready. It's going to be a busy night. Watch out for roaming hands and obnoxious mouths."

"Seriously?" She shook her head. "Noah lectured me about the same thing on the way over here."

"Can we help it if we worry about you?" Freddy said.

"Thank you," she said. "But I can take care of myself."

She walked into the small room behind the bar that served as the locker room for employees. She put her purse into one of the small compartments and removed the apron that hung on a hook. After tying it around her waist, she met Freddy at the cash register, and he handed her the change she needed to get started.

Noah was already behind the bar. A woman standing on the other side was chatting with him while waiting for a drink. Abbie didn't like the way the woman leaned over the bar just enough to give him a peek at her cleavage. To his credit, he never even glanced at the woman. His eyes stayed on the tap as he filled the mug.

The sudden desire to dump the woman's drink over her head took Abbie by surprise. She had never been jealous before. It was silly to be jealous now. Although they spent a lot of time flirting with each other, Noah didn't really think of her like that, and she had no business thinking of him that way. After all, she would only be here long enough to meet Stacy, and he would never leave his ranch. What kind of future would they have?

She forced her gaze away from the bar and walked across the room to greet the first table. "How is everyone doing today? Does anyone need anything?"

The young cowboy gave her a charming smile. "We're doing a whole lot better now that you're here. For now, I could use another beer, but later I might need something else." He winked at her.

She returned the smile. "The beer I can handle. You're on your own for everything else."

The other men at the table laughed and ribbed him before giving her their own orders. She walked up to the bar and told Noah what they wanted.

Noah was watching the table. "You managed that pretty well. But you know, when he gets a little more alcohol in his system, he may not want to take no for an answer."

Abbie nodded. "I have boots with pointy toes and I'm not afraid to use them."

He laughed and handed her the drinks.

The next few hours flew by. She barely had time to deliver one order when another table called for her attention. It was a good thing she was so good with math. Everyone at the tables tossed her their money and expected the correct amount of change even before she could give them their total. Soon she had a system down, and as her speed increased, so did her tips.

Abbie was putting money into the cash register and recording the orders when Freddy stopped her.

"I wanted to let you know that you're doing a great job." He nodded toward the cash register. "Most of my servers just bring the money to me or Noah and let us put it into the cash register to make the change."

Abbie's chest swelled with pride. It was the first compliment she had received about her math skills that hadn't come from her father.

"Thanks. I've always been good with numbers."

Noah leaned close to Freddy. "You're talking to a college graduate with a degree in accounting."

Freddy's eyebrows raised in surprise. "Really? I've got you working in the wrong spot then, haven't I?"

Her heart pounded. "I'd be happy to help you out with your books if you need it, or give you any tax advice you want."

"Thanks, but my current bookkeeper might be offended if I tried to replace them."

Heat flooded her neck and face. "Of course. I didn't mean that you should hire me instead of whoever you're already working with. It's just nice to get a second opinion sometimes, so I was just saying if you ever need anything—"

"Abbie," Noah interrupted her. "He was joking. His wife is the bookkeeper."

"Oh." She took a breath. "I better get back to work."

ALL NIGHT, Noah kept one eye on his work, and one eye on Abbie. So far, she had done really well. She was friendly without being overly flirtatious. Plenty of men flirted with her, and she managed to put them in their place without embarrassing them enough to make them angry.

The band started to set up, which meant things were going to get loud and rowdy. He scanned the room looking for Abbie. She was standing next to a table of hotshots. He recognized the man talking to her. His name was Shane, and he thought of himself as quite the ladies' man. He said something that made Abbie laugh and Noah bristled.

Had he ever made her laugh? She made him laugh every day, but he couldn't recall making her laugh—at least not in the way that Shane was.

"Noah! Noah." Freddy tapped him on the shoulder.

He took his gaze off Abbie and realized the mug he was filling was overflowing. He closed the tap and set the beer on the counter.

Freddy handed him a towel. "I never thought I would see the day that a woman had you so twisted up."

He dried his hands and started to clean up his mess. "You don't know what you're talking about."

"Then where is your head, *mijo*? It's certainly not on your work." Freddy's gaze followed Noah's. "You could do a lot worse than her."

"I couldn't get her on my best day," Noah said with a snort.

"And why not?" Freddy looked offended. "You're a hard worker. Honest. Trustworthy. And pretty good-looking according to my daughters."

"I'm also a high-school dropout and a rancher on the verge of losing his ranch." His eyes lingered on Abbie for another moment. "She's a college graduate from a rich family. There is nothing I can offer her that she couldn't have any time she wanted it."

Freddy clapped him on his shoulder. "Love, *mijo*. You can't buy love."

What did Noah know about love? His dad had bailed on him. His mother was so desperate for love she chased every cowboy who looked at her twice. When he was a teenager, the girls wouldn't give him the time of day. At least not the ones he was interested in. Those girls wanted a man who could give them a future. He was not that man. Not then. Not now.

The band started and the atmosphere was electric. More than once he saw a man stand up and attempt to get Abbie out on the dance floor. She managed to shrug them all off without offending them. But with each offer she had, Noah's patience decreased just a little.

He noticed that for as many admiring looks as she was getting from the men, she was getting an equal number of glares from the women. One thing about small towns: the women didn't like competition. And Abbie took competition to a whole new level. At a small table in one corner he noticed Kelsey Barton and Cora Lancaster leaning close to each other and whispering. Every so often one of them glanced over at Abbie.

While he had never been the object of either of their affections, he had seen the two women in action and knew what they were capable of. He didn't want Abbie to have to experience what small-town jealousy could do.

The next time she came up to the bar to get drinks, he leaned over and said to her, "You need to be careful."

Abbie groaned. "I told you, I don't need you to protect me."

"It's not the men you need to worry about." He nodded at Kelsey's table. "Women around here can be pretty catty. And there are some tigers out there who are dying to sharpen their claws on you. I don't want to see you get caught up in their games."

Her mouth dropped open. "Why would they have a problem with me? I'm not leading anyone on. And I'm not interested in any of their men."

He clicked his tongue at her. She had a lot to learn about small-town life. "You don't have to do any of that. You're young, beautiful and new in town. That's all that is needed to have every male in this place interested in you and every female hating on you."

"That's silly," she said. "I haven't done anything to any of them."

"I'm just warning you to watch your back."

"I appreciate that, but I have a little more faith in wom-ankind than that."

"I hope you're right," he murmured as she placed the drinks on her tray and hurried away.

Noah kept a close eye on her the rest of the night. She made a point of stopping and talking more to the women at the tables than the men. Most of them responded well to her, although there were some eye rolls and chuckles between a few of them when she left the table. Kelsey and Cora didn't even try to be friendly to her.

He relaxed as the night went on, although every time he saw Kelsey and Abbie exchanging words, he tensed up. Kelsey was walking off the dance floor as Abbie walked by. Noah saw her exchange a glance with Cora and knew something was up.

Kelsey moved over and bumped Abbie with her shoulder. He couldn't hear what was being said, but he moved to the edge of the bar. If Kelsey said anything to upset Abbie, he'd throw her out. Before he could take another step, Kelsey tossed her hair over her shoulder and sashayed away.

Abbie stepped up to the bar. "I need three beers and a shot of tequila."

Noah nodded toward Kelsey's table. "What was that about?"

"Nothing." She shrugged. "She was just welcoming me to town."

Her answer didn't put him at ease. He didn't relax until Kelsey and Cora got up and left a little while later.

The crowd thinned out, and the band prepared to wrap up. It appeared they'd made it through the night without an incident.

Abbie balanced a tray full of drinks with both hands as she weaved around tables and people on her way to deliver the last drinks of the night.

Without warning, two men at the pool table started fighting. One man shoved the other one, who stumbled backward right into Abbie. Her tray went flying, and the people at the table closest to her got drenched in beer.

Abbie looked horrified. "I am so sorry," she said. She ran to the back and grabbed towels, then started cleaning up the mess.

As soon as the first shove happened, Noah picked up the phone and called the sheriff's office. Freddy's rule was to never get in the middle of drunk customers when they were fighting. Noah would stop a fight if he had to, but usually, a sheriff's deputy could get there before too much damage was caused.

Apparently, no one told Abbie about that rule. She waved her hands and tried to stop them. One of the guys picked up a chair and hit the other guy with it. He stumbled into Abbie, knocking her into a table. Glass shattered as the table fell over.

Noah hung up the phone and leaped over the bar. He grabbed one of the men from behind and threw him halfway across the room. When the man charged at him, he had no choice except to defend himself. One uppercut to the jaw and the man fell to the floor in a heap.

Sirens wailed in the distance, and everyone started scrambling to get out. Noah rushed over to Abbie. He pulled the table off her.

"You're bleeding." He ran his fingers over her scalp.

Her green eyes clouded with confusion. "What happened?"

His heart raced as he looked for the source of the blood. Head wounds tended to bleed a lot even if they weren't serious, but until he could find the wound, he wouldn't know.

He placed a towel over the area the blood seemed to be coming from and held it tight.

"She okay?" Sheriff Tedford appeared beside them.

"Yes."

"No."

He and Abbie spoke at the same time. "She might need stitches."

"Did she get hit?"

Abbie glared at Noah. "I can speak for myself. No, I didn't get hit. I was too close while they were fighting and got knocked down. That's all."

He nodded. "Do you think the two of you can come by tomorrow to give me a statement?"

"Sure," Noah said. "I just want to get this bleeding stopped right now."

Abbie pushed his hand away and felt her scalp. She parted her hair, exposing the cut. "Can you see it?"

He signed with relief. The cut didn't look too bad. "It's small, but it may be deep. We should probably go to Springerville Hospital to check."

"No." She pleaded with her eyes. "My parents will freak out if they see another hospital visit on their insurance."

"If it hasn't stopped bleeding by the time Frank leaves, I'm taking you in."

The bleeding stopped, but it didn't keep Noah from worrying that she might have a concussion.

He left Abbie sitting on a chair and went to talk to his boss. "I'm really sorry about this."

Freddy waved it off. "It happens. I'm just glad no one was seriously hurt. How's Abbie?"

"She says she's fine, but I'd like to take her home to

make sure." He looked around the bar for the first time since the fight began. "I'll come back in the morning and clean up."

"Don't worry about it." Freddy was already picking up a broom. "I'll take care of this. Take Abbie home and make sure she's okay."

Abbie was waiting for him by the door when he turned around. He wrapped his arm around her and half walked, half carried her to the truck. He opened the passenger's-side door and lifted her into the seat.

After he got in on his side and shut the door, she laid her head on his shoulder. "Let's go home," she mumbled.

Home. His pulse thrummed as quickly as a humming-bird's wings. For the last ten years, he'd been so busy try-ing to save his home that he hadn't given much thought to what kind of home it should be. He gazed down at the woman leaning against him and he knew what he wanted. He also knew, without a doubt, that he could never have it.

CHAPTER THIRTEEN

Abbie OPENED HER eyes and felt like her head was about to split open. Her hand went to her scalp, but all she could feel was matted hair. She threw the covers back and rolled out of bed. She looked down and realized she was still in the same clothes she'd been wearing yesterday. At least she hadn't fallen asleep with her boots on.

A soft sound came from the living room. She walked over to the sofa and looked down to see Noah sleeping soundly. Her heart sped up just a little as the events from the night before flooded back.

He had carried her from the truck into the cabin and gently pulled off her boots before covering her up. She vaguely remembered being woken up several times throughout the night. Each time he woke her, he said something about making sure she didn't have a concussion.

She took the opportunity to stare at him while he was asleep. He had told her she was beautiful, but nothing could be more beautiful than he was. Her fingers itched to brush a strand of hair away from his face, but she didn't want to disturb him.

As quietly as she could, she made coffee and started breakfast. He sat up and stretched. She poured him a cup of coffee and carried it to him. "Good morning."

He took a long drink from the cup. "How long have you been up? How's your head feeling?"

"It's still pounding, but I don't see spots in front of my eyes anymore." She sat down on the sofa next to him.

"I still think we should take you to the doctor. You probably have a concussion."

She snorted. "What can the doctor do for me if I do? Nothing. Why waste the time and money when we don't have to?"

Noah stood up and stretched again. "I better get to the barn and feed the horses."

Abbie walked over to the stove to check on the food she was making. "We can go after breakfast. It's almost ready."

"We?" Noah shook his head. "*We* are not going anywhere. *I* am going to feed the horses and *you* are going to stay here and relax."

Abbie stirred the potatoes in the pan. She wanted to argue with him. She needed to argue with him. But her head was starting to spin a little, and she knew there was no way she could clean the stalls today. "Fine, but at least wait until after you've had breakfast."

"I'm the one who should be making you breakfast, not the other way around."

She handed him the spatula. "Okay. You can finish cooking."

Noah took the spatula and started to stir the potatoes around. Abbie stepped back and watched him for a minute. "You look right at home in the kitchen."

"I should. I started cooking for my brother and myself when I was ten."

Abbie nudged him out of the way and took her spatula back. "I was just kidding about you finishing up breakfast. Why did you have to do the cooking? Where was your mother?"

He leaned on the counter with his elbows, staying close to her. "She wasn't around much. Sometimes she disappeared for months at a time and Grandpa was sure she was dead in a ditch somewhere. Then she would show up again."

"Where did she go?" She couldn't imagine a mother leaving her children for that length of time.

"We stopped asking after a while." He got two plates out of the cupboard and placed them next to the stove. "My mom hated the ranch. She hated being tied down. She hated being a mother."

"But not you. She couldn't hate you." Abbie's heart hurt for how his twelve-year-old self must have felt. First their father abandoned them, and then, for all intents and purposes, so did their mother.

"No. She told us how much she loved us every time she came home. But sometimes I wonder if it was just because she knew Grandpa was leaving the ranch to us and not to her. She wanted to make sure she had some kind of influence over us when that happened."

Abbie opened the refrigerator and removed a carton of eggs. While she scrambled a couple of them together, she wondered how her life would have been if her biological parents hadn't died. Would her mother have been doting and kind, or would she have been more like Noah's mom?

"What happened when you got the ranch?"

Noah shook his head. "She tried everything she could to convince us to sell it."

Abbie put the food on plates and they sat down at the table. Something Emily said came back to her. She'd said that when it came to Noah, no one could ever compete with the ranch. When they were done eating, Abbie took the plates to the sink.

She turned around and leaned against the counter. "The girls in this town must be nuts to let you get away from them."

His face got a pained look for a moment. "Most of the girls who grew up here have one goal—to get out of this little town. I'm never leaving, so that takes care of those women. The rest of them might want to stay, but they want someone who can take care of them and buy them things and take them places. They know I'll never be able to do that."

"Why would anyone think you couldn't take care of them? You take care of me all the time. As for the rest of it, I don't believe all women are as shallow as you think. I'm sure there are lots of women around here who would love to have a man like you."

"I didn't even finish high school, Abbie." He rubbed the back of his neck with his hand. "I'll never be able to afford the finer things in life. While some women are okay with simple things, they still like to think things could be different in the future."

Anger swelled in her chest. Is that really what he thought of himself? That he wasn't good enough for anyone? "So that's it? You're just planning on being alone for the rest of your life?"

He nodded. "I've never planned on life working out any other way."

She reached down and took his hand. She ran her fingers slightly over his callused palm. It was a reminder of how hard he worked. Suddenly, she felt very inadequate. "Are you okay with that?"

"I used to be." His brown eyes stared into hers, and she could barely breathe.

"But not now?" Her voice was barely a whisper.

He lifted one hand and traced her jawline with the backs of his fingers. He licked his lips. "Lately I've been wondering what it would be like to have something more."

"More?" Her gaze focused on his lips. "Like what?"

"Like this." His head bent down and his lips covered hers.

The kiss was soft and gentle at first, but soon it was not enough. She wrapped her arms around him and poured everything she felt into that kiss. She wanted to tell him that she wanted nothing more than who he was.

He broke the kiss but kept her trapped in his arms. "I have to go feed the horses."

She was afraid if he left, she wouldn't see him again for the rest of the day. "What are you going to do after that? Do you have to go to the garage today?"

He tucked a piece of her hair behind her ear. "It's Saturday. I don't work there on Saturday. I need to go out to my ranch today. Would you like to come?"

"Yes." Her heart sang with the knowledge that he wanted to spend the day with her, too.

His brow furrowed. "How does your head feel now? Are you dizzy at all?"

She'd forgotten all about her headache. "I'm fine," she said. "Never better, actually."

"Good. I'll pick you up in a little while. If you start feeling sick or dizzy, don't try to do anything. I'll help you when I get back."

"Okay. I promise. Just hurry."

FOR THE FIRST time in his life, Noah took shortcuts with his work. He fed the horses and put them out in the pasture, but he only cleaned up the worst portions of the stalls before throwing down new straw. Time moved slowly without Abbie there to help him. Even with him taking shortcuts, it was almost noon before he finished.

He was nervous about letting Abbie see his ranch. Would she like it? Would she be disappointed? Most importantly, did she think it was someplace she could ever live?

Before picking her up, he went to his own cabin so he

could shower, shave and change. As he was climbing the stairs to her cabin, his stomach was tied in knots. He felt like a kid going on his first date. He hadn't gone on that many. None of the girls he went to high school with were allowed to date him after he quit school. It didn't matter that he dropped out in order to take care of his grandfather while he was sick and to work to support the family. Their parents thought only delinquents quit school.

She opened the door before he could knock. She'd showered and braided her hair. "Hi. Are you hungry? Do you want something to eat before we leave?"

As if on cue, his stomach growled.

"I'll take that as a yes." She left the door open and went to the kitchen. "I make a really mean grilled cheese sandwich."

He was anxious to get to the ranch, but his stomach won out. "I haven't had a grilled cheese in years."

Noah leaned against the counter while she sliced two pieces of bread off the homemade loaf. "How long have you been making your own bread?"

"Since I was ten." She reached into the refrigerator and took out the butter and sliced cheese. "I wasn't allowed to do sports or anything like that, but my mom did let me take some classes at the country club. I took a baking class and I was hooked."

He'd already tasted her rolls, and he imagined her bread would be just as good.

"How often do you go to the ranch?"

"I try to go every Saturday. But sometimes people want to go on trail rides, so I have to stay close to the campground. I haven't actually been out there in a couple of weeks."

Her nose scrunched. "Why don't you just live at the ranch and drive here?"

"I thought about it," he said. "But with the way gas prices are going up, and as much gas as my old truck uses, I decided it would be better to stay here."

She flipped the sandwich over in the pan. "How does the ranch manage if you live here?"

"Easy. There's nothing to take care of there." Saying the words out loud ripped his heart in two.

"Yet."

He turned his head to stare at her. "Sorry, what?"

She wrapped his sandwich in a paper towel and handed it to him. "I said 'yet.' There's nothing to take care of *yet*. But there will be."

His heart felt like it would burst in his chest. She believed in him. Other than his brother, no one had believed in him before.

"Come on." She waited for him at the door. "You can eat on the road. I want to see this ranch."

Noah opened the door for her and Tom jumped in, too. He waited for the cat to hiss at her again, but he curled up in a ball between them. Even Tom was completely under her spell.

When they got close to town, both of their cell phones started to buzz. He pulled over on the side of the road to read the text messages. "I got a text from Stacy."

Her eyes brightened. "You did? Are they coming back soon?"

"Not yet." He showed her the message.

Return home has been delayed. Bringing home a surprise. Keep my sister there and tell her I can't wait to meet her.

Abbie squealed. "She really does want to meet me, then."

He raised his eyebrows. "Did you think we were lying?"

"No." She wrinkled her brow. "For the last year, I was too scared to look for her because I was afraid she wouldn't want to know me."

He couldn't imagine anyone not wanting to know her. Before he could say anything, though, her phone started ringing.

Her expression clouded when she looked at the screen. "Hi, Mom."

His truck was really loud, so he turned the engine off so she could hear. While she talked to her parents, a whole new set of doubts crept into his mind. Her parents wouldn't approve of him at all. What parents would? He wouldn't want his daughter to marry a man with no real job, no income and no future.

His fingers gripped the steering wheel. *Marry?* Why had that word slipped into his thoughts? He couldn't afford to pay off his ranch. How would he afford a wife?

He was so lost in his thoughts, he didn't hear Abbie hang up the phone.

"Noah." She rubbed his arm with her hand.

He pulled himself out of his daze. Her eyes were glassy, and he knew she was trying not to cry.

He put one arm around her and pulled her in tight. "It's okay to miss them. Even if you don't agree with them all the time, it's okay to miss them."

"I know." She swallowed. "Every time I talk to them, I feel they're more and more disappointed in me."

"Because you haven't come home yet?"

She nodded. "My mom seems to think that me wanting to find my biological sister means that I think she's a terrible mom."

"That doesn't make any sense." He turned the ignition and got back on the road.

"That's what I told her." She shook her head. "But she

insists that if she had been a good enough mom, I wouldn't feel this need to find Stacy."

"She's probably scared of losing you." He understood that fear. How long would it be until he lost her?

THEY STAYED ON the highway and drove past Coronado. Abbie had never walked past the junction between the highway and main street, so it was all new to her. Just past the town limits, donkeys grazed in a field. One of the donkeys had the longest hair she'd ever seen.

"I've never seen a donkey like that." She pointed it out to Noah.

"It's called a Poitou donkey." He pointed to a sign ahead: Coronado Donkey Sanctuary.

They passed an RV park, and a little while later a sign advertising a lodge. The land began to look less and less like the mountains around Coronado. The trees changed from pine and aspen to cedar and mesquite Finally, Noah slowed down and turned onto a dirt road.

"Look!" Abbie pointed to the hillside. "Are those elk?"

He slowed the truck down to almost a crawl, and she opened the camera app on her phone. "They're huge."

"Don't you have elk in New York?"

"No. They've tried to bring them back a few times, but so far it hasn't worked." The closest she'd ever come to wildlife were the raccoons and deer that hung around the lodge they rented in the Catskill Mountains every summer.

They turned onto another dirt road. Abbie sat up as a house and outbuildings came into sight. The house was built of hewn logs and had a wraparound porch. Green shingles on the roof stood out in contrast to the red-tinted logs. Rosebushes flanked the steps leading up to the porch.

A barn, larger than the one at the campground, stood not too far from the house and was surrounded by several smaller buildings. At one time, this had been a huge productive ranch.

Noah pulled up the gravel driveway and parked the truck. As soon as she opened the door, Tom jumped out and ran to the barn. She walked to the front of the house and looked at it. "Noah, you live here by yourself? This is so big."

"When my great-grandfather added on to the existing house, he expected to raise a dozen children. Most of them boys, of course. But they were only able to have three children. My grandfather was the only one who lived to adulthood."

She could just imagine the home filled with children. At Christmas it would be large enough to have family come in and stay. She couldn't imagine a more perfect home. "You have to show me the kitchen."

Noah laughed and took her hand to lead her to the door. He didn't let go of her hand to unlock the door. Or when they stepped into the giant entryway. Double doors opened up on each side. He took her into the living area first. The room was cozy even if the furniture was old and worn. A large fireplace was the centerpiece of the room. Faded carpet protected the wooden floor, and a staircase was on the far side.

They went back through to the double doors on the opposite side of the entryway. A formal dining table stretched in front of multiple picture windows. One wall was decorated with shelves that held decorative plates.

Abbie stopped and looked at them but was too afraid to touch them. "Did these belong to your grandmother?"

He shrugged. "Probably. They've been there as long as I can remember."

The house was like a museum. Everywhere she turned,

remnants of an older way of life greeted her. Bringing in anything modern would ruin the home.

A swinging door led from the dining room into the kitchen. Noah held the door open for her. Except for the refrigerator and stove, she felt like she'd stepped back in time. The old wood-burning stove was still in one corner of the kitchen. She rushed over to it and ran her hands over the metal.

"I can't believe you actually grew up here. This place is like a dream."

"You don't think it's too far away from civilization?"

She shook her head. "I think it's perfect."

A funny look came across his face, and she was afraid she'd said something wrong. "What is it?"

"You're the first person who's been able to appreciate the house for what it is."

"I don't believe that." She walked around the kitchen some more. "I can't believe that you haven't sold off some of this stuff, though." She pointed to the wood-burning stove. "Do you know how much some of this stuff is worth? Some of the dishes in that dining room are probably worth more than your truck."

Immediately, she knew she had said the wrong thing. Noah's eyes, which were a soft brown a little while ago, darkened. The muscles in his jaw flexed.

"Now you sound like my mother. Every time things got hard, she wanted to sell off pieces of the place. Who knows how much stuff she snuck out of here when no one was looking?" His tone was as cool as his eyes.

Abbie toyed with her locket. "I'm sorry. I didn't mean to suggest that you should sell any of this. I'm glad you didn't. It belongs here, with you, with this house. But most people wouldn't hesitate to sell it off when they needed extra cash."

He relaxed a little bit, and Abbie let out a sigh of relief. She tried to lighten the mood. "You know what I think we should do now? Those rosebushes in the front looked really thirsty. Can I water them?"

"Sure. You can do that while I check on the barn."

Together they walked back through the house and outside. He didn't hold her hand this time. She tried not to read too much into it, but she couldn't help but feel that he was holding back again.

He pulled a long hose over and connected it to the outside faucet. Then he left her to water the flowers while he walked out to the barn.

She had just finished watering the roses when Noah came back. "Are there any animals left here?" she asked him.

"Not domestic ones." Noah nodded toward the barn. "There are a few barn owls and some feral cats that we were never able to tame. But the cattle and chickens have been gone for a while. Both the horses are at Whispering Pines."

They walked around a little bit longer before finally heading back to the truck. As they drove away, she watched Noah's face. It never showed any signs of emotion. Now she could see why he was working so hard to hang on to the ranch. But she was also a realist. The longer he left the place vacant, the harder it would be to bring it back to what it once was.

She watched the house fade in the rearview mirror. What would happen to Noah if he lost the place? She had the feeling that he would fade away, too.

CHAPTER FOURTEEN

THE NEXT MORNING things felt awkward. Abbie had hoped that it was mostly her imagination, but she could sense that Noah's guard was back up.

She hadn't gone to the Watering Hole the night before. Emily heard about what happened and insisted on working for her. She waited up for Noah, but when he got home, he just waved and told her to go to bed.

On the surface, everything seemed fine. While they cleaned the barn, Noah was friendly. He moved more quickly than usual and pushed her to do the same. More than once she caught him checking his watch. But when he dropped her off at the cabin afterward, she knew for sure her fears were not unfounded.

Noah parked his truck in the usual spot, but he didn't shut off the engine. Before she got out he said, "I can't give you a ride to the hardware store today. I have some things I have to take care of."

Alarm bells rang in her ears. "Okay. I understand."

Then he drove away. With every step she took toward her cabin, she felt like she was walking away from him. Why had she said anything about selling items at the ranch? That had to be what upset him. He had been fine until then.

Her emotions were all in a jumble. Partly from Noah being upset with her and partly from yesterday's conversation with her mother. She had told her mother everything about her life in Coronado. Of course, she'd been horrified to learn that her daughter was spending every morning mucking out stalls. Every conversation with her parents was a reminder that her real life wasn't in Arizona. At some point, she had to figure out what she was going to do with her life and move on.

She stopped to look at the calendar hanging on the wall. Tomorrow would mark two weeks since she arrived in Coronado, but it felt like she'd been there forever. Her car would be ready in another two weeks. Then what would she do? There was still no word from Stacy about her return date. How long was she expected to stay? She took her time getting ready to go to town. She wasn't meeting Mr. Morgan and Emily at the hardware store until after they got out of church, so there was no rush. She kept glancing out the window toward Noah's cabin. Where was he? He didn't go to work at the garage because it was closed on Sundays.

There was still no sign of Noah at the cabin when Abbie got ready to walk over the ridge to town. She didn't see Mr. Morgan's pickup at the hardware store. He must not be out of church yet, so she stopped at the market to get a soda.

Vince looked up from behind the cash register and smiled. "We haven't seen you in here for a while. I thought you'd snuck back to New York without telling us."

A twinge of guilt hit her. She'd thought about it. "I've been really busy. Have you heard from Stacy lately?"

"Talked to her yesterday. Sounds like she won't be here till the end of the month."

That was about the same time her car would be done. It was perfect timing. She could spend a few days with her sister and go back to New York. That was the entire purpose for her trip here. So why did the end of September hover over her like a giant doomsday clock?

She grabbed a paper cup from the dispenser and filled it with ice and soda. As she was checking out, the two older ladies from the post office walked in.

"Good afternoon, Abbie," the sisters said in unison.

The pink-haired sister squeezed Abbie's hand. "We've been expecting you for tea."

Her sister smiled. "We usually have tea on Monday, but Margaret and I have eye doctor appointments tomorrow, so we're doing it today. Will you be able to make it, dear?"

Abbie had forgotten all about their previous invitation. "I wish I could, but I'm on my way to the hardware store to help Mr. Morgan."

"Well, isn't that wonderful," the other sister said. "We haven't spoken to Denny in ages. How about we bring the tea to you?"

Abbie faked a smile. "Great. I look forward to it."

She left the market and walked across the parking lot to the hardware store. Mr. Morgan's pickup was now parked out front. "Hi, Mr. Morgan."

The man was sitting behind the counter reading the newspaper. "I didn't hear that rattletrap of a truck outside."

"I walked today. Noah had something to do."

Mr. Morgan slid his glasses down his nose and looked at her over the rims. "Trouble in paradise?"

"Everything's fine." She walked behind the counter and woke up the computer screen. "Did you enter the ledger numbers this weekend?"

He folded the newspaper and set it on the counter before coming to stand next to her. "I did, but the numbers at the bottom aren't coming out right."

Abbie opened the ledger book and went over the numbers he entered. For fifty years, he'd entered every transaction into a ledger by hand, she was surprised that he was taking to the computer so quickly. She suspected Emily had been giving him lessons.

The simple accounting program she had installed was similar to the ledger he did by hand. If she could teach him to enter the information into the computer, then Emily could use a different software program to run reports, update his taxes and order inventory. She just hoped that he would continue to use it when she left.

She scanned the numbers. "Everything looks good. Which numbers did you think were wrong?"

A few minutes later, Emily walked in, pushing Wyatt in a stroller. "Hi, Abbie. Hello, Grandpa." Emily had set up a play area for her son behind the counter. She put Wyatt in the playpen and handed him a toy before coming over to the computer.

Mr. Morgan busied himself with entering numbers into the computer, while Abbie put the software on her personal laptop into training mode. She gave Emily some numbers to practice with.

"I ran into the Reed sisters at the market earlier," Abbie told Emily. "They're bringing tea over this afternoon."

"Here?" Emily's eyes widened and she glanced at her grandfather. "This should be entertaining."

"Why?"

"You'll see." Emily chuckled and went back to work on the computer.

AT TWO O'CLOCK on the dot, Margaret and Edith Reed knocked on the door to the hardware store.

"Here we go." Emily chuckled and went to unlock the door.

The sisters hurried inside. Margaret was carrying a picnic basket and Edith carried a box.

Mr. Morgan scowled at them. "What in tarnation are you two busybodies doing here?"

Abbie looked at the man in shock. She had never seen him be unpleasant to anyone. Grumpy, yes.

Edith placed her box on the counter and opened it to reveal well-packed teacups and saucers. She pointed a finger at Mr. Morgan. "Don't you start your nonsense with me, Denny Morgan. Your Opal had tea with us every Monday. Now these young ladies want to join us but you won't let them off work, so we're coming to them."

"That's right," Margaret added. "We even brought your favorite finger sandwiches. So, sit down and enjoy them, you old goat."

His eyes opened wide. "Cucumber and tomatoes?"

"What else?" Margaret placed some sandwiches on a saucer and slid them in front of him.

Mr. Morgan picked up his plate and carried it into his office at the back of the store. Probably so he could eat in silence.

Edith smiled. "Let that be a lesson to you ladies. Even the grumpiest man can be tamed with his favorite food."

Emily pulled some extra bar stools over for the sisters to sit on while Abbie moved the laptop to make room on the counter. As soon as Abbie sat down in the chair next to Emily, the two old women began bombarding them both with questions. Most of the questions for her seemed to revolve around Noah, while Emily's questions were about her son.

"Emily, it's a shame you weren't at church this morning. Jessica Kilpatrick's grandson is visiting. He's such a handsome young man." Edith took a sip of her tea.

Margaret nodded. "Yes. He's about your age, too."

Emily shot Abbie a pleading look.

Edith sat her teacup on the saucer. "He's going to be

at the community center for square dancing lessons on Wednesday. He needs a partner so I told him that you—"

"Wednesday?" Abbie interrupted. "I'm sorry. Emily is driving me to Springerville on Wednesday. I need to pick up a few things, and my car isn't out of the shop yet."

"Why can't Noah drive you?" Margaret leaned forward in her chair. "You two have been spending a lot of time together."

Abbie looked the older woman straight in the eye so she would hopefully take the hint. "He's really busy at the campground right now."

"That boy works too much," Edith said.

"Yes," Margaret agreed. She gave Abbie a pointed look. "You know, he took care of his grandfather for years."

"And his brother," Edith added. "Until he up and deserted Noah, just like their parents did."

"Luke didn't desert him," Emily said. "Noah told him to chase his dream before it was too late."

Margaret nodded. "Sounds just like something Noah would do."

Abruptly, Emily stood up. "I'm going to check on my grandfather."

The sisters exchanged glances with each other. Edith leaned close to her sister. "I do believe we touched a nerve."

"I believe you're right, sister." Margaret nodded.

A few moments later, Emily reappeared, carrying the plate her grandfather had carried to his office.

The two women stood up and began packing up. Edith gave Abbie a quick hug. "Thank you both for keeping two old women company this afternoon."

"Thank you for the tea and cookies." Emily went to unlock the doors for them.

Edith hugged Emily again. "When you get time, swing

by the house. We have a box of baby blankets and clothes that we've been knitting just for you."

"Thank you." Emily hugged her back, then opened the doors for them.

After they left, it seemed very quiet. "Thanks for helping me out." Emily shook her head.

"I don't know," Abbie said. "I feel kind of guilty. What if I just caused you to miss out on meeting the love of your life?"

"This is the love of my life." She picked up Wyatt and blew raspberries against his cheek.

"Is it safe to come out?" Mr. Morgan stuck his head out of his office. When the girls nodded, he walked back into the store, shaking his head. "I never cared much for those two gals, but my Opal thought the world of them."

Abbie could understand why people either loved them or hated them. "Now that the party's over, let's get back to work."

It was after five o'clock when Abbie finally made her way back to the cabin. She wasn't scheduled to work at the Watering Hole tonight. Would she be able to spend the entire evening with Noah? Would he even want to?

Her hopes sank when she saw that Noah's truck wasn't at the cabin. Was he avoiding her? She walked up the steps to her cabin and paused to unlock the door.

"Excuse me." A woman's voice stopped her just as she was about to go inside.

Abbie turned around to see a middle-aged woman sitting on Noah's porch. The woman's hair was too red to be natural, but it had been professionally styled so Abbie had to assume it was intentional. From the top of her head to the tip of her manicured toes, the woman was immaculate.

Abbie assumed she was a guest at the campground. "Yes? Are you looking for the maintenance man?"

"I'm looking for Noah."

"He's not here right now, but if you let me know your cabin number, I'll send him over when he gets back."

The woman shook her head. "I'm not a guest. I'm his mother."

"Oh." Abbie walked over to her and held out her hand. "I'm Abbie. A friend of Noah's."

"Friend?" She shook Abbie's hand. "I'm Colleen."

"I don't know when Noah will be back, but you're welcome to wait in my cabin if you like."

Colleen accepted and walked into the cabin with Abbie. After everything Noah had said about his mother, Abbie hadn't expected to like her. But after an hour of chatting with her, Abbie was surprised by how personable she found Colleen to be.

A little after six o'clock someone knocked on her door. She knew it wasn't Noah because his truck would have made itself known a mile away. Probably someone who was actually looking for the maintenance man, she thought. She opened the door and Noah filled the doorway.

"Surprise!" He stepped back to reveal her car parked in the driveway.

"My car!" Abbie stepped outside, closing the door behind her. "I thought it wasn't going to be ready for another two weeks!"

Noah shrugged. "Bear let me know yesterday that the last part had come in early. So, I got there as soon as I could and worked on it all day so it could be finished."

She covered her heart with her hands and smiled at him. "That's why you couldn't wait to get away from me this morning?"

"I never want to get away from you," he handed her the keys. "I was thinking we have the night off. Let's go for a ride. Maybe go watch the sunset at Big Lake?"

She bit her lip and glanced at her cabin door. "I would love to, but I have a surprise for you, too."

"Really?" He pulled her close and gave her a quick kiss. "What is it?"

"Hello, Noah." Colleen had stepped out onto the porch and stood next to the door. She raised a manicured hand and waved at her son.

His eyes sparked with anger and darted between Abbie and his mother. "What are you doing here, Mom?"

Colleen smiled. "Can't a mother come see her boy?"

"No." He crossed his arms. "You only come around when you need something. So what do you need?"

"Nothing." Colleen pressed her lips together. "I went out to the ranch, but no one was there. I had to find out where you were from Luke. You could've told me you were staying here."

"Why? You never tell me where you are."

"That's not true," she said. "I told you I live in Snow-flake now. I even wrote the address in your address book."

"That was two years ago."

Colleen nodded. "And I'm still in the same spot."

"That's a first," Noah muttered.

"I don't need anything, but I would like to talk to you about something."

The tension between mother and son was palpable. Abbie hadn't always gotten along with her parents but this was a different level than anything she'd experienced.

Noah glanced at her. Was he wanting time alone with his mother? Or was it a plea for support? She couldn't tell.

She opened the door to the cabin. "Dinner's almost ready. Come inside whenever you're ready."

Nodding at them, she went inside and closed the door, giving them privacy, if they wanted it.

The murmured voices on the porch were too low for her

to make out words, but at least Noah's voice didn't sound angry. And he couldn't leave. His truck wasn't here and he'd already given her the keys to her car.

A moment later, Colleen came inside.

"Where's Noah?" Her heart rate jumped. He wasn't above walking to the barn if he needed to get away.

"He got a phone call. Is there anything I can do to help?" Relief flooded through her.

"You can set the table for me. The meatloaf will be done any minute."

Everything was on the table by the time Noah entered the cabin. He was grinning.

Abbie raised one eyebrow. "Good phone call?"

"Yes." He took her face in his hands and kissed her. "And I have you to thank for it."

"Well? What was it?" She joined Colleen at the table and waited for him to sit down as well.

He almost bounced with excitement. "I called the number on the card you gave me."

"The one about the wild horses?" She picked up a bowl of mashed potatoes and handed it to Colleen. "You said it wouldn't help you."

Noah sat down at the table. "I decided you were right and it wouldn't hurt to look into it. It's a different program than what I thought. If I can get the contract, it'll pay enough to take care of the bank loan. I'm not sure if anything will come of it but it can't hurt to meet with him, right?"

"I think it's a good idea to keep all your options open. When do you meet with him?"

"Tomorrow morning. He's only in town for a few days. He's interviewing a couple of other ranchers, too, but my ranch is the only one with enough space available for what they need."

Colleen passed Noah the mashed potatoes. Her expression was tight. "Who are you meeting with?"

Noah gave her an exasperated look. "Gerald Thomas, from the White Mountain Wild Horse Management Program."

Colleen's face paled. "That's a great program."

"I hope so." Noah plopped a spoonful of potatoes on his plate. "Before my phone rang, you said you had some good news you wanted to share."

Colleen paused. "Um… I got a promotion at work."

"That's it?" Noah looked skeptical.

She shrugged. "I get a week's vacation and thought you might want to go to Nashville with me to see Luke."

"I'll think about it." He picked up a plate with Abbie's rolls. "You have to try these. Abbie makes them from scratch."

The tension in Abbie's shoulders relaxed a little. The phone call seemed to have put Noah in a good enough mood that he was able to relax a little and enjoy dinner.

Colleen offered to help Abbie with the dishes, but Noah stepped in. "I'll help Abbie. You go ahead and go back to my cabin. I'll be there in a little while."

Abbie washed the dishes and Noah dried them.

"We didn't get to go on that drive," Noah said as he put the last dish away. "How about driving me down to pick up my truck?"

"Sure."

"If we hurry, we can make it to the market before it closes and rent a movie."

Abbie frowned. "I didn't know they had rentals."

"They have a pretty good selection, but they get picked over pretty quick." Noah held open the door for her.

She caught Noah glancing at his cabin as they walked

toward her car. "Do you really want to watch a movie, or are you trying to avoid your mother?"

He opened the driver's-side door for her. "No harm in killing two birds with one stone, is there?"

THE NEXT MORNING, Noah shut the door to his mother's bedroom. He made his coffee and heated up a couple of breakfast burros before putting on his boots and heading outside.

Abbie was waiting by his truck. "Your car is finished," he said. "You don't have to clean the barn anymore."

"I wanted to talk to you about that." She leaned against the truck. "The car may be done, but someone had to pay Bear for it. My guess is it was you."

She reached into her front pocket and pulled out a wad of cash. "It's not enough, but by the time I leave, I should have it all for you."

He eyed the money in her outstretched hand, but didn't touch it. "Where did you get that?"

"It's my tips from the tavern."

"I don't want your money."

Her brow furrowed. "But you paid for my deductible. I owe you five hundred dollars."

"You've earned every bit of that," he said. "By taking over the stalls, I've been able to get to the garage at least three hours earlier than usual. Instead of using that extra money to pay you for working, I put it straight toward your car. Would you feel better if I had paid you cash and let you pay Bear yourself?"

Her face scrunched as she thought about it for a moment. She opened the door to the truck and climbed in. "By my calculations, I still owe you five days of work."

He walked around to the driver's side and got in. "How do you figure that?"

"My deductible was five hundred dollars. I work about

four hours a day, so if you were to pay me, I would make about ten dollars an hour, or forty dollars a day. I've worked eight days. That equals more than half of what I owe you. But I still need four and a half more days."

It didn't surprise him that her calculating mind had come up with a system for repayment.

"Your numbers are flawed," he said. "Minimum wage is more than ten dollars an hour in Arizona."

"I know." She grinned. "But I'm taking into account what I would have left after federal and state taxes, social security and unemployment taxes. You're getting a bargain, really."

He laughed and started the engine.

She put one hand on his arm. "I think we need to clear the air about something else, too."

"About what?"

She swallowed. "If you're still upset with me for suggesting you sell some of your family heirlooms, I'm really sorry. I wasn't thinking and—"

"Abbie." He stopped her. "Is that why you were so quiet yesterday? You thought I was still upset about that?"

The comments she had made at the ranch about selling some of his things had hit a little too close to home, but she didn't say anything other people hadn't already told him. He wanted so badly for her to like his home. Maybe even enough to make it her home someday.

Relief filled her face. "I was just quiet because I thought you were angry with me."

Noah reached across the cab and cupped her cheek with his palm. "Next time you think I'm mad, just ask me. You can't fix something if you don't know there's something to fix."

She covered his hand with her own. "Okay."

She leaned over and brushed a kiss across his lips. Noah's heart skipped a beat, and he caught her lips with his and deepened the kiss. He broke it off. "We better go feed the horses."

"How did things go last night?" Abbie asked. "With your mom."

"She was in bed by the time I got home. I still haven't figured out why she's here, but at least she hasn't asked for money or cried on my shoulder about her latest heartbreak."

"Maybe she just wants to spend time with her son."

That would be the day. "My mother doesn't do things for no reason. And she didn't come here to invite me to Nashville. Something else is going on. She's just waiting for the right time to spring whatever it is on me."

When they got to the barn, he broke his burro in half and offered her part of it.

She wrinkled her nose. "Does it have jalapeños in it?"

"It has green chili in it. Why?"

"Remember my first day here? You left a burrito for me?"

"I remember."

She wrinkled her nose. "My tongue burned for an hour after trying to eat that thing."

He chuckled. "I should have realized you city girls can't handle a little heat."

Abbie gave him a playful punch. "Any idea how long she's planning to stay?"

"No." He hoped she didn't stay too long. He wasn't sure how much longer he was going to have with Abbie, and he wanted to spend as much time as he could with her. He could worry about his mom later. "Speaking of staying, have you made any plans yet?"

Abbie shrugged. "Not yet. I didn't think my car would be ready for two more weeks, and I was hoping Stacy would be back by then, so I hadn't made any plans. You fixed my car early. Does that mean you're ready for me to leave?" Her tone was light and teasing, but her somber eyes told him she was serious.

"No. Not at all." He had only wanted to surprise her. "But I want you to be free to make the choice about when you leave." *Or if*, he wanted to add.

"I do need to go home. I need to start applying for jobs and find a place to live." She took a breath. "Vince said Stacy should be back by the end of the month."

"And you can't wait that long?" Noah knew she would have to leave eventually, but he wasn't ready for her to go yet.

"I was already planning to wait until the end of the month. I see no reason to change that now. But if she's delayed any further, I may have to leave. The only reason I wanted to stay until she got back was so I could tell her who I am in person." She smiled at him, but the smile didn't quite reach her eyes. "Now that she knows, I don't need the element of surprise. I can come back to see her anytime I want."

His stomach sank. "So when do you want to leave?"

She worried her bottom lip, something he noticed she did when she was trying to decide something. "I can't leave until I get Emily trained and finish Mr. Morgan's books. If I leave before then, all the work I've done this far will be for nothing."

"How long will that take?"

"I should be able to finish by the end of the month." Her green eyes searched his. "That gives us almost three weeks."

He swallowed. That wasn't nearly enough time, but he wouldn't make her feel guilty. "Well, what do you want to do next weekend, then?"

She shrugged. "I haven't done much in Coronado except work. Maybe you can show me some of the sights?"

"Well, you can't come to the White Mountains and not go fishing. That's practically against the law."

She laughed. "We can't have that now, can we?"

"I have to lead a sunrise trail ride Saturday morning. Why don't you come on that first, then we can go fishing afterward."

"A trail ride? Like on a horse?" She grimaced.

Noah stopped in front of the barn and shut the engine off. "It's time we got you over your fear of horses, too. You're definitely going on that trail ride."

"I'd rather not learn how to ride in front of a bunch of strangers." Abbie opened the door.

"Good point," Noah said. "How about tomorrow morning? We can go for a trail ride before cleaning the barn."

He followed her into the barn. She paused at the first stall, where Maze, Stacy's horse, was waiting to greet her.

"Okay." Abbie stroked Maze's nose. "I'll do it."

Once inside the barn, they fell into their work routine. He cleaned the tack room while she worked in the stalls. There was a big family reunion being held at the campground that upcoming weekend, and in addition to the sunrise ride, there were several others planned. Coy and Becky would be in town and would take care of the rest.

Abbie hummed while she worked. He stepped out of the tack room to watch her. Her ponytail swung back and forth as she pushed a wheelbarrow full of dung outside. He leaned against the wall and waited for her to return.

On her way back inside the barn, she caught him watching her. She smiled. "What?"

"I've never seen someone so happy about shoveling poop."

"There's no shame in shoveling poop," she said. She

parked the wheelbarrow and came over to him to brush a kiss across his mouth. "And I am happy. I don't know when I've ever been this happy."

Then don't leave, he wanted to say. But it would have to be her choice. Maybe if he had more to offer her, it wouldn't be such a hard decision.

The phone in the office started to ring. Noah went to answer it. "Hang on for a minute."

Ten minutes later, he emerged from the office and checked on Abbie's progress. She was almost done, so he ducked into the tack room to finish polishing the saddles.

"Who was on the phone?" Abbie hung her pitchfork and shovel on hooks on the back wall.

"Gerald Thomas. He wanted to move our meeting up to eleven-thirty."

"You better go shower." Abbie nodded at his dirty jeans. "I'll finish up here."

"Are you sure?" His limbs trembled, and he was so excited he felt like he could float away. This was his last chance to save his ranch. Once his ranch was safe, maybe he would have something to offer Abbie.

"What are you worried about?" Abbie gave him a puzzled look.

"My mom." *How could he ask her to keep an eye on his mom?* "I don't want her to know why I'm doing this. If she finds out how much trouble the ranch is really in, she's going to try to get me to sell it."

"The ranch is in your name, right? She can't do anything without you."

Noah shrugged. "The ranch belongs to me and Luke. He doesn't want it and tried to sign it over to me, but I wouldn't let him. I wanted to be able to pay him for his half."

"You think your mom might talk Luke into wanting to sell it?"

"I wouldn't put it past her. Luke always was a mama's boy, so he might listen to her."

"Don't worry. I'll keep your mom company, and I won't tell her a thing."

After Noah met with Gerald Thomas, he went to work at the garage. When Noah got back to the cabins, his mother and Abbie were nowhere to be found. Abbie's car was gone, so he could only assume they had gone somewhere together.

Almost two hours later, Abbie's car pulled into the campground. Abbie and his mother got out and both of them had shopping bags in their hands. They giggled like little girls as they walked up the path to Noah's cabin.

He stepped out onto the porch and crossed his arms. "Where have you been?"

"Springerville." His mother patted him on the cheek. "We've been having some girl time." She climbed the steps and brushed past him into the cabin.

He sighed. It was just like his mother to go shopping, even when she didn't have the money for it. Thank goodness Abbie was different.

Abbie stood on the path between the cabins. He nodded at the bags she was holding. "I'll take those in for you."

"Oh, these are mine." Abbie took a step toward her cabin. "I had no idea Springerville was so close to Coronado."

Close? It was over a forty-five-minute drive. His stomach twisted. Maybe she was more like his mother than he thought. One of the reasons his mother left was because there wasn't enough to see and do in Coronado. Abbie had been in Coronado without shopping until now. If she stayed, how long would it be before Springerville was no longer enough?

He followed her into her cabin. "You bought a lot of stuff. I guess you're not worried about money anymore."

She dropped her bags on the sofa and turned to face him. "What's that supposed to mean?"

"Nothing. But you're leaving in three weeks. Shouldn't you be saving that money to get home on? What if you have another accident or something?"

Her eyes sparkled with anger. "I used my tip money from the bar. The money you wouldn't let me pay you with. I wouldn't touch the money set aside to pay my bills and get home. Why shouldn't I be able to splurge occasionally?"

Noah knew exactly what she was going to say next. He had heard his mother say it thousands of times. "And you deserve it, right?"

Her eyes narrowed and she crossed her arms. "I'm not sure I like your attitude right now."

"Then we're even, because I don't like yours either." He stomped across the cabin and went outside.

He couldn't go into his cabin because his mother was in there. What he needed was to go for a ride. He climbed into his truck and headed for the barn.

CHAPTER FIFTEEN

THE NEXT MORNING Abbie got up and walked to the barn before Noah came out of his cabin. Partly because she was still angry with him. Partly because she didn't want him to be angry with her. And partly, because she hoped he hadn't forgotten his promise to take her riding today. When he got there, she had already fed the horses and had her stuff ready to go. She was just waiting to see what he was going to do.

Despite working around them for the last couple of weeks, she was still a little scared of the horses, especially Paddy. He liked to stamp his feet and snap his teeth when she walked by. Did horses get jealous?

She brought him a treat today. Her first attempt at a truce with the horse. She approached cautiously, keeping her eyes on him. When she was within touching distance, she extended one arm and opened her fist to reveal apple slices.

Paddy wasted no time in plucking the fruit from her hand. Abbie grinned. "See, I'm not so bad."

"Are you bribing my horse?"

Her gaze met Noah's. "I thought if I brought him a treat, he might not stomp at me all the time."

He stopped in front of her. "Are you still mad?"

"Yes." She lifted her chin. "Are you?"

"No." He took her hands in his. "I'm sorry. I was angry

with my mother and I took it out on you. I don't want to ruin our last few weeks together."

Her heart jumped a little. The fact that he was willing to apologize spoke volumes to her. "I'm sorry, too. I don't like fighting with you."

"Since you're trying to make nice with my horse, does that mean you're still willing to go riding with me?"

"Yes. As long as we go slow." Her heart rate increased just thinking about it.

"You can ride Stacy's horse, Maze. She's very gentle."

"Okay, I'll try, but I'm not making any promises."

"Good."

Taking her hand, he led her to the tack room. He pointed out things she'd never paid attention to and explained what they were and why she needed them.

She followed Noah from the tack room to the stalls, Maze's bridle over her shoulder and a grooming brush in her hand. She watched him go into Paddy's stall and slip the bridle on. He led Paddy out of the stall and to the hitching posts next to the tack room.

"Your turn." He nodded his head toward Maze's stall.

With shaking hands, she opened the gate and stepped inside. Maze dropped her head and leaned into Abbie's hand when she reached up to scratch the horse behind her ears. She tried to slip the bridle over Maze's nose, like she'd seen Noah do, but it didn't fit correctly.

Noah pointed at a strip of leather. "It's upside down. That goes under her head." He pointed to a thicker, shorter piece of leather. "That's the brow band and it goes above her eyes."

Abbie nodded and slid the bridle around until she was able to pull it over Maze's head.

Once it was on, Maze followed her outside to the tack

room. Noah started brushing Paddy and Abbie imitated his movements with Maze.

She had to admit, brushing the horse was therapeutic. There was something soothing about the long strokes and soft fur. Why hadn't she tried brushing the horses before?

Noah didn't let her try to saddle the horse herself, although she did put the saddle blanket on.

Finally, they led the horses behind the barn, where the trails started. Abbie clutched the reins in her hand, not sure what to do.

Noah dropped Paddy's reins to the ground and took Maze's reins from her hand and placed them over the horse's neck.

He moved to stand behind Abbie. "Hold onto the saddle horn with your left hand."

His mouth was next to her ear and his warm breath sent shivers across her neck. He stood close enough behind her that she could feel the heat from his body and she fought the urge to lean back and rest against him.

"Now put your left foot in the stirrup. Then step up and swing your leg over."

Abbie nodded. She'd done that once before. Only when she stepped up, she'd been behind Noah and not up there by herself. His hands gripped her waist, ready to assist her. She swallowed her fear and followed his directions.

A second later, she was sitting in the saddle. "Wow," she gasped. "It's so high up here."

Noah chuckled and handed her the reins laying across the horse's neck. "Hold these."

A moment later, he'd mounted Paddy and was next to her. He carefully explained how to steer the horse. And most importantly, how to make her stop.

She gripped a rein in each hand. "I think I have it. Pull right to go right. Left to go left. Pull both back to stop."

"Basically," he said. "Let's go."

He kicked his horse slightly with his heels and she did the same.

"Whoa." She squeaked. Maze stopped. She gave Noah a frantic look. "Why did she stop. I didn't pull the reins."

"You said 'whoa.'" Noah turned in the saddle to look at her. "*Whoa* means stop."

"Oh," she laughed. "I just meant it like whoa, it's a long way down."

She nudged the horse with her heels again and Maze resumed walking. The rhythmic movement of the horse made it easy to relax. "This isn't that hard."

Noah pointed to a break in the brush. "The trail starts there. If you start to get scared, just pull the reins and wait until you're ready to go."

Abbie nodded. So far, riding was a piece of cake. She wasn't sure why she'd been so scared of it.

They approached the beginning of the trail and Abbie caught her breath. The path looked barely wide enough for a person, much less a horse. Brush and grass grew up on either side of the trail and it was no longer straight.

She managed to keep up with Noah as the trail twisted and turned through the brush, but when the trail began to go downhill, she pulled back on the reins.

Noah stopped and turned in the saddle. "Relax. Horses are way more sure-footed than we are."

"But it's so steep."

"Trust your horse," he told her. "And trust me. I wouldn't take you anywhere dangerous."

She looked into his dark eyes and that was all she needed. Taking a deep breath, she urged Maze ahead. After a few steps, she discovered that gripping the saddle horn helped her keep her balance and she clung to it for dear life.

It wasn't long until the trail reached the bottom and a

lush, green meadow spread out before her. She could hear water rushing from the middle of the meadow.

"It's beautiful."

Noah grinned. "Come on. I want to show you something."

He waited until Maze was even with Paddy and they walked side by side. "Look there."

Abbie's gaze followed the direction he pointed. The mountain ahead seemed to be divided in half. Part of it held giant pine trees, lush green grass, while the other half was bare with only sticks seeming to point out of the ground.

"That line is where the Hot Shots were able to hold back the wildfire and keep it from destroying Coronado."

Abbie remembered his stories about the wildfires from several years ago. There was even a memorial to the fire-crews that fought it inside the Bear's Den Café. "I didn't realize the fire got so close to town."

"It could have gotten a lot closer," he said. "It was ten years ago, and the mountain is still bare."

Abbie studied the landscape. "It's trying to recover. I see some baby trees. Some grass. There's hope."

He gave her a sad smile. "I've looked at that mountain a hundred times and all I've ever seen is devastation. You look at it once and you find hope."

"Is that a bad thing?"

The leather of his saddle creaked as he leaned close to her. He cupped the back of her head with one hand. "No. It's a good thing. The world needs more people like you."

Her pulse increased when his thumb traced her bottom lip. "What about you?"

"I need you, too." He closed the gap between them and kissed her.

AFTER NOAH HAD dropped Abbie off at the cabin and left for the garage, she decided to go to his cabin and invite

Colleen over for lunch. The older woman gladly accepted her invitation.

Colleen was as taken with Abbie's homemade bread as Noah was. She took a second bite and closed her eyes, savoring the soft, chewy morsel. "Seriously. You should sell this."

"You don't know how badly I wish I could. But I'm sure making bread at home for fun is very different from making it for a store." Abbie put the dishes in the sink. "How long are you planning to stay in Coronado?"

"I'm not sure yet." Colleen wiped crumbs from her fingers. "I see that my son has told you about my track record."

"Not much," Abbie said. "He did say you move around a lot."

"That's an understatement." Colleen shook her head. "You're being kind. I'm sure Noah's words weren't so favorable."

"He just really wants to know why you're back."

Colleen sighed. "Can you keep a secret?"

Abbie shifted uncomfortably. "Not if it's a secret you want me to keep from your son."

"Yes and no." Colleen walked over to the sofa and sat down.

Abbie followed her, a sinking feeling forming in the pit of her stomach. She didn't want to be caught in the middle between Noah and his mother.

"It's only a secret because I don't know what to do." A smile spread across Colleen's face. "For the first time in my life, I'm really, truly, hopelessly in love."

What was it Noah had said about his mother? That she was always chasing her next love?

Colleen waved one hand. "I know what you're going to

say, but I can promise you this is different from anything I've ever felt before."

It wasn't Abbie's place to judge. "Tell me about this man."

"We've been seeing each other for over a year now." Colleen hugged a sofa pillow across her middle and leaned back with a dreamy look across her face. "If Noah told you much about my past, then you know that except for his father, I've never stayed in a relationship that long."

Abbie didn't answer. What could she say? That her son made her sound like a tramp?

"He has asked me to marry him. I said yes, of course, but he won't marry me without Noah's approval."

"So what's the holdup?"

Colleen's face clouded. "We've hit a bit of a snag."

"What kind of snag?"

"My fiancé is the one in charge of the program. I believe he met with Noah yesterday."

"Oh," Abbie said. "Did he pick Noah because he's your son?"

Colleen pressed her lips together. "He didn't know he was my son. I changed my name back to my maiden name when Karl and I divorced. He asked me if I wanted to come to Coronado with him while he interviewed a rancher for his program. I thought it would be a good chance for me to make amends with Noah for being a lousy mother. Gerald also wanted to meet my son and get his blessing."

Abbie's chest was tight. "So he knows now, right?"

"I didn't realize it until Noah got that phone call before dinner. Gerald didn't realize it until Noah's interview."

"Okay. So, you tell Noah and we celebrate your wedding."

Colleen shook her head. "You don't understand. If I marry Gerald, Noah won't be eligible for the contract."

Abbie's heart sank. "Why not?"

"Because of a nepotism clause. No one with any family ties can be awarded a contract."

"But Noah's counting on that contract."

"I know." Colleen sighed. "Gerald says Noah's chances of getting the contract are excellent…if it wasn't for me."

"What are you going to do?"

"I don't know yet. What I do know is that right now I'm in a position where I have to choose between my son and the man I love and want to spend the rest of my life with."

Abbie hugged her. "Don't worry, it will all work out."

As soon as Colleen left, Abbie got in her car. She drove to town and pulled into the parking lot at the post office.

She took out her phone and stared at it for a long time. With shaky fingers she scrolled through her contacts and found her dad. She hesitated. She knew what Noah would think about her interfering. But what other choice did she have? She couldn't let his mother sacrifice her happiness. And she couldn't let Noah miss out on the chance he had to save his ranch.

She took a calming breath and hit Call.

Her father answered after the second ring. "Hi, sweet pea. What's up?"

Her shoulders relaxed a little. When he called her by her nickname, he was in a good mood. "Hi, Dad. I need to talk to you about something."

The other end of the line was silent for a moment. "You're not calling to tell me that you're eloping with your cowboy, are you?"

She laughed. "No. I—"

"Because if you elope, it'll kill your mother. She's been planning your wedding since the day we adopted you."

Abbie frowned. "You wouldn't care if I married Noah?"

"If you love each other, that's all that matters."

"I'm glad, but no, that's not why I'm calling. I want to see what I have to do to withdraw some money from my trust fund."

Silence.

"Dad?"

"Is he asking you for money?"

She gasped. "No. Oh, goodness, no. And he wouldn't take it even if I offered."

"Since you haven't submitted your résumé at the firm, I'm going to assume you don't want the job. Did you find something there? Is that why you need your money?"

Guilt hit her in the chest. "One day, I would like nothing more than to work with you. But you and I both know I'm not experienced enough for that position. If I applied, I would get it and everyone would know it was because you own half the firm."

"What's wrong with that? Is it terrible to want to give my child a leg up?"

"Nothing. Except that I'd never earn the respect of my colleagues. And I'd never know if I was really good enough to work for you."

"Hmph," he said. "You've made your point. But you didn't answer my question. Are you wanting money so you can move to Arizona."

"No." Did she cling to the hope that someday Noah might want her to be a permanent part of his life? Of course. But so far, he hadn't tried to talk her out of leaving.

"Is it your sister? Does she want money?"

"Daddy," she sighed, "why do you think every person I know is trying to get money from me?"

"Okay. So what do you want it for?"

She explained Noah's situation the best she could. She started with his trucking idea, explained the fire and ended with the wild horse contract.

"So if he pursues the contract, his mother can't marry Gerald. That's his name, right?"

"And if he doesn't get the contract, he'll lose his ranch."

"He sounds like a proud man. Too proud to accept money. So we'll offer him a loan. No special privileges, just a straight across loan."

Abbie was willing to try anything. "Do you think he'd do it?"

"I think it's worth trying," her father said. "I know I was upset when you left, but this trip was good for you. You've really grown up. I'm proud of you."

She swallowed the lump in her throat. "Thanks, Dad. That means more than you could ever know."

NOAH PULLED IN front of Coronado Hardware. He got out and went inside. Usually when he stopped by, Abbie was behind the counter working on the computer. He didn't see her there and walked around the store looking for her.

He heard her laugh and followed the sound. She was standing with a man at the far end of the last aisle. The guy's back was to him. A ping of jealousy shot through him even though he knew there was no reason for it. Abbie looked up and saw him. She waved him over.

"You know Gerald Thomas, right?" Abbie motioned to the man standing in front of her.

The tension left Noah's body at the sight of the older, familiar man and he shook his hand. "Nice to see you again, Mr. Thomas."

"I was just telling Gerald that he needs to see your ranch. How about getting together for dinner sometime this week?"

Gerald Thomas was likely close to sixty-five, but he appeared to be in better shape than some men half his age.

"You have my number," Gerald said to Noah. "Give me a call as soon as you decide the day."

"How about tomorrow?" Abbie asked.

"All right. See you then."

Noah waited for the man to walk away before turning to Abbie. "Dinner at the ranch? Do you think that's a good idea?"

She shrugged "I'm not sure. But it can't hurt. Besides, it'll give me a chance to cook in your kitchen."

Noah shoved his hands into the front pockets of his jeans. "I finished early today. Want to go fishing when you're done here?"

Her eyes flickered with excitement. "Absolutely. But I'm not putting a worm on a hook."

Before they could head to the lake, they had to stop at the bait and tackle shop to buy Abbie a short-term fishing license. She stared at it as they got back into the truck.

"I had no idea you could buy a fishing license for just a day."

"Arizona has a lot of out-of-state visitors. This way they get to enjoy the great outdoors without having to buy one for the whole year."

The drive from Coronado to Big Lake was longer than the drive to his ranch, but it went by fast with Abbie sitting next to him. Abbie was fun to go anywhere with. She had a way of pointing out little things that he'd never noticed before. And she found excitement in the things he did notice but didn't pay much attention to.

It had been quite a while since he had taken the time to go fishing. The road ahead curved, and he recognized one of the side roads. Slowing down, he turned onto it.

The lake wasn't too far now. A couple more miles and they rounded the curve that led to the large man-made body of water. He parked in a spot close to the lake's edge.

"On the weekends it's hard to get a parking spot anywhere this close to the lake." Noah retrieved a couple of fishing rods, a tackle box and a bait box from the back of the truck.

Even though they were able to park close, they still had to walk down a winding trail to get to the edge of the water. He handed Abbie one of the rods.

"Are these hooks big enough to catch a fish with?" she asked, holding the tiny hook in her hand.

"Trout have little mouths, so they don't need big hooks. And today the bait of choice is Power Bait, so no worm-wrangling required."

Once they'd walked out to a point at the edge of the lake, they sat on a large rock to bait their hooks. Noah opened the bait box and slid it toward Abbie. "What color would you like to try?"

Abbie picked up the different jars. "Why are there so many colors?"

"Because trout are very finicky. They prefer one color today and a different color tomorrow, so you need all of them to be prepared."

"I'm supposed to keep trying them until I find one that works?" Abbie looked skeptical.

"Either that or ask someone what they recommend."

He waved at a couple of guys sitting on fold-up chairs on the other side of the point. Cupping his hands around his mouth he yelled, "What color?"

One of the men responded, "Orange!"

Noah smiled at her. "See? Try orange."

He showed her how to put the tiny balls onto the hook, but teaching her how to cast the line into the water was a bit trickier. Abbie flicked the rod like he showed her, but the line went behind them and caught in a bush. On her next attempt, the line dropped straight in front of her.

After several attempts she was finally able to get her line a decent distance in the water.

She gave him a triumphant smile. "Now what?"

"Now we wait for the fish to bite."

Abbie sat still for a while, her eyes watching the end of the fishing rod. Before too long she started stretching. Noah could see that her patience was running thin.

"How do people do this all day?" Abbie stood up and bounced on her toes.

Noah stood up as well. He should have brought some chairs for them to sit on. The rough rocks were not very comfortable.

"Noah, I think something is happening."

He looked at the end of her rod and sure enough, something was giving the line a slight tug. "When you pick up the pole, wait for one more tug. When you feel it, jerk the line back."

Abbie nodded, completely mesmerized by the dancing line on the end of the fishing pole. She moved slowly, as if the fish could see her. When she felt a tug, she did what Noah had told her and jerked the rod back. "What do I do now?"

"Start reeling it in." Noah left his pole on the bank and went over to stand next to Abbie.

It took her a few minutes, but she was able to reel the fish in close enough to the shore that Noah could lean down and scoop it up. Abbie pulled out her phone and handed it to Noah. "Take a picture of me with my first catch."

He removed the hook from the fish's lip, then showed her how to hold the fish by placing her thumb just inside its mouth. Then he handed her the trout. She gripped the fish just like he had told her and posed long enough for him to snap a picture.

As soon as she was able, she handed the fish back to Noah. "What do we do with the fish we catch?" she asked.

"If we were going to be here for a while and catch a lot, I would put him on a stringer to take home and cook for dinner. But since it'll be getting dark soon, we don't have time to catch many more. This one's not big enough for both of us to eat, so I suggest we give him his freedom."

Abbie nodded her agreement, so Noah lowered the fish into the water and let it go.

The sun was setting by the time they had loaded everything back in the truck. Abbie stood at the edge of the lake and stared at the sunset. The sky looked like it was on fire and cast an orange glow on the tops of the mountains. The clouds ranged from hues of orange and pink to gold.

Noah came up behind her and slipped his arms around her waist.

She leaned against him. "That's the most beautiful thing I've ever seen."

He laughed softly in her ear. "Doesn't the sun set in New York?"

"Not like that." Her voice was sad.

Then stay. He kept the words to himself.

What for? Should she stay so she could muck out stalls and work at a bar to help him make ends meet? No, that wasn't fair to her. She deserved everything she wanted. She deserved the best. And until he could give that to her, he couldn't ask her to stay. He just needed that contract with Gerald's wild horse management program. Then maybe he could start to think about asking her to stay.

CHAPTER SIXTEEN

"Do you really think this will work?" Colleen wrung her hands in front of her.

Abbie added the last of the sugar snap peas to the salad she was making. "Yes, I do. Even Gerald thinks this is the best way and the best place to tell him the news."

Colleen shook her head. "I still don't understand how I can marry Gerald and not cost my son his ranch."

"I'm still working on some of the details," she said. The check inside her front pocket was as heavy as lead.

Noah was meeting Gerald in town so he could follow Noah to the ranch, while Abby and Colleen came out earlier to start dinner. They should arrive at any moment.

If she couldn't convince Noah to accept a loan from her father, Colleen would never get to marry the man she loved. And the man Abbie loved might lose his ranch. Despite Colleen's past, Abbie was convinced she loved Gerald as much as she claimed to. And Gerald was certainly smitten with her.

Colleen set down the spoon she was holding and walked over to her. "You're working so hard to make sure I get what I want. What about you? What do you get out of this?"

Abbie squeezed Colleen's hand. "I get the satisfaction of seeing a woman I like and admire get to marry the man she loves."

Colleen looked at her for a long moment. "What about you? You love Noah, don't you?"

"I do." Her heart swelled. It felt so good to admit that to someone.

"Then why are you going back to New York?"

She pushed down the lump that threatened to choke her. "He hasn't asked me to stay."

"Would you?" Colleen's brown eyes, so much like her son's, were full of sympathy.

"Yes." Her heart sang with the truth. "I would."

She didn't care that the chances of her getting an accounting job in Coronado were next to none. She didn't care if she had to muck stalls for a living. All she wanted was Noah.

Colleen squeezed Abbie's shoulders. "Then stay."

Abbie cleared her throat. "I've given him lots of opportunities to give me a reason, but he's never asked me to stay."

"Maybe he's scared."

"Of what?" Abbie didn't understand. "He has to know how I feel about him. If he doesn't, he's an idiot."

Colleen laughed. "All men are idiots, honey. Sometimes they need some sense knocked into them. But more importantly, they need to hear the words. Have you told him how you feel? Have you told him you want to stay?"

"Not in so many words, no." Didn't her actions tell him?

"Don't forget," Colleen said, "Noah hasn't had the best examples to live by. His dad bailed on him. Then I did. My dad did most of his raising. And I loved the man, but warm and cuddly he was not. Noah's grandpa was old-school and ruled with an iron fist. Maybe that's why I tried to get away so much."

The slamming of the front door caused them to jump apart. Colleen went to the stove and started stirring the green beans. Abbie peeked in the oven.

"Something smells good in here," Gerald said.

Noah came in right behind him. He looked around the kitchen. "You sure made yourself at home quick." He winked at Abbie.

She grinned. "It's easy in a kitchen like this."

A few days ago, she had harbored hopes that this kitchen would be hers someday.

Noah motioned to his mother. "Gerald, this is my mother, Colleen. Mom, this is Gerald Thomas. He's in charge of the wild horse management program in these parts."

Abbie noticed that both Colleen and Gerald had panicked looks on their faces. It was one thing to keep their secret until Noah was ready. It was quite another to lie to him.

Gerald spoke up. "We've met."

Noah's eyes widened. "Where? When?"

"Snowflake," Colleen said. "We actually work in the same office building."

"Interesting," Noah said. Abbie could tell that his suspicions had been raised. She wasn't sure if her nerves would make it through dinner.

Noah sniffed the air. "What are we having?"

"Lasagna," Colleen announced. "Abbie wanted to cook her favorite meal for you before she leaves."

"Are you going somewhere?" Gerald asked.

Noah answered. "Abbie is from New York. She's just here to visit her sister and will be going home soon."

Abbie swallowed. Hearing the words come from Noah's mouth made it so much more real. And so much more apparent that he wasn't going to try to stop her.

"Oh." Gerald frowned. "I assumed you two—"

"How about setting the table?" Abbie handed Noah a stack of plates.

Once the dining room table had been set, all that was

left to do was to take the food in. She handed the salad bowl to Gerald. Noah grabbed the green beans and Colleen carried the lasagna, while Abbie pulled fresh-baked rolls from the oven. Within a few minutes, dinner was on the table and everyone had taken a seat.

Gerald took a roll from a plate and passed the plate around. "How did you two meet?"

Noah told him about how Abbie had wrecked her car dodging a wild horse and ended up having an asthma attack in the middle of nowhere.

"That must have been so scary," Colleen said. "Didn't you have an inhaler with you?"

Abbie shook her head. "I hadn't had an attack in over two years. Honestly, I thought I'd outgrown it."

"How long has this ranch been in your family?" Gerald asked Noah.

"My great-grandfather bought the land in 1915, or 1916." Noah paused, as if trying to remember the year. "It took him three years to build the house."

"Nineteen fifteen." Colleen passed a plate of rolls around. "He bought it from a Mormon settler who needed enough money to go to Utah. The settler charged Grandpa twice what it was worth because he convinced him that the railroad would be coming through and the value of the land would skyrocket."

Noah stared at his mother. "I didn't know that."

Colleen laughed. "It doesn't surprise me. My grandmother was the one who told me about it. Grandpa didn't want anyone to know he'd been played for a fool. He always got so mad when Mama tried to tell that story."

Noah laughed and Abbie laughed with him. Gerald asked a few more questions about the history of the ranch. Noah answered most of his questions, but Abbie was surprised that Colleen answered almost as many. Noah had given her the impression that Colleen didn't care to know anything about the ranch.

"You have some gooseneck trailers parked by the barn. Are they yours, or do you drive a truck for someone?"

"They're mine," Noah told him. "I had to sell the big rig after the fire, but the cattle trailer belonged to my grand-dad and I traded an old tractor for the flatbed. I haul cattle for some of the local ranchers, and I occasionally get hired to pick up feed and other things with the flatbed. I was hauling logs for Reed's Mill, but the wild horses put a stop to that."

Gerald nodded. "So you're hoping to go back to work if we can round up all the horses."

"I'd rather go back to ranching full time," he said. "But I get enough side business with my truck that I can manage until that day comes."

"What about your future plans?" Gerald's gaze darted between Noah and Abbie. "I mean, other than the ranch. What kind of personal plans do you have?"

Abbie's heart lodged in her throat. She held her breath, waiting for Noah's answer.

Noah frowned. "My only plans are for the ranch. Until that gets taken care of, I don't have time for personal plans."

Her heart dropped from her throat to her feet. Emily was right after all. Nothing could compete with the ranch. It was all he cared about. Didn't he know she would help him? Didn't he understand that his dreams had become her dreams, too?

When the business talk started to wane, Abbie and Colleen looked at each other and Colleen winked at her. It was time to put their plan in motion.

Abbie stood up. "Is anyone ready for dessert?"

Gerald patted his stomach. "Not yet. I need to walk some of this off first."

Noah put his napkin on the table and stood. "I'll be happy to show you around the ranch. That should give you plenty of exercise."

"Noah." Abbie put her hand on his arm. "Why don't we let your mom show him around? I need your help in the kitchen."

Before Noah had the chance to argue, Colleen and Gerald both stood. Gerald offered his arm to Colleen. "Shall we?"

The two of them had left the room before Noah could say a word. He gave Abbie a puzzled look. "What are you thinking?"

She stepped closer to him and wrapped her arms around his waist. "Mostly, I was thinking about how I could get you alone."

Maybe Emily was right and Noah would never care about anything except the ranch, but maybe Colleen was right, too. Maybe she needed to tell Noah exactly what she wanted.

He rubbed her back and held her against his chest. She could hear the steady beat of his heart.

"I wish I could record that sound," she whispered.

Noah pulled back to look at her. "What sound?"

"Your heart," she said. "I could listen to it forever."

"Hmm." He hugged her a little tighter. "I think that went well, don't you?"

"Yes. My cooking is amazing, so what did you expect?"

Noah's laugh vibrated against her cheek. "I should go join them."

He had a one-track mind. She shook her head and pulled herself out of his embrace. "No, what you should do is help me clear the table."

He did, although every few seconds his gaze darted out the window, searching for his mother and Gerald.

"What are you so worried about?" She was trying to gather up enough courage to talk to him about her offer. But he wasn't going to pay any attention to her while he was distracted.

NOAH WAS A little put off by her question. She knew how much he had riding on this. And she knew how his mother was. Come to think of it, Abbie had been acting a little strange all day. She seemed jumpier than usual, and her fingers rarely left the locket around her neck. When she was nervous, she played with the necklace. When she was worried, she bit her lip. He looked at her again. What did it mean when she did both?

Noah's gaze drifted to the doorway that his mother had gone through. "I'm worried because I don't think it's such a good idea to send her off with him. I can't believe you invited her. I don't want him to think I put my mother up to charming him in an effort to get the contract."

"And what would be so wrong with that?" Abbie brushed a kiss across his mouth. "It couldn't hurt if she charmed him just a little, could it?"

Noah stepped away and went to look out the window toward the barn. "Sure, she's charming and all smiles now, but what happens when he sees her true colors? It will ruin any chance I have of getting that contract."

Abbie let out a huff of air. "You're putting a lot of hope in that contract. What if you don't get it?"

"I have to." He walked away from the window. "I'm out of options. If I don't get this, I'm done for."

She swallowed. "There is one more option."

"If there is one, I haven't found it."

She took a deep breath. "You can get a loan to pay off the bank."

Noah burst into laughter. "I thought you were an accountant. Don't you advise against getting one loan to pay for another? Besides, what bank in their right mind would give me a loan?"

Abbie crossed her arms. "Not a bank. A person."

The blood in his veins turned to ice. He squinted at her. "I really hope you're not going to suggest what I think you're going to suggest."

Her jaw tightened. "And why not?"

"I will not borrow money from you." His head swam with fury.

Abbie reached into the front pocket of her jeans and pulled out a folded slip of paper. She opened it up and showed it to him. "Not from me. From my father."

"I thought you had vowed not to use your father's money. Or now that you're going back, it's okay?"

"That's not fair," she said. "It's not like I'm asking him to buy me a pony. I told him about your situation, and he thinks you're worth the risk."

"Wonderful. I'm so glad you told him about the deadbeat rancher who can't make ends meet. Did you tell him I'm a high-school dropout, too?" He pinched the bridge of his nose in an effort to calm down.

"It's not like that. He thinks you made a smart business decision that just didn't pan out. It wasn't your fault."

Her words didn't dispel his anger any. He picked up the check and looked at it. It was blank.

"I wasn't sure how much you might need. After you fill in the amount, we'll draw up the loan papers. It's not a favor. It's the same type of loan he offers to his clients. The same terms—"

"I'm not one of his clients." A blank check? How many

people in this world had the ability to give someone a blank check and not worry about the amount? Exactly how rich was her father? He handed the check back to her.

"Thanks, but no thanks." He nodded his head toward the window. "Once I get this contract, I won't need anyone else's money."

Abbie stared at the check. "What you really want to say is that you don't need me."

"No. I don't need you." Did he want her? Yes. With every fiber of his being. But as soon as he allowed himself to need her, then he would lose her.

Abbie pressed her lips together. "What if you don't get the contract?"

"You keep saying that. Do you know something I don't know? Is there a reason I wouldn't get the contract?"

Something flashed in Abbie's eyes.

Noah shook his head. "No." He didn't want to believe it. "Is there already something going on between Gerald and my mother?"

The look on Abbie's face was answer enough. He let the door slam behind him as he headed to the barn. He could hear Abbie chasing after him, but he didn't slow down.

There was no sign of Gerald or his mother in the corrals, so he opened the barn door and slipped inside. He walked quietly down the center aisle of the barn. There was no sign of them anywhere.

He walked around the corner to the wash area and there they were, all wrapped up in a passionate embrace. "What is going on here?"

They jumped apart. His mother at least had the decency to look guilty, but Gerald put one arm around her and pulled her closer to him. "We didn't mean for you to find out this way, son."

He took a long cleansing breath trying to control his temper. "I need to talk to my mother."

Gerald shook his head. "Whatever you want to say to her, you can say in front of me."

Colleen placed her hand on Gerald's chest. "It's okay. Go back to the house and wait for me there. I'll be there in a minute."

Abbie burst through the doors of the barn, her chest heaving. Noah momentarily put his anger on the back burner. "I can hear you wheezing. Do you have your inhaler?"

She put her hands on her knees and gasped for air. She nodded. "In my car."

"We're not done yet," he said to his mother. He started toward Abbie when his mother spoke up.

"Gerald, could you please walk Abbie to her car to get her inhaler? My son and I have some things to discuss."

Noah shook his head and moved to Abbie's side, but she waved him away. "No. Talk to her," she managed to say between gasps.

After Gerald and Abbie left the barn, he turned to face off against his mother. "You want to explain what's going on?"

Colleen gave him a wistful smile. "I love him."

"So?" Noah had heard her say that so many times it no longer had an impact.

"I came to Coronado to ask for your forgiveness," she said. "And your blessing. Gerald asked me to marry him."

Noah crossed his arms. He couldn't do either one of those right now. "So why didn't you just tell me when you got here? Why didn't Gerald tell me when we met the other day? Why go through this whole dog-and-pony show of bringing him out here so I can look like a fool?"

Colleen laced her fingers together. "He didn't realize you were my son until after he'd already interviewed you."

"How could you do this to me?" he asked.

Her brow wrinkled. "This has nothing to do with you."

Noah ran his fingers through his hair. "You're right. It never had anything to do with me. You never cared about me or Luke. All you've ever worried about is yourself."

Colleen took a deep breath. "You're right. I haven't been a good mother to you boys. I don't have an excuse for my past behavior. All I can do is tell you that I've changed."

"A tiger doesn't change its stripes."

"What?" Colleen looked confused.

"That was something Grandpa used to say to us a lot."

Colleen crossed her arms. "I'm not a tiger. And I have changed."

"You know, the best thing you ever did for us was bring us here. At least Grandpa wanted us. He taught us how to take care of ourselves and survive without you." Noah gave her a stoic look. "I guess he knew we would never be able to count on you."

Colleen shook her head. "I'm not proud of my past and there are a lot of things you don't know, but right now I want to focus on the future"

"I've heard it all before, Mom. You love him, you've finally found the one. You're so much happier than you've ever been before. And you want to tell me this time it's different?"

Colleen crossed her arms. "It is."

"You know, at first, I thought maybe you were flirting with him to help me get the contract. It made me mad, but at least I thought you were on my side."

"I am," she whispered.

"Are you really going to marry him?" Noah swallowed.

"Only if you can give us your blessing."

He felt like a two-ton weight was pushing down on him. "I'll lose the contract. I'll lose my ranch. I'll lose any hope I have for a future with Abbie."

Colleen's mouth dropped open. "Do you want a future with her? Do you love her?"

He ran his fingers through his hair. "I'm not talking to you about this."

Her face broke into a smile. "Don't you see? She loves you, too. If you marry her, you won't need Gerald's contract."

He couldn't believe what he was hearing. Was she actually suggesting that he marry Abbie for her money? "You *would* want me to do that. I'm not like you. I'm not going to use her for her money."

He took a couple of steps toward the door, then stopped and looked back at his mother. "Tell Gerald I'm withdrawing my application. Go ahead and marry him. Then stay out of my life. I don't ever want to see you again."

NOAH DIDN'T GO back to the house for a while. He wanted to give his mother and Gerald plenty of time to leave. He was tired of worrying about his mother's decisions. He was tired of figuring out how he was going to save the ranch. He was tired from working three jobs and from not getting enough sleep. He was just tired.

Colleen had said that Abbie loved him, too. Did she? If he asked her to stay, would she give up everything for him? Maybe she would. But how long would it take before she regretted it? How long would it be before she missed the life she left behind so much that she would leave him? If that happened, he couldn't deal with the heartbreak. How many times had he wished his father would come back? How many times had he pleaded with his mother not to leave again? He'd learned the hard way that no one stays if they really want to leave.

No. He would not ask Abbie to stay yet. He'd planned to get out of debt, build his ranch back up and go get her when he had something to offer her, but now it looked like that hope was gone, too. There was no way he would get the contract now. Without it, the bank would have his ranch by the end of the year and then what would he be left with? Nothing.

He walked down to the end of the pasture. He picked up some rocks and skipped them across the pond. Finally, he decided it was time to go home.

The front of the house was dark when he entered. He could hear noise from the kitchen. Was Abbie still there?

When he walked into the kitchen, Abbie was wrapping plastic around plates of food and putting them into the refrigerator. She looked up and saw him standing there. She plucked an apple from the bowl on the counter and threw it at him.

He ducked as it whizzed by his head. "What was that for?"

She glared at him. "You kicked your mother out?"

"Yes." Noah kept an eye on her hands in case she decided to throw something else. "I don't need her in my life."

"Of course not. Because big, strong Noah doesn't need anybody except himself." She shook her head. "You don't know what you've done."

"Why are you defending her? I told you what she was like." The anger started to build again. "And you knew about her and Gerald. You knew and didn't tell me. Instead, you let me get my hopes up about that contract and the entire time, you knew I wasn't going to get it."

"I only found out yesterday. And I promised not to say anything." She lifted her chin.

He paced around the kitchen. "My entire life was at stake, and you just stood by and let it happen because of a promise you made to my mother."

"I promised not to tell you because she wanted to tell you herself."

"When was she going to tell me?" He threw his hands in the air. "After they got married? You know I can't get that contract once they get married."

"It's because of me." She lifted the check and waved it in front of his nose. "I asked them to wait until I could give you another option. They know if they get married, you're ineligible for that contract. I gave you another option, but you're too bullheaded to take it."

"My mother should know me well enough to realize that I would never take a loan from you or anyone else."

"She does." Abbie shook her head sadly. "That's why she broke up with him. Congratulations. Your mother is giving up her last chance at happiness for you."

ABBIE WAS TOO upset to talk with him right then. She picked up her purse and keys and walked to the door.

"Don't go," Noah said.

"I have to." She reached up to touch his cheek with her hand. "Emily told me not to get involved with you. She said I would never be able to compete with the ranch. Just so you know, I never wanted to compete with the ranch. I wanted to be part of it."

Abbie didn't look back until she got in her car. When she did, she saw Noah standing on the porch, watching her pull away. That's when she let the tears flow. Maybe someday he would forgive his mother. She hoped so because neither one of them realized how much they needed the other one. Just like she hadn't realized how much she needed her own parents until she witnessed Noah and Colleen's relationship. She didn't want that kind of relationship with her parents.

It would be good for her to go away for a while. She would return as soon as Stacy got home. Maybe by then Noah would be ready to admit that he loved her. Maybe by then he would have apologized to his mother. Or hell would have frozen over.

She was just close enough to town to get cell phone service. Her phone started to ring. She pushed the button on her steering wheel to connect the call to her bluetooth, but it didn't work. Something must have happened to the connection after the accident. She pulled over to the side of the road to retrieve the phone from her purse on the floorboard. Maybe it was Noah. She glanced at the caller ID. It was a number she didn't recognize. A number from New York.

"Hello?"

"Hello. May I speak with Abigail Houghton, please?"

"This is she." Probably a telemarketer. She got ready to disconnect the call.

"This is Dr. Bruner at St. Joseph's Health Hospital. Your mother asked me to give you a call."

She gasped. "What's wrong? Is she okay?"

"Your mother is fine," the voice continued. "I'm afraid it's your father. He suffered a heart attack and was brought into the hospital this morning."

Her heart seemed to stop. Her hands began to shake. "Is he—"

"He's in the ICU right now. He's in critical but stable condition."

"Why didn't she call me herself?" She swallowed the lump building in her throat. Her mind raced. It would take her several days to drive home and she had no idea if she had enough money to purchase an airline ticket.

"Your mother is in shock right now," the doctor said. "We've given her some sedatives to help her calm down, which is why I'm calling you. She also said to tell you she'd put enough money in your account for you to get here as quickly as possible."

"Tell my mother I'm getting on the next plane home," she said before she hung up.

NOAH SPENT THE night at the ranch. It felt good to sleep in his own bed again. Besides, he might not get to do it for much longer. He was trying to accept the fact that he was probably going to lose his ranch.

The next morning, he fixed himself a cup of coffee and sat on the porch to drink it. Tom came out of the barn and moseyed over to him. He needed to apologize to Abbie. And whether he wanted to admit it or not, he needed to apologize to his mother.

He had let his emotions get the better of him. It was time for him to come up with a new plan. A better plan. One that wouldn't leave him drained. And maybe one that wouldn't leave him alone. He walked around the house looking at all the things that his family had passed down over the generations.

He picked up a plate and looked at it. He had never looked at it before. Turning it over, he noted the inscription on the back. He went into his office and got on the computer. A couple of searches later and he realized that Abbie had been right: some of the things in his house were worth a lot of money. Pride and stubbornness had caused him to hang on to everything for all these years. Would he rather have his ranch or a few trinkets?

He got his phone and walked around the house taking pictures of everything that he treasured but never even looked at. He uploaded the pictures to an antique dealer and entered his information. He closed his laptop with satisfaction.

His mother was right: people could change. Now he needed to go tell the people who mattered to him the most.

He drove straight to the cabin. Feeding the horses would have to wait until he talked to Abbie.

Her car was gone. He parked in front of her cabin and went to the door. Maybe she had gone to town. Maybe she went to clean the barn. He pushed the door open and walked inside.

Everything was gone. Her closet was empty. Her dresser drawers were empty. All the bathroom stuff was gone.

He couldn't believe she would leave without telling him goodbye. Maybe that was what she was trying to tell him last night. He walked out of the cabin and slammed the door.

His father had been the first person to leave him, then his mother. Now Abbie had left him, too.

CHAPTER SEVENTEEN

⌐ IT WAS DAWN by the time Abbie reached the hospital. She left her car in a garage at the Phoenix Sky Harbor Airport. She didn't know how long she could park there and right now she didn't really care. They could tow the car. She just needed to get to her dad.

She stopped at the first counter she came to and told the gentleman behind the counter she needed to get to New York as fast as possible. After listening to her story, he made a few phone calls and had her booked on the first flight to Syracuse. He even explained that her car would be fine until she could make arrangements for it. Too bad he couldn't help her get over the fear of flying.

Only love for her father outweighed the panic that gripped her when she sat down on the plane.

Once she landed, she caught the first taxi she could get and headed straight for the hospital. Tiffany Houghton was waiting for her in the lobby.

"Mom!" She threw her arms around her as tears began to flow. "How is he doing? What do the doctors say?"

"He's made it through the night, which surprised the doctors," Tiffany said. "Not me. Henry's a fighter and he's not going to—"

"Mrs. Houghton." A nurse approached them. "Dr. Bruner says you can go up to see him now."

Abbie let her mother go into the room first. After thirty-five years of marriage, she deserved some time alone with her husband. Through the hallway window, she could see her mother talking to him at his bedside. A few minutes later, her mother looked toward the window and motioned for her to come in.

Although she'd spent almost as much time in hospital rooms as she had at home as a child, she wasn't prepared to see her father in one. Tubes and hoses stretched from him to the machines next to his bed.

She sank into the chair next to her mother, her throat tight. "Hi, Dad. It's me. I'm here." She took his hand in hers.

Her mother quietly got up and went into the hall. The only sound in the room was the steady *blip, blip, blip* of his heart monitor. The sound both comforted her and tormented her. Less than twenty-four hours ago, she'd listened to Noah's heartbeat, wishing she could record it. Now, she listened to her father's heartbeat and prayed it didn't stop in front of her.

"Is this how you felt every time I was in the hospital?" She didn't know if he could hear her, but she needed to say some things. "I can't imagine how much I put you through. I'm sorry I took you for granted. And I'm sorry for leaving the way I did."

"He knows." Tiffany put her hands on Abbie's shoulders.

"Mom. I didn't hear you come back in."

"The nurses said we need to leave now." Her mother waited for Abbie to press a kiss to her dad's forehead before she repeated the same gesture. Fear and sadness threatening to overwhelm her, Abbie reluctantly followed her mother out the door.

"You came straight from the airport?" Tiffany asked when they were in the hallway.

Abbie nodded. "Yes."

"Where is your luggage?"

"I left it there," Abbie said. She'd been in such a hurry to get to the hospital, she hadn't bothered going through baggage claim. "I left my car in the parking garage at the Phoenix airport, too."

"That'll cost a fortune to get out." She looped her arm through Abbie's and headed for the elevator. "I'll call Corbin and have him pick up your luggage."

"What about my car?"

Tiffany took a deep breath. "Well, I guess you can pick it up when you go back to meet your sister. I'm sure your father will be out of the hospital by the time she gets home."

Abbie's heart pounded. "So you're okay with me going back?"

"Of course I am, sweetie," her mother said, squeezing her arm. "Stacy went all the way to Georgia, looking for you. You can't just leave her hanging now, can you?"

The elevator door opened, and they walked into the lobby. Her mother asked the receptionist to call a cab for them. While they were waiting, her mother apologized for being difficult regarding her sister.

"I was so worried that once you met her, you wouldn't want anything to do with us."

Abbie hugged her mother. "How could you think that? I love you. Meeting Stacy isn't going to change that."

"I know," Tiffany said. "Your father told me the same thing."

The cab ride was quiet. Her mother was still worried about her father. Abbie checked her phone every few minutes for a message from Noah, but one never came.

When the cab dropped them off in front of their house, Abbie took three steps and stopped.

Tiffany unlocked the door and looked at her. "What are you doing?"

"Looking for stars." Her head was tilted back, searching the sky. What she wouldn't give to be able to make a wish on a falling star tonight.

ABBIE HAD ONLY been gone two days, but it felt like years to Noah. There was a giant hole in his chest. Everything reminded him of her. Especially the stars.

This morning he had led six riders on a sunrise trail ride. For one of them, it was their first time on a horse. All he could think about was Abbie. Had it only been a few days since she'd ridden for the first time?

Becky and Coy had arrived shortly after he returned from the trail ride. They would cover the rides for the rest of the weekend, leaving Noah to wallow in his misery. When the next group of riders left, Noah took advantage of the empty barn by washing out all the stalls with the power washer. It needed to be done occasionally, and he needed something to do to keep his mind off Abbie.

He was putting the equipment away when he heard a vehicle drive up. When he walked to the door, he saw Gerald getting out of his truck.

"What can I do for you?"

Gerald leaned against his truck. "I saw you withdrew your application."

"Seemed like the best thing to do," Noah said. Without his application in the way, there was nothing to stop Gerald and his mother from getting married.

"I appreciate that." Gerald opened the front door of his pickup and removed a packet. "Here. I thought you could use these."

"What is it?"

"It's all the organizations in the state that are looking for ranches to partner with. Some of them pay a lot of money."

Noah flipped through a few pages. A couple of donkey sanctuaries. Lots of horse rescues. Even a llama home. "Thanks. I'll look into it."

Gerald gave him a pointed look. "Go see your mother."

"Why? Is something wrong?" He had apologized to his mother a couple of days after the dinner incident. He even told her she could stay at the ranch as long as she wanted. Or at least as long as he still owned it.

"Yes, something's wrong. She deserves more than an apology over the phone, don't you think?"

Noah ducked his head. "I'll go to see her soon."

"Soon's not good enough. Today." Gerald shook his head. "And when are you going to come to your senses and go after that girl?"

"She doesn't want me. She didn't even say goodbye."

Gerald snorted. "Shows how much you know." He turned around and headed back to his truck.

"Wait. What do you mean?"

"Go see your mother and maybe you'll find out." Gerald started his truck and drove away.

Had Abbie come back? His heart raced. Maybe she was at the ranch right now, waiting for him.

It took him less than fifteen minutes to put away his stuff, shower and set off for the ranch. When he got there, he jumped out of the truck and ran to the front door.

His mother opened it.

"Where is she? Is Abbie here?"

Colleen shook her head. "No. She's in New York."

His heart sank again. "Oh. I thought maybe Gerald was trying to tell me something."

"She did leave something for you." Colleen turned and went into the house.

He followed her into the office where she pulled a manila envelope from the top of the desk and handed it to him. "What's this?"

"It's the loan documents she told you about." She crossed her arms. "She told me where she left them when she called to say goodbye."

Noah stared at the envelope but did not open it. He looked at his mother. "She called you to say goodbye?"

"No, she called to tell you goodbye. I just happened to answer the phone."

"If she had just waited a little bit longer," Noah said, "she could have told me in person."

Colleen's mouth fell open. "You don't know, do you? I thought for sure you would have called her by now."

Noah shook his head. "Know what?"

"Her father had a heart attack. The night we were all here for dinner." Colleen cocked her head and looked him straight in the eye. "That's why she couldn't wait around to tell you goodbye in person."

"Did he…?"

"No. But he's still in the hospital."

His heart felt like it started to beat again. She hadn't left without saying goodbye, after all. Somehow that changed everything.

"While you're here—" Colleen walked over to a side table by the sofa "—that antique store owner from Phoenix called to arrange a time to come give you a quote."

"You know more about that stuff than I do. Can you meet with her?" He ran his fingers around the edge of the envelope. "And Mom, I'm really sorry about how I treated you and the things I said. Can you ever forgive me?"

"I forgave you the minute they came out of your mouth," she said. She nodded toward the dishes. "Are you sure you really want to sell that stuff?"

"Yes. I think I've held on to the past for a little too long. It's time to start fresh."

IT WAS ABBIE'S turn to sit with her father. It was the only way to get her mother to leave the hospital occasionally. Her father had been moved to a private room now that he was no longer in ICU, so she was allowed to sit with him for most of the day.

During his brief moments of alertness, she told him all about her trip to Coronado. He laughed along with her when she told him about the Reed sisters. And he listened while she talked about Noah.

"I hope I get to meet him someday," he told her.

She had the feeling that would never happen. Every time her cell phone made a noise, her heart skipped a beat. But it was never Noah. Had he forgotten her already? How had things gone with his mom?

When it wasn't her turn to sit with her father, she tried to keep herself busy. She put together some job applications to send to local accounting firms, but she was hesitant about sending them out. She wouldn't start a new job until her father was out of the hospital, and she had no idea how long that would be.

One afternoon, Abbie stopped by her father's accounting firm.

Monica Tucker, her father's secretary, greeted her. "Hello, Abbie. How are you holding up?"

"I'm well, thanks for asking," she said. "Dad wanted me to grab a few things from his office. Would that be alright?"

"Yes." Monica motioned for her to follow her. "We have a basket of things he can do from his bed. Puzzle books, things like that. I was going to bring it by, tomorrow, but you can take it, if you want."

"Great, he'll like that." She looked around the office.

It hadn't changed a bit since she worked there two summers ago.

"Monica, I can't get this account to…oh, hello, Abbie." The vice-president of the firm, Charles Schugart, nodded at her, balancing a stack of files.

"Do you need some help with that?" She nodded at the files dangerously close to sliding to the ground.

She removed half of the stack and followed him to his office.

"Thank you," Charles said. "Things have gotten crazy without your dad here to keep us all on track."

"Don't tell him that," Abbie joked. "He'll be calling and shouting orders over the phone."

Charles picked up a file off his desk. "We could really use some help around here. Didn't you intern with us for a while?"

"Yes. Why?"

For the next week, if she wasn't at the hospital, she was at the office, helping to cover some of the extra work caused by her dad's leave of absence. And every moment in between, she was struggling to keep her mind off Noah.

A couple of times she called his number. She knew he wouldn't answer because there wasn't any service at the cabin, but she liked to hear his voice anyway. She always hung up before it was time to leave a message.

She and her mother stayed up late at night talking about Coronado. And Stacy. And Noah. "Don't give up on that man yet," her mother said. "Sometimes men need a little time to themselves to figure out what's really important."

"I hope you're right."

Her mother gave her a smile. "Trust me. And when your dad gets home, ask him about the time that I left him for six months."

Abbie's mouth dropped open. "You left Dad?"

Her mother winked. "How do you think I got him to marry me?"

CHAPTER EIGHTEEN

IT WAS THE last week of September. Abbie had been home for two weeks and Coronado seemed like a lifetime away. Her heart still ached for the small town. Emily called her a few times, mostly to ask questions about the software she was using, but they always talked for a while about random things. She was very careful not to ask about Noah.

While her father wasn't out of the hospital yet, he was getting stronger every day. Meanwhile, Abbie was still helping out at his office and by the end of the first week, she had been officially rehired. Her father was thrilled. He even joked about making her a full partner, but she wasn't ready for that yet.

It felt weird to be home. It felt weird to work at a job without the smell of horses, manure and dirt surrounding her. She missed it so much.

She was trying her best to settle into the life she was supposed to have, but it didn't feel right. "Mom, I'm home!" she called as she returned from the hospital.

Tiffany appeared at the top of the steps. "You should check the mail. There's something in there from Arizona."

Abbie ran to the table next to the entryway where all the mail got stacked. She recognized the manila envelope that she had left for Noah before she got on the plane. She ripped open the envelope. Inside were the loan documents.

Stuck on the front page was a yellow sticky note. It read: "I'm sorry. I can't."

Her heart felt as if it cracked into a million more pieces even though she didn't know how that was possible. She looked at the sticky note again.

What he was really telling her was goodbye. She took a deep breath. That was that. It was over.

"Mom," she said, being careful to control the tremor in her voice. "I think I do want to go apartment hunting this evening after all."

"Uh-oh." Tiffany gave her a concerned look. "What happened?"

"Nothing." She dropped the envelope and all of its contents into the trash can.

Her phone started ringing and for the first time in two weeks, she didn't care if she answered it or not. With a sigh, she pulled it out of her purse and her heart started to pound. It was an Arizona number.

"Hello?"

"Hi. Is this Abbie?"

"Yes."

"Oh, my goodness. I can't believe I'm really talking to you. This is Stacy, your sister."

A flood of emotions rushed through her. A lump lodged in her throat, keeping her from being able to talk. She took some deep breaths. "Hi. Are you home now? I'm sorry I couldn't wait for you to get back. My dad—"

Stacy interrupted her. "I know. Noah told me. I'm so sorry that I wasn't able to get back while you were still in Coronado. How is your dad?"

Noah was the one who had told her? So he knew why she left but he still hadn't called her. Her stomach seized.

"How was your trip? I feel terrible. If I had just called you when I found you and hadn't insisted on driving to Arizona to meet you in person, you wouldn't have had to go overseas."

"Don't you dare feel bad. It wasn't a wasted trip. And…
the reason I was so late returning was because Caden and
I met two sisters at the same orphanage we were at. They
reminded me so much of us that I fell in love with them
immediately."

"Are you telling me that you adopted two little girls
from Georgia?" Abbie couldn't believe it. "I guess that
makes me an aunt now!"

"It sure does," Stacy said. "As soon as your father gets
better, I hope you can come back to Arizona to see us."

"I can't wait! He should be able to come home next
week. I'll look into some flights now."

"One more thing," Stacy said. "If you could arrange to
be here on October 7, Colleen would appreciate it. She's
going to be calling you to ask you to be the maid of honor
in her wedding."

"Colleen and Gerald are getting married?" At least
somebody got their happily-ever-after. She was dying to
ask Stacy about Noah, but she didn't dare.

She had barely hung up the phone when it rang again.
This time it was the number to the landline at the ranch.
Could it be Noah? "Hello?"

"Abbie? This is Colleen. How are you? How is your
dad?"

"He's doing better. He may get to come home next week.
I just talked to Stacy and she told me the news. Congratulations!"

"Thank you. I'd really like you to be here to be my maid
of honor, but if you can't, I understand."

"I'm going to do everything I can to be there." Abbie
swallowed the lump in her throat.

She wasn't sure if she was ready to face Noah again, but
maybe it would bring her the closure she needed.

"Noah, what are you doing up here?" Colleen's head appeared in the opening to the attic stairs. Her body emerged into the low-ceilinged space, and she approached where he sat cross-legged on the dusty floor. "Just looking at old pictures."

He showed her the photo album he'd found. It was full of pictures of his childhood.

Colleen sat down next to him. "I forgot about these albums." She flipped through some of the pictures.

The book fell open to a picture of Colleen and Karl on their wedding day. Noah looked at the picture for a long time. "What happened? You look so happy there."

"I was," Colleen said. "I was seventeen and in love with the idea of being in love."

"So you're saying you weren't really old enough to know what you were doing?" He wanted a clue as to why their marriage failed so he never repeated it.

"I was definitely young and immature," she said. "And most of all, I wanted out of this house."

"Why?" They were so different. He didn't want to leave, and she didn't want to stay.

"My dad." Her voice was quiet. "He was different with you boys than he was when I was growing up. He was so determined to be a better rancher than his father that it was all he cared about."

Her eyes took on a faraway look. "I think he resented me for being a girl. He wanted big strapping boys who would carry on the Sutton family legacy."

"I never knew why you didn't get along."

"When I met Karl, your grandpa was giddy. He was finally getting a son that he could pass down his knowledge to. The problem was Karl had no interest in being a rancher. He was drawn to the bright lights of the city."

Noah nodded. "That must be why you were drawn to him. You always liked the city, too."

"Probably." She shrugged.

He stared at the picture of his father. "Grandpa said he borrowed a bunch of money from him and couldn't pay it back. That's why he left."

"Every time we saw my dad, all Dad talked about was that loan. It finally drove Karl away."

Noah chuckled. "That wasn't too smart of Grandpa. He never did get paid back."

"Yes, he did." Colleen lifted her chin. "I paid him back. Every penny."

"You did? How?" He didn't remember his mother holding a job for more than a few months.

"That's why I left you." Colleen's face was somber. "I got a job as a flight attendant. It paid good money, but I knew I would be gone a lot. My dad and I had our differences, but I never doubted how much he loved you and Luke. So we made a deal. I would go to work and pay him back everything Karl owed him, as long as you boys always had a home."

Noah's heart thudded. "Why didn't you tell us?"

"I thought you knew. I didn't know my dad had told you horrible stories about me." A flicker of anger flashed in her brown eyes. "He wanted to make sure you never left the ranch, and the best way to do that was to get you to hate me."

"Why didn't you tell us?"

"You loved your grandpa. And I loved you. You already had to deal with your dad abandoning you. I didn't want to risk ruining the relationship you had with your grandfather."

Guilt roiled in his stomach. How many years had he

spent being angry at his mother when he shouldn't have been? "I'm sorry, Mom. I had no idea."

"It's okay." She wiped a tear from the corner of her eye. "That's why I always pushed you to sell the ranch. I didn't want it to destroy you like it did him."

The blood in his veins ran cold. "It almost did."

She ruffled his hair. "But it didn't. You're stronger than that."

He put the photo album away and followed his mom out of the attic and back to the kitchen. Wedding decorations were scattered across the table.

"Do you think she'll come?"

Colleen squeezed his hand. "Abbie? She already RSVP'd."

He picked up the notepad on the kitchen counter. His mom had written down the phone number for Abbie's parents' house. Colleen told him that Abbie had been working at her father's accounting firm during the week. Tomorrow, while Abbie was at work, he would call her parents and put his plan into motion.

"Mom, I'm home." Abbie came into the house and dropped her carryall on the floor next to the sofa.

"In here." Her mother's voice came from down the hall.

The light in one of the guest bedrooms was on. She pushed the door the rest of the way open and saw her father sitting up in an adjustable bed with her mother standing behind him. "Dad!" She threw her arms around him and hugged him tight. "Are you sure it's okay for you to be home so soon?"

"Yes," her mother said. "I think he was so grumpy the nurses were ready to kick him out."

"Well, if they would feed me like a real person, I wouldn't get so grumpy," her dad said, and smiled. "I could sure use one of my daughter's famous grilled cheese sand-wiches right now."

"Of course!" She headed down the hallway to the kitchen to make a sandwich for her dad.

It reminded her of the night she'd made a grilled cheese sandwich for Noah. Thinking of him made her a little angry now. How could Noah just forget her so soon?

"You're thinking of him again, aren't you?" Her mother came to stand behind her. She put her hands on Abbie's shoulders and squeezed.

"It's not just him, it's everything about that place. Can you believe I even miss shoveling horse manure?"

Her mother stood so she was facing her and put one finger under Abbie's chin, lifting her daughter's face to look at her. "I think that when you find the place you're supposed to be, nothing else matters."

"Are you trying to tell me I should go back?" Abbie shook her head. "I can't. There's nothing for me there. I said I missed shoveling horse manure, not that I want to do it for a full-time job. And that's about the only work there is for me in that little town."

"What I'm saying is I hope you're not holding back on account of us."

"No. I'm not going back because there's nothing to go back to."

Her mother tilted her head. "Are you sure about that?"

"Yes. It's been almost three weeks, and I still haven't heard from him." She used the spatula to flip the grilled cheese sandwich onto a plate, and her mother cut the sand-wich in half before picking the plate up off the counter.

"I'll take this to your father. I printed a flight schedule for you. It's on the desk in Dad's office. That wedding is this weekend."

"I don't think I'm ready to face him yet."

"Well, too bad. You already promised Colleen that you would be there." She flinched at the firmness with which her mother said the words. "Until you go, you'll never get closure and you'll never be able to move on."

After her mom left the kitchen, Abbie walked into the office and picked up the flight schedule from the desk. A thrill of anticipation went through her. She would go. She would go and give Noah a piece of her mind. Then she could come home and get started on the rest of her life.

CHAPTER NINETEEN

"ARE YOU SURE you don't want us to pick you up at the airport?"

Abbie couldn't help but smile every time she talked to her sister. "No. My car is still in the parking garage there, and that's a long way to come with little ones. I'll be fine. I'll see you tomorrow."

"Okay," said Stacy. "I can't wait to finally see you in person."

"Me neither." Abbie disconnected the phone call and turned to her parents one last time.

"Are you sure it's okay for me to leave?" Her dad was still in a wheelchair but finally able to get out of bed and join the family for meals.

"Don't you worry about us. We'll be fine. You have a safe trip, and we'll see you in a couple of weeks."

She hugged her parents goodbye and got into the taxi headed for the airport.

Her mother had offered her some anxiety medication for the flight, but Abbie refused. If she was going to have a relationship with her sister, she would need to get over her fear and learn to deal with it, because she would be flying back and forth a lot. Somehow, just acknowledging the fear seemed to help. She still felt a jolt of fear when the plane began taxiing down the runway, but once in the air, she was able to relax a little.

The plane ride to Arizona was both too short and too

long. Too short because she needed more time to think about seeing Noah again. She didn't know what she would say to him when she saw him again. And she would see him again. Unless he decided to boycott his own mother's wedding. And it was too long because she was eager to meet her sister.

Of course, after she got off the plane she would have a four-hour drive to think about it.

After her plane had landed and she paid the outrageous parking fee at the airport garage, she was ready to get back on the road. Before leaving the airport, she gave Stacy a quick call to let her know she'd made it.

"That's great. We'll see you in the morning. Your old cabin is ready and waiting for you. I'm so excited—I don't know if I'll be able to sleep!"

"I know! Me neither. See you in the morning!" She disconnected the call.

As she approached the outskirts of Coronado, Abbie's hands gripped the wheel a little too tightly. This time she kept her eyes open for signs of horses or elk.

When she pulled into the campground, she noticed that the light was on in her cabin. Out of habit, she glanced at Noah's cabin. It was completely dark. And his truck was gone.

Of course. With Stacy and her husband home, Noah wasn't needed there anymore. She parked her car and got the suitcases out of the back. She carried them to the cabin. It was nice of Stacy to leave lights on for her. Juggling a small suitcase in one hand and pulling a larger suitcase with the other, she opened the door and went inside.

A woman with golden brown hair was asleep on her couch. A lump lodged in her throat. She approached the sofa cautiously and touched the woman on the shoulder. "Stacy?"

The woman's eyes flew open, and she smiled. She threw her arms around Abbie's neck and hugged her tightly. Abbie sat down next to her and for a few minutes, they both cried.

Stacy grabbed Abbie's hands and wouldn't let go. "I just couldn't wait until tomorrow to see you… You don't know how long I've looked for you! I had given up all hope. And the orphanage refused to give me any information over the phone or by mail."

Abbie frowned. "I don't understand. When I sent them a letter, they sent a big box back to me with all the information I wanted and some personal items that had been left at the orphanage."

"When I got there, I found out why." Stacy's voice was strained. "But I'm not sure if I should tell you."

"Now you have to tell me," Abbie said. "What was the problem?"

"In order for information to be shared, both parties had to agree. When my—our—father left me at the orphanage, he signed papers authorizing them to release my information to you or your parents if it was ever requested. When the Tedfords adopted me, they had to sign a paper either leaving the agreement in place or revoking it. They agreed to it."

Abbie's mouth dropped open. "But my parents didn't. So you weren't able to get any information from the orphanage."

Stacy reached over and touched Abbie's locket. Then she reached under the collar of her own shirt to reveal a matching locket. "This is the last thing our biological father gave us before we went to the orphanage."

Abbie stared at the necklace that was an exact replica of her own. "I still can't believe you're real."

The two sisters stayed up and talked until it was almost

dawn. Abbie couldn't believe how much Stacy had been through. Her adoptive mother had been sick for years before dying from Huntington's disease. Her father, Vince, had been an alcoholic and had even abandoned Stacy and her mother at one point.

Abbie was a little surprised to hear about Vince's past. He had been so kind to her. She was glad that he was sober now and back in her sister's life. She felt guilty that her life had been so much easier than her sister's. But none of that mattered now. Now they were together.

Stacy looked at her watch. "I can't believe I've kept you up all night. You must be exhausted. The girls will be getting up soon, so I should get back—"

"I'm coming with you!" Abbie said, cutting her sister off.

Stacy gave her a questioning look. "Don't you want to rest?"

"It's okay. I slept on the plane. I'm too wound up to sleep now, anyway." Abbie grinned. "I can't believe that you can still speak Georgian. I guess that's a good thing since your daughters don't speak English yet."

"They'll learn fast. I did."

"That had to be hard. Coming to a new country after losing your entire family. And then not knowing the language." Abbie had been so young when she came to the United States, she didn't have any memories of not understanding English.

Maybe that's why she'd been so shy as a child. She'd always assumed it was because her parents had been so overprotective.

"My parents have a friend from Georgia, Nina, who lives here in Coronado. She was over at our house a lot when they first brought me home. She translated for me.

Vince even learned to speak a bit of Georgian after they adopted me, so he's loving that he can dote on the girls."

"I wish I knew how to speak it." Abbie sighed.

"The girls will learn English fast enough," Stacy said. "And I'll teach you to say whatever you want in Georgian."

They walked over the ridge to the apartment where Caden, Stacy and the girls were living until they built their house next to the campground.

The girls, who were two and four, were beautiful, although a little shy. Abbie sat on the sofa and watched them interact with their new mother. Marina, the two-year-old, was a little more outgoing. She approached Abbie with a book and handed it to her. Abbie took the book and snuggled the little girl on her lap.

Khatia, the elder sister, preferred to stay close to Caden. She trailed close behind him as he brought Abbie a cup of coffee. "Lots of cream and lots of sugar?"

"Yes," she said. "How did you know?"

He shrugged and smiled. "Runs in the family."

During breakfast, she caught Stacy yawning more than once. "I'm going to go to the hardware store and check on Mr. Morgan and Emily. You take a nap." She stood up from the table.

"Don't forget you have to go to the ranch this afternoon to make sure your bridesmaid dress fits," Stacy said, yawning again. "You should probably take a nap before then, too."

Abbie waved to the girls and walked across the parking lot to the hardware store.

"Abbie," Mr. Morgan greeted her with more enthusiasm than she'd ever seen. "Welcome back!"

"Hi." She hugged the elderly man. "How are things going? Is the computer software working out okay?"

"It's doing great," he said. "Of course, Emily does most of the work."

Emily bounced a fussy Wyatt on her hip. "Grandpa is actually learning to put the numbers in pretty quickly, too. He can't run reports yet, but he's doing the bulk of the ledger entries."

"That's great, Mr. Morgan." Abbie grinned at him. "I'm proud of you."

"How long are you going to be in town?" Emily asked her.

"The wedding is tomorrow and I fly home the next day."

Emily glanced at her grandfather before lowering her voice. "Have you talked to Noah?"

"No. Not since I left. I don't understand. Things were going so well."

Emily scrunched her face. "The Sterlings are good at walking away without an explanation. Take my advice. You corner him at that wedding and demand to know why he never called you."

Abbie cocked her head and looked at her friend. "You sound like you've got experience. Did Luke do that to you?"

"No," Emily said quickly, her face turning red. "But I went to high school with him, so I know how he is."

"Are you going to Colleen's wedding?"

Emily shook her head. "No. Wyatt's had a cold, so I don't want to leave him with my aunt."

Abbie couldn't help but notice that Emily looked unusually tense. "Are you okay?"

"I'm fine. But Luke and I didn't exactly part on the best terms, so even if Wyatt is feeling better, I don't think I should go."

"What do you mean? Were you two dating?"

"Nothing like that," Emily said. "We just had a difference of opinion. On everything. Have fun at the wedding."

Abbie gave her a hug and walked outside. Before going back to Stacy's apartment, she needed to get some answers from her parents.

She checked her phone to make sure she had a good signal, then called the house phone.

"Hi, sweet pea," her father answered the phone. "You're on speaker with me and your mom."

"You sound good, Dad," she said.

"How was your flight? Was it terrible?" Anxiety laced her mother's voice.

"It really wasn't that bad, Mom. I'm glad you're both on speaker because I need to know something."

"What is it?"

"Did you fill out some papers that kept Stacy from getting any information about me?"

Her father was the first to answer. "What? Why do you ask that?"

"Because I was able to get lots of answers from the orphanage, but they wouldn't give Stacy any information. I want to know why."

She heard her mother's voice mumble something in the background. "What was that, Mom?"

"You must be talking about a request to release records."

"Yes," Abbie said. "The Tedfords signed it, but you didn't. I just wanted to know why."

"Our lawyer told us not to," her father said. "Our lawyer was afraid that your biological father would try to blackmail us for money."

Abbie sucked in her breath. "That's it? That's the only reason?"

"What other reason could there be?"

"You never wanted me to search for my biological

records. I thought you didn't want me to find out about my family."

Her father's voice came on the line first. "When we adopted you, we had no idea you even had a sister. All we were told is that your mother had died and your father couldn't take care of you."

"So it wasn't because you wanted to keep me from my sister?" The tension in her chest began to release.

Her mother was the one to answer. "Of course not. If we had known about her, we would've adopted her, too."

That made her feel better.

"How are things going?" Abbie could hear the tension in her mother's voice. "Was meeting your sister everything you hoped it would be?"

Abbie hadn't realized how scared her mother really was about her meeting Stacy. "It was wonderful. It's amazing how much we have in common. But you're still my parents. I love you."

"We love you, too."

She couldn't see her mother's face, but she knew she was crying. "I have to go. I'm going to the ranch to try on my bridesmaid dress."

"Will Noah be there?"

"No." Abbie had already asked Colleen that. "He and his brother took Gerald fishing for the afternoon."

"You have to face him at some point. What are you going to do?"

"I don't know, Dad." Abbie sighed. "I just don't know."

Abbie hung up the phone. It relieved her to know that her parents hadn't kept the adoption records secret out of malice. They had just been scared and overprotective.

She didn't stop at the store. Just like Stacy, she needed a nap, too. She headed up the trail to the campground.

It was amazing how much the scenery had changed in

just a few weeks. The leaves on the aspens had turned brilliant shades of gold and orange. The air was crisp and cold, but the sun was shining, promising warmth later in the day.

The closer she got to her cabin, the heavier her heart got. She was thrilled to see her sister, but she wasn't ready to face Noah.

Maybe Emily had the right idea. Maybe she should confront him and demand to know why he hadn't contacted her.

Her cabin came into sight, but it was the empty cabin next door she couldn't take her eyes from. It was empty, just like her heart felt. She drew in a long breath. She was going to get some answers from him before she left, no matter what.

NOAH PEEKED OUT the door for the hundredth time. The backyard had been transformed into a beautiful wedding venue. The trees popped in shades of red and gold. He scanned the crowd for Abbie.

"You've opened that door fifteen times." His brother poked him. "Who are you looking for?"

"He's looking for Abbie," Gerald said. "Pastor Curtis said it's time to take our places."

Noah turned to look at his soon-to-be stepfather. "You nervous?"

"Nah."

"Are you sure? Your vest is on inside out."

"What?" He scrambled to fix it.

Luke and Gerald took their places and Noah went to his mother's bedroom and knocked on the door.

"Come in."

He opened the door. "Wow, Mom. You look amazing."

"Thank you." She placed one hand over her heart. "I'm just so happy that you're here."

The rest of the wedding party was making their entrance. Noah watched Luke escort Abbie down the center of the aisle. It was the first time he'd seen her since she left Coronado a few weeks ago. He pushed down the jealousy of seeing her with someone else, even if it was his brother.

When the wedding march began to play, his mother took his arm and they exited the French doors into the backyard.

Everyone stood as they approached. Noah wasn't sure exactly who all was there that he knew; he was too busy staring at Abbie. As he approached the altar, she didn't look at him, but kept her eyes focused on the bouquet she was holding.

When the pastor asked who was giving the bride away, he didn't hear it because he was busy trying to catch Abbie's eye. His mother pinched his arm. "Oh. Sorry. I do."

He took his mother's hand and joined it with Gerald's. He tried to focus on the wedding vows, but his mind was only on the woman he'd allowed to slip through his fingers.

After the ceremony, every time he tried to talk to Abbie, something got in the way. First it was pictures. Then they needed him to help carry a table for the refreshments. People were spread out all over the backyard.

At last, he spotted her. She was holding her two-year-old niece on her hip. Abbie's cheeks were puffed up and full of air. The little girl was taking her hands and tapping her cheeks so that Abbie would let out the air in a big puff. The little girl giggled.

"Hi," he said.

"Hi." She barely glanced at him.

"Can we talk?"

Stacy took the little girl from Abbie. "Come on, Marina. Let's go get cake."

"You look beautiful," he said, as Stacy and Marina headed off, leaving the two of them standing alone.

Abbie avoided looking at him. "Thank you."

This was going to be harder than he thought. "Will you take a walk with me?"

Her shoulders slumped. "What do you want, Noah? Whatever it is, just say it and be done."

He didn't like hearing the pain he'd caused in her voice. "I want to show you something. Please."

She nodded. He held out his hand, but she refused to take it. He led her away from the crowd in the backyard and down the path to the barn.

In the very back of the barn, he stopped. "Do you see that?"

She looked in the direction he was pointing. "What?"

He moved some hay to the side and revealed initials carved into the wood: K.S. + C.S.

"Who is that?"

"Those are my parents' initials. They carved this when they were in high school. They were high-school sweethearts, you know. My father dreamed of running his own business," Noah said. "Shortly after they were married, my mom talked Grandpa into loaning them the money to buy a motorcycle repair shop in Phoenix. But my father wasn't a very good businessman. Every year he lost more and more money. And every time they came to visit, my grandpa wanted to know when he was going to pay the loan back. Between my grandpa staying on my father's back about the money, and my mother, who just wanted to spend more than they made, he couldn't take it anymore. He abandoned his wife and his children because he was too ashamed to face them anymore."

Abbie swallowed. "Why are you telling me this?"

Noah took her hands in his. "If I took the loan you offered me, I might save the ranch for a few years, but there's no guarantee I could save it forever. Eventually, I could lose the ranch, and you. I can live with losing the ranch, but I can't live with losing you."

Her eyes welled up with tears, and she blinked them away. "Why didn't you call? I waited and waited for you to call, but you never did."

"Call and say what?" he asked. "Hey, I'm still here. I still have no income. I'm still a loser."

"You're not a loser," Abbie said. "Don't ever say that."

He lifted her face to his. "I couldn't call because I couldn't bear telling you that I still had nothing to offer you."

"I don't care about any of that. I just wanted you."

"I know," he said. "But I want to be someone you can be proud of. Someone your father would want to marry his daughter."

"And you're telling me now because…"

"Come on, I need to show you something else."

She let him take her hand this time, and he led her across the yard and into the house. He stopped in the middle of the living room.

"Notice anything?"

She looked around. "It seems emptier."

"Right." He took her to the kitchen. "And here?"

"You cleaned out some of the older things?"

"No. I sold them."

"You didn't." Her mouth dropped open. "Why?"

"I discovered that I could either hold on to a few keepsakes and lose everything, or I could sell them and save what matters most."

Her gaze danced around the kitchen. "Did you get much money for them?"

He gave her a smug smile. "Thanks in large part to my grandpa's excellent taste in music and his extensive vinyl collection, I got enough to pay off my bank loan completely."

"That's great." She bit her bottom lip. "I'm happy for you."

He could see the conflict on her face. "You don't sound happy."

She looked at him, pain radiating from her green eyes. "You sold enough things to keep your ranch."

Noah's heart pounded in his chest. "That's not what matters the most."

Abbie swallowed. "I don't understand."

"Don't you see? It's you." He took her by her shoulders. "I held on to the ranch, so I would have something to offer you. It doesn't mean anything without you."

Abbie's breath hitched. "What are you saying?"

"I don't want there to be anything between us, like there was with my parents. I don't want you to ever wonder if I was using you to keep my ranch, like my dad used my mom to get money.

"I had to save the ranch so it wasn't hanging over our heads. I love you. And if you want me to sell it tomorrow and move to New York, I will. But I love you. And I think you love me, too." He clasped both her hands and held them to his chest.

Abbie nodded. "I love you, but—"

"We can figure out all the buts later." He cupped her face with his hands and kissed her until she couldn't breathe.

When he finally broke the kiss, she touched his cheek. "You didn't let me finish. I love you, but I would never ask you to give up your ranch. I told you once I didn't want to compete with it. I want to be part of it."

Noah kissed her again. Then he dropped to one knee and pulled a ring from his pocket. "I love you, Abigail Houghton. And one day I hope to be worthy of being called your husband. Will you marry me?"

She wiped the tears that were freely streaming down her face. "Yes. Yes, of course I will."

She threw her arms around him and kissed him. Noah was only too happy to kiss her back.

ABBIE STARED AT the ring. It was beautiful. It had belonged to Noah's great-grandmother. Hand in hand, they walked to the backyard and found themselves surrounded by their friends and family.

"It's about time." Gerald slapped Noah on the back.

"You gave her the ring." Colleen kissed her son on the cheek.

"Wait. Let's see the ring," Stacy said. She looked at Noah. "You weren't supposed to do that until tomorrow."

Abbie gave Noah a puzzled look and then glanced back at Stacy. "You knew he was giving me the ring?"

"Girl," Stacy drawled, "this has been the biggest and best surprise this town has ever pulled off. I'm pretty sure the whole wedding was just a setup to get you back here."

"Hey," Gerald protested, "I think I had some say in that."

Colleen wrapped one arm around him. "Don't act like it wasn't your idea to begin with."

"When's the big day going to be?" Stacy asked, as she balanced Marina on her hip.

Abbie didn't know what to say. "We don't know yet."

Noah piped up. "The date is yet to be determined."

"I don't want to wait too long," she whispered in his ear. "What about a winter wedding?"

Noah pulled her a little away from the crowd. "I love you, Abbie. And I want nothing more than to be your husband. But we can't get married for a while."

"I don't understand."

"I have the bank paid off," he said. "But my ranch isn't back to working status. And I still don't have a steady income."

"I don't care about that." Abbie touched his cheek. "You could lose all the money in the world three times over and you wouldn't lose me."

He kissed her soundly on the lips. "That's good to know. But I'm still not going to marry you until I know I can be a good husband."

Abbie was left a little confused. How could she go from such a high to feeling bad again in such a short period of time? He loved her, yes. But he was holding himself up to a standard that was impossible to attain.

"Don't look so down," he said. "I wouldn't have proposed if I didn't have a plan. It just may take a while."

"What is your plan and how long will it take?"

"Gerald put me in touch with a few organizations that are looking for ranches. With any luck, I'll have a contract by spring."

"Spring?" Abbie whined. "I don't want to wait that long to marry you."

"Me either—" he pressed a kiss to her nose "—but I'm not going to marry you without being able to offer you a better future than mucking out stalls."

She pressed her lips together. "I liked mucking stalls."

"The only stalls you will ever muck are the stalls on our own ranch. And that will be because you want to, not because you have to."

The band started to play, and the wedding guests gathered around to watch the bride and groom's first dance. As soon as the dance floor opened up to everyone, Noah swept her out onto the floor. And as he held her, all her worries went away.

THE DAY AFTER the wedding, Abbie, Stacy, Caden and the kids drove back out to the ranch to help clean up. Colleen and Gerald had left for their honeymoon early this morning. Luke, who had to be back in Nashville, drove them to the airport.

On the drive over, Stacy and Abbie discussed all things wedding related.

"I would love to get married right here at the ranch," Abbie said, "but it depends on my parents. I'm not sure when my father will be able to travel."

Stacy nodded. "If he can't, do you think you would do it in New York?"

"Yes. I can't get married without my parents being there." She let out a sigh. "The wedding probably won't be for a while, anyway. Noah has some grand ideas about when he will be 'worthy enough' to marry me."

They pulled up to the front of the ranch house. They had started to walk around the side of the house to the backyard when Noah opened the front door. "Abbie, can you come in here first? I have a surprise for you."

She raised her eyebrows at Stacy, and they headed for the front door. She had only taken a couple of steps inside when she saw her parents sitting on the living room sofa. She rushed over to them.

"What are you doing here? I thought Dad wasn't able to travel yet."

Her dad shrugged. "I wasn't going to let some doctor's orders stop me from seeing my little girl get engaged."

"How did you know…?" She looked at Noah.

Her mother took her hand and admired the ring. Then she looked at Noah. "Noah called us last week and let us know in no uncertain terms that you would not be coming back home. He said he loved you and wanted to marry you. Then he offered to fly us out here to see if we might want to move here, too."

"Are you serious? You would be willing to move to Arizona?"

"Your mom told me that I have to retire. My doctor told me I have to retire. So, I guess I'm going to retire," her father said. "I hear Arizona is a pretty good place to do that."

She looked around and noticed that everyone else had slipped away, leaving her alone with her parents.

Her mother picked up Abbie's hand. "The ring is beautiful. Have you set a date for the wedding?"

"Not yet." She sighed. "This might be a long engagement."

"Why?"

"Noah refused to marry me until he has a steady source of income."

Her father smiled. "I knew I liked him."

"Oh, Henry," Abbie's mother said, "you go talk to him right now and tell him that's nonsense. We need to set a date. There's so much to plan!"

LATER THAT EVENING, the backyard had been cleaned up and Noah was grilling steaks for everyone outside. So far, things had gone perfectly. Abbie's parents were open to the idea of moving to Arizona. He still couldn't believe Abbie had agreed to marry him.

He hadn't planned on proposing until her parents arrived, but once he saw her, he couldn't wait.

"The sunsets here are just beautiful," Tiffany exclaimed.

"Wait until you see it from the lake," Abbie said. "Dad, you'll love fishing there, too."

"I can't wait to try it." Henry gave his daughter a long look. "Have you given any thought to what you're going to do? Job-wise, I mean. I hope you aren't going to let your degree go to waste."

Noah stiffened, but didn't turn from the grill. Was Henry going to suggest moving to Phoenix? He held his breath, waiting to hear Abbie's answer.

"I'm not sure. I have some ideas, but I haven't talked them over with Noah yet."

Ideas? What kind of ideas? Noah glanced at her over his shoulder and she smiled.

"Well," Stacy said, "if you decide to open an accounting office in Coronado, you'll have my business. I hate doing bookwork. I'll build your website and do the marketing, but I hate numbers."

Caden nodded. "I'm pretty sure you'd get Denny Morgan's business as well. That man thinks you walk on water."

Abbie smiled. "I will do your books for you all day long. I'll do Mr. Morgan's too, but I don't think two businesses would justify me opening my own accounting firm."

Noah removed the steaks from the grill and placed them on a couple of large cookie sheets. "That's not a bad idea, though. You might even pick up some business from Springerville."

"Really? You think so?" Abbie frowned. "I was thinking more along the lines of a bakery."

"A bakery?" Henry scoffed. "And throw away your degree? Nonsense."

Noah almost laughed when Henry's face turned red.

"I could do both." Abbie shrugged. "Besides, after I get married, I don't know if I'll be able to work full-time."

"Why not?" Tiffany raised one eyebrow. "Are you planning on starting a family right away?"

Abbie's face turned red and she flashed Noah a smile. "We haven't talked about that yet, but running a ranch is a full-time job. It comes first. If I have time for another job, that's fine, but I expect this place will keep me pretty busy."

Noah's chest swelled with pride. He stepped over to where she was sitting and brushed a kiss across her lips. "Sounds like I turned my city girl into a rancher."

He straightened up. "Steaks are done. It's getting dark, so I suggest eating in the house to avoid the bugs."

Everyone agreed. Henry took one of the cookie sheets with steaks while Caden and Stacy carried their daughters. Abbie hurried ahead of everyone and started setting the rest of the food on the table.

"This is just the biggest kitchen I've ever seen," Tiffany declared. "Abbie, you must be in heaven."

"There are lots of leftovers from the wedding, so heat up whatever you want." Abbie waved at all the containers. "There's beans, corn on the cob, potato salad and more."

Just as they were sitting down to eat, the house phone rang, and Noah excused himself to answer it. A few minutes later, Noah returned. His pulse was racing.

"You said you wanted a winter wedding? What day exactly?"

Abbie swatted his arm. "Stop teasing me. You already said we couldn't set a date for a while."

Noah shrugged. "I said we couldn't set a date until I had a steady source of income for the foreseeable future."

She cocked her head. "Who was on the phone?"

"A wild horse rescue organization out of New Mexico. They need a place to keep their horses and someone who can help train them."

"Can you do that?"

"Yes. I can do that." He glanced at Caden. "I might need some help. Didn't you tell me you used to ride wild broncos?"

Caden grinned. "Let me at 'em."

"Wait," Abbie said. "Does this mean we can set a date?"

He twirled her around. "Yes. Any date you want."

Abbie let out a whoop and jumped into his arms.

Noah looked over at Abbie's mother. "You realize she's not as excited about marrying me as she is about getting my kitchen."

Abbie ran her fingers through his long hair. "I wouldn't trade my cowboy for a dozen kitchens."

EPILOGUE

ABBIE WRAPPED A blanket around herself and stepped out onto the porch of the ranch home. Her home. Tom rubbed against her leg, waiting for her to sit on the porch swing. As soon as she did, he jumped in her lap and wiggled under the blanket.

The stars sparkled in the night sky and in the distance she could hear the occasional nicker of horses, calling to one another. Her breath came out in soft white puffs. Winter was definitely here. A light frost had already set on the ground.

Noah was making his way toward the house. He paused mid-stride when he saw her. "What are you still doing up?"

"Watching the stars and waiting on you." She moved over, inviting him to sit next to her. "How's the mare?"

"She's going to make it."

Abbie could hear the relief in his voice. The mare had arrived at the ranch sick and the vet recommended she be put down before infecting the rest of the herd, but Noah refused to give up. He had been nursing the horse day and night for a week.

"Are your parents asleep?" He wrapped one arm around her and pulled her closer.

"Yes." She snuggled up to him. "Are you sure you don't mind them staying with us until they close on their house?"

"Of course not. Besides, your dad is really helping me out with the bookwork for the ranch."

Abbie elbowed him. "I'm still mad you asked him to do that. I was managing it just fine."

He kissed the top of her head. "I know. But you're baking bread for the market, the Bear's Den *and* Paisley's Tea Garden. And you're still helping Emily at the hardware store."

"Speaking of," she said, "I was dusting pictures in the den today and saw some pictures of you and Luke when you were little."

"Yeah."

"Emily's son is the spitting image of Luke at that age."

Noah shrugged. "Don't all babies look the same?"

"No." She shook her head. "Do you think it's possible?"

"No." He scratched Tom's ears. "Luke knows what it's like to grow up without a father, and he would never do that to his kid."

"Maybe Emily didn't tell him."

"Impossible." He pointed at the sky. "Look. A falling star. Make a wish."

"I don't need to." She nuzzled his neck. "All my wishes have already come true."

"That makes two of us." He covered her mouth with his and kissed her.

* * * * *

WESTERN

Rugged men looking for love...

Available Next Month

Falling For Dr Maverick Kathy Douglass
Her Cowboy's Promise Cheryl Harper

....

The Rancher's Christmas Reunion Brenda Harlen
A Sweet Montana Christmas Jeannie Watt

....

Snowbound With A Baby Melissa Senate
The Cowboy And The Coach Anna Grace

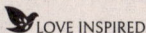

....

LOVE INSPIRED

Redeeming The Cowboy Lisa Jordan
Her Cowboy Inheritance Danica Favorite

Larger Print

Subscribe and fall in love with a Mills & Boon series today!

You'll be among the first to read stories delivered to your door monthly and enjoy great savings.

WE SIMPLY LOVE ROMANCE